A DIFFERENT RIVER

by

Jo Verity

D0987915

HONNO MODERN FICTION

First published in 2018 by Honno Press, 'Ailsa Craig', Heol y Cawl,

Dinas Powys, Vale of Glamorgan, Wales, CF64 4AH

1 2 3 4 5 6 7 8 9 10

A catalogue record for this book is available from the British Library.

Published with the financial support of the Welsh Books Council.

ISBN 978-1-909983-76-2 (paperback)
ISBN 978-1-909983-77-9 (ebook)

Cover design: Graham Preston
Cover image: © Rebekka Ivacson/Shutterstock Inc.
Text design: Elaine Sharples

SHE WANDERS THROUGH THE HOUSE, struggling to remember how it used to be before those cheery, burly men packed everything into boxes and took it all away.

Sounds ricochet off bare surfaces. Shoes on the quarry tiles. Keys tossed on the work top. The latch on the larder door. Hostile. Inhospitable. And after tomorrow's 'deep clean' that vaguely *dirty* smell which greets her whenever she opens the front door – coffee, garlic, toast – will be replaced by the wholesome anonymity of Domestos.

Things happened here. Momentous things. And things that weren't in the least bit momentous. Clues are everywhere if she has the courage to look. The cup-hook in the ceiling. The pear-shaped stain on the stair carpet. The clothes peg, wedging the sash window. The mound of pebbles at the far end of the garden. Evidence of the lives (and lies) that once inhabited this house.

On the bedroom mantelpiece is a box she won't be taking with her. Made of dark wood, it is the size of a house brick. The first time she lifted it she was shocked by its weight, its heft. Now she carries it through to the bathroom and perches on the edge of the bath. Over the weeks, a plan has been taking shape at the back of her mind and today it has elbowed its way to the front, testing and taunting.

She removes the lid of the box, revealing pale grey granules mixed with larger flakes. This would be the time to say something. 'Shit to shit' perhaps. Short and to the point. And yet, once spoken aloud the vindictive words might turn on her, damage her, and so she remains silent.

Start and there will be no going back. But it has to be done. Standing up, she tilts the box, watching her husband trickle into the lavatory, the noise of his hitting the water like oil hissing in a hot pan. He wasn't a big man but the steady, slithering stream goes on forever.

The first flush has no effect, the ash remaining stubbornly in the pan, grey scum floating on the water. (Sand-filled knickers after a day at the beach should have taught her this would happen.)

Second flush – no better. If anything the stuff consolidates, taking on the appearance of black concrete. Hysteria bubbles beneath her breastbone, threatening to erupt as she imagines it setting and causing a blockage. Try explaining that to the plumber.

Taking the lavatory brush, she agitates her husband whilst simultaneously flushing. The cistern takes an interminable time to refill but she keeps at it, repeating the process half a dozen times, each time the mass in the pan reducing, reducing, until Sam Siskin is no more than a spoonful of sludge.

Part I

1

THEY BOWLED UP PUSHING BUGGIES. Dragging toddlers flushed with sleep. Manhandling bikes and scooters. Carting toys and waterproofs. Mums, dads, nannies, child-minders. Grandparents (like her). Grouping and regrouping. Greeting one another as though a lifetime had passed since they last met. Swapping party invitations and snippets of information – cake sales, after school clubs, play-dates. The latest gossip on The New Teacher.

At three-thirty on the dot, a tide of little people smelling of disinfectant, powder paint and hair-that-could-do-with-washing flooded out through various doors, teachers and classroom assistants checking (with what seemed to Miriam a desultory glance) that each child paired up with the designated adult. The waiting army went into action. Doling out apples and biscuits and muesli bars. Calming tantrums. Praising paintings lethal with gobbets of wet paint. Enticing their fractious charges home with promises of chocolate or loom bands or Panini cards. It was the same every weekday and Miriam had become trapped in the predictable loop of it.

As usual Max was out first, racing towards her, anorak worn Batman-style, its hood concealing his dark hair.

'Gam,' he yelled, 'Gamma,' as if she might overlook him.

'Hello, sweetheart.' She stooped to kiss his pungent forehead.

'Did you remember—?'

'Of course,' she said, producing from her jacket pocket a cockroach (or something equally repulsive) encapsulated in a cube of resin.

Max held it aloft, rotating and scrutinising it from every angle, a faraway look in his eyes. 'It's my best thing.'

'Gamma.' Rosa came pelting across the playground, coat fastened on the wrong buttons, socks round her ankles. 'Can I go to Julia's? Just for a bit. Mum won't mind.' She scowled, anticipating refusal.

'Not this evening.'

She stamped her foot. 'You're so mean. Mum would let me go.'

Miriam was accustomed to Rosa's *modus operandi*. Persistence. Defiance. Noise. So different from her biddable younger brother.

'It's Wednesday,' she said. 'Piano lesson. Remember?'

Rosa threw back her head, screwed up her face and shouted 'I *hate* the stupid piano.'

Several adults were watching to see how she would deal with her granddaughter's developing tantrum. When she grabbed Rosa's hand and yanked her towards the school gate, she sensed an intake of judgemental breath from the spectators.

The kitchen was snug, filled with the smell of chicken casserole. The muffled sound of piano scales, faltering then beginning again, came from the living room. Max was sitting at the table absorbed in his drawing, the tip of his tongue visible between his lips.

'That looks exciting,' Miriam said, pointing at a tangle of colourful shapes.

'It's Goliath,' he said. 'The bit where he gets eaten by aliens.'

He grinned and she loved him with a fierce ache that made it hard to breathe. The world he'd been born into was precarious. Filled with malevolence and despair. It was intolerable to think of his being bullied or frightened or harmed in any way, yet unrealistic to imagine he wouldn't.

'I'm *starving*,' he said. 'What's for tea?'

'Chicken, green beans and mashed potato,' she said.

'Yummy.'

She tickled the silky skin on the back of his neck and he scrunched up his shoulders and giggled.

The piano had stopped and Rosa and Luke were laughing.

Miriam thought back. Every Monday, after school, as her friends were dawdling home, she had set off in the opposite direction, for her own weekly piano lesson. She'd made little progress with the impossible instrument, and if she and her teacher, Miss Halse, had ever laughed together she certainly didn't remember. (But the old lady's eau-de-cologne-and-sherry smell, and the touch of the bony hands lifting her wrists and forcing her fingers onto the keys, had stayed with her for fifty years.)

'Sounds like they've finished,' she said. 'Off you go and wash your hands.'

The children were both good eaters and had soon cleared their plates. Throughout the summer, they'd played in the garden after supper but it was November and they were confined to indoor activities. Rosa wasn't good at amusing herself and her default was tormenting Max but this evening she was happily threading beads on a cord and Max was immersed in a complex Lego project. As Miriam pottered in the kitchen, it was easy to forget that she was sixty-one years old and the children murmuring in the next room were not her own.

When Miriam first moved in, she'd waited to eat supper with her daughter and sometimes it was nine o'clock before they'd cleared away the dishes. Lately she'd taken to eating with Rosa and Max. This suited her digestive system and the children were better behaved when they had adult company.

Naomi came down from kissing her sleeping children. 'Both out for the count, thank God.'

'I've kept you some food,' Miriam said, and while she ladled chicken casserole into a bowl, Naomi moaned about work and her colleagues whom Miriam heard about regularly but would never meet. Naomi's job ('in PR') was a mystery to her but she listened with what she hoped was a sympathetic expression, now and again muttering a strategic 'oh, dear'.

When Naomi ran out of steam, it was Miriam's turn to report on domestic matters. Not for the first time she felt as if her life had flipped back thirty years, Naomi replacing Sam as head-of-the-household whilst once again she, Miriam, played the supporting role.

'There's a parcel for you. From Amazon,' Miriam said.

'I put it on your chest of drawers. Oh, and Rosa's been invited to a birthday party.' She flattened out the sheet of paper which had obviously been in Rosa's coat pocket for days. 'Sunday. Eleven o'clock. At the Leisure Centre. "Tom's Trampoline Party". She's quite excited about it.'

'Well she won't be able to go,' Naomi said. 'David's taking them to his mother's for the weekend.'

'She won't like that.'

'I'm afraid she'll have to lump it.'

Naomi's phone chirped an incoming text. 'It's Sally. She wants to know if I'll go out for a drink tomorrow evening. That's okay, isn't it?'

Miriam hesitated. 'Actually I'm going out.'

'Really? Where?'

'The cinema. Sorry.'

Naomi sighed. 'I'll just have to tell her I can't make it.'

Rosa and Max delivered to school and a wash in the machine, Miriam rooted out the Arts Centre programme. The film showing that evening didn't appeal but she needed to spend the evening away from the house and the Arts Centre was as good a place as any.

She felt bad about lying to Naomi. Such a spineless, juvenile lie too. But now and again it became necessary to remind her daughter (and herself) that she wasn't endlessly available. Recently she'd come across the term 'mission creep'. She wasn't entirely sure what it meant but it seemed to fit the way her life was being smothered.

Of course she should have considered all the angles before accepting Naomi's offer to move in with them, but at that point she'd been incapable of deciding what to wear, let alone how to salvage her life. Medication had eased her through those first grim weeks and, looking back, she couldn't help wondering whether things – *vital* things – had been discussed, agreed upon, when her brain had been candy floss.

She was wrestling her duvet into a fresh cover when the phone rang. Without fail, her parents called her on Sunday evening so seeing their number flash up on this, a weekday morning, was cause for concern. For octogenarians they were remarkably on the ball but they were also worryingly frail. A fall or a chest infection – and that would be it.

'Dad?' she said. 'Everything okay?'

'Can't I ring my only daughter for a chat? Does something have to be wrong?'

Her parents hadn't changed in twenty years. They were frozen in time like Max's cockroach. She didn't need Skype to know that her father was kitted out in shapeless grey trousers and pilled cardigan; her mother in a beige (or taupe or brown) dress, dab of rouge on each cheek, scant hair coaxed into a French pleat.

'Of course not. It's always lovely to hear from you.'

'Can you believe it's a month since you came to see us,' he said.

Her parents lived a hundred miles away. Did they expect her to pop in every five minutes? But sunlight was flooding the room, turning dust motes into powdered gold, and she wasn't going to spoil the day with an argument.

'Really? I don't know where the time goes,' she said.

'You don't have to tell *us* that.'

Her mother was whispering in the background.

'What's Mum saying?' she said.

'I'll put her on.'

She pictured her mother taking the receiver, handling it as if it were a piece of the finest porcelain.

'Hello? Miriam?'

'Hello, Mum. What's the problem?'

'It's not really a problem, dear. Well... We're defrosting the freezer. We've got a piece of beef that needs eating. It's too much for the two of us. We thought you might come and help us out.'

Miriam swished her hand through the shaft of light, setting the motes spiralling. Easier and cheaper to bung the wretched meat in the bin, but such a suggestion was unthinkable. 'Actually I'm a bit busy this weekend, Mum.'

The children would be off with David, and Naomi had plans to go gallivanting with friends. 'Busy' amounted to having the house and weekend entirely to herself – a rare treat.

'Oh. Oh. I see. Well. Never mind.'

She heard her father's voice demanding 'What did she say?' and her mother's 'She's busy.'

'Miriam?' Her father had retrieved the phone. 'Busy? It's the weekend.' His voice dipped as he ratcheted up the pathos. 'Why can't you come and see your old mum and dad?'

Her second's hesitation allowed her father to jump in. 'So that's settled then. We'll see you on Saturday morning.'

'Afternoon,' she said, salvaging a few precious hours of her weekend.

2

THE GOLDEN MORNING HAD GIVEN way to gusting winds and torrential rain. The last sheddings from limes and horse chestnut trees had dammed gutters and blocked drains. Street lights and headlights glistened off the wet road, creating a gaudy, disorientating kaleidoscope.

As Miriam swerved to avoid a mini flood, a motorcyclist loomed up from nowhere, hustling to overtake, forcing her to veer towards the pavement. Her front wheel nudged the kerb and the noise and the spew of water set her heart racing. At the first opportunity she turned into a side street and stopped the car, waiting until her breathing returned to normal.

It shouldn't be like this, skulking around on foul nights, concocting excuses to leave the house. But she had not even the germ of an escape plan.

Sam had never been keen on the Arts Centre. 'Faux arty,' he'd say, pointing at paint-spattered dungarees, clay-daubed shoes and unkempt hair. But she'd always liked the place. Its bustle and buzz. Its comfortable shabbiness. Its welcoming informality. Its promise of the unconventional.

Sam had been a suit person. He'd never looked at ease in old clothes. Any item of clothing that was even part way to looking shabby went into the charity bag. Whenever he'd embarked on a messy task – decorating or gardening or simply polishing his shoes – he'd change into an overall. An acquaintance went as far as to mention it in a condolence letter – 'Sam always looked so dapper'.

She bought a coffee and found a seat at a refectory-style table where she could read and people-watch, and she was settling into chapter six of *On Beauty* when she became conscious of a figure standing on the far side of the table.

'Excuse me. Is this taken?'

The man pointing at the seat opposite and slightly to the left of hers was, she guessed, in his mid-forties.

She smiled. 'Not as far as I know.'

He shrugged off his leather jacket and draped it on the back of the chair. 'I wonder if you'd mind keeping an eye on my bag.' He plonked a stained canvas satchel on the table. 'I promise it contains nothing sinister.'

'That's a shame,' she said.

He smiled and offered his hand. 'Callum Robertson.'

'Miriam Siskin.'

'Hello, Miriam.' He nodded towards the counter. 'Can I bring you anything?'

She detected a twang. American? Irish?

She was already awash with coffee but the prospect of adult conversation prevailed. 'A black coffee would be lovely.'

She watched him make his way to the counter, nodding to people as he went, laughing with the girl operating the hissing Gaggia. It seemed Callum was a regular. She returned to her book but found herself glancing up between sentences, anticipating his return.

He was soon back and when she tried to pay for the coffee, he waved away her money. 'Your turn next time,' he said and she found the implication that they might meet again rather agreeable.

Whilst he tucked into vegetable curry and she avoided drinking her coffee, she established that he was a painter and he taught at the local art college. His wife, Lara, was a relationship counsellor and they had ten-year-old non-identical twin sons.

'So tell me about you,' he said. 'Tell me about Miriam Siskin.'

And maybe because he had an open face, or because he'd shown an interest, or simply because he'd called her by her name, everything came tumbling out. Sam's betrayal. The loss of her home and her job. The crushing banality that currently defined her life. (Not the bit about Sam's ashes – no one knew about that.)

'Sorry,' she said when she'd finished. 'I don't generally bare my soul to strangers.'

'Oh I do,' he said.

'Really?'

'Strangers are impartial. They have no stake in your soul.'

She laughed. 'Sounds Dracula-esque.'

'Look,' he said, 'you mustn't get demoralised. Eight months isn't long. And you've had a heckuva lot to deal with. Don't despair. You'll hit on the answer.'

'You can't be sure of that,' she said.

'I can. I'm a fully paid-up clairvoyant.' He nodded towards her book. 'Good book?'

14

'It took a while to get into but I'm enjoying it,' she said.

They talked books, Callum doing his best to persuade her that graphic novels were 'literature' and that Shakespeare, were he around today, would have taken to Twitter 'like a swan to the Avon'. It was light-hearted nonsense. Fun. It was a while since she'd been treated as a person in her own right, rather than an adjunct to someone else.

They'd moved on to films when a jangling came from Callum's jacket. 'Excuse me,' he said, taking out his phone.

He turned away from her and, although she couldn't see his face, the way he was massaging his forehead indicated that the news wasn't good.

'Something wrong?' she said when he'd finished.

'Not wrong, exactly. Bloody inconvenient. My life model has buggered off to Spain.'

'Oh dear. Did she not—'

'He.'

'Did *he* not give you a hint?' she said, the image of a fig-leafed youth flashing through her mind.

He shook his head. 'Viktor's always been flaky. I don't blame him. It's not the most stimulating job. And the pay's lousy. It would have been nice to have a bit more notice, though.' He glanced at his watch. 'I'd best be off. See if I can call in a few favours.'

'Well thanks again for the coffee. And the chat. It's been very pleasant.'

'It has.' He took a card from his satchel and handed it

to her. 'This is me. Let me know how things pan out.' Then, as if he could read her mind, he added 'I'm not just saying that.'

'I will,' she said. 'And good luck finding a replacement model.'

'Have you seen Rosa's trainers?' Naomi said as they passed on the landing. 'Oh, and how was the film?'

'I didn't go,' Miriam said. 'At least I *went* but when I got there I didn't fancy it. Mmm. Trainers. I think I saw them in the downstairs cloakroom.'

Miriam chose this moment to come (almost) clean as in the hurly burly there would be no time for a post-mortem. School mornings were a series of crises. Missing games kit, unpractised spellings, misplaced reading books. Naomi hunting for her phone or a pair of un-snagged tights. By the time they next met, something else would have overtaken her daughter's irritation at her missed night out.

Miriam had slept fitfully. The conversation with Callum Robertson, although light-hearted, had resurrected a tranche of disturbing issues. Brought them bubbling to the surface where they were impossible to ignore. Eight months would soon become a year, then two, and Miriam Siskin would be permanently defined by her tripartite role – daughter, mother and grandmother.

After the house had been sold and Sam's gambling debts cleared, she'd been left with a small sum of money. It might buy her a tiny flat if she weren't too particular where she lived but it wouldn't cover her living costs. She didn't need to earn a fortune, simply enough to pay her way. Sixty-one wasn't the ideal age to embark on a new career and she examined her options for the umpteenth time, hoping there was a possibility she'd overlooked.

Returning to teaching – standing in front of judgemental, apathetic teenagers, enthusing about George Eliot or the romantic poets – was out of the question.

Librarian. She could be a librarian. She had a degree in literature and knew how to put things in alphabetical order. But libraries – those that hadn't been closed – were now 'Learning Hubs'. She guessed that involved advising people with 'issues' and helping them acquire IT skills. She was neither qualified nor wished to do either of those.

Did *The Lady* – if it still existed – have its 'situations vacant' section? Acting as paid companion to an old dear couldn't be that difficult could it? Although on second thoughts…

What else? M&S? 'Sorry to keep you waiting.' 'D'you want the hanger?' *Oh, God.*

Last week she'd spotted an ad in the paper inviting applications for MI5. Curious and disbelieving, she'd visited the website where a link took her to their 'investigative challenge'. Over the years, she'd absorbed enough John le Carré to know which of the multiple choices to tick and had done well enough for them (or an algorithm) to suggest she might be 'investigative officer material'.

So. Her future lay somewhere between espionage and selling underwear, which covered pretty much everything.

Her day progressed without incident or interruption.

No one called to invite her to go swimming or offered her a theatre visit or suggested a trip to the garden centre – commonplace events before she'd become Miriam, the gullible widow who'd caved in under the strain of it. Miriam the failure.

By the time she was standing in the playground, isolated in the midst of a chattering crowd, she was feeling exceedingly sorry for herself.

3

WHEN SHE ANSWERED THE DOOR she found David on the doorstep. 'Miriam. Lovely to see you.' He leaned forward to kiss her and she caught a whiff of cigarettes beneath his cologne. 'How are you?'

David Garrett was a gentle, thoughtful man. Miriam had always got on well with him and she missed his being around. Naomi seemed less bothered than she did by their separation, and the children had accepted the set-up as if seeing their father at weekends were normal. (She did wonder whether Rosa's outbursts were a result of his absence – although the child had been angry from the day she was born.)

'I'm well,' she said. 'You're off to visit your parents, I believe.'

His looked tired and she noticed he was missing a button from his jacket.

'It's easier for us to go to them,' he said. 'There's space for the kids to run around. And Mum loves having a houseful.'

She didn't know the ins and outs of it but Naomi had mentioned that he was living in a small flat on the far side of town. From what she'd gleaned from the children, there was no garden and it was 'miles and miles' to the park.

'Where is everyone?' he said.

'Upstairs. Arguing about what they should bring.'

He glanced towards the stairs and, lowering his voice, said, 'It's a great comfort knowing that you're here, looking out for them.'

David might like the idea that she was keeping an eye on them but it wasn't fair to expect her to dedicate her life to mopping up the mistakes of others.

'You do know that this is a temporary arrangement?' she said. 'I'll be moving as soon as I get something sorted out.' It sounded brusque and, to be truthful, slightly delusional but it was essential to keep reminding everyone – particularly herself – that she wouldn't be living here forever.

She still clung to the hope that Naomi and David would get back together. Their marriage had seemed rock solid, the two of them such good friends. When, without warning, they'd announced their parting, she and Sam had spent hours trawling the past, looking for evidence of cracks. When they'd asked Naomi, she'd trotted out vague, generic reasons. 'It isn't working' and 'people change', and the more loaded 'only two people know what goes on in a marriage', but, to Miriam's way of thinking, nothing to justify throwing in the towel. In the light of what followed a matter of months later, it was embarrassing to recall how she and Sam had offered to mediate – as if their marriage set the gold standard for honesty, trust and tolerance.

David hovered on the doorstep and she wondered whether to invite him in. Offer him a coffee. Give him and Naomi a few minutes together. They needed to keep talking – stay connected – if there were to be any hope.

He must have guessed what was running through her mind. 'It's okay, Miriam.'

He squeezed her hand and she noted the trace of yellow-brown stain between index and middle finger. What a shame. He'd been so pleased with himself when he'd kicked the habit.

Before she had a chance to say any more, he shouted, 'C'mon you two. Let's get this show on the road.'

Rosa and Max came hurtling down the stairs and, scooping them into his arms, he pulled them close. 'Hi. Have you had a lovely week? What have you been up to?'

The children began gabbling, voices growing louder as they tried to outdo each other.

Naomi appeared with two backpacks. 'Rosa, Max. Your things.'

'Hi.' There was caution in David's smile. 'How are you?'

'Frazzled. Tired.' Her folded arms signalled *keep your distance* and, for the umpteenth time, Miriam wondered what could have happened to cause and sustain this rift.

'Well, enjoy your quiet weekend.' There was the hint of a dig in his remark, as if he sensed Naomi was planning quite the opposite. 'Right, kids. Coats on and we'll be on our way. What time d'you want them back, Mum?'

'Not too late. They'll need baths and hair washes.'

'Okay.'

'Check they clean their teeth, David. And not too much TV. Oh, and seatbelts. Be sure they—'

'I have a vested interest in these children too,' he said.

'Have a lovely time,' Miriam said. 'And please remember me to your parents, David.'

'Will do.'

He herded his children down the path, both of them tugging at his jacket, instantly switching allegiance from one parent to the other, employing a child's inborn tactic for self-preservation.

The car pulled away and Naomi, miraculously energised, hurried upstairs to get ready for her day out. But Miriam stayed in the kitchen, remembering a time when they'd been a proper family. Before David left, and Sam had the bloody cheek to kill himself. When she'd been an interesting person. How readily they'd taken it all for granted – the wonderful normality and nurturing ease of it. What a mess they'd made of everything.

Her father consulted his pocket watch. 'You're early. What happened to all that *stuff* you had to do?'

'I did it,' she said, 'but I can go away and come back later if you like.'

Her father cupped her cheeks and peered at her face. 'You look pale.'

'I've been driving for two hours, Dad. A cuppa and I'll be right as rain.' She shrugged off her coat. 'Where's Mum?'

'Changing. Let's get the kettle on.'

The washing up had been done and everything tidied away but the kitchen still smelled of fish and cauliflower. A joint of beef in its frosted wrapping stood on a platter on the worktop. From her mother's description, she'd pictured a quarter of an ox but it probably weighed less than a kilo.

Her father filled the kettle and took three mugs from the shelf. He dropped one tea bag in the pot, considered, then added a second. When she was a child, there had been 'men's work' and 'women's work' and she'd never got used to seeing him perform these domestic duties.

'I'm glad I've got you on your own,' he said.

'Oh, dear.'

He laid his hand on her arm. 'You must stop assuming that all news is bad news. You're going to make yourself ill again.'

She waited, allowing him to concentrate on pouring boiling water into the tea pot, his skinny wrist shaking with the weight of the kettle.

'You have to let it stand for a couple of minutes,' he said, a mantra to the process. 'Come.'

She followed him into the dining room now used only on special occasions. Close her eyes and she would smell the Sabbath candles, the sulphurous coal smouldering in the tiled grate. He took a key from his pocket and unlocked the drawer of the dainty desk in the alcove at the side of the chimney breast.

'This is intriguing,' she said.

He took a bulky manila envelope from the drawer and handed it to her. 'Here.'

She held the envelope, its top folded over and secured with several rubber bands. 'What is it?' she said, knowing yet not knowing exactly.

'Nothing. Eight thousand pounds.'

She laughed. 'Dad, you can't—'

'A bond matured. What are we going to do with it?

Go jet-setting? You'll get it when we die so you might as well have it now. When you need it.'

'But—'

'Tsk, tsk, tsk. Not another word.' He pointed to the envelope. 'Put it away before your mother comes.'

Her parents had adored Sam. They'd been instrumental in her meeting him. In her marrying him. From the word go they'd treated him as their second son. Their *first son* after that final bust-up with Danny. When Sam died, and the truth came out, they'd been knocked sideways. On her previous visit she'd noted that Sam's photograph had been relegated to the back of the collection on the dresser, obscured by the rest of the family.

'I'm okay, Dad. Honestly.'

'Miriam, you have no income.'

'I'll get a job. I'm feeling much, much better.'

'That's good to know.' He held her with a steady gaze. 'Put it somewhere safe. It'll be there if you need it.'

'Lionel?' Her mother was coming downstairs. 'Is she here? Why didn't you call me?'

'We're in the dining room, Freda,' her father called, flapping his hands to indicate that she should conceal the envelope.

Her mother looked more insubstantial each time Miriam saw her. Her clothes – even her shoes – looked a size too big. Only arthritic knuckles prevented her rings from slipping off her fingers. Her skin had the translucence of a newborn. Rather than making her look healthy, the artless dabs of rouge on her cheeks gave her the appearance of a feverish doll.

'Hello, Mum.'

'You look peaky, dear,' her mother said.

And they went over it again – her early arrival, the tiring drive – ending up back in the kitchen making a fresh pot of tea.

Miriam dumped her holdall on the chair and switched on the lamp. This room had been hers from the age of thirteen, an acknowledgement of her coming of age. The yellow and indigo scheme she'd thought so avant garde had been over-painted several times with serviceable 'neutrals'. Her collection of gonks and her Joni Mitchell wall were long gone but the circular mirror and the Anglepoise lamp remained. And the desk at which she'd done her homework and written love letters to her schoolboy sweetheart still stood there, alongside the armchair where she'd curled up reading *The Group* and *The Female Eunuch*, making sense of neither until she'd plucked up the nerve to explore her own body. The elation, misery and uncertainty of adolescence, all lurked here, primed, ready to explode and pepper her with memories.

After her father had retired she'd encouraged them to look for somewhere smaller, where they'd worry less about heating bills and the garden and the awkward stairs. But they'd always come up with reasons to stay put. She'd lived here for her first twenty-one years; he'd retired twenty-one years ago. The symmetry felt significant. Beginnings and endings, perhaps.

She took the envelope from her bag and emptied it onto the bed. The cash was in eight bundles, each held with a red rubber band. Her father picked up these bands

– the postman's discards – when he went for his morning newspaper and took delight in his growing cache which sat in a jam jar on the window sill in the hall. Eight thousand pounds. In twenty-pound notes. What did these pieces of paper represent? A decent second-hand car. One of those fancy-pants chronometer thingies that Leonardo DiCaprio advertised. More tempting, a ticket on the Trans-Siberian Railway. Or maybe enough to keep her solvent for a year or two if she were prudent. (Sam would have doubtless put it on a horse and lost the lot.)

Of course she couldn't take the money. Not because it would leave her parents short. It wouldn't. Her father's pensions, coupled with a lifetime's habit of collecting rubber bands and the like, ensured their dwindling needs were covered. And there was no escaping the facts. Her parents wouldn't live forever and, unless they went on a spending spree of epic proportions, she would eventually inherit a substantial sum. This spacious house near an 'outstanding' state school – she had no idea what it might sell for. One thing was certain, it would be snapped up before the estate agent had time to put up a board. But it wasn't good to drift along as she was, pocketing advances on her 'great expectations'. It wasn't good to become the family charity case which threatened to go hand-in-hand with being the family carer.

She returned the bundles of notes to the envelope. Her father had ordered her to put it somewhere safe. Under the mattress? On top of the wardrobe? In the end she left it on the desk, challenging fate to deliver a bolt of fire or a burglar.

4

EIGHT THOUSAND POUNDS AT THE bottom of her holdall, the remains of the beef in a Tupperware container on the passenger seat, Miriam set off to drive home. The sun had failed to break through all day and, within half an hour of leaving, the light had gone. Traffic was atrocious on Sunday evenings but she was familiar with the road, and with Radio 4 to keep her company, the miles were soon clocking up.

She'd negotiated the weekend reasonably well. Better than on her previous visit, when she'd lost her temper with her parents for no reason other than their being old, frail and indecisive. This time she'd taken several deep breaths when they'd come out with absurd pronouncements. (Admittedly, ATMs weren't without security issues but her father needed to face the fact they were here to stay, and using them had to be safer than stowing his cash in a shoebox at the bottom of the wardrobe.) They'd spent Saturday evening watching television, sticking with the safety of *Strictly Come Dancing* and Lucy Worsley. On Sunday morning she had, under her father's instruction, doused the garden paths with MossKleer and pruned spindly rose bushes whilst her mother cooked 'dinner'. The money wasn't mentioned again and she decided to do as her father had suggested – hold on to it 'just in case'.

At the halfway point of her journey, the tug of filial

duty gave way to that of maternal obligation. Naomi had been the result of carelessness and the assumption was that subsequent babies would come along to order, but several miscarriages had taken their toll and by the time Naomi started school, they had accepted she would be their only (much loved) child. Sam and Naomi had always been as thick as thieves. Three is a tricky number at the best of times and she'd often felt excluded. Now she and Naomi must find a way of talking to each other. Honestly and openly. It was easier to continue fumbling blindly along, skirting around the devastation that Sam's death and addiction had inflicted upon them but it would surely damage them if they failed to address it.

It was past the children's bedtime by the time Naomi got back, but they were still rampaging around.

'David winds them up then dumps them back on me,' Naomi said. 'He does it every time. It drives me crazy.'

Abandoning hopes of an early night with her library book, she smiled. 'How was your weekend? Did you have fun?'

'I did. We got *sooo* drunk. And I spent *sooo* much money.' Naomi frowned and pointed at the ceiling. 'They're bouncing on the bed. You couldn't pop up…?'

The children greeted her with great gusto. David and his parents had packed more than seemed possible into their weekend. Finally Miriam bribed them into bed with the promise of the next chapter of *The Hobbit*. Max soon drifted off but Rosa refused to let go and, lulled by the monotony of her own voice, Miriam was in danger of falling asleep before her granddaughter.

Eventually Rosa's breathing slowed to a steady snuffle. To be on the safe side, Miriam gave it a couple more minutes before easing herself up from her beanbag seat. She looked at her sleeping grandchildren. Max barely visible beneath a mound of soft toys. Rosa, arm flung back, parted lips revealing front teeth that looked several sizes too big for her petite mouth.

She kissed them, switched off the bedside lamp and tiptoed to the door.

When teaching had occupied too much of her life there were things she'd longed, but hadn't the time, to do. Now Miriam was on the other side of the playground, the hours between drop-off and pick-up dribbling away in sham busy-ness. She was treading water and it was wearing her out.

Jonathan Tate, her GP, had prescribed 'happy pills'. Two weeks ago he'd reduced the dosage, congratulating her on progressing from 'moderate' to 'mild' clinical depression. Hoo-bloody-ray, she'd said, waving an imaginary flag. But Doctor Tate – a self-contained young man with shaky hands and scuffed shoes – hadn't cracked a smile.

To anyone encountering Miriam Siskin – or 'Naomi's mother' as she was better known – she probably appeared busily and willingly occupied. *Retired woman. Helping her daughter forge a career. Two beautiful grandchildren to look after. Must love every second of it.* Was it selfish to want more? She berated herself. *Come on, woman. Write a book. Learn Mandarin. Take up… bell-ringing. Make something – even if it's a mistake.*

What she lacked was a friend. A candid, caring friend who demanded nothing of her. A confidante with whom she could speak freely and openly. Someone who wouldn't judge her when she admitted she wished her parents would die (together, peacefully, in their own beds). Or that Naomi and David would get back together. Or bemoan forty years of marriage to the wrong man. Even confess that she'd flushed his ashes down the loo. In fact every single thing she felt guilty about admitting to herself.

The silly thing was she had just such a friend but they had become disconnected. She and Frankie Slattery had met on the stomach-churning first day at grammar school when they were allocated adjoining desks. It shouldn't have worked. Miriam Edlin, biddable, diligent, forgiving. Frances Slattery, sharp, witty, reckless. (Amoral, although Miriam didn't recognise that until years later.) But it did work. Through those years of bras, periods, unreasonable parents, boyfriends and, eventually, sex, they'd shared the highs and lows.

Frankie had gone through boyfriends at the same rate she went through stockings, never giving a thought to what lay beyond the next party or the next pair of heels. Miriam wasn't good at flirting and consequently found herself with boys who knotted their school ties correctly and handed in homework on time. This natural division had eliminated competition – quite something at that critical age.

They'd drifted apart when Frankie, no longer content with 'boys', had switched her attention to men. Once in a very blue moon, she received a postcard – from Amsterdam or Barcelona – 'having a marvellous time' or something similarly uninformative scrawled in Frankie's flamboyant hand. Frankie had visited a few times, making sure to be out of the way before Sam came home as they didn't get on. Miriam had mailed her when he died, and again when she moved in with Naomi. She'd heard nothing which was disappointing but not entirely surprising. Despite her unreliability, Miriam still considered her to be her best friend and when she next turned up, she would offload the whole lot.

Miriam half-hoped she'd lost Callum Robertson's card. It would rule out the crazy idea which had wormed its way into her head as she'd lain, sleepless, in her old bedroom. But there it was, in the fruit bowl, a small rectangular omen.

She thumbed his number and he picked up right away, giving her no chance to waver.

'Hello?' he said.

'Callum? This is Miriam Siskin. We met the other—'

'Of course. Hello again.'

'I'm not interrupting anything?'

'Nothing important. It's good to hear from you.' His soft burr was more evident on the phone.

Outside the window, a blackbird was mercilessly yanking a worm out of the lawn, persisting until its pinkish-brown victim lay squirming at its feet.

'I expect you're wondering why I'm phoning,' she said. 'I've an appointment near the art college tomorrow.

Would it be okay to call in? See what goes on. That's if I wouldn't be in the way.'

The bird was pecking at the worm, snipping it into pieces, each piece still writhing.

'Terrific,' he said, 'I'd love to show you around.'

She decided on her grey linen trouser-suit, teamed with a white shirt. Her size had remained constant for the past thirty years. There had been other changes, of course. Her hair, worn at the nape of her neck, Virginia Woolf-style, had turned from near-black to near-white. She had her share of wrinkles but dark eyebrows and strong, white teeth gave her a vigorous look. Her breasts were no longer firm, and the flesh on her arms was flabby, but she still looked reasonably okay in a swimming costume. She wasn't vain but to have lost her looks as well as everything else would have been too cruel.

The art school had once occupied an imposing Victorian building in the centre of town. The turquoise patinaed dome and crisp, red brickwork had made it a distinctive landmark. But, as part of 'essential cuts', the council had sold the building to developers. It was now 'luxury apartments' whilst the art school had been relegated to what amounted to a warehouse on the outskirts of town.

'Moving here must have been a wrench,' she said when Callum collected her from Reception.

'It was for me. I loved the old building but the students don't seem bothered,' he said.

'I would have thought art students would be sensitive to their surroundings.'

'Art students? Sensitive?' He laughed. 'Come and see for yourself.'

The building was a series of featureless, interconnecting spaces. In the first, three boiler-suited youngsters were struggling with rusty metal rods and a girl was fiddling about with wire mesh. In the next a man was tearing up pieces of foam rubber whilst another filmed him. There was a strong smell of adhesive. The sound of metal striking metal and classical music filled the air.

'It's not at all as I imagined,' she said. 'None of it.'

'No? You weren't expecting easels and canvas were you?'

'I'm not sure what I expected. I must admit I can't see where life drawing fits in.'

'Making marks on paper is vital to the process. "Drawing makes you see things clearer, and clearer and clearer still, until your eyes ache",' he said.

'Gosh. How very poetic.'

'I'll come clean,' he said, 'Hockney said it. But it's absolutely true.'

She followed him down a corridor and he explained that, as well as studios, the college had suites of rooms dedicated to video and audio projects.

'So does *no one* paint anymore?' she said.

'I do. But best not tell anyone.' He pointed to a door. 'My room's through here.'

They entered a pokey room with frosted glass windows. A leather armchair occupied one corner and the walls were a chaos of posters, photographs and drawings. A mobile consisting of geometric shapes dangled from the ceiling.

'This is homely,' she said.

'My retreat from the twenty-first century. Coffee?'

He motioned her towards the chair and she watched as he filled the reservoir of an espresso machine and slipped a capsule into the compartment.

'Did you have any luck finding your model?' she said.

'Afraid not. I can fake something up for this week's classes. I'll get them each to pose for five minutes. Sketching the human form quickly and accurately is a useful skill.'

She cleared her throat. 'Actually I know someone who might be interested. In life modelling, I mean.'

He looked up. 'Really?'

She was poised on the highest diving board, raised on her toes, ready to launch herself into the unknown yet still able to take a step back.

'Me.' Her voice was barely loud enough to hear, let alone believe. 'I don't have any experience but…'

She felt shy. Embarrassed. Exposed. If talking about it made her feel this way, how would she feel standing naked in front of strangers? Why didn't he say something? Maybe she'd got it wrong. Maybe he was looking for a lissom young thing with pert bosoms and buttocks and perfect skin.

At last he spoke. 'Why would you want to do this, Miriam? It's exhausting. Boring. The money's rubbish. Six hours a week. Ten pounds an hour. It's hardly a fortune.'

'That's sixty pounds more than I'm earning now.'

How had she expected him to react? Certainly not by

warning her she would be bored. To her it seemed the least boring thing that she could possibly do.

'Aren't you going to mention the nakedness aspect of it?' she said.

'Do I need to? You've looked at paintings of nude figures. The first thing you must have considered was "the nakedness aspect". Assuming, therefore, that you aren't horrified by the idea of nudity, you need to understand what else the job entails. It's not as easy as you think. Models sometimes faint from standing still. And it can get bloody cold in the studio.' He handed her a cup of coffee. 'Yours is black, if I remember.'

'Thanks,' she said.

He slotted another capsule into the machine. 'Has this got anything to do with what you were telling me the other evening?'

'Of course it has. I want to do something… brave. To test myself. To see myself differently. I want to become a different person. I wouldn't tell my family. Does that sound bonkers?'

He threw his head back and began to laugh.

'Why are you laughing?' she said.

'No one says "bonkers" these days.'

'So you'll let me give it a try?'

'Let's both mull it over for a few days. Talk again at the end of the week.'

5

'YOU LOOK... DIFFERENT,' NAOMI SAID.

'In what way?'

'I don't know. Perkier.'

'Maybe it's these.' Miriam rattled a tub of vitamin tablets. She did feel 'perkier' but she doubted it was a result of vitamin pills. 'I'm going swimming after I drop the children off.'

'Lucky you.' Naomi was, as usual, flicking her phone. 'Could you collect my coat from the cleaner's, Mum? The ticket's on the fridge.'

'I'll try.'

Naomi glanced up, but Miriam offered no explanation for her uncertainty, the first small but significant marker in her self-rehabilitation.

She didn't care for the leisure centre. It was unwelcoming. An intimidating fervour prevailed. People in clingy sportswear, gripping holdalls and 'power' drinks, stomped about, grim-faced, as if under military orders. They tended to be on the thin side, too – an endorsement of what they'd achieved here or, as she was more inclined to think, testimony that the people who *should* be here, weren't.

She paid her money and pushed through the turnstile. After the crisp November air, the heat was sapping. The acrid smell of chlorine and the echoing shrieks of swimmers filtered through from the pool, catapulting her back into the panic of childhood swimming lessons and eroding the courage she'd spent hours summoning up.

The changing room bustled with strident women (young, old, middle-aged) and a crop of noisy, uncooperative toddlers. Her impulse was to find a dimly-lit corner in which to wriggle out of her clothes and into her swimming costume. But that would defeat her objective.

Numbered lockers lined the Spartan room. A bench with coat hooks above and a shallow gutter beneath, ran down its centre. She stationed herself at the midway point and, looping her rucksack on a hook, began to undress, slowly and methodically. Jacket. Shoes. Socks. Cardigan. Jeans. Shirt. Until she was left in her underwear.

The heat was overwhelming and, as she removed her bra and knickers, she was overcome with giddiness. Breathing deeply, she grasped the rail, steadying herself and waiting for the wooziness to pass, acclimatising to public nakedness as her breasts, thighs, buttocks came in contact with the dank air.

The women continued nattering, taking no notice of her. Maybe they were being polite. Discreet. Or maybe they thought her unhinged. (She might have thought so too had she found herself standing next to a naked woman.) So far, so good. But for this to be a true test of nerve, she needed these women to look at her. Engage with her.

She made a neat pile of her clothes and transferred them to a locker. Fishing out two fifty pence pieces from the zipped compartment at the front of her rucksack, she walked slowly towards a gaggle of women, all fully clothed.

'Excuse me,' she said. 'Would you by any chance have a pound coin? For the locker?'

They seemed unfazed by her nudity and one of them took a handful of change from her pocket and sifted through it. 'There you go, love.'

Miriam swapped the two fifty pences for a single coin. 'Thanks.'

She donned her black swimming costume, locked the locker and fastened the key-strap around her wrist. Then she went through to the pool and stood in the shallow end, waiting for her heartbeat to return to normal.

Next day she spent an hour in the art gallery which was part of the town's museum. Sometimes she brought the children here but they preferred the natural history section with its mangy stuffed rabbits and animal skeletons and she had rarely had a chance to study the paintings in detail. She dawdled past uninspired landscapes, characterless bowls of fruit and stuffy-looking military men whose gaudy medal ribbons were the only relief to their khaki uniforms and brown leather armchairs. She wouldn't have given any of them wall space.

She was heading for the café when, in a side room, she spotted what she'd hoped to find. A painting of a nude woman. In fact two of the same woman. In one, she was coming down a very ordinary flight of stairs. In the other, going up.

She consulted the card fixed to the wall alongside the

canvases. 'J. L. Knox (1899-1943). Oil on canvas. 1934.' The woman was naked apart from a pair of red pumps. Her short, dark hair, cut in a bob, bore out the date but the titles 'Woman on the Stair – I' and 'Woman on the Stair – II' gave nothing away.

At first glance, they were purely studies of a nude woman. Yet, take a few minutes to consider, and the pumps and lack of any other artefact (even a stair carpet) created a conundrum. Were she pushed to concoct the narrative, it might be a summer's morning, the woman pausing on her way downstairs (to boil the kettle or feed the cat), pausing again on her way back to bed or to get dressed. Miriam had never wandered downstairs naked but it wasn't unthinkable. The unimaginable factor was that someone would be waiting at the foot of the stair, ready to capture the moment in oil paint.

She took a closer look. Sturdy. Small bust, wide hips. Fortyish? Not young, anyway. In the descending version, her head was turned slightly to her right, eyes cast down as if glancing over the banister, into the hall. Perhaps making sure there was no one about. Pausing to listen. Or to have second thoughts. A few minutes (or hours) later she pauses again, on her way up this time, head turned enough to reveal the tip of her nose beyond a curtain of sleek hair. But it was the birthmark below her left shoulder blade which caught Miriam's eye, bringing this unknown woman to life more than either her nipples or near-black pubic hair.

Were she to pursue this life modelling job, *her* nakedness would be studied in forensic detail. Art students must be accustomed to nudity. Would they be critical of her shape? Her age? Would they see her as decrepit stripper or more a compilation of elements, some of which – hands, she imagined – were trickier to draw than others? Callum had said it was easier to bare your soul to strangers than to someone known to you. Baring your body might be easier, too.

She took a couple of steps back. So who was she, this 'woman on the stair'? Knox's wife? Lover? She certainly couldn't imagine anyone painting their mother, or daughter, naked – although hadn't she read somewhere that Lucien Freud…?

The young man at the desk could give her no information on the painter or his – her? – subject. And, back at the house, when she googled 'J. L. Knox artist' the best it could come up with was James Knox, CEO of a painting and decorating firm in St Louis.

'I've been doing some research,' she said when Callum phoned.

'Research?'

She explained about the changing rooms. 'I'd like to give it a go.'

'Right,' he said. 'Well I've been doing some thinking, too. Let's start with head and shoulders. You've a good face. Timeless.'

'You mean old.'

'I mean *timeless*,' he said. 'I've okayed your appointment with the college. We can sort out the paperwork when you come in.'

40

'When d'you need me?' she said.

'Tuesday and Thursday mornings. Nine-thirty to twelve-thirty. Does that suit?'

What if the children were ill? And there were those tiresome 'INSET' days…

'Yes,' she said. 'What should I wear?'

'Something unfussy.'

'A T-shirt?' she said.

'Perfect.'

Miriam's worldly goods sat in a sprawling hangar on the industrial estate. The interior of AAA Storage was something to behold. Row after row of what amounted to lock-up garages. CCTV cameras scanning. Forklift trucks scuttling up and down the alleyways, laden with boxes and sofas and white goods. All accompanied by the sporadic clatter of metal doors. Sometimes, when she lay awake in bed, she imagined the place, vast and echoey, shadowy figures creeping about.

She was free to access her possessions whenever she liked. A keycard allowed her into the building and a four-digit code, chosen by her, opened the door to her container. She made a point of going there every couple of weeks, needing validation of her old life and confirmation that something else lay ahead.

Deciding what to take to Naomi's had been like packing for a holiday without knowing where she was going or how long she'd be away. Eight months down the line it was gratifying to know she hadn't been far adrift with her selection.

Occasionally she needed to retrieve this or that and she was heading back to the car with a couple of books and a clip-on lamp when someone called her name. Turning, she saw a woman hurrying towards her across the car park.

'It *is* you,' the woman said.

Yes, it was her. But who was this, holding her arms out in a welcoming gesture? She smiled, waiting for the appropriate part of her brain to spew out the answer but the woman got there first.

'It's Stephanie,' she said. 'Goodness me. It must be five years.'

Stephanie. Stephanie. Stephanie.

'Steph,' Miriam said. 'What are you doing here?'

'We had to bring the car to the body shop.' She indicated a row of prefabricated buildings off to her left. 'I had a slight contretemps with a bollard.'

'But I thought you'd—'

'We did. But we're back. Doug got a big promotion.'

Stephanie and Doug. She taught geography. He was something in the bank.

'You're still at Kelsey,' Stephanie said – a statement rather than a question.

The news of Sam's death, the scandal surrounding his gambling and her 'illness', had circulated more quickly than Miriam would have dreamed possible. By the time she'd felt up to facing the world, Naomi had made sure those who should know did know. She grown accustomed to friends and ex-colleagues crossing the road or diving into shops, uncomfortable at the prospect of meeting her, but Stephanie's ignorance caught her off balance.

'I'm not actually,' she said.

Stephanie's smile gave way to a questioning frown. 'Oh. So…?'

'I'm at the art college.'

'Art college? What on earth are you doing there?' Stephanie had always been unsubtle.

'Pastoral stuff. Admissions. Admin. A bit of everything.'

She'd rehearsed this fantasy ready to break the news of her new job to Naomi, nevertheless when it popped out so readily, and so plausibly, she was impressed with her quick reaction.

'Really?' Stephanie said. 'I'm surprised. You were such a brilliant teacher—'

'Was I?' she said. 'I can't imagine where you got that idea from.'

'Everyone… You always…'

She felt empowered by Stephanie's floundering but her smugness was short-lived.

'Actually I'm meeting up with the old crowd tomorrow evening,' Stephanie said. 'You should come along. We can have a good old catch-up.'

Miriam hadn't seen 'the old crowd' since Sam's funeral when she'd been pretty much out of it. Afterwards, several of them had tried to contact her but Naomi had fended off their calls and they'd soon given up. Occasionally she might glimpse one of them in Marks's or Waterstones, and they'd doubtless seen her, but it was easier to walk in the opposite direction.

'Shall I give you a piece of advice?' she said.

Stephanie smiled a vague, expectant smile and nodded. 'Never look back,' she said and headed for her car.

'But what about the children?' her father said when he made his usual Sunday phone call.

'It's only a couple of mornings a week, Dad. They're at school 'til three-thirty. My mornings are free.'

He paused and she waited for his next question. 'Don't they need someone in the office full-time? How will they manage when you're not there?'

'I have no idea.'

'I'm surprised you didn't ask.'

'They must know what they're doing. I'll find out all the details next week.'

'So how much are they paying you?' her father said. 'You've got a degree. You're over-qualified for clerical work.'

'That's not what this is about, Dad,' she said.

Naomi had accepted the news of her job without this cross-examination but she should have known her father would demand chapter and verse.

Time to play her trump card. 'Aren't you pleased I feel well enough to take on a job?'

'Of course I am. I just think you could do better.'

'Let's see how this goes first,' she said.

By the time they were saying goodbye, she almost believed that she was going to be answering emails and dealing with student applications.

6

CALLUM WAS WAITING FOR HER in the foyer. 'You look a bit frazzled.'

They'd got halfway to school when she'd remembered Max's consent form for his upcoming trip to the city farm and she'd had to rush them back to the house, Rosa wailing that they'd be late. By the time she'd seen them in to school and struggled across town through the morning traffic, she was feeling like a rag.

'I'm fine,' she said.

The building was throbbing with people, everyone knowing where they had to be and what they had to do. They carried things – rucksacks, portfolios, lengths of timber. One girl was struggling along with what looked like a giant dartboard.

'We're on the first floor,' Callum said.

She followed him up the stairs and along a gloomy corridor. One or two of the students stopped to speak to him but no one took any notice of her. Since leaving the house, she'd had a distinct sense of detachment and their failure to acknowledge her accentuated this to the point of her wondering whether she was really there.

The room Callum led her to was high-ceilinged, distorting its proportions and making it seem smaller than it was. Running along one wall, tall windows – north-facing she assumed – sprang from a high sill. Lights with conical metal shades dangled from long chains. The creamish walls were scuffed, the parquet floor spotted with paint. Easels were arranged in a rough semi-circle focused on a podium – half a metre or so above floor level – on which stood a chair and low table. They might have time-travelled back a hundred years.

Callum pointed to a door in the corner. 'That's the model's room – more of a cupboard actually – if you want to dump your stuff. And the loos are at the end of the corridor.' He glanced at his watch. 'We've got five minutes.'

'You'll have to tell me what you want me to do,' she said.

'We'll warm up with quick poses. Fifteen minutes for each, with a short break to give you time to stretch. We'll take a coffee break around ten-thirty and use the second half of the session for one pose – again we'll break every fifteen minutes.'

Students started to arrive, chatting and laughing, dumping their bags and coats on the floor.

He helped her up on to the podium and pointed to the chair.

'How d'you want me to sit?' she said.

'However feels comfortable. You don't have to keep absolutely still. Try not to tense up or your muscles will ache. Okay?'

She nodded. 'I think so.'

She sat down, pushing the small of her back against the chair, facing straight ahead, her eyes fixed on the light switch on the opposite wall.

The students, eight or nine of them, brought their easels nearer, adjusting the angle and height and fiddling with drawing materials.

Callum clapped his hands. 'Okay, people. This is Miriam. She's our model today.'

A murmur of welcome ran around the group and she felt the colour rising in her cheeks. He explained what he wanted from them and how the morning would be structured and, as they started drawing, the room fell silent.

She was breathing too quickly and, before a few minutes had passed, her shoulders began to ache. She took several deep, slow breaths and willed her mind to wander but her thoughts failed to escape from the silent room. By the time Callum called 'Let's stop there' her every muscle was taut.

The second session was easier. This time she slumped a little and altered the angle of her head. The students had swapped places so as to have a different viewpoint and she could see more of their faces. There were nine of them. Six girls and three boys – although some of them were too old to be 'girls' or 'boys'.

As they continued, Callum wandered amongst them, pausing now and again, glancing between whatever was on their easel and her face. They seemed at ease with his silent scrutiny.

'Let's get a coffee,' he said after the fourth session.

'It's very different from how I'd imagined it would be,' she said. 'Time drags and then suddenly it rushes on. Very odd.'

By the time they returned, the students had reassembled. The mood in the room was more relaxed, or maybe she felt more confident. This time Callum directed her pose, tilting her head a little this way and that. Once he was satisfied, the students moved their easels and off they went again.

She imagined her ex-colleagues at their Friday-night get-together. Stephanie's account of their meeting in the car park. They'd soon put her right on how things had been – or how they imagined they'd been. No one would ever know the whole story.

After each short break Callum made sure she adopted the same position. Her neck and her back ached and her hands were cold through lack of movement but she was finding it easier to give herself up to her thoughts. The stop-start of the process chopped her musings into chunks and, each time she resumed, it was as if she'd started reading a new chapter. Stephanie. Getting Rosa and Max to school on time. What the new owners might have done to her beautiful home.

Callum called a halt at twelve-thirty and the students shuffled out, a couple of them casting a quick 'thanks' towards her.

'So?' he said.

'It's made me realise how infrequently I sit still doing nothing.'

On her way out she called in at his room and he gave her several forms to complete. 'You can bring them on Thursday,' he said. 'You are coming back?'

'Won't they get fed up with drawing the same face?' she said.

'Different group on Thursday,' he said.

'How was it?' Naomi said.

'Interesting. A bit tiring. But it's always like that when you tackle something new, isn't it?'

She waited for Naomi to come back with more questions. Her father would have demanded every last detail but as long as it didn't interfere with childcare, her daughter clearly wasn't interested in her mother's 'little office job'.

Next morning she did a big Sainsbury's shop, prepared meals for the next two days and made a batch of bolognese sauce to put in the freezer. She cleared her ironing pile and phoned British Gas to arrange a boiler service, and switched her dental check-up from Tuesday to the following Monday.

Her phone rang whilst she was hanging her shirts in the wardrobe. The screen showed 'Louise T', one of the 'old crowd' as Stephanie called them. They must have had a good old gossip about her at their get-together. Maybe they'd drawn straws to decide who would phone her. She let the phone ring through to voicemail, thankful that Louise left no message.

Yesterday had gone well enough. But next week the students were expecting a nude model. The ones who'd attended the session had taken their work seriously. If anyone were looking for a quick thrill, there were easier ways to ogle naked women than signing up for art school. The students weren't the problem here. She was. And if she were in any doubt whether she would be able to stand naked in front of them, it would be only fair to tell Callum right now.

She went up to her bedroom and quickly stripped off her clothes. Standing in front of the wardrobe mirror, she assessed her body, making sure not to draw in her stomach or push out her breasts or stand straighter than was comfortable. She studied herself from all angles. Front. Side. Back. She turned again, more slowly, imagining herself the focus of nine pairs of eyes. And not for a couple of minutes but for three hours – although those first minutes would surely be the most uncomfortable.

She went to the top of the stairs and started down, stopping and planting her bare feet side by side roughly where the woman in the painting had stopped. The natural thing was to steady herself with a hand on the banister rail but the woman's arms had been at her sides. She dropped her arms and turned her head a little to her right. It wasn't long before her head began to swim. It had been her intention to continue to the bottom but instead she did a kind of shuffling turn until she faced the stairs, her back to the void – was that how it had happened that day in 1934? She resolved to return to the gallery soon and take a closer look.

Thursday morning's session followed a similar pattern but this time the students were livelier, chatting as they worked, inspecting each other's work. They showed surprise at having an older and fully clothed model. One young man told her that she had an unusual face 'in a good way'.

'How are you feeling about next week?' Callum said when she returned the college forms.

'I think I'll be okay.'

'Good. I think so too.'

'Any tips?' she said.

'You might want to bring along a robe. You can slip it off once you're in position. That's what life models generally do.'

'Right.'

'It means you don't have to walk across the room with nothing on. It minimises the titillation aspect.'

She'd remained calm until now but his insensitive aside caused her to blush.

On the way home she stopped at a small boutique and spent well over her week's earnings on a satin robe – plum-coloured with orange piping. Not something she'd wear at home but she could see that the trick to all this was to compartmentalise her life.

On Monday night, she found it hard to get to sleep and then a raucous cat fight woke her at 5am. At breakfast time, the children played up, squabbling over a puzzle printed on the back of the cornflakes box. The tussle resulted in a bowl of cereal crashing to the floor. They murmured apologies but showed scant remorse, unperturbed by the shards of pottery and splatter of milk. Her subsequent scolding, made more ferocious by anxiety, reduced Max to tears and sent Rosa into a rage: 'I hate you, I hate you, I *hate* you.' Had she not been about to get into a car, she would have taken a nip of brandy.

She was getting used to the college's hustle and bustle; its layout; the faint but persistent smell of glue and paint and sawn timber. When she reached the studio, she was nonplussed to see that a chaise longue affair, draped with a dark green blanket, had replaced the chair on the podium. A couch suggested lying, lolling, lounging – a different proposition from perching primly on a straight-backed chair.

The model's room was gloomy, illuminated only by a sliver of window, tight up against the ceiling. To make matters worse, it was glazed with frosted glass as if to foil giant Peeping Toms. The room was furnished with a table and two chairs, the walls lined with shelves stacked with saggy cardboard boxes. It must once have been a stockroom. She hung her jacket on the back of the chair and placed her bag on the seat. Today she was wearing jeans and an old sweater – easy to slip off and on and more in keeping with the ambience of the place.

The sound of laughter seeped into her cupboard. Students were arriving. She checked the time. Five more minutes. Long enough to go to the loo.

'Hi, Miriam,' one of the girls called as she attempted to slide unnoticed out of the room.

'Oh, hello.' She could have been greeting one of her A-level students.

On the way down the corridor she bumped into Callum. 'Back in a sec,' she said, pointing towards the cloakroom door.

Max had read somewhere that one day an asteroid would wipe out Planet Earth. The idea troubled him and she'd spent some time dispelling his fears but today – right here, right now – annihilation would be a blessing. *Get a grip, woman.* If she couldn't hack this, she should walk away. No one – no one she cared about, anyway – would be any the wiser. She fished inside the dispenser for the end of the loo roll. Not true. She would know. This whole business was about being brave and bold. Raising two fingers to her crappy life. Fail at this self-imposed challenge and she might as well abandon all hope of escape.

Callum was talking to two of the students and he smiled and raised a hand as she disappeared into the room. *Right. Okay.* She took a deep breath and hastily stripped off her shoes and clothes, dumping them on the table, making a point not to look down at her body. When she pulled on the robe, it felt cold and slippery. She could hear Callum instructing the students. 'Take a few minutes to find your viewpoint. You can reposition in the breaks if you like but Miriam will be holding the same pose throughout.'

She opened the door, simultaneously allowing her consciousness to detach itself and fly up to hover above the woman in the shiny robe. There she was. Miriam Siskin. Walking towards the podium. A prizefighter in a shiny robe, heading for the ring. She stepped up onto the podium and, with her back to the room, slipped off the robe. And, believe it or not, the world didn't end. In fact the students went on chatting and clattering about as though nothing had happened.

Callum was at her side. 'If you could sit down, both legs up. Ankles crossed.'

She sat on the couch, legs extended, crossed at the ankles.

'Perfect,' he said.

She smiled, her face feeling stiff as it did when the dentist gave her an injection.

He coaxed her right hand across her stomach until it was resting on her left thigh. His touch was reassuringly clinical. 'Just here. Good.'

He held up a stubby crayon. 'Face paint,' he said, tracing swiftly around her hand, marking where it lay on her thigh and where one ankle crossed the other. 'This'll help locate your position after you've taken a break.'

'Where should I look?' she said.

'Up to you. Wherever feels natural.'

She raised her chin so that her body was outside her field of vision. 'This okay?'

'Spot on,' he said.

Every so often he gave a time check, more for her benefit, she imagined, than the students. Her mind and her body took turns to grab her attention. Her feet grew colder and colder until she could barely feel them. She pictured her parents chatting over a late breakfast, wondering how she was getting on in her new job. Her knees ached and the rug she was sitting on prickled the skin on her buttocks. Oh, God. Had this blanket been washed since what's-his-name – *Viktor* – sat on it?

Callum called a break. Her muscles had stiffened in the course of twenty motionless minutes, and when she stood up she couldn't help letting out a groan. She'd noticed how her parents emitted random moans and groans every time they got up from a chair or climbed the stair. It sounded to her like a constant and irritating plea for attention. Now, heaven forbid, she was doing the same thing.

Turning away from the students, she pulled on her robe and headed for her little room. Callum was right. She would have felt embarrassed weaving her way between the easels without something covering her nakedness.

There was a gentle knock on the door. 'Can I get you anything?' Callum said. 'I generally have a coffee mid-morning,' he said, 'but if you'd like one now...'

'I'll leave it a while,' she said, not wanting him to come in and destroy her illusion of disconnection.

When she tried rubbing the life back into her feet, she saw that the bottoms were filthy. Next time she must bring her Birkenstocks.

7

A TAP ON THE BEDROOM DOOR and a whispered 'Miriam? Are you asleep?'

Her mother was hovering on the landing, holding a cup of tea. She had swapped her beige dress for something identical in bottle green, the marcasite brooch at the neck the only thing that indicated she was going out.

'Lovely. Thanks, Mum.'

'Dad wants us to leave at eight,' her mother said.

Miriam didn't want to go. *Really* didn't want to go. She didn't want to strip off her cosy sweater, her cords, her woolly socks. She didn't want to struggle into tights, dress, party shoes. She didn't want to accompany her parents over the road to see in the New Year with a crowd of geriatric strangers.

'Oh,' her mother said, 'you haven't changed yet.'

'Plenty of time.' Miriam held up a bottle of bath bubbles. 'First I'm going to have a soak. Rosa gave me these for Christmas.'

'Oh dear.' The response was potent with reproach and anxiety.

Her mother never failed to give the impression that she was incapable of working anything out for herself. It made Miriam cross and sad, and she wanted to shake her. But shaking old ladies wasn't allowed and instead she stirred things a little. 'Then I have to ring a few people. If

I wait until midnight, they'll be too drunk to make sense. But you two go ahead. It's you and Dad they want to see, not me. I'll pop over later.'

Her mother fiddled with her brooch. 'I don't know…'

She caught a whiff of the floral scent her mother dabbed on her wrists on special occasions and, repenting, kissed her cheek, the skin beneath her lips soft and pliable like putty-coloured chamois leather.

She lay back in the bath, breasts, belly and knees breaking the surface of the water in a glistening archipelago. Her father's voice was rumbling on in the kitchen below. Occasionally her mother murmured something. She couldn't make out what they were saying but she knew they were conducting a post-mortem on her reluctance to conform to their schedule.

After the first few modelling sessions, nudity had become shockingly easy. Either she'd lost every ounce of self-esteem or she'd gained an astounding new confidence. Whichever it was, she looked forward to her mornings at the college. On the practical side, things were running smoothly. Naomi wasn't the least interested in how she spent her days as long as she was at the school gates in time to meet the children. Taking a sponge, she trickled water across her neck and shoulders. Forty years ago her future had rested in this body. Love. Marriage. Motherhood. Now her body was a business asset. Her means of income. Compared with her teaching salary, the pay was a pittance but she'd opened an account with the Halifax and was insanely proud of her blue passbook and its mounting balance.

Something flashed in the darkness beyond the window, followed by a barrage of muted pops and crackles. New Year's Eve. The first of the fireworks. This time last year, she and Sam had been getting ready to go to a party. Full of hope, they'd kissed and raised their glasses to 'the future'. This evening, the best she could hope was that nothing too awful would happen in the coming year. The odds were stacked against it. This morning she'd spotted her father fiddling with a pill-dispenser. When he saw her he'd shoved it into his sock drawer and when she sneaked back to check, it had disappeared. Her mother had, several times during the course of her week-long visit, stopped mid-sentence and looked around as if someone else had been speaking. If illness or old age didn't get them, there was always a wonky paving slab or a runaway bin lorry. A wave of non-specific anxiety swept over her.

Most of the houses she could see from the bedroom window were still festooned with Christmas lights. No inflatable Santas or flying Rudolphs in this staid street. God forbid. Yet there were elements of one-upmanship in the tasteful displays. And so many lights. All those the meters whirring round. Npower must love Christmas.

The children had persuaded David to decorate the trees in their front garden. Watching him gather up tools, duct tape and such like, Miriam had been filled with sadness. When he'd finished, Rosa had pressed him to stay for lunch. 'I don't want to impose,' he'd said, his eyes fixed on Naomi who had seemed happy – well, not *un*happy – to go along with it. The children had hopped around the kitchen, screeching with delight. In that instant she had become an outsider in their little family unit and, leaving them together, she'd gone out for the afternoon.

Earlier on, she'd lied to her mother. She wasn't planned on calling anyone this evening – mainly because she had no one to call. She'd already spoken to Naomi. Finding a babysitter for tonight had proved impossible and her daughter was hosting a party for similarly stymied friends and their offspring. Naomi promised to keep the door to the 'granny annexe' closed but with a house full of sugar-high children it was hard to see how her domain would escape invasion.

There must be someone who'd appreciate a New Year greeting. She scrolled through her contacts. Who would she choose from the 'old days', Stephanie? Louise? Their old neighbours? Too weird, too needy-seeming after her long silence. And from the 'new days'? Callum was her only recent contact and, although he saw her naked twice a week, phoning him didn't seem quite the thing.

She crawled under the duvet and pulled it over her head. She missed Sam but she hated him, too. Deceiving her was one thing, but killing himself – that was indefensible.

It was well past ten-thirty by the time she got there. A wisp of a woman opened the front door. 'Come in, dear. Here, let me take that.'

She took off her coat and handed it to her hostess. 'I'm Miriam. Lionel and Freda's daughter.'

'I'm afraid I can't introduce you to everyone. I don't remember who half of them are.' The old lady seemed proud of her deficiency.

Her parents were in the far corner of the living room, talking to an elderly woman who appeared to be dressed for the opera, right down to velvet choker and fur wrap. When her father spotted her he tapped his wristwatch but she waved, pretending not to understand, and went in search of a drink.

She spent the next hour doing the rounds, explaining who she was and how she came to be at the party. The guests were diminutive and insubstantial, clones of her parents, and amongst them she felt like a giant. They all seemed to know Lionel and Freda Edlin which she found surprising. Whenever she pictured her parents, they were in their house, alone.

'Shall I tell you a little secret, dear,' her hostess said when Miriam returned to the kitchen for a refill. 'My husband and I spent the whole afternoon in bed.' She tittered and held arthritic hands to her cheeks.

Whether the memory was hours or decades old, it still delighted the old lady and Miriam smiled. 'Good for you.'

She watched her parents and their friends, doggedly partying on whilst all she wanted was to sleep. In the course of her many conversations with Doctor Tate, he'd spoken of a study showing that if you made it beyond seventy-two there was no reason why you couldn't live to be a hundred. He'd probably imagined this would be a comfort to her.

The kitchen door led into the garden and, lured by the

sound of fireworks, she ventured outside. Rockets burst across the sky, shooting fiery tadpoles in all directions. Bangers carumphed like artillery shells.

She checked her phone for the umpteenth time. David had texted – *H N Y Dx*. A sign that matters were improving between him and Naomi? More likely he felt sorry for her on this, the trickiest of nights.

The door opened and a woman came out. 'Mind if I join you?'

'I'm watching the fireworks.'

'Terrible waste of money,' the woman said. 'You'd think we'd have had our fill of explosions, wouldn't you? Iraq. Afghanistan.'

'True. But they are lovely, aren't they? And the smell. It takes me right back.'

They stood without talking. Watching and listening.

'What's the time?' the woman said after a few minutes.

Miriam glanced at her phone. 'Four minutes to midnight. I suppose we should join the party.'

In the bright kitchen, she had a chance to study her companion. The woman was roughly her age. Dressed in jeans and a sweater, she looked as if she should be gardening or walking the dog.

'You don't have a glass,' Miriam said.

'I'm driving. Who'd have thought the day would come when I'd be collecting my mother from a party?' The woman peered at her. 'Don't I know you?'

Before she had time to answer, a chorus of voices began the countdown. In the living room, a ragged circle had formed and Miriam was in time to link hands with her parents as they broke into *Auld Lang Syne*. After the first round, the tempo increased and they started careering in and out, welcoming in the coming year, recklessly challenging it to finish them off. The circle finally disintegrated and Miriam hugged her parents.

'You cut it fine,' her father said.

'And a happy New Year, to you too, Dad,' she murmured.

As if someone had blown the end-of-play whistle, the guests set about rummaging for coats.

'I *do* know you,' the woman said as they were making their way out. 'You're Miriam Edlin.'

'I used to be. Sorry but—'

'You wouldn't. I was two years below you at school.' She held out her hand. 'Angela Terry. Used to be Fielding.'

Miriam shook her hand, trying and failing to picture her as she might have looked forty-odd years ago.

'I hated you,' Angela said, smiling.

'Really?'

'Yes. In fact I wished you dead.'

'Gosh. Any particular reason?'

'I had a massive crush on Paul Crosby. I couldn't bear that he was going out with you instead of me. Of course he was unaware of my existence, but we're not rational when we're fifteen are we? And he was incredibly handsome, wasn't he?'

Paul Crosby. Paul. Her Paul.

'I suppose he was.'

'Have you kept in touch?'

'No,' Miriam said. 'Paul went to med school in London and… it sort of petered out. I've no idea what happened to him after that.'

Angela raised her eyebrows. 'So you haven't heard?'

'Heard what?'

'He's joined a GP practice. Here. In the city centre. I know because a friend of a friend is the practice nurse. I gather he's recently divorced.'

Her parents were heading for the door, signalling her to get a move on.

'I'm sorry but I have to go,' she said.

'That's a shame,' Angela said. 'Why don't we meet for coffee? Are you around tomorrow?'

'I'm afraid I'm off home. But maybe next time I'm here.'

She scrawled her number on a scrap of paper and gave it to her new acquaintance.

'Who's that woman you were talking to?' her father asked when they got back to the house.

'Angela Terry,' she said. 'We were at school together.'

'That's nice,' her mother said, unpinning her brooch.

'Are you alright, Miriam?' her father said. 'You look drawn.'

'I'm tired, that's all. I'm off to bed.'

Her mother patted her arm. 'Sleep well. No need to rush off in the morning. Have a lie in.'

She hurried up to her room and, without undressing, got into bed.

Paul. Here. In this city.

8

IT WAS DARK. HER DRESS was tugging beneath her arms. Her skin itched where her tights gripped her waist. Pushing away the duvet, she groped for her phone. Six-forty on the first day of a new year. Desperate for a cup of tea, she tiptoed past her parents' door and down the stairs. The house was chilly but were she to advance the heating, the noise of the ancient system bursting into life would wake them. Taking her coat from the hall stand, she shoved her feet into her father's slippers and, whilst she waited for the kettle to boil, she pondered Angela Terry's revelation.

Her iPad lay on the worktop where she'd left it charging. Sitting at the kitchen table, she typed 'Paul Crosby GP UK' into the search box. A list of links came up suggesting she check LinkedIn, Facebook, Wikipedia and the like. Scrolling down she spotted something promising and a tap on the screen took her to an announcement in the local online paper. 'Dr Paul Crosby has joined Monkton Square Surgery as a general practitioner'. A few sentences followed explaining that 'Dr Crosby was a pupil at the local grammar school before going on to study medicine in London. He has worked all over the UK, most recently in Scotland'.

Within thirty seconds of trying, she'd found Paul Crosby and discovered where he'd been for the past forty-two years. A second tap and she was looking at a map showing the location of the practice. She pulled the coat around her and leaned back, staring at the red marker. Technology made everything dangerously easy. How could a blob induce such... such... agitation? Heart-stopping information like this should be harder-earned.

She made a mug of tea and took a packet of digestive biscuits from the tin, dunking one after another, taking comfort from their soggy sweetness. Did her parents know he was back? They read the local paper. They gossiped with neighbours. It was perfectly possible. They'd looked so harmless last night, telling her to 'sleep well', perhaps knowing that the young man they'd ruthlessly eliminated from her life had returned and was working a mile or two away. Fuck their toxic vulnerability. She would wake them and demand an answer.

But as she stood at their bedroom door, she felt her rage giving way to frustrated acceptance. Even without their interference, it was unlikely she and Paul would have made it through those student days. She'd been over it often enough to convince herself of that. Was there any point in revisiting a mistake made all those years ago?

The sun had not yet risen. Frost rimed the lawn lending it a ghostly luminosity. Her breath fogged the air. The car windows needed de-icing and it took half a dozen attempts before the engine stuttered into life. The only living thing she encountered on her short drive was a black-and-white cat, a wraith streaking across the road, yellow eyes catching her headlights before it vanished over a garden wall.

Monkton Square. A shabby public garden enclosed within a dog-proof fence and surrounded by three-storey buildings. The houses had started life as homes for affluent Victorian families but now, judging by the nameplates, they were occupied by solicitors, dentists and architects. She drove slowly around the square until she came to number eighteen. Stopping, she leaned across the passenger seat and peered at the sign. 'Monkton Square Surgery'. It was light enough to see his name on the list of practitioners, 'Dr Paul Crosby', followed by a string of letters. She got out of the car. The thermometer on the dash was showing minus three and she could well believe it. She pulled up her coat collar, buried her nose in her scarf and studied 'Surgery Hours for the holiday period' on the noticeboard. The practice wouldn't open again until next Monday. Three whole days.

Of course Angela might have got it wrong. Maybe Paul wasn't divorced. Or maybe he *was* but he had a new partner. He could have been married several times. Doctors – real and fictional – held limitless potential for romance. Doctor Zhivago. What's-his-name in *Brief Encounter*. The whole cast of *ER*. If Paul had retained even a modicum of his good looks, he would have women throwing themselves at him.

She had dressed in a hurry, foolishly choosing the thin-soled pumps she'd worn to the party and her feet were numb. With her phone, she took a picture of the practice details and returned to the car where, abandoning her duty to the environment, she sat with the engine running and heater at full blast.

What should she do? What *could* she do at eight o'clock on New Year's Day morning?

Slipping the car into gear, she drove on around the square but, when she reached the turn that would take her home, she kept going and, for the second time, stopped outside number eighteen. Opening the glove compartment, she took out the spiral-bound pad she kept for making shopping lists and jotting down interesting bits she heard on the radio. Whilst she was here, she might as well leave a note. What harm could it do?

After several false starts, she was reasonably happy with what she'd written.

Dear Paul

I only heard last night that you've moved back. I shan't attempt to précis the past forty years. Suffice it to say, I was widowed last year. My parents live in the same house and I visit them often.

I hope life has treated/is treating you well.

Best wishes,

Miriam

She added a single kiss, her mobile phone number and, after some deliberation, her address. She couldn't simply push it through the letterbox for anyone to read – although it was perfectly innocuous. She rooted through her bag and found a tatty but unused envelope. Putting her note inside, she sealed it and addressed it in bold letters. 'Dr Paul Crosby – PERSONAL'. Before she could change her mind, she shoved it through the outsized letterbox.

She was getting back in the car, when a figure appeared from nowhere, muffled from head to toe against the cold, shuffling along the pavement towards her. As the figure drew nearer, Miriam saw that she – from the UGG-type boots, she guessed it was a woman – had a white rabbit tucked beneath her arm.

'Hello,' she said as the woman drew parallel with her. 'What a gorgeous rabbit.'

Ignoring her, the woman shuffled on.

Only eight hours old, this new year was already proving interesting.

By the time her parents came downstairs, Miriam had showered, dressed (properly this time) and was stirring a pan of porridge.

'You enjoyed the party?' her mother said.

She gave a noncommittal smile. 'Your friends are very chatty. I got all the local gossip.'

Was she mistaken or did a frisson of unease pass between her parents?

'I could have sworn your car was parked facing the other way,' her father said.

'I'll make the toast,' her mother said. 'After breakfast there's something you can give me a hand with.'

Her mother had taken it into her head that a glass-fronted cabinet in which she kept her best china needed moving from one side of the fireplace to the other.

'I need to give everything a good rinse,' her mother said as they emptied the contents onto the coffee table.

Miriam was tempted to remark that it couldn't

possibly be dirty but washing cups and saucers seemed as good as any way of passing the few hours before she could leave for home. 'Why not?' she said.

Her mother muttered something which she only half caught.

'The better the… what?' she said.

'The better the day, the better the deed. My grandmother used to say that.' Her mother's face took on a faraway look. 'She had the loveliest voice. And the tiniest feet.'

As Miriam stood at the kitchen sink, swishing fragile, never-used porcelain in sudsy water, she took the opportunity to ask, 'Did I see Dad with a pill dispenser?'

Her mother was drying a tea plate, turning it round and around, seemingly hell-bent on erasing the gold paint from its rim.

'Mum? Is Dad okay?'

Her mother looked bewildered, and it struck Miriam that her father might be shielding his wife, protecting her from bad news, and she let the matter drop.

Callum phoned from Scotland where he and his family were visiting friends. He wished her a 'Good New Year'. It was nice to hear from him, sweet of him to think of her, but his voice wasn't the one she wanted to hear. She pictured her shabby envelope, thrown out with a pile of junk mail or scuffed under the doormat by a patient scurrying in from the cold. Anything was preferable to his ignoring her note.

Rosa and Max weren't due back at school until Thursday.

Naomi had arranged a couple of 'play dates'. Playdates. Sleepovers. The inexorable creep of Americanisms. And, rather too cheerfully, her daughter had returned to work. Miriam didn't object. To be truthful it was good to have something to take her mind off her silent phone. The children were hooked on the Monopoly set David's parents had given them for Christmas and were happy to play for hours on end as long as she played too.

On Wednesday morning, she woke around six-thirty. The duvet had slipped to one side and her shoulders were cold. It was dark yet an unusual brightness penetrated the narrow gap between the curtains. The customary morning noises – a car reversing off a driveway; the hum and rattle of the milk float; a dog barking in a neighbour's garden – were absent. The world was silent.

Pulling on her dressing gown, she went to the window and drew back the curtain. Snow. Heaps of it. Meringue toppings on cars and wheelie bins and garden walls. Hedges and shrubs bowing and sagging under their white burden. Unblemished pavements crying out to be trampled. Indigo shadows, almost as dark as the sky, spilling across the garden. And the snow was still coming down, small flakes swirling in front of the streetlights. It was impossible not to marvel at it.

The children were delirious, bolting breakfast and pestering Naomi to dig out the toboggan before she left for work.

'You'll take us to the park, won't you Gamma?' Rosa said.

'I'm going to make the best snowman in the world,'

Max said. 'Have you got a carrot, Mum? And some coal?'

The low, grey clouds hung heavy and the local radio station was warning of more to come, reeling off lists of impassable roads and cancelled buses, advising against 'non-essential travel'.

'How will you get to work?' Miriam said. 'The car's half-buried.'

'If push comes to shove, I can walk.'

'It'll be hard going.'

The children were impatient to be outside. Miriam, too, felt the compulsion and soon the three of them were togged up. First they went into the back garden kicking up the snow, churning around in it, laughing and shrieking, despoiling its perfection.

Naomi came out to say her boss had phoned telling her not to come in and to check again tomorrow.

The children started on their snowman but the snow was powdery and each time they rolled a snowball, it disintegrated before it had reached a decent size.

'It's not working,' Rosa wailed aiming a hefty kick at yet another failure.

'How about using a shovel?' Miriam said.

But Max would have none of that. 'Dad *always* starts with a snowball,' he said. His cheeks were scarlet, roughened by the wind. Trails of clear snot ran from his nostrils. 'I wish he was here,' he whispered.

Most of the time, the children coped well. But if things went awry, or when the present didn't live up to the remembered past, it became too much. Max was six years old. Poor little boy. He couldn't be expected to understand what she, after a lifetime of ups and downs, could not.

'Why don't we give it a try?' she said.

The children trailed after her to the garden shed, watching doubtingly as she rummaged around. Once she'd found the plastic spades they used at the beach, she returned to a corner of the lawn where the snow lay undisturbed and began shovelling snow into a conical mound, slapping each new layer with the flat of the spade trying to get it to stick.

The children watched from a distance, firing off negative comments. 'That's a sandcastle, Gamma, not a snowman.' 'Where's his head?' 'It's too small.' She carried on, hoping that, by magic, the unimposing heap of snow might be transformed into something acceptable. It was starting to snow again. Staring at the tiny flakes whirling across the garden induced mesmerising dizziness.

'My feet hurt,' Rosa moaned.

Stray wisps of hair not covered by her hat were dripping icy droplets onto Miriam's neck. 'What we need is a hot chocolate,' she said and they trouped back into the house.

They were peeling off layers of soggy clothing when her father phoned. 'What's it like there? We've had a smattering but I've been watching the news and looks a lot worse where you are.'

Miriam hadn't given her parents a thought. 'We've had a good few inches. And it's still snowing. Naomi's been told to stay home and the kids aren't due back at school until tomorrow.'

'Your mother wants me to ask if you've got plenty of food in,' he said.

'We're absolutely fine, Dad. How about you?'

'Every time there's "two-for-one", your mother stashes one away. We won't starve.'

She visualised her parents' larder, tins and packets relentlessly passing their use-by dates, shelves stacked with more food than they would live to eat.

'So how's our granddaughter?' he said, 'and our great-grandchildren?'

'Everyone's fine,' she said, catching Naomi's eye and pointing at the phone.

Naomi grimaced and shook her head.

'When are they coming to see us?' he said.

'Soon,' she said. 'They get booked up at weekends what with activities and birthday parties, but I'll pop up again as soon as the weather improves. Promise.'

Warm, dry and full of hot chocolate, the children were soon angling to be outside again, fretting that the weather might change and the snow melt. She was doing her best to convince them that a game of Monopoly would be just the thing, when the doorbell rang. It was David towing an obviously new and very swanky toboggan.

'I've given myself the day off,' he said. 'I thought the kids might like a trip to the park.'

Naomi didn't seem surprised to see him and Miriam guessed he'd okayed it with her before coming.

'Don't stand there with the door open,' she said. 'You're letting the warm out.'

David stepped into the hall and slipped off his boots.

'Why don't you come with us?' he said to Naomi. 'It'll be fun.'

'Yes. Please come, Mum,' Rosa said.

Max screwed up his face, stressing the earnestness of his entreaty. 'Pleeeease.'

'I suppose I could,' she said. 'Okay. Why not?'

Miriam dug out dry gloves and socks for the children and helped them back into their outdoor gear, glad that Naomi and David seemed to be finding ways of getting to know each other again. Having waved the four of them off, she took a cup of tea and yesterday's half-finished crossword up to her bedroom. Every now and again, when a clue was getting the better of her, she glanced out at the back garden watching the steady, persistent snow restoring the lawn to marshmallow perfection.

Thanks to a meteorological something-or-another, by Saturday the snow had all but disappeared and life was returning to normal. Naomi had taken the children into town to spend their Christmas book tokens and Miriam was sorting through her laundry basket when her phone rang. The screen showed 'unknown caller'.

'Hello?' she said. All that she could hear was a whispery sound that could be the wind. 'Hello? If you're trying to sell me double-glazing, I've already got plenty. And I've never worked in a noisy environment or bought PPI.'

The caller – a man – exhaled, as if he'd been holding his breath for a long time. 'Miriam?'

'Who is this?' she said.

'It's me. Paul.'

She sat on the bed, eyes tight shut, leaning forward until her forehead rested on her knees. 'Gosh. Hello.'

'Gosh indeed,' he said, laughing the laugh she'd not heard for forty years. 'It's wonderful to hear your voice. How have you been?'

'Me? Oh. Fine, thanks. You?' He must be able to hear the pounding of her heart.

'I'm fine, too,' he said. 'Look, sorry I've not phoned sooner. I only got your note yesterday. I've been in Manchester. On a course.'

'Anything interesting?'

'Cross-infection control. Riveting stuff.' He paused. 'Where are you at the moment?'

'At home. Sitting on my bed. In a kind of granny-flat tagged on the side of my daughter's house. I live with her and my grandchildren.' It was the sort of thing a needy old woman might come out with. *Aren't I lucky? My family lets me live with them.* 'It's a temporary arrangement. Until I find something that suits me better.' Now she sounded ungrateful.

'What can you see from your window?' he said.

'The front garden. The street. Why do you—'

'Go to the window. Tell me what you see.'

A car was parked opposite, a man standing in the road, leaning against the driver's door. He wore a long, navy overcoat and a red scarf. His gloved hand was raised to his ear and he was looking up at her window. His lips moved and Paul's voice sounded in her ear. 'Hello, Mim.'

'This is crazy,' she said. 'What if I'd not been here?'

'But you are.'

He walked across the road and stood on the pavement outside the gate. 'It's freezing out here.' He was close enough for her to see his face. To recognise him. 'Any chance of a cuppa?'

Part II

MIRIAM EDLIN YANKED A PAPER TOWEL from the dispenser and wiped the condensation from the mirror above the mucky wash basin. Tossing the wad of paper into the bin, she checked her reflection. Her nose was shiny. And her hair – straightened earlier with the help of several applications of heavy-duty lacquer – was reverting to the careless waves she spent hours failing to tame.

'Bing's shoes are gruesome.' Frankie's voice came from the cubicle next to the one Miriam had vacated.

She turned on the tap, letting cold water trickle across her wrists.

'Mim? Did you see Bing's shoes? They look like they belong to his dad.'

The driving beat of *The Locomotion* was coming from beyond the cloakroom door. She pressed her hands against her cheeks, enjoying the shock of the cold. She hadn't noticed Paul Crosby's shoes. Her attention had been held by the strip of Elastoplast covering his eyebrow.

'What's happened to his face?' she said.

'God, *I* don't know. And I honestly don't care.' The cubicle door opened and Frankie emerged. 'It's something to do with this afternoon's rugby match. I swear he's keener on groping his mates than groping me.'

Miriam laughed. 'What are you on about?'

'Rugby's just an excuse for boys to touch each other up. It's a well-known fact.'

Miriam watched as her best friend leaned toward the mirror, fussing with the flicked-up ends of her hair.

Scowling and pouting. Checking lipstick and mascara. She'd given up measuring herself against Frankie. Blond hair that stayed where it was supposed to. Neat nose. Slim ankles. Size four feet – D-fitting.

'Let's get back,' Frankie said. 'Barbara's been making eyes at Bing all evening. Sly cow.'

On Saturday evenings they came to *Betty Hudson's School of Ballroom and Latin Dance*. Not to learn to foxtrot or tango (although Miriam had convinced her parents this would be an asset) but for the 'modern free' which came after the soft-drinks break. This boiled down to a selection of singles played, full blast, on an ugly but efficient record player. Hardly cutting-edge stuff but it gave them the opportunity to flirt. To hold sweaty hands. To rub against each other. To become aware of the lumps and bumps that lay beneath their Saturday best. To get a hint of mysteries yet to be revealed.

Although Miriam wasn't keen on these febrile Saturday evenings, she was conscious that friendships were forged through collective experience. Friday evening youth club. A Saturday job. A place in the tennis team. But she was excluded from these activities because she wasn't released to join her friends until after lunch on Saturdays. This made coming to *Betty's* all the more important. Frankie called her a ninny for putting up with the curfew. Told her she was old enough to decide how she lived her life. But Miriam had watched her father and Danny fight over the self same issues until things became so bad her brother stopped coming home. She couldn't put them through that again.

The girls linked arms and made their way to the far corner of the hall where the others – Bing, Barbara, Colin, Little Pete, Emms, Lisa and Judith – were standing in a loose circle. The boys were laughing about something, and the girls were laughing because the boys were laughing. Frankie uncoupled herself from Miriam and took her place at Bing's side, standing close to him, their arms touching.

Neil Sedaka was next up and Frankie took Bing's hand and dragged him onto the dance floor. Lisa and Judith were already jiving together. They spent hours rehearsing their routine – a sequence of quirky, jerky manoeuvres repeated with single-minded precision and blank faces. Without debate, the rest of the group paired up, leaving Miriam to the mercy of Emms.

Glyn Emms – a gangly, narrow-faced boy with chewed finger nails – had made it known that he 'wouldn't mind going out with' Miriam Edlin. Of course he hadn't said as much to her. Such propositions were conveyed by a third party (in this case Colin) who acted as go-between until the matter was resolved, one way or the other. She wasn't flattered by Emms's attention. He wasn't desperate to go out with *her*. He was desperate to go out with a girl. *Any* girl – as long as she had lips and breasts and something mysterious in her knickers. That's what all these boys were after. It was demoralising and depressing.

'Dance?' Emms directed his invitation over her shoulder, as if he were talking to someone a few feet behind her.

With no good reason to refuse, she nodded and they

spent the next three minutes dancing a foot apart, avoiding each other's eyes. As they danced, Miriam edged nearer Frankie and Bing, grimacing and mouthing 'help' when she caught her friend's eye.

As soon as the music stopped, she pulled Frankie to one side. 'Keep talking. Don't let Emms muscle in.'

Emms was watching her, a soppy smile on his face. 'Oh, God,' she said. 'He winked at me.'

'He's such a creep,' Frankie said. 'I'll get Bing to warn him off.'

'How?'

'I don't know. He could tell him you're... you're... frigid. That should do it.'

Miriam wasn't clear what frigid meant but she knew it wasn't complimentary. To be on the safe side, when the last dance started up – the smoochy number that established pairings for the coming week – she made sure to be in the 'Ladies'.

They spilled out of *Betty's* and headed for the coffee bar next to the bus station. For years and years it had been a seedy little café where people went to keep warm while they waited for a bus. Recently it had changed ownership and had been fitted out with leatherette seats and a flashy Italian coffee machine, and now it was called 'Presto'.

They ambled along, Miriam and Frankie arm in arm, Bing and Emms lagging at the back, probably discussing her frigidity.

'Is Bing okay with this?' she said.

'Of course,' Frankie said. 'My every wish is his command. Besides, he thinks you're too good for Emms.'

She was surprised to hear this. As Frankie's best friend, she was often in Paul's company but she couldn't recall ever having a conversation with him. In fact she'd always felt intimidated by Paul – 'Bing' – Crosby, the golden boy of the Lower Sixth. As well as being handsome, he was clever. And sporty. *And* he'd passed his Grade 7 piano exam.

At the coffee bar they squeezed into adjacent booths. Miriam sat with Frankie, Bing and Colin. Emms was on the next table, facing away from her. (Whatever Bing had told him had done the trick.) She wasn't keen on coffee but she ordered it just the same, spooning in enough brown sugar to offset its bitterness. Again the boys dominated the conversation, making jokes she didn't always understand but laughed at anyway. It was fun being here in the coffee-scented warmth with her friends, knowing that Bing thought she was too good for Emms.

Frankie nudged her, nodding towards two young men who had come. They were older – perhaps in their early twenties. One wore his dark hair in a ponytail. The other had a moth-eaten crew cut. Both were wearing donkey jackets and the orange boots favoured by workmen and art students. Crew-cut sat at the table across the aisle, reading a tattered paperback, while Ponytail went to the counter.

'Time for another coffee, I think,' Frankie said and, manoeuvring past Bing, she went up to the counter and stood behind the young man as he placed his order.

Miriam saw her friend tap the man on his shoulder. He turned around and, smiling, took something from his pocket, swapping it for whatever she had in her hand. *She'd asked him for change.* Then they were chatting away as if they were old friends. Bing was grumbling about his father's refusal to pay for driving lessons, talking too loudly, pretending not to notice that his girlfriend was flirting with a stranger.

'Where's your coffee?' Bing said when Frankie returned empty-handed.

'Changed my mind,' she said. 'I'm allowed to, aren't I?'

Miriam was in her bedroom when the doorbell rang.

'Someone to see you,' her mother called.

She hurried down, expecting to find Frankie in the hall. But it was Bing.

'Hi,' he said. 'Am I disturbing you?'

'I was getting ahead with some reading for next week,' she said. 'Nothing that can't wait.'

'Can I get your friend something to drink?' Her mother directed the question at her as though Bing weren't there.

'Not for me, thanks,' Bing said. 'I'm Paul, by the way. Paul Crosby. I'm at school with Miriam.'

'She's never mentioned you.'

'Paul does science, Mum,' Miriam said. 'We don't have lessons together.'

'Ahhh. So you're going to be a scientist.'

Bing cleared his throat. 'Actually I'm hoping to become a doctor.'

'A *doctor*. Goodness me.' Her mother's lips, squeezed in a prim smile, conveyed her scepticism.

Miriam shot her a go-away glare but she stood her ground.

'Miriam very kindly lent me bus fare the other day,' he said. 'I was passing so I thought I'd drop it in.'

He jangled the coins his pocket which appeared to satisfy her mother. 'I must get on,' she said and disappeared into the kitchen.

'I don't think she likes me,' he said.

'It's not you. She's the same with everyone.'

Bing ran his hand through his hair. 'You can guess why I'm here.'

She nodded towards the kitchen where her mother was clattering pans. 'Let's go outside.'

She slipped on her coat and they went into the front garden and sat on the wall.

'Frankie and I have had a bit of a set-to,' he said. 'I assumed she would have told you.'

When they'd left the coffee bar she'd seen Frankie and Bing standing in the corner of the bus station and it was obvious they were arguing. 'No. I haven't spoken to her today,' she said.

He swivelled to face her, the dressing on his eyebrow making him look simultaneously heroic and vulnerable. 'Apparently I'm boring. And immature. And uncreative – whatever that means. Oh, and possessive. I almost forgot possessive.' He looked up and down the street. 'Fancy a walk?'

'Okay,' she said, suddenly and unaccountably wanting to spend time with this boy whom she scarcely knew.

'Shouldn't you tell your mum?' he said.

It was considerate of him to suggest it, but her mother would probably raise an objection and she didn't want to risk it.

'It's fine,' she said.

He levered himself off the wall and dropped down onto the pavement. 'Where shall we go?'

Wanting to prove she had a mind of her own she said 'Let's go to Bellevue Park.'

'The park it is.' He offered her his hand as she jumped down. 'Blimey. You're freezing.' He pulled a pair of woolly gloves from the pocket of his duffle coat. 'Here.'

They walked, and talked about Frankie. He wanted to know about the Slattery family and what Frankie was planning to do when she left school. She was surprised how little he knew about her considering they'd been together for months. She answered as best she could, careful not to let slip anything that showed Frankie in an unfavourable light – or herself to be an unreliable friend.

Bellevue Park – a grand Victorian endeavour – dropped down the hill towards the canal. It was a popular destination for a post-Sunday lunch stroll, offering a tropical greenhouse, ponds with water lilies, goldfish and miniature waterfalls, tennis courts and a bandstand. A notice stated that the play area was for 'under twelves' but the park keeper was nowhere to be seen and she and Bing sat on adjacent swings, swaying back and forth whilst, all around, children slid and jumped and twirled and yelled.

They urged their swings higher. Leaning backwards, legs extended; bending forwards, legs tucked under. The swings were soon out of synch, and they exchanged snippets of conversation as they flew past each other.

'I used to come here with my brother,' she said. 'Once he got flung off the roundabout and broke his collar bone.'

'You have a brother?'

'Yes. Danny. He's five years older than me.'

'What does he do?' he said.

The truth was, she had no idea what Danny did, or where he was. The last time he wrote, he was in California 'with a group of like-minded pilgrims'. (When her father read this he'd hit the roof.) That was months ago.

'He's travelling,' – as she flew forward. 'You have two older sisters,' – as she plummeted back.

'How d'you know?'

'Frankie told me.'

He dragged his feet on the tarmac, bringing his swing to a standstill, waiting for her to do the same. 'How come you two are friends?' he said. 'I don't get it.'

She could ask him the same question but from what she'd just heard he and Frankie weren't friends. Not *friend* friends, anyway. So she didn't, instead describing her first nervous day at grammar school. How she and Frankie had ended up sitting together. How, although they weren't the least alike, neither of them quite fitted in. Frankie – opinionated and rebellious. She – a bit 'square' and from a different culture. How they complemented and supported each other. She told him how she sometimes did Frankie's homework for her and recounted several of her friend's crazier escapades, embellishing the stories to make them more amusing. She made him laugh, and she liked that she could do that.

'Watch out. Parkie.' Bing pointed at the park keeper who was blowing his whistle and heading in their direction. Grabbing her hand, he pulled her off the swing seat and they ran, laughing, out of the play area, along the terrace towards the bandstand, keeping going until they could no longer hear the shrill whistle.

Monday morning, and the girls' cloakroom was buzzing with weekend gossip.

'Guess who I was with last night,' Frankie said as they were changing into their indoor shoes.

Miriam shrugged. 'Who?'

'Remember the guy in the coffee bar? The one with the ponytail?' Frankie rolled her eyes. 'And guess what? He's got a car.'

'But Bing? You can't just—'

'Mim. We're seventeen. We can do whatever we like.'

Throughout the week, Frankie talked of little else but Gregg. She'd cheated on previous boyfriends but never on Bing – not to Miriam's knowledge, anyway. She couldn't help wondering why a man like Gregg would bother with a schoolgirl. But she said nothing, and it was several days before she discovered that Frankie had told him she was nineteen and had a job as a secretary in a solicitor's office.

'So what about Bing?' Miriam said.

'What *about* Bing?'

'He's bound to find out.'

'Only if someone tells him.' Frankie said.

The week trundled by. Miriam saw Bing in the distance – twice – and he smiled and raised his hand but they didn't speak. When she asked Frankie if she was going to *Betty*'s on Saturday, she came back with a vague 'That depends.'

'On…?

'Whether I get a better offer. And I've been thinking, Mim. Maybe Gregg could fix you up with his friend.'

'*Abso*lutely not.'

Frankie grinned. 'Only joking. Will you go?'

She'd never gone to *Betty*'s without Frankie. The other girls could be stand-offish and, when it came to the boys, she lacked Frankie's confidence.

'Depends,' she said.

'You should,' Frankie said. 'You can keep Bing company.'

On Saturdays, Frankie worked on the counter at Swift's Bakery and, as soon as the Edlins had finished lunch, Miriam went to find her, loitering outside until the shop was empty.

'Did you get your better offer?' she said.

'Indeed I did.' Frankie glanced over her shoulder and lowered her voice. 'We're going to a party. Can I tell Mum I'm staying at yours?'

Mrs Slattery was a careworn woman – nothing at all like Frankie. Mr Slattery had walked out on the family (Frankie had two younger brothers) before the girls met and Frankie never spoke of him. Miriam guessed this went a long way to explaining her friend's two-fingers approach to life. Danny's leaving had taken its toll on the Edlins but, if anything, it had made them cling together more tightly. Grow more inward-looking. But it might have been very different had her father been the one to leave.

'I don't know…'

'Come on, Mim. What's your problem?'

'*My* problem? I rather think it's *your* problem. What if there's an emergency and your mother phones my house? And there's Bing. What if he asks where you are?'

'What if… what if an asteroid – or do I mean a meteor – smashes into the earth?'

The shop door opened and two women came in, curtailing the girls' conversation.

Frankie dropped a jam doughnut in a paper bag and handed it to Miriam. 'I'll ring you when I finish here.'

The class was ten minutes into the foxtrot when Miriam arrived. She'd hung on at home as long as she could in case Frankie changed her mind.

Pairings for the 'ballroom' session were more to do with matching heights than romantic intent. If you didn't sort yourself out, Betty did it for you. This evening, girls were in short supply and, as soon as she walked into the hall, Betty pushed her towards a boy she'd not seen here before. He was nondescript and had nothing to say for himself but he had a good sense of rhythm and was able to count in his head – quite a bonus. As they moved around the room – *slow, slow, quick, quick* – she took stock. Lisa and Colin. Judith and Little Pete. Emms, standing in the corner. And was that Bing over there, with Barbara?

The foxtrot led on to the waltz, and the waltz to the tango. Everyone kept the same partners. When it came to the half-time break, the boy thanked her and wandered out of the door.

'Where's Frankie tonight?' Lisa said.

She'd rehearsed her story. 'Babysitting. It came up at the last minute.'

'Well *someone's* pleased she's not here.' Lisa inclined her head towards Barbara.

Miriam gazed at Bing, willing him to look her way. Almost at once he glanced at her, smiled and came to join her. She felt dizzy with the nearness of him.

'I won't ask where she is,' he said.

'She has these mad moments, Bing. I'm sure she'll come to her—'

'I don't want to talk about Frankie.'

Clattering signalled the lifting of the roller shutter and with that everyone began drifting towards the counter where refreshments were on sale.

Bing caught her arm. 'Let's get out of here.'

We're seventeen. We can do what we like.

'Okay.'

While their friends were buying pop and crisps, they collected their coats and slipped out of the hall. After the sweaty fug, the air was shockingly cold but Miriam's uncontrollable shivering had as much to do with nerves as with the temperature. Barely speaking, they hurried past Presto, keeping going until they reached the railway station. The café in the ticket hall was still open, picking up trade from late travellers and those with nowhere to go on a cold Saturday night.

'Coffee?' he said.

'I've a confession to make,' she said. 'I don't actually like coffee. Can I have tea?'

He smiled. 'You're funny.' He waved away the coins she offered. 'You get them next time.'

Next time.

'Before you say anything,' he said when he returned, 'I know about Frankie.'

'Oh.'

'It's that bloke from the coffee bar, isn't it? The one with the stupid ponytail.'

She'd got the wrong end of the stick. She was here to lend a sympathetic ear.

'I went to meet her from work,' he said. 'He was in the shop with her. She spotted me through the window. And d'you know what she did?' He paused. 'She kissed him.'

Had anyone else been the injured party, she might have excused Frankie. But Bing – it wasn't on.

'That's a rotten thing to do,' she said. 'I don't know what comes over her sometimes. I'm sure she'll come to her senses—'

'She doesn't deserve a friend like you.'

She blushed and looked down. An oily film had formed on the surface of her tea. The station announcer's tinny voice was reeling off a list of stations.

'Actually it's fine,' he said. 'You see I went to the shop to tell her it's over.'

He was no longer wearing the sticking plaster and she could see stitches, like three black spiders, running through his eyebrow. The blemish made his face more beautiful.

'The thing is,' he said, 'I've met someone else.'

'Oh. Right.'

'Can you guess who?'

'Barbara?'

'No, silly. Not Barbara. *You.*'

Instead of catching the bus, they walked. Bing positioned himself on the edge of the pavement, between her and passing traffic. Her father did that when he walked alongside a woman and it made her feel grown up. She was no longer the least bit cold because Bing had his arm around her, holding her close. They talked non-stop. Shop window displays. The chrome on a monster motor bike. An old man walking four podgy dogs. Litter. Whether chips tasted better with ketchup or brown sauce, which led naturally on to the question of vinegar. She liked it, he didn't.

When she could put it off no longer, she said, 'What's Frankie going to say.'

'About…?'

'*Us.* What's she going to think?'

'*Us* has nothing to do with her. She's made it crystal clear she doesn't give a toss about me. She can't expect me to hang around on the off chance she'll change her mind.'

He was right. But Frankie Slattery wasn't the most rational person in the world.

'Shouldn't we at least wait until you've spoken to her?' she said.

'Don't worry. I was always going to be a stepping stone to someone else.'

'So why did you put up with her?'

'The same reason you do. She's funny. Disrespectful. Dangerous. It's thrilling at first but you can have enough of that sort of thing.'

As they neared the house, she grew apprehensive. Light was filtering through the closed curtains of the living room. Her parents would be watching TV and glancing at the clock on the sideboard. She had to be in by ten-thirty and her father was a stickler for punctuality. Danny used to joke that if he didn't get in five minutes early, he got a 'rollicking' for being late.

They stopped in the deep shadows of the evergreens that framed the front gate. 'I'd better go in,' she said. 'I don't want my father coming out to look for me.'

'Now you're scaring me,' he said.

He pulled her towards him and kissed her, gently at first and then more insistently, his tongue probing deeper and deeper. A tingle, barely noticeable at first, spread through her body, building and building until it she could think of nothing else.

Next day, Sunday, Miriam heard nothing from Frankie. Neither was she in school on Monday. She'd mitched off before but she'd never been out of touch for this long – especially baffling knowing what she'd been planning for Saturday night. But surely if Frankie had disappeared or anything terrible had happened to her, Mrs Slattery would have been in contact. Most days, the two girls dawdled homeward together, going their separate ways when they reached St John's Church. Today she stopped at a phone box and dialled the Slatterys' number. If Mrs Slattery answered she risked a tricky conversation about Frankie's supposed night at her house. But she needn't have worried because there was no reply.

Frankie turned up at school on Tuesday with a note 'from her mother'. Apparently she'd been laid up with period pains – the good old standby. It wasn't until they were walking home that Miriam had a chance to question her. 'Where have you been? I was getting worried.'

'After the party we went back to his flat. Then on Sunday we drove to London. In. His. Car. It was brilliant. His friends live in a squat. We smoked pot and drank vodka and listened to music. It was the best thing ever.'

Miriam couldn't see beyond the practicalities of Frankie's two-night absence. 'What did you tell your mother?'

'That your parents were going away, and they'd asked me to stay at yours to keep you company. She thinks the sun shines out of your bum so she was fine with that.'

Miriam gasped. 'That's *outrageous*.'

Frankie ran a few yards ahead then turned to face her. 'So… do I look different?'

For months Frankie had been preoccupied with losing her virginity. Reading about it. Talking about it. Fantasising about it. All the same, Miriam was shaken by her decision to surrender to a stranger, even if he did have a car and a ponytail.

'Not really,' she said.

'Well I *feel* different. And that's because I *am* different. I've been liberated.' Seizing her satchel by its strap, Frankie twirled around, the buckled bag inscribing a horizontal circle. 'Sex is a million times better than I imagined.' She twirled a few more times then let go, releasing the satchel to fly through the air and land with a thump in the middle of the road.

Miriam had spent the best part of two days worrying about divulging her news. But Frankie's recklessness infected her and out it spilled. 'Bing's asked me to go out with him.'

Disbelief flitted across Frankie's face. 'And?'

'And I said I would. That's okay, isn't it?'

She grinned. 'It's more than okay. It's perfect.'

They were interrupted by the blast of a car horn as a motorist swerved to avoid the satchel. The din attracted the attention of several pedestrians who watched Frankie saunter into the road, pick up her bag, raise her middle finger to the driver, and saunter back again.

'Let's give the nosey old biddies a fright,' she said and plonked a swift, rough kiss on Miriam's lips.

Initially her parents' disapproval of her friendship with Bing amounted to nothing more than a negative undertow. She put this down to their reluctance to accept that she was old enough to have a real boyfriend. Paul Crosby standing in their hall waiting for her, and her flushed cheeks when he brought her home, were proof that she was no longer their 'little girl'. She hoped that the more they saw of him, the more accepting they would become. He was hard-working, courteous and dependable. He was going to be a doctor, for goodness sake. What more could they ask? But as the weeks and months passed, their resistance stiffened. He rarely made it further than the front door where he was met (usually by her father) with frostiness. It got so that she was on pins before he came to collect her and, to protect him from their hostility, she waited for him in the porch.

His parents, on the other hand, couldn't have been more welcoming. Julia and Angus Crosby were doctors with a laissez-faire approach to domestic chores, homework, bad language, hairstyles, bed- and mealtimes – matters which obsessed her parents. The family lived in a grand but ramshackle house which hummed with interesting people doing interesting things. If she happened to be there when a meal was in prospect, a place would be set for her at the vast kitchen table. (Never a tablecloth which she found daring and thrilling.) No one interrogated her about school or her plans for the future. No one batted an eyelid when she and Bing went up to his bedroom. The same went for his sisters and their boyfriends, when they were around. She wondered whether, immersed in illness and death, his mother and father understood how important it was to live in the now.

'Don't you feel like doing mannish things sometimes?' she said.

They were in Bing's room. The door was open, a babble of voices drifting up from the kitchen where a game of brag was in full swing.

'*Mannish*?' he said. 'Is that even a word?'

'You know what I mean. Drinking. Telling dirty jokes. Chatting up birds. Seriously. You're surrounded by women. Me. Your sisters. Doesn't it get you down?'

'I love it,' he said, 'although now you come to mention it, I feel like doing a *mannish* thing right now.'

He closed the door and switched off the light. 'Come here, you.' His arms folded around her and she breathed in the smell that was becoming as familiar to her as her own. Tangy shampoo. Lanolin from his sweater. A hint of sweat – not unpleasant.

They kissed, the ache she'd grown to crave spreading to her most secret places. Next, as though by accident, his hand brushed the front of her sweater. Back and forth, back and forth, causing her breasts to tingle and her heart to race. (All the time, kissing, her skin getting hotter.) Easing up inside her sweater, his practised fingers undid her bra. He stroked her back, keeping her waiting until, when she thought she would scream, his hands moved around to cup her breasts whilst his thumbs circled her nipples until they were hard and sore and she felt faint. This was their ritual and she had become addicted to it.

'I love you,' he murmured and pulled her down onto the bed and they carried on, pressing against each other, their legs entwined and she felt him hard and hot through his trousers. Suddenly he was sneaking his right hand inside the waistband of her skirt, past her suspender belt, moving down, tracing the lacy border of her knickers. Edging closer and closer.

Once upon a time, before she'd experienced this visceral sensation, when sex was something baffling, she'd made up her mind to save 'below the waist' for the man she married. Once upon a time, that had seemed so clear-cut, so easily achieved.

'Stop,' she murmured, pulling away.

He stopped, his hand resting on her thigh.

'I want to. Honestly I do,' she said.

Retrieving his hand cautiously as if removing the fuse from a ticking bomb, he rolled away.

'I'm sorry,' she said. 'It's just…'

'You don't have to explain, Mim. It'll happen one day. We'll know when the time's right.' He reached for her hand. 'Frankie and I… we didn't go all the way.'

She pictured Frankie's satchel soaring through the air. 'I know and I'm glad.'

A muffled roar came from the card-players downstairs. Hard to believe there was a world beyond this room. She turned on her side. Her eyes had grown accustomed to the dark and she could make out his profile and, on his bedside table, his alarm clock, the hands clearly visible against its white face. Twenty-to-nine on Saturday evening. The image of her parents, settling down to watch television, flashed, uninvited, into her head.

In the spring and without warning, Danny turned up. For a while they were all on their best behaviour. Her mother fussed, offering to wash his clothes, churning out plates heaped high with what she insisted were his favourite meals. Her father was more guarded, clearly waiting to see why his son had chosen this moment to return. Conversations skimmed the surface, veering away from anything that might prove provocative. With Miriam he was overly polite. The five years between them, a chasm when they were children, should have mattered less now but it seemed as unbridgeable as it had ever been. She longed to get him alone and ask him where he'd been and what he'd seen. But he spent a great deal of time in his room with the door shut and, when he came downstairs, her parents were always around.

They made it through four whole days before the first barney. Her father asked Danny whether he went for regular dental check-ups. Harmless on the face of it, but perhaps not the thing to ask a son who'd left home because his parents were 'suffocating' him with their attention. The row progressed rapidly from the bad impression caused by decaying teeth to the folly of smoking, Danny coming out with, 'What's the point of making old bones? Look at you two. Are you happy?'

The second row began as small talk over their evening meal. An elderly neighbour had died a few months earlier and, that morning, an estate agent's board had appeared in the front garden.

'We'll be getting new neighbours,' her mother said.

'I hope they'll fit in,' her father said. 'We don't want any trouble.'

Danny looked up from his plate. 'Trouble?'

'Well, this is a respectable neighbourhood. The wrong type of people could be detrimental to house prices.'

'Define "the wrong type of people",' Danny said.

'You know quite well what I mean. People who play loud music. Or have hordes of children.'

'Funny cooking smells,' her mother murmured.

'Ahhh. I get it. You mean *foreigners*.'

'Well. Outsiders don't understand how we do things.'

Daniel shook his head. 'Given this family's history, I'd have thought you'd be more understanding – compassionate – towards *outsiders* as you call them.'

'You don't understand.'

'I do. That's the problem. You're a bigot, Dad.'

Her mother sniffled into a handkerchief and her father looked as if he might have a seizure. Miriam felt sick. She wanted to scream at them to stop it. Instead she ran upstairs and shut herself in her bedroom.

Later that evening, Danny knocked her door. She was lying on her bed trying (and failing) to focus on *Middlemarch*.

'Can I come in?' he said.

She sat up, pushing her skirt down to cover her bare knees. 'Of course.'

'How's it going?' He drew up a chair, as if she were an invalid, he a visitor.

'D'you mean school? Or…'

'I mean life. How's your life? Are you happy?'

Nothing for days and suddenly he was asking if she were happy.

She drew her legs up and clamped her arm around them. 'I'm okay. Well. Okayish.'

He raised his eyebrows, encouraging her to continue.

'They expect too much of me,' she said. 'Not academically. That's not a problem. It's like they messed up with you and now they're pinning their hopes on me.'

'Hopes of what?'

'Turning into a carbon copy of them, I suppose.' She closed her eyes and leaned her forehead on her knees. 'I wish I hated them. It'd make things so much easier.'

'Poor Mim. I'm sorry I landed you in it.'

'And now you're going away again, aren't you?'

'I can't stay here. You can see that, can't you?' He was silent for a few seconds and she could see he was making his mind up about something. 'Can I trust you with a secret?'

She looked up. 'You're not dying are you?'

He gave a sad smile. 'We're all dying. The important thing is how we live. We have to be true to ourselves.'

'Frankie's always telling me that.'

'Then you should listen to her.'

'It sounds a bit selfish to me. What if being true to yourself hurts the ones who love you? That doesn't seem right.'

'If they really love you – *you*, not their idea of you – they'll want you to be happy.'

'Mum and Dad do love you. They were devastated when you left. Mum cried for days. I know they're quick to criticise. Especially Dad. But you can't expect them to approve of everything you say and do.'

'I've never asked them to *approve*. But they've never even listened to my side of things. You and I don't exist merely to fulfil Dad and Mum's ambitions. It's not selfishness, it's self-preservation.'

More than anything she wished he would lean over and hug her or squeeze her hand, or do something physical to prove that he was her brother and that he cared.

'So what's this big secret of yours, anyway?' she said.

He dug in his shirt pocket and brought out a photograph. It showed a woman with olive skin and lustrous black hair. She was holding up a chubby, laughing baby.

'Who are they?' she said, although she already knew.

'Ava and Pearl, my wife and daughter. What d'you think?' He might have been showing her a picture of his new car.

You've abandoned me twice, that's what she thought. What hope she'd had of his coming back to save her had been snatched away by this Ava and Pearl.

'Why didn't you tell us?' she said.

'I needed to do it in person,' he said. 'That's why I came.'

'So why *haven't* you?'

'I had this crazy idea that they'd have mellowed. Dream on, as they say.'

'You will tell them though?'

'After all that stuff about "outsiders" and funny-smelling food?' he said. 'Can you imagine their reaction? No. They don't deserve to know.'

'So why are you telling me?' she said.

'In case anything happens to me. It's important that someone knows Danny Edlin has a wife and child.'

'You're unbelievable,' she said. 'You've dumped your secret on me and now you're going to disappear again. Can't you see what an impossible position this puts me in?' Her anger flared. 'You're selfish and cowardly. Fuck off back to America. I'll be fine.'

Danny left and, overnight, her parents aged ten years. It had been bad the first time but lingering somewhere in the background had been the hope of reconciliation. This time there was none. His absence tainted the household with the bleakness of bereavement. Indeed there were times when she wished he *had* died. At least then they could have talked about him. Because they didn't. Not to her anyway.

The new neighbours – a middle-aged couple – moved in. He was a bank manager and she did 'good works' of some kind. They kept themselves to themselves and Miriam wasn't aware of any weird cooking smells coming from the house. Despite this, her parents treated the world as an increasingly hostile place. Everyone, and everything, was conspiring against them. They went out only when it was necessary. Her mother fretted about every little thing. Their conspicuous misery piled pressure on her to be a dutiful child. To compensate for their prodigal son. It wasn't fair. Nevertheless, she did her best to please them because, in spite of everything, she loved and pitied them.

Frankie dyed her hair the colour of Ribena and moved on from Gregg to his crew-cutted friend, Andy. Most afternoons she went straight from school to Andy's flat which meant the two girls rarely walked home together.

Frankie had stopped pretending she was nineteen and Andy was doing his best to persuade her to leave school. The friends' worlds were diverging. But Miriam's life was made bearable by Bing.

As she grew more dependent on him, her parents' opposition became even stronger. He wasn't welcome in their house; they didn't like it when she went to his. They dreamed up reasons why she must stay in, or why she had to be home early. She became convinced they were spying on her, sneaking in to her room looking for clues of... what she wasn't sure. She took to leaving her desk drawer slightly open, not sure whether she was pleased or not to come home and find it as she'd left it. They said mean things about the Crosby family's 'bohemian' lifestyle hinting that, by associating with them, she was risking her reputation.

Had the Crosbys treated her like that she would have given up, but Bing took it on the chin. 'They're vile to you,' she said. 'I don't know why you bother with me.'

'Well, whatever they say and whatever they do, I'll keep turning up.'

When life at home became intolerable, she dreamed of joining Danny in America. After the bust up with her parents, he'd disappeared without saying goodbye, but when she opened *Middlemarch* she found a sheet of paper with his address (964, Harding Street, Fairfield, CA – she'd committed it to memory before destroying the evidence) and the sentence 'For your eyes only.' She'd resisted for a whole month before writing to him. Her letter was short – a bit about school and her new Joni

Mitchell album. In a PS she'd added 'best wishes to Ava and Pearl'. She'd used Frankie's address in the hope he would reply. But she'd heard nothing.

End-of-year exams done, the freedom of summer stretching ahead, she and Bing were foraging for raspberries in the Crosbys' jungle of a garden. The day was humid, the air alive with flying insects. Bing's T-shirt was stained with raspberry juice. His hair, damp with sweat, was curling at the nape of his neck and, in that instant, she was overwhelmed with love for him.

'Here.' He was holding a perfect raspberry between his thumb and forefinger. When she opened her mouth, he dropped it on to his own tongue and they came together in a raspberry-flavoured kiss.

The garden baked in the sultry heat and before long they were lying on the grass, hidden from the house by a dense box hedge.

This was the right time.

Her father arranged for her to spend August with his sister, Adele, in Boston. Most girls would have given their eye teeth for such an opportunity but Miriam had reservations about spending a month away from Bing. Her parents behaved as if in agreeing to go she'd done something clever and as a reward they bought her several outfits and a new suitcase. Their being so keen to send her to the same place as their missing son was bizarre. She'd checked the map. Thousands of miles separated Boston from Fairfield but at least she'd be on the same landmass as Danny – assuming he still lived in America. (He never replied to her letters.)

On the day before she left, she and Bing made love three times. Her parents thought a crowd of them were hiking to the local reservoir. His parents were at work and his sisters who were somewhere in the house failed to notice what was going on. ('They're probably up to the same thing,' he said.)

Her aunt and uncle couldn't have been kinder. And her cousins – older than she – went out of their way to include her in whatever they were doing. She did all the right things. Saw a baseball game at Fenway Park. Drove around in an open-topped car. Drank milk shakes, played tennis and went to the 'movies'. The weekend after she confessed to a passion for *The Great Gatsby* – the book and the man – they drove her the two-hundred-odd miles to Long Island. She missed Bing. But there was so much going on she didn't have time to mope.

Bing demanded to hear every detail of her stay in Boston and she found herself underplaying it, not wanting him to think that she'd had too good a time. He kept returning to the boys she'd encountered while she was there. Worrying away at it. Names. Descriptions. Whether any of them had tried to get off with her. This irked her and culminated in their first ever falling out.

'You said you didn't mind my going,' she said.

'I didn't think I would.'

'Don't you trust me?' she said.

'Of course I do. I just can't bear to think of you even speaking to another man.'

'That's ridiculous. In a few weeks you'll be in London and I'll be in Manchester. How's that going to work if we don't trust each other?'

'Don't rub it in. The moment you're out of my sight, I know some bastard will snap you up.'

'You don't have much faith in me, do you?' she said. 'Besides if we're going down that route, I could point out that you'll be spending your life examining naked women. Prodding and poking their breasts and fannies. How d'you think that makes me feel?'

'Don't be daft.'

'Oh, I see. I'm being daft and you're being rational.'

Without waiting to hear any more she ran home and spent a miserable afternoon in her room. When her mother called her for supper, she said she wasn't hungry.

Around seven-thirty the doorbell rang and, recognising Bing's voice, she hurried to the top of the stairs. He was in the hall and her father was telling him that she was in bed, unwell and unable able to talk to him. Bing was wearing a suit and had a perfect parting in his hair. Aside from the bunch of daisies in his hand, he looked as if he were on his way to a job interview. He glanced up and gave her a tentative smile, and with that her exasperation dissolved. In a moment of recklessness, with her father looking on, she planted a kiss on Bing's freshly shaven cheek. *So there.*

Her mother gave her a notebook with family recipes and instructions for washing woollens. Her father coached her on the correct way to write a cheque and clean her shoes, and warned of the repercussions of attending student demonstrations. When neighbours asked if she were looking forward to university, she murmured assent, and put the whole business out of her mind.

Their parting had been a mirage, flickering on the horizon. If they mentioned 'leaving home', it was as if it were going to happen to two characters from a book but when a cabin trunk appeared in the spare room, and a cheque book addressed to Miss Miriam Edlin turned up, there was no escaping the reality. They would be living two hundred miles away from each other. (She'd checked in her father's AA book.) They would spend weeks and weeks apart. And this would continue for years and years. University felt like a punishment not an opportunity.

Bing's term started a week before hers. They'd planned a romantic 'last evening' but, due to a last-minute crisis at the surgery, his parents had to drive him up to London a day early. They ended up saying goodbye on the pavement outside the Crosbys' house, whispering pledges of love whilst his father packed his stuff into the boot of the car.

They exchanged explicit letters which they wouldn't have wanted anyone else to read. Miriam kept hers in a wooden box, its lid inlaid with mother-of-pearl. She read them, in chronological sequence, every night when she got into bed, wallowing in the misery of separation, tears boosting their potency.

It became obvious that letter-writing didn't come easily to Bing. He struggled to find new ways of saying that he missed, loved and desired her. As the weeks rolled by, she couldn't escape the fact that his letters were becoming repetitive. When a letter arrived, she scanned it for something fresh, informative. An account of his meals. Or a description of a lecturer. An amusing or bizarre incident – he was a medical student, for heaven's sake. Most of all she longed to hear that he hated his course and his fellow students. But he rarely touched on these matters. *I miss you, Mim. I love you. I can't wait to make love to you.* Yes. She knew all that. There must be things he wasn't telling her. Parties he'd been to, people – girls – he'd met. How readily doubts crept in when they relied on words to convey complex feelings.

They lived in halls. There *was* a system for phone calls but it involved Bing ringing the warden's office where the minion on the switchboard directed the call to the correct floor. From there on it relied on a random inmate picking up the phone and coming to find her. A similar process applied when she phoned Bing. If the phone outside her room rang, Miriam always picked up. But there had been the odd occasion when, on discovering it wasn't Bing, she'd replaced the handset, depriving some poor girl of her phone call. When they did make contact, their conversation – a succession of tentative questions, halting answers and miserable silences – petered out in *peep-peep-peep* as the money ran out.

Half way through the term, she went to London. The journey was time-consuming. A chunk of her grant went

110

on a new dress – he said he liked her in blue – but, surrounded by his worldly friends, she felt overdressed, provincial. The visit had been arranged for weeks, yet he seemed surprised when she turned up. He asked what she wanted to do, where she wanted to go. She'd been to London only twice before and could suggest nothing, and they wasted hours drifting aimlessly and irritably, spending money they could ill afford. Bing persuaded one of his friends who lived in a flat, to let them sleep there. Their bed was a couch in the living room. She had nowhere to leave her things, nowhere private to undress. The others in the flat looked at her as if she were an exhibit in the zoo. It was humiliating and uncomfortable and, to be honest, she was relieved when her train pulled out of Euston.

They limped on towards the end of term, Miriam hanging on to the hope that things would revert to normal once they were on home ground. She'd read that soldiers returning from battle were reluctant to talk about their experiences. To begin with, they were like that – not knowing how to pick up the threads; each shielding the other from something they wouldn't understand. But within days they were back in step. Miriam was re-absorbed into the familiar chaos of the Crosby household, whilst her parents made no attempt to conceal their displeasure that she and Bing were still together. They spent hours in his bedroom, 'listening to records'. (This fooled no one. More to the point, it *shocked* no one, and Angus Crosby proved this by leaving a bumper pack of condoms on Bing's bedside table.)

There were Christmas parties and New Year parties with the old crowd from *Betty*'s. Little Pete, Barbara, Colin, Judith – they'd all changed a little but the changes were tempered with affection. She even felt warm towards Emms – although that might have been the cider. And there was Frankie, when she wasn't busy with her new man. Friends were as good as family. Certainly easier. She had nothing to prove and that was a great relief.

Then term started, and the whole thing lurched off kilter again.

Part III

9

'COME IN,' SHE SAID.

He stepped inside, scrubbing his perfectly clean shoes on the muddy doormat. He looked weary. Stooped. His hair had turned from dirty blond to nothingy grey. But eyes and voice, and the tilt of his head – those hadn't changed.

'Wonderful to see you,' he said.

Heart thudding, she fumbled a hug whilst he aimed a peck at her cheek, and they laughed to cover their awkwardness.

'Let me take your coat,' she said.

She made space on the hall stand, rearranging anoraks and duffel coats and woolly hats, conscious that he was watching her. *Near-white hair. Broadened hips. The beginnings of jowls.*

'Have you eaten?' she said.

He said something about sandwiches and motorway services but her mind was skittering about, dispersing his words so they didn't quite make sense.

'Why don't I put the kettle on?' she said.

The kitchen smelled of fish fingers. A basket of washing stood next to the tumble drier and the floor could have done with mopping. While the kettle boiled, she wittered – the weather, his journey, the state of the kitchen – collecting dirty crockery and piling it next to the sink to form a neater muddle.

'Tea? Coffee?' she said.

'Tea, please.'

'Sugar?' How could she have forgotten?

'I gave it up at med school,' he said. And without warning they were lurching towards the past and she was nowhere near ready for that.

He must have felt the same way because he nudged them towards safer territory. 'You live here with…?'

'Naomi, my daughter. And my grandchildren. Rosa's eight and Max is six. They've gone to the cinema. A treat before term starts on Monday.'

'D'you have other children?'

She shook her head. 'Just the one. You?

'One son and two daughters.'

'Grandchildren?'

'Not quite. My older daughter's due in six weeks. I'll be glad when it's over. I know too much about childbirth.'

'Let's find somewhere more comfortable,' she said, leading him across the hall to her sitting room, explaining about the extension and David's absence and her hopes that he and Naomi would soon patch things up.

They sat opposite each other – he in the armchair and she on the sofa – not knowing what they were supposed to do next.

'So your parents are still alive,' he said.

'Just about. They're scarily frail. Yours?'

'Both dead.'

Julia and Angus Crosby. Ahead of their time and no longer in the world.

'I'm sorry to hear that. They were always kind to me.'

'I should hope so,' he said.

A beat. She should mention her parents' treatment of him but again he steered them away from the past.

'Your note came as a surprise,' he said. 'I had no idea you still had connections there.'

'Only Mum and Dad.'

'Your husband died,' he said.

'Sam. Yes. Last year.'

'Was he ill?'

'No. It was a car crash.'

He raised his eyebrows but there was a lot of ground to cover before they came to that.

'You know I'm divorced?' he said.

'Angela did say something.'

'We should have done it years ago.'

'How long were you together?'

'We almost made our thirty-fifth. You?'

'Not quite forty.'

The sat for a moment.

'What's your ex-wife's name?' she said, not sure why this was relevant.

'Eloise. She's French.'

A sylph-like woman with jutting cheekbones and dark glossy hair cut in a geometric bob. Miriam wanted to punch her on her perfectly-straight nose.

'So your children must be bilingual?' she said. 'That's a great asset.'

'It is.' He smiled. 'You haven't changed, Mim.'

She raised her hands to her cheeks, feeling them warm

beneath her palms. 'Apart from white hair and wrinkles and—'

'I'm talking about the *you-ness* of you. The *essence* of Miriam.' He leaned forward in his chair. 'I've thought about you every single day.'

She fiddled with the cuff of her sweater. 'Oh, dear. You're embarrassing me.'

'Nothing to be embarrassed about. It's the way it is. Thinking of you is part of my daily ritual.'

'Like brushing your teeth?' The words sounded flip. 'Sorry. I'm rather thrown by all this.'

She'd thought of him too. Every day in the beginning and again, after Sam died. But there had been weeks – months – when she'd locked Paul Crosby away in a dark corner, out of thinking distance. Had he been free to meander, she couldn't have coped.

He jumped up. How trim he was. Unlike Sam, he showed no hint of a beer belly, or a double chin.

'I have something for you,' he said. 'It's in the car.'

She stood at the front door watching him cross the road, reluctant to take her eyes off him in case he disappeared as suddenly as he'd arrived. The neighbours had drawn their curtains and streetlights were coming on. Naomi was due back in an hour, expecting a meal and an explanation for this stranger. *An old school friend. Out of the blue.* True, as far as it went. It was naughty of him, turning up like this. He should have warned her. On the other hand, she'd had no time to agonise over what to wear or what to cook. How to *be.* The car bleeped and flashed and he was coming back with a package beneath his arm. She'd expected flowers, or a bottle of wine but this was obviously neither.

'It must be way below freezing,' he said, brushing her cheek with the back of his hand. It would have been the most natural thing in the world to twist her head and kiss it but she resisted.

'Here.' He handed her the package.

It was solid, and heavier than she'd anticipated. *A book?* She stripped off the silver gift-wrap to reveal an expensive-looking wooden frame. The photograph it contained showed a group of youngsters outside a café.

'Oh my God,' she said.

She moved her finger across the glass. Bing. Emms. Colin. Barbara. Judith and Lisa scowling in unison. Little Pete at the back, holding up two fingers. She and Frankie in the middle, arms linked, laughing.

'Like it?' he said.

'I *love* it. We're all there. So who took the photo?'

'We must have asked a passer-by. I still have the negatives.'

'I remember that camera of yours. Every time I looked round, you were pointing the wretched thing at me.' She held the photograph at arms' length. 'We thought we knew it all, didn't we?'

'Perhaps we did,' he said. 'Have you kept in touch with Frankie?'

'I see her once in a blue moon. She's extremely elusive.'

They sat together on the sofa, studying the photograph, remembering friends and clothes and school.

'What happened to them?' she said. 'All those hopes and

dreams. Judith and Lisa – d'you think they were gay? And Little Pete, didn't he go to the Royal College of Music?'

'Easy enough to find out,' he said. 'A few clicks. A few feelers on Facebook.'

'You're very up on that stuff.'

'It has its uses,' he said. 'Did you never google me?'

'Only after the party.'

'Were you never curious?'

'Of course.'

'So why didn't you?'

'To be honest, it was easier not knowing.'

Her phone rang, letting her off the hook. 'It's my daughter,' she said. 'Won't be a sec.'

She went into the hall and pulled the door behind her. 'How was the film?'

'Soporific,' Naomi said. 'We're on our way to the car. Do we need anything? I can swing by M&S.'

'No need,' she said. 'There's bolognese in the freezer and we've yoghurt to eat up.' In the background, she could hear Rosa and Max singing. 'Oh, by the way, I've got a visitor. An old school friend.'

'That's nice. Will she be staying for supper?'

'*He*. His name's Paul. And I haven't invited him yet.'

'*Paul.* Intriguing.'

'Not at all. As I said, he's an old friend.'

'They're on their way back from town,' she said when she returned to the living room. 'Will you stay for supper?'

'I don't want to put you to any trouble,' he said.

'Don't be silly. I should warn you, though, it can get messy.'

He looked confused and she laughed. 'My grandchildren are enthusiastic spaghetti twirlers.'

The children were wired, recounting every detail of the film, their voices getting louder as they tried to outdo each other. Max shot wary glances at the outsider whilst Rosa played big sister, correcting her brother at every opportunity. Paul gave them his undivided attention, asking pertinent questions as if there were nothing in the world more natural than a panda whose aim was to become a master of kung fu.

When they'd exhausted film talk, Max turned his attention to the photograph which was standing on the window sill. 'What's this, Gamma?'

Miriam explained that the photograph had been taken a very long time ago when she was a schoolgirl. 'That's me,' she said, 'and Frankie. You remember Frankie, don't you? And there's Paul.'

'You were pretty,' Rosa said, 'and your hair was brown.'

'I like it white,' Max said, reaching out to touch her hair.

God she loved this child.

'Shall I tell you a secret?' Paul said. The children nodded and drew a little closer. Dropping his voice he said, 'Your grandmother was the most beautiful girl in the school. In fact she looked a lot like you.' He winked at Rosa and she was eating out of his hand.

Naomi, too, was clearly charmed by the handsome stranger whom her mother had never mentioned. *He's gorgeous*, she mouthed when Paul's back was turned.

Max was sprawled on the floor, arranging his

collection of miniature zoo animals into a parade. 'What's for tea, Gamma? I'm starving.'

Before Miriam could say anything, Paul snapped his fingers. 'I've just had an idea. Why don't we get a takeaway? My treat.'

The children's faces lit up and they turned to Naomi, seeking approval. She laughed and shrugged and agreed – 'If that's okay with Paul' – and Miriam felt a surge of pride in this 'gorgeous' man who had, within minutes of meeting her family, won their hearts.

He turned to the children. 'What d'you fancy? Pizza? Fish and chips?'

A while back, when the children were staying with David, he'd ordered Chinese food. This had arrived in a cardboard box shaped like a house, complete with pitched roof, the handle forming the chimney. Rosa and Max recalled nothing about the food but the box – now in the shed – had become an object of great desire. That's what they wanted. 'Chinese' in a house-box. They didn't know *which* establishment the meal had come from but, loath to let them down, Miriam called David and discovered it was (of course) The Chinese House. As they were winding up the conversation, Miriam considered inviting him to join them. He and Paul would get on famously. Then, in the background, she thought she heard a woman, singing softly, and let it go.

Paul asked The Chinese House if they could possibly deliver the meal in *two* houses. They did, and Rosa and Max – now each the proud possessor of a *new* greasy, smelly cardboard box – were mightily impressed by this person who was able to fix anything.

'You're not driving back tonight,' Naomi said when they were in the kitchen rinsing out the foil containers ready for recycling.

'It only takes a couple of hours,' Paul said. 'I'll be home by eleven.'

'We won't allow it, will we Mum?' Naomi said. 'The kids can double up in Rosa's room and you can sleep in Max's bed.'

'It's very comfy,' said Max who, despite appearing to be reading, was listening.

Miriam turned the clock-radio to face away from her, not wishing to be reminded that it was two-seventeen. She was exhausted but could not let go. Hardly surprising considering all that had happened in the past twelve hours. Was Paul asleep or was he too mulling it over? It was a little different for him. He'd made the decision to come and had had time to prepare himself. All the same he must have wondered how she would take his appearing on her doorstep. And what would he have done if she'd not been there? Or had a new partner? Turned around and gone home again?

She rolled on to her front and shoved her arms beneath the pillow. For the first few minutes it seemed sleep might finally be on its way, but her neck – twisted to one side – began to ache and she fidgeted onto her side, pulling the duvet over her head to form a soft, dark cave.

When she'd pushed the note through the surgery letterbox, she'd imagined he might email or even phone. Perhaps suggest they meet for a drink next time she visited her parents. When she'd heard nothing, she'd been disappointed but not surprised. After all they'd not parted on the best of terms. But Paul Crosby, whom she'd last seen when she was twenty, had chosen to forget or forgive and driven a hundred freezing miles on the off-chance of finding her. Now he was here, sleeping in her grandson's bed, on the other side of her bedroom wall.

In the brief time before Naomi returned, she'd discovered that he and Eloise met at a medical conference in Geneva. She'd been part of the team organising the event. They'd married in 1973 when Eloise was four months pregnant. Two more children. A peripatetic life as a hospital doctor and then a GP.

Then it was her turn. She told him, in the broadest terms, how Sam's death had knocked her for six and she'd been forced to give up teaching. 'I've got a job at the local art college. Part-time.' 'Doing what?' 'Oh, this and that.'

How could she explain her life with Sam when it no longer made any sense to her? And the modelling job. Did she want him – or, come to that, anyone else – to know? It wasn't that she was ashamed of it. Her reason for doing it was to have something entirely her own. A secret. Proof that she had it in her to surprise herself. Would he understand that?

Lives were way-marked by momentous days. The predictable – births, marriages and deaths – and those acts of fate that altered everything. Seeing Paul walk across the road towards her would always be a landmark. Now everything was happening so quickly. Too quickly? Naturally she wanted him to get to know her family.

Maybe not quite so soon – and not quite so well. Before introducing him to them, she'd have liked to time to catch up on the missing years. To take stock. To let her feelings settle. But it was perfectly fine. In fact, considering how smoothly it had gone, it was probably a good thing that it had been taken out of her hands.

At bedtime, they'd kissed and said polite goodnights on the landing but she'd half-expected him to concoct some excuse to knock on her bedroom door. With that in mind, she'd discarded her cosy pyjamas for her sexiest nightdress and dabbed scent between her breasts. What had she been thinking? Curled up in her snug cave, she went over it for the umpteenth time. Seeing him. Touching him. Smelling him. *Wanting* him. She was shocked how much she wanted him. In a few hours they would be eating breakfast together and… well, she had no idea where it might go from there. One thing she knew for sure, if she didn't get some sleep soon she would look like nothing on earth.

10

PAUL LEFT AFTER LUNCH, THE whole family standing at the front gate, waving him off as if he belonged to all of them. He'd offered Miriam a lift – 'Come with me. It'd be a chance for you to see your parents'. She could think of nothing she'd like more than to be cocooned in a car with him, talking and talking for a hundred miles. But her parents would throw a fit if she turned up unexpectedly. Besides, she had to be back in time for school drop-off. As soon as she got there, she would have to start making her way home again – not straightforward by public transport.

A couple of hours later Paul phoned to let her know he was home. And again after supper to wish her goodnight.

'I meant to ask you,' he said. 'Why "Paul"? Why not "Bing"?'

'It seemed... I don't know... as if I were taking something for granted.'

'Mim,' he said, 'it's me. It's us.'

'He's absolutely gorgeous,' Naomi said after his second call. 'How come you've never mentioned him?'

'Why would I?'

'It sounds like it was pretty intense.'

'Don't be silly. We were school kids. Everything's intense when you're seventeen.'

'How long were you together?'

'Oh, I can't remember,' she said. 'We were constantly swapping and changing. Before me, he went out with Frankie.'

'So who dumped who?'

'*Whom*,' Miriam corrected her. 'When we left school, we went our separate ways. And can you stop the interrogation, please?'

The children went back to school, Naomi to work and Miriam prepared to settle back into term-time routine. But everything was different. Pushing her trolley down Sainsbury's aisles, or chopping vegetables for minestrone soup, or ironing Rosa's school blouse, she imagined herself wandering with Bing (of course he was 'Bing') through Montmartre or along white-sand beaches. And when no one was around to read her mind, they tumbled together between fresh cotton sheets.

His gift took pride of place on the mantelpiece and she returned to it again and again. He must have more photographs from those sixth-form days. She did. She'd not exactly hidden them from Sam but for years they'd been in the loft, at the bottom of a box of linen tablecloths which she never used. When she had a moment, she must go to the storage place and fish them out.

'Good Christmas?' Callum said.

'It was,' she said. 'I bumped into an old friend and it's reminded me of the person I used to be. How about you? Did Father Christmas bring the right things for the twins?'

He told her about the Robertson family's trip to Scotland and how he'd spent best part of three days helping his sons with the Airfix kits Father Christmas had delivered. 'Then we had to get them home in one piece. Not straightforward with two boys and an over-exuberant dog in the car.

He started to walk away then turned back. 'Oh, I almost forgot. I was with a painter friend last week. Bob Moat. He's on the lookout for a life model. A "mature person".' He hooked the air with his index fingers. 'I said I'd mention it to you.'

'Me? Gosh.'

'He'd pay well. Better than this place, anyway.'

She was flattered. Sitting for a professional painter was a step up from a class of students, and Callum wouldn't have suggested it unless he thought her up to it.

Today she was standing, extended left arm supported on a tripod-affair (not to be included in the drawing). It was a demanding pose. Now, for instance, her lower back and the muscles in her arm were beginning to twitch. The heating system was struggling against the January chill and Callum had rustled up a couple of heaters which he'd stationed close to her but they weren't quite doing the job.

She had plenty to take her mind off her aches and goosebumps as she reached out into thin air. Bing had suggested a weekend get-together. He was on call which meant her going there. Her parents would be thrilled, if somewhat bewildered, to see her so soon. She must be up front about her reunion with Paul Crosby. They might not like it but they'd have to put up with it. They'd lost the right to object. After all, their preferred candidate had turned out to be a shit. They must accept at least some responsibility for what Sam Siskin had inflicted on her. Come to think of it, why should she worry what they thought? Over the years, their outlook had grown narrower and narrower, excluding everything not directly related to their own survival.

And now there was Callum's flattering proposition. Were she to accept, it wouldn't be for the money. Of course that would come in handy but she could probably earn as much without taking her clothes off. *The artist's muse.* Wouldn't that be something? When Bing asked what she did at the college, she'd fudged her answer. What would he make of it? A doctor couldn't be shocked by nudity. On the other hand, naked *ill* people weren't at all the same thing as naked *well* people. He might not like the idea of her being alone, unclothed, with a man. And why was she worrying what Bing thought, anyway? It was for her to decide.

'The Moat thing sounds interesting,' she said when she and Callum were walking to the car park.

'Why not have a chat with him?' he said and scribbled Moat's number on the back of a flier.

They arranged to meet in the museum café. She made a point of getting there early, sitting at the table in the corner, screening the customers as they trickled in. *Bob Moat.* The name evoked a boxing promoter but Google images showed a stout, middle-aged man, more librarian than artist. He warranted a Wikipedia page. His work was held by various galleries and he'd been awarded several commissions. His paintings (without exception, the human figure) were, from what she could make out on the screen, visceral. Energetic. Flurries of swirling brush strokes. The man was definitely not a 'Sunday painter'.

He arrived five minutes late, wearing a fake-fur hat with ear flaps.

'Moat,' he said, pulling off the hat to reveal a balding head, fringed with sandy-coloured hair. 'And you're Miriam Siskin.'

'That's me. How did you—?'

He glanced around. 'Let's be fair, you're the only middle-aged woman here.'

There was something unsettling about his face. His features were spread out leaving, what seemed to Miriam, too much space between them, these gaps emphasised by pale, uncannily smooth skin. He took off his overcoat and draped it over the back of the chair. Beneath it he was wearing a suit teamed with a black shirt and pale blue tie. He rubbed his hands together and she noticed his nails were painted a matching blue.

'Coffee?' he said.

Without consultation he went to the counter and was soon back with two Americanos, a jug of warm milk and a pile of Danish pastries.

He plonked down the tray. 'I'm looking for a model. Female. About your age. How old are you, by the way?'

'Sixty-one,' she said.

He nodded. 'Much as I guessed.'

'How old are you?' She knew from her Google

research but she could see she needed to stand up to this odd little man.

He grinned. 'Fifty-two. Only child. Parents dead. Never married. No children. No pets.'

And that was all she was going to get out of him.

He set about an apple Danish as if he hadn't eaten for days, swilling down each mouthful with a slurp of coffee. He might have been performing for her benefit but it was more likely he gave not a fig what she thought of his table manners.

'Any objection to my sitting in on Callum's class?' he said when he'd finished eating.

She was nonplussed by his request (yet impressed by his handling of the gerund and possessive). 'I suppose not. If it's okay with Callum…'

'Good. Now. Anything you want to ask me?'

She'd jotted several questions on an A4 sheet, but before she could read them, he whipped it out of her hand and rattled through the answers.

'Twice a week. In Torrington Street, near the market. I was thinking fifteen pounds an hour. "How many sittings?" Mmmm. As many as it takes.' He folded the paper and handed it back to her. 'Anything else?'

'I have sessions at the college twice a week. And I pick up grandchildren from school every day. Would that suit your schedule?'

'We can work around that,' he said and pointed to the remaining pastries. 'Help yourself.'

After he'd gone, she stood for a while studying the 'Woman on the Stair'. She could not by any stretch of the imagination be described as sexy. Yet it was impossible not to weave an erotic story around her. (Those red shoes?) Bing had said the answer to everything was a few clicks away. But she'd tried that and come up with nothing. It seemed 'Woman' was determined to keep her secrets.

Moat turned up in the same suit. Callum, very properly, checked that she was happy to have him sit in on the session. When he introduced Moat to the students, a frisson of excitement ran around the room.

Callum had her adopt a sequence of short poses – standing, sitting, lying down. Ten minutes each. He was putting her through her paces for Moat's benefit. As the students worked, Moat wandered around, looking at her and inspecting the work on the easels, now and then murmuring something or pointing something out. The usual relaxed atmosphere was replaced today by a sense of concentration and eagerness. In her breaks, she retreated to her little room to stretch and warm herself against the radiator. When she came out for the final pose he'd gone.

'He apologised for scooting off,' Callum said. 'Optician's appointment or something.'

'The students were impressed,' she said.

'He's something of a star. Anyway, you've got the gig if you want it.' He paused. '*Do* you want it?'

'Can I ask you something before I make my mind up?'

'Fire away.'

'He's… above board isn't he?'

'Don't be put off by the flimflam. You'll be perfectly safe with Moat.'

Naomi expressed delight when Miriam told her she was visiting Paul. (She wasn't ready yet to share his nickname with anyone.)

'How romantic,' Naomi said. 'You'll stay at his?'

'Of course not. I don't know why you're getting so exercised about this.'

Naomi threw her arms around her. 'You're allowed to be happy, Mum. None of it was your fault.'

Miriam dipped her head against her daughter's shoulder. They rarely mentioned Sam and when they did it tended to be inadvertently, as if the rule of silence had slipped their minds. Occasionally Rosa and Max remembered they'd once had a Grandpa Sam. They appeared to have taken his death in their stride and perhaps that was no bad thing. One day they might be curious about him, and the circumstances surrounding his death and, if the time were right, she would tell them.

Naomi rubbed her back. 'If this guy helps you to feel better, that's fine by me.'

'I must admit it's a relief being with someone who didn't know what happened,' Miriam said. 'Is that a dreadful thing to say?'

'Surely he's asked about Dad.'

'He knows he died. That's enough for now.'

'I miss him, Mum. There were happy times, weren't there?'

It was easy to forget that Naomi, too, had lost something but Miriam had to look out for herself. 'I can't think about that at the moment,' she said. 'One day, perhaps.'

Naomi pulled away. 'I'm sorry but I can't pretend he didn't exist.' She tore off a length of kitchen roll and blew her nose.

'I don't expect you to. But you have to understand I'm not ready to let him back in to my life. Maybe I never will be. Oh, dear. We've ended up talking in clichés.' She went to the sink and filled the kettle. 'Tea or coffee?'

But Naomi wouldn't let it go. 'I know it's not your thing, Mum, but mightn't it be a good idea to talk to someone?'

'We've been through this,' she said. 'I don't think it would help. In fact I'm beginning to think things are turning around.'

'That's wonderful but maybe talking to someone would speed things up.'

'You mean a psychiatrist?'

'I mean someone who understands what you've had to deal with.'

'I think you'll find the only person who understands that is me,' she said.

'No need to snap my head off. I'm trying to help.'

'I know. And I am grateful. But everyone seems to think we can all – every one of us – be happy all of the time. Well we can't, and perhaps the sooner we accept that it's okay to be sad or angry or whatever, the better.'

Bing persuaded her to drive up on Friday evening.

'No need to disturb your parents,' he said. 'Come straight to mine. I've got stacks of room.'

He had a point. Turning up after dark on Friday would raise too many questions. She'd join them for coffee on Saturday morning and let them assume she'd just arrived. She told Naomi her plan. This seemed wise on three counts. Naomi could cover should her parents phone after she'd left. The shared confidence would act as all-girls-together olive branch following their prickly conversation about Sam. And whatever resulted from her reunion with Bing would stand a better chance were Naomi part of it right from the off.

By Friday lunchtime, she'd arranged with Moat to be at his studio on Wednesday morning at nine-thirty for the first sitting, and packed and repacked a weekend case. For a brief visit like this she would normally take a couple of changes of socks and underwear, jeans, a spare shirt and an extra sweater to combat her parents' stinginess with the heating. Today her case was full to bursting. Pyjamas and the sexy nightie. Jeans and neat black trousers. The linen suit she'd worn to her art college interview. A casual shirt and a silk blouse. And the heels Naomi had insisted she take. Clothes to suit all eventualities. Tonight she would spend with him, of course. *With him.* The English language was at times extremely coy.

Whilst the children were eating supper, she phoned her parents.

'Still okay for tomorrow?' she said.

'Your mother's baking,' her father said as if that were irrefutable proof of her visit. 'You're phoning at peak time.'

'I'm going out later so I thought I'd best do it now. But Naomi will be here if you need to pass a message.'

'Why would I do that?'

'No reason. I'll see you tomorrow. In time for coffee.'

11

SHE COULDN'T STOP HER THOUGHTS drifting to what lay ahead and she had little recollection of whole stretches of the journey. After the second near miss she pulled in to a petrol station and bought a double espresso from the machine, pacing the forecourt, waiting for caffeine and the sub-zero temperature to revive her. She glanced up at the spatter of stars. Orion's Belt? Ursa Major? On one occasion Sam had lost patience with her when she'd said it was possible to join a few random stars and call it anything you liked.

Were she to draw a Venn diagram of her life, it would consist of two circles. *Family* and *Modelling*. The circles would not overlap, a fact she found empowering. Sam must have persuaded himself of the same thing. In his case there would have been three circles. *Family*, *Work* and *Gambling*. The difference being, of course, that *Gambling* had expanded until it not only overlapped with but consumed the other two. His secret had demanded every ounce of his energy. And his cunning. That was what got to her. His ruthless cunning. By comparison, her secrets were harmless.

She shoved her empty cup in the bin and returned to the car, unable to resist etching ME ♥ PC in the rime on the windscreen, swiping it away before fate or a CCTV camera had time to register it.

She called him. 'I'll be about forty minutes.'

'Wonderful,' he said. 'So when you reach the ring road, go straight across the roundabout—'

'And take the second left, past B&Q. I know. I have your email on the passenger seat.'

'Sorry. I'm fussing.'

'No,' she said, 'I shouldn't have snapped.'

His painstaking directions led her to a development of small, pinched houses, each detached from its neighbour by no more than a couple of metres. *Street View* had shown houses grouped around cul-de-sacs named after birds. She parked outside 5, Sparrowhawk, switched off the headlights and unclipped her seat belt. A niggling pain had started up where she imagined her appendix to be and she shifted in her seat, hoping it would ease. While she waited, she checked her phone. *go for it mum x.* (No capitals, no punctuation.)

Naomi had said she was allowed to be happy, as if she were constantly punishing herself. Was that the impression she gave? A flagellating widow? That wasn't her intention. All she wanted was to sever connection with the phoney life she'd lived with Sam. To start again. Ambitious, perhaps, but her expectations of this born-again life were modest. It was too late to embark on a different career even if she were able to summon the energy. But, thanks to Callum, she'd set off in an unforeseen direction – one that Sam couldn't, in a million years, have imagined her taking. That, in itself, made it a victory. She'd been edging cautiously but steadily into her new future when Bing turned up. The past made flesh, as it were, phoning and texting and pressing her to visit. Surely they couldn't pick up where they left off? And yet. Here she was, along with her fanciest underwear and sketchiest nightie, her stomach aflutter.

She glanced at the house and saw a figure silhouetted in an upstairs window. She waved and by the time she'd unloaded her case and locked the car, he was halfway down the front path.

'Hello, you,' he said and kissed her lightly on the lips.

The house was welcoming, filled with the smell of cooking. She shrugged off her coat and he hung it next to his. He was wearing the same navy sweater and brown cords he'd worn last weekend.

'Journey okay?' he said.

She yawned and shivered. 'Not too bad.'

'You're bushed,' he said.

'I think I am. May I use the bathroom?'

'Top of the stairs. Your room's to the left.'

She'd forgotten what a child-free bathroom looked like. No soap splashes on the mirror. No bin brimming with heaven knows what. No slimy flannel on the rim of the bath. No fleet of plastic toys, puddled with last night's bath water.

After using the loo, she washed her hands and splashed water on her face. The strip light above the mirror was unforgiving, lending her skin a sallow cast. Her scarf failed to disguise her scrawny neck. Leaning in closer she saw that her right eye was bloodshot near the tear duct. If she closed her eyes, she was floating on a gentle sea swell.

Her suitcase was waiting for her on the bedroom chair. She glanced around. Double bed. Sharp creases in the plain white, obviously-new linen. Blue towels – also new – on the bed. Unopened box of tissues and, a bizarre touch, the current issue of *Homes & Gardens* on the bedside table. Immaculate yet lifeless, like a hotel room. She flipped back the lid of her case. Everything she needed for tonight was to hand – toilet bag, nightdress, underwear for tomorrow, book (she'd chosen *Dr Zhivago* – a doctor, star-crossed lovers, a reunion).

His voice drifted up, easy and familiar. 'I've poured your wine.'

'Down in a sec.'

Pulling the tortoiseshell slide from her hair, she brushed it until it crackled. Loose or pulled back? The latter. (Nothing worse than pretending she was still a schoolgirl.) To counteract the schoolma'am look, she opted for frivolous earrings – cascades of silver stars and turquoise beads. She aimed a squirt of scent at each wrist and, lifting her chin, pulled herself up to her full height. Last night she'd scrutinised her body in the mirror, as she had before accepting Callum's job offer, this time assessing the woman staring back at her as a potential lover. Bing had last seen her naked when she was twenty and blossoming into womanhood. Now here she was – skinny and slack – sliding into old age. An artist might consider bare flesh as 'the body's history' – Callum's words – but to lovers, it was foreplay not backstory.

The door across the landing stood ajar and she pushed it open. A reading lamp shed low light across a smallish bedroom. Clothes heaped on a chair. Mug, spectacles and a remote control on the bedside table. Television on top of a chest of drawers. Desk strewn with papers and journals. Laptop. Brief case. Pretty much what she'd expected – but for the single bed.

Bing's room in the Crosby house had been her favourite place in the world. Once they were inside, door shut, no one else existed. But it was more than a hideaway. The room was enchanting and enchanted. Shabby furniture that might have started life in Russia or Morocco – certainly not the department store where her parents went for their prosaic G Plan stuff. The mishmash of games kit and schoolbooks, fossils and beer mats. A record player and records stacked upright in a wicker hamper. Sports trophies. Photographs of the Crosby family on the beach or in the garden. They'd lain on his double bed, dreaming of making this room their home – all they'd need was a kettle and a gas ring. (The room was never dusty although it had been hard to imagine Julia Crosby wielding a duster.)

Bing was in the kitchen humming along to Radio 3, surrounded by fallout from his cooking efforts.

'Find everything?' he said.

'Yes, thanks. The room's lovely.'

'I can't take the credit,' he said. 'Jenny sees to all that. She's my cleaner-cum-miracle-worker. I couldn't function without her.'

How he coped with the daily round – shopping, cooking, washing, cleaning – hadn't crossed her mind. She felt an instant and fervent dislike for this indispensable

Jenny who changed his sheets and tidied his underwear drawer.

He handed her a glass. 'What shall we drink to?'

He would be expecting something consequential but all she could come up with was 'To us.'

'To us... and to the future,' he said.

The future. They weren't youngsters, starting from scratch. At their age and with their history, bumbling along, seeing how things panned out, wasn't the way to go. Before long they would need to have a frank conversation about this, this... whatever it was.

'Can I do anything?' she said.

He patted the seat of a chair. 'Talk to me.'

She sat at the table whilst he sliced carrots, occasionally reaching across to steal a piece from the colander, all the time watching and remembering. Flat, square finger nails. His habit of whistling through his teeth when he concentrated. The scar across his eyebrow. There was something of his father about him which hadn't been there when he was nineteen. Maybe it was more in his manner – his confidence – than his anatomy.

He moved on to shredding cabbage, his knife tapping rhythmically on the chopping board. On the radio, a string quartet playing something slow and sad. *Haydn? Schubert?* Her hands were beginning to disconnect from her arms – the not-unpleasant sensation that sometimes preceded sleep.

'Hey.' He touched her shoulder. 'Dinner's ready.'

'Resting my eyes,' she said.

She hadn't realised how hungry she was until she was

well into her second helping of beef bourguignon. As they ate, the conversation jumped from this to that. Rosa and Max. A film they both wanted to see. A cold-calling scam that was causing a rumpus. Blizzards in America.

'How was your week?' he said.

She'd deliberated long and hard over what to tell him about her job. He knew she worked a couple of mornings at the college and how she spent her time there made no difference to anything. She would let it ride for a while longer.

'Much as usual,' she said. 'Yours?'

'Unremarkable.'

'You're a doctor,' she said. 'A *real* doctor.'

'So they tell me.'

'Aren't you constantly worrying you'll get it wrong?'

'Ninety-nine percent of it's straightforward. Hernias. Tonsillitis. Athlete's foot. *You* could diagnose most of my patients.'

'But aren't you terrified you'll miss something?'

'When in doubt I refer them to a consultant.'

'I'm sure there's more to it than that,' she said.

'My parents said doctors were glorified mechanics. It was a case of identifying the knocking sound in the engine.'

'Do you see much of your children?' she said.

'Blimey,' he said. 'We're covering the ground.'

'Do you?'

'Not as much as I should.' He frowned. 'They seem to have decided their mother needs them more than I do.'

'Where does she live?'

'Lyon. But let's not talk about her.'

'What did your sisters do in the end?' she said. 'I liked them very much. I always felt they were on my side.'

'Caroline died of meningitis. When she was twenty-four. That was really difficult for all of us. Then Helen got religion big time. She's a nun, would you believe?'

'That's so sad. Don't you ever—'

'Can we do this on a need-to-know basis?' he said.

The clock on the digital radio showed ten-twenty. She really should go to bed.

'I told Dad I'd be with them for coffee.' She paused. 'I was hoping you'd come with me.'

'Have you told them we're in contact?'

'I haven't got 'round to that yet.'

He was gathering up the plates, scraping debris from the meal into the bin and he stopped what he was doing and turned to face her. 'What happened last time... I don't think I could go through that again.'

This reference to her parent's rejection and, obliquely, to her betrayal was painful but he had every right to bring it up.

'They've changed,' she said. 'Staying alive takes every jot of their energy. They're selfish but they're not stupid. They know if they fall out with me, they'll be completely on their own.'

'What happened to your brother?' he said.

'Danny? Remember he went off to America? Well, he never came back. One day I'll bore you with the whole thing.'

'You really want me to come?'

'Could you bear it? You needn't stay long. I'll explain you're on call.'

He looked sheepish. 'About that.' He picked up a J-cloth and made a few swipes at the work top. 'I swapped with a colleague. I needed a reason why you had to come here.' He worked at a blob of gravy. 'Nice though they are, I didn't think I'd be able to make love to you with your family under the same roof.'

She felt her cheeks burning.

'Poor Mim. I've shocked you, haven't I?'

'No. Well. A bit.'

'What did you hope would happen when you left that note?' He spoke softly as if coaxing the truth from a child.

'I don't know.'

'I think you do.'

She took a deep breath. 'I hoped you'd get in touch, of course. But I wasn't sure you'd want to. Not after the way I treated you.'

'You were in an impossible position,' he said.

'Don't be too understanding or I'll cry.'

He caught her hand. 'May I kiss you?' he said. '*Properly* kiss you.'

The first kiss was tentative, questioning. The next, gentle at first then becoming greedier. He was holding her tight against him, crushing her breasts, his belt buckle pressing into her stomach. She smelled the earthiness of his hair, not quite concealed by tangy shampoo. The chemistry that had never failed was instant and potent.

'Like riding a bike,' he murmured, as if he could read her mind.

She placed a hand on his chest and pushed gently. 'Maybe we should—'

'Please don't suggest we slow down.'

'But—'

'When I give patients the bad news, the first thing they ask is, "How long have I got"?'

'You're not ill?' she said.

'No. But neither of us knows how long we've got.' He paused. 'Sorry. That was tactless.'

He was imagining that she was still raw after Sam's death. Another conversation they would have to have.

'Go on,' she said.

'When you reach our age, I reckon it's time to speed up not slow down. And it's not as if we're strangers. I know you can't stand spinach and you fancy – or used to – Robert Redford. God I wanted to strangle that man.'

'Spinach still makes me gag,' she said.

'See. I always remember the things that matter.'

'Is it that simple?'

'Yes.' He folded her in his arms again and she relaxed against him. 'This is a heart not head thing.' He ran a hand up and down her spine. 'You're too thin.'

'I love you,' she said. 'Shall we go to bed now?'

'If you're sure.'

'I am.'

12

IT WAS SEVEN MINUTES PAST eleven when Miriam rang the doorbell.

'Bad traffic?' her father said.

She ignored the snipe. 'Where's Mum?'

'Sitting down. She's feeling woozy.'

Her mother was in the living room, ensconced in the winged chair which she and Sam had given her for her eightieth. When she saw Miriam she smiled and reached out her hand. 'There you are.'

Miriam took her hand, feeling its bird-bone fragility. 'How are you feeling?'

'Better for seeing you.'

'Did you eat a proper breakfast?'

Her mother looked towards her husband as she so often did when asked a question.

'We had porridge and toast,' he said.

'Why don't I make us some coffee?' Miriam said. 'You stay here. I'll bring it through.'

Once in the kitchen, she phoned Bing.

'Most likely low blood pressure,' he said. 'Encourage her to move around a bit. Get the blood pumping.'

'That doesn't sound very scientific,' she said.

'Like I said, medicine is largely suck-it-and-see.' He paused. 'Have you told them I'm coming?'

'I'll do it soon. I promise.'

A tray stood ready on the kitchen table, coffee granules in three of the 'best' cups, biscuits arranged in a swirl on a plate. She made the coffee and carried the tray into the living room. Setting one of the nest of tables alongside her mother's chair, she sat on the floor near the hearth where a meagre fire was generating next to no heat.

'Is anyone else chilly?' she said, taking the tongs and piling on coal from the brass scuttle.

Despite the profligate use of fuel, her father seemed relieved that someone else had taken the reins and, as he nibbled a digestive biscuit, he sneaked longing glances towards the door.

They chatted, covering well-worn ground. The snow. Naomi and the children. The new neighbours who'd had the gall to tear out the laurel hedge and replace it with a fence.

'D'you remember Paul Crosby?' she said when they'd run out of chit-chat.

'The boy you dumped for Sam?' her father said. 'Tall. Fancied his chances.'

'It wasn't quite like that, Dad.'

He waved his hand, swatting away her protestation. 'What about him?'

'Well, he became a GP. He's worked all over the place but now he's come back here. To a practice in Monkton Square.'

'Doctor Oates is our doctor,' her mother said. 'If she can't fit us in we see Doctor Sherriff.'

'What's this got to do with us?' her father said.

She ploughed on. 'He called at the house last week.'

'He didn't come here,' he said.

'Not *here*. Naomi's. He got my address from a mutual friend.'

'Who would that be?'

'That's not important, Dad. The thing is, he's going to drop in later. That's okay, isn't it?'

She'd anticipated a rant, or at least a dig. Instead her father directed his attention towards the newspaper. 'As long as he doesn't tire your mother.'

Remembering what Bing had said, Miriam suggested it might be an idea for her mother to stretch her legs. She helped her up from the chair and they made their way into the kitchen whilst her father escaped to the dining room.

'You remember Paul, don't you?' Miriam said as she washed the coffee cups.

'Of course. A nice-looking boy.'

Her mother, tea towel in hand, was staring out at the winter garden. 'The snow's nearly gone,' she said. 'We did what we thought was best. For you and for Danny.'

Miriam let it go. It was too late – years too late – to have this conversation.

'You were fond of this Paul, weren't you?'

'Yes I was. And I still am. He's fond of me, too.'

Her mother pointed. 'Look. There's a robin on the feeder.'

'I said Paul and I are—'

'I heard you, dear.'

The doorbell rang and Miriam hurried to answer it. Bing was holding a bunch of bronze chrysanthemums.

'How's it going?' he whispered.

Before she could answer, her father appeared from the dining room. Caught between the two men, the old anxiety took hold.

'Hello, Mr Edlin,' Bing said, smiling over her shoulder.

After an exchange of niceties, they ended up in the kitchen where her mother was fiddling with the wrapper on a sliced loaf.

'I don't know why you've brought your visitor into the kitchen,' she said.

'Nothing wrong with the kitchen, Mrs Edlin,' he said. 'It's the heart of the home.' He held out the flowers, their sharp scent filling the room. 'Only chrysanths, I'm afraid.'

'For me? How lovely. And they last.'

Miriam hunted for a vase whilst her mother fussed about, trimming stems and stripping off leaves.

'Miriam tells us you're a doctor,' her father said.

'That's right.'

'Would that be private or NHS?'

'Dad…'

Bing shot her an *I've got this* glance. 'NHS, Mr Edlin. The state educated me and it's my duty to serve the state. That's the way I see it.'

Her father nodded approval. They talked for a while about the 'flu outbreak and the closure of a nearby hospital. Bing was deferential, addressing her father as 'Sir'. He picked up additional brownie points when he volunteered to look at the dripping lavatory cistern.

'He's very handsome,' her mother said after the men had gone off to diagnose the problem. 'It makes a difference when a man keeps his hair.' She leaned closer. 'Anyone can see that he dotes on you.'

Bing's presence appeared to inject her parents with a surge of vitality. They became animate. Even frivolous. Perhaps they considered a doctor in the house to be a safety net against medical crises. Miriam was astounded at their readiness to accept the man whom they had once banished from her life. Bing amazed her too. Warm. Reassuring. Letting them have their say. Bonding with the people who had, in effect, stolen her from him. Lunch went well. Her mother had prepared her speciality – chicken soup with barley. They ate in the kitchen which made it feel very much a family affair. Miriam allowed herself to relax a little. After they'd finished, she and Bing offered to do the washing up whilst her parents napped by the fire.

'You're a miracle worker,' she said. 'I was sure it would end in tears but they've taken you to their bosom. Ironic, don't you think?'

'If they have, let's be grateful,' he said.

He was at the sink, hands immersed in washing-up water, and she came up behind him and leaned against his back, clasping her arms around his chest.

'I'm frightened I'll wake up and this will all be a dream,' she said.

When they could put it off no longer, they joined her parents in the living room. Her father had banked up the fire and switched on several table lamps although it was still light.

'I was hoping you could spare Miriam this evening,'

Bing said. They were sitting primly on the sofa, a couple of adolescents in an era when parental permission was obligatory for everything. She'd spotted salmon fillets and a tiny piece of lamb in the fridge – this evening's supper and tomorrow's lunch. It would be unkind to abandon her parents, and possibly reignite hostilities and she wished he'd thought to mention his intention to go out.

'I'll have supper here with you first, of course,' she said, 'then maybe Paul and I could pop out for a quick drink.'

'We like to be in bed by ten,' her father said.

Bing caught Miriam's hand in a demonstration of intent. 'We'll be quiet coming in, won't we, Mim?'

'He's divorced, you say,' her father said after Bing had left.

She was prepared for the post-mortem. 'Yes. Not long ago. But he and his wife separated quite a while before that.'

'Have you two been in touch all these years?' He was watching her intently.

She shook her head. 'We made a clean break when I started seeing Sam. I had no idea what had become of Paul until your neighbour's New Year party.'

The reference to Sam might prick his conscience. And laying her reunion with Bing at their door – she'd never have gone to that party were it not for them – would do no harm. Now he'd quiz her about who had contacted whom, and the ins and outs of Bing's visit to Naomi's, but at that moment an ember tumbled onto the hearth rug, causing a kerfuffle and curtailing the inquisition.

Thanks to her parents' habit of eating supper before six, everything was cleared away when Bing called for her at seven.

'Your ears must be on fire,' she said, 'in a good way. They think you're wonderful.'

'Can't imagine why. Perhaps I'm no longer a threat to the family's reputation.'

They were sitting in the car outside the house and he reached across and jangled her earring. 'Shall we go to mine?'

When they arrived at his house, a bottle of champagne, still chilled, and two glasses stood on the table next to the bed.

She laughed. 'You're very sure of yourself, Doctor Crosby.'

He opened the bottle cautiously, barely spilling a drop. 'Here. Doctor's orders.'

When they'd drunk enough champagne, he sat on the bed and patted the place next to him. 'Come and lie next to me.'

The lay side by side, and before too long, the champagne and the smell of his skin and the touch of his lips, made lovemaking easy and inevitable.

Afterwards, they talked.

'When shall we tell them?' he said.

'Whom? What?'

He circled her breast with his finger. 'The whole world that we're in love.'

'Have you said anything to your children?' she said.

'Not yet.'

She wondered whether he'd ever told Eloise about her – his first lover. Men weren't inclined to that sort of revelation. It had been obvious from Sam's skill in bed that he'd been with women before her, but they'd never gone into it. He must have known she and Bing had been lovers but he'd never mentioned it.

'They'll think you've taken leave of your senses,' she said.

'Probably.'

They lay together, silent and content. Destiny – fate – fortune – whatever people wanted to call it, no longer seemed an absurd construct. Their coming back together had been inevitable, she saw that now. Bing belonged to her, she to him. It was hard not to regret all those missed years. But he was right. They mustn't waste time raking over what might have been. Besides, there were consolations. Had life taken the less circuitous path, Naomi, Rosa and Max wouldn't exist, and that was unthinkable.

Neither of them was fit to drive and Bing called a cab. She was quite able to get herself home but he insisted on going with her, saying the walk back to his house would clear his head. They paid off the taxi and, for old-time's sake, lingered in the shadows near the gate.

'Tomorrow?' he said.

'I'll drop in for a cuppa on my way home.'

'I trust that's a euphemism,' he said.

'I think you'll find it's a hot drink.'

'You're a hard woman.'

'I've had to be,' she said. 'Now off you go.'

As she crept up the stairs, she wished there were someone she could talk to about this miracle that was unfolding. Frankie was the only one who'd understand. Maybe Danny too. He'd surely be pleased for her. Her parents' bedroom door was ajar and she paused to listen, picturing them lying like marble effigies on a medieval tomb. Her father was snoring, steadily marking the passing time as he and his wife drew nearer their end. It was too sad.

Thanks to her 'cuppa' with Bing she was late getting back and didn't have chance to talk to Naomi until breakfast time.

'So? How did it go?' Naomi said.

'Fine. Granddad and Grandma seemed to like him.'

'Why wouldn't they?'

'Oh, you know how they get in a tizz about any kind of change.'

Naomi was remarkably accepting. When it had emerged that Sam wasn't the heroic dad she'd believed him to be, she'd been knocked sideways. The revelation had come not long after she and David separated, when she was already fragile. Miriam had been going through her own agony, in no fit state to help. Only now was she was beginning to appreciate how difficult it had been for her daughter, struggling to keep herself and her family afloat. What she'd seen as selfishness had been Naomi's coping strategy. She appreciated that now. One day she might be able to tell her the whole story. Bing. Sam. Even the part her parents had played in it.

'Are you seeing him next weekend?' Naomi said.

'Yes. If that's okay with you.'

'Of course. It's David's turn to have the kids. Why not invite him here? I'll say hello then make myself scarce. I wouldn't want to play gooseberry.'

'Don't be silly. We're long past all that.'

'I sincerely hope not.'

13

'NO TROUBLE FINDING ME?' MOAT said.

She shook her head. 'I sometimes come this way to the market. I've always admired these houses.'

'Late Victorian. Nothing out of the ordinary. But it suits me.' He took her coat. 'Let's have coffee and I'll talk you through the project.'

He'd swapped his eccentric garb for sweatshirt and jeans. His language was less arcane, his manner less arch. He seemed altogether more relaxed and she felt that perhaps having seen her naked he trusted her to see him as the plump, balding man that he was. He ushered her down the tiled hallway to an untidy kitchen. He gestured towards a chair and, whilst he ground coffee beans in an old-fashioned hand grinder, she sneaked a look around. There was enough crockery on the shelf for a family, and mounds of fruit in the bowl. But no plants or photographs, or those odds and ends that revealed a woman's touch.

'I wasn't sure you'd come,' he said.

'Neither was I.'

Driving home yesterday, she'd almost changed her mind. Things between her and Bing were progressing at a pace. Why fill her life with unnecessary complications? And yet. Since working at the college she'd begun to mend. There had been months when she'd doubted such a thing could happen – maybe hadn't wanted it to. But this off-the-wall job had enticed her back into the world. *Naked Widow Rising from a Sea of Despair.* So, yes, she would do the Moat thing, see out the term at the college, and then take stock.

'What swayed you?' he said.

'I realised it's not good to base decisions on what another person – people – might think.'

She expected a follow-up question or, at the very least, an observation but either out of tactfulness or lack of interest, he offered neither.

'Let's get down to business,' he said.

He folded his arms and stared at the ceiling. 'You'll be standing, looking straight at me. Life-size, so it'll be a biggish canvas. No gimmicks. Success or failure rests entirely on the quality of the painting.' He drummed his fingers on the table and she noted the absence of nail varnish. 'What else?'

She gave it a few seconds then said, 'I'm wondering why you want a middle-aged model.'

'Fair question. Apparently, when they reach a certain age women become "invisible". Every time I open a magazine, that's what I read anyway. I think it might be interesting to investigate that assertion, through painting.'

'I'm not sure I want to be the invisible woman.'

'Miriam. You didn't listen. I said I wanted to *investigate* the idea. Show people a middle-aged woman and let them decide for themselves. I could get a friend to sit but that wouldn't work. The model needs to be unfamiliar to me. Callum spoke highly of you, and as soon as I saw you I knew you were right. You have a certain vulnerability that professional models don't. I'm after authenticity. I'm not explaining myself very well am I?'

'You want to paint a vulnerable, middle-aged stranger,' she said, 'who might or might not prove to be invisible.'

'That's pretty much it.'

She couldn't imagine why he would wish to do this, yet something made her want to be a part of his venture.

'I'll show you where we'll be working.' He stood up. 'Come.'

He led her up two flights of uncarpeted stairs to what was obviously a recent loft conversion.

'This is my studio,' he said. 'It can get chilly up here but I'll turn the thermostat up when we get started.'

Did he imagine room temperature was her main concern?

She'd expected his studio to be cluttered with bric-a-brac. Stippled with paint. A curiosity shop of artiness. Quite the opposite. Units, complete with worktops and a stainless steel sink ran down one side. Grey vinyl flooring. Off-white walls. Outsized roof lights. It might have been a dental surgery awaiting delivery of the chair. It was conspicuously devoid of colour apart from an enormous flag draped over a screen in one corner. Three broad vertical stripes in green, white and red and, dead centre, a circular emblem.

'Mexico, isn't it?' she said.

'Correct. I bet everyone wants you in their quiz team. I picked it up in a junk shop near the bus station.' He traced the emblem with his index finger. 'What d'you make of this?'

She took a closer look. It depicted an eagle sitting on a cactus, tearing at a snake. 'What a bizarre thing to put on your flag.'

'I think so too,' he said, and she felt childishly pleased to have given a satisfactory opinion.

He had her stand in the centre of the room looking straight ahead. He told her to ignore him – not easy as he circled like a predatory shark. Now and then he came right up to her, removing the clip holding her hair back and tilting her chin this way and that.

'A few close-ups of your face and we're done for today,' he said.

He produced an expensive-looking camera and rattled off a quick succession of shots. *Chunk. Chunk. Chunk.* After checking the screen he said, 'You're not wearing make-up.'

'I used to but I don't anymore.'

'Good. Your face needs no enhancing.'

His comment was without guile. The more time she spent with him, the more she respected and trusted him.

'One more thing,' he said. 'I'm going to ask you something and I want you to say the first answer that comes to mind.'

'It's not one of those psychological tests?'

He smiled and shook his head. 'In the painting, you'll be wearing one item of clothing. So. What will it be?' He snapped his fingers. 'Quick.'

'Shoes. Red pumps.' It was out before she had time to think.

He clapped his hands. 'Miriam Siskin, you amaze me.'

She found herself laughing. 'D'you want to know why?'

'Absolutely not. It must be an enigma to everyone, me included. Does that make sense?'

'Perfect sense,' she said.

When she was leaving he asked whether she wanted paying with cash or a cheque. The college paid her wages into her bank account and she'd overlooked this embarrassing detail. 'Oh. Gosh. I don't mind.'

'Cash then,' he said producing a roll of notes from the back pocket of his jeans. 'Fifteen pounds an hour, wasn't that what we said?'

He handed her thirty pounds and she blushed.

'Don't be embarrassed,' he said. 'You've earned it. Don't forget to bring the shoes next time.'

Red pumps shouldn't be hard to track down. And they needn't be top quality. She would never wear them outside Moat's studio. The thirty pounds she was holding should cover it.

'How did you get on with Moat?' Callum said when she turned up for the Tuesday session.

'It all seemed straightforward,' she said. 'I rather like his house.'

'It was his mother's. He moved in a few years ago, after she died.'

'Did he grow up there?'

'Haven't a clue. Moat's not one for small talk as you must have discovered by now.'

To account for her additional absences, Miriam had

given Naomi the impression she'd taken on extra hours at the college. Obviously she needed to be better organised than she had been. No aimless meandering or little naps in the afternoon. But that was a matter of time-management, something which had never been a problem when she was teaching full-time as well as taking care of her family and the garden.

The studio was warm as he'd promised it would be. He'd pulled the screen away from the wall and found a chair for her clothes. A large canvas, painted pale brownish-yellow with rough brush strokes leaned against the wall. Tubes of paint were set out in ordered ranks on the work top.

'Could you manage twenty minutes?' Moat asked.

'I'll try.'

'Okay. Let's get started.'

She went behind the screen and began undressing. She was accustomed to doing this in her little room at the college but it felt different here in this airy room, flooded with light.

Last night, as she was packing a rucksack ready for her first session with Moat – red pumps (a snip from Top Shop at £19.99) and a robe to put on during breaks – she'd considered what she was about to do. Going to a stranger's house and stripping off her clothes was, on the face of it, a reckless act. Were Naomi to do such a thing, she – Miriam – would freak out. Yet this was precisely what she was doing, and she knew she would be safe – far safer than when she crossed that nasty bit of dual carriageway to get to the shops.

Moat was pottering about on the other side of the screen. She could hear him opening and closing cupboard doors.

'Should I wear the shoes?' she said.

'Yes. People hold themselves quite differently when they're bare-footed.'

She pushed her feet into the shoes. They were stiff and thin-soled, no use at all for walking in. *Robe on or robe off?* She dithered for a few seconds before putting it on. Taking a deep breath, she stepped out from behind the screen.

'Your hair's very distinctive,' he said, 'the way it contrasts with your eyebrows. I wonder whether it should be tied back as it is now, or loose. How do you usually wear it?'

'Like this,' she said.

'Let's go with that. I want you to feel as much like yourself as possible.'

He pointed to a chalk mark on the floor. 'There. Feet together.'

He held out his hand and she took off the robe and passed it to him, and stood, feet together, looking straight ahead as instructed.

Bing was hell-bent on driving down as soon as he'd finished his Friday evening surgery. Miriam was eager to see him but didn't like the idea of his setting off when he would be tired especially as the temperature had dipped again and roads were treacherous.

'Don't make me worry,' she said. 'Come first thing on

Saturday morning. We can all have breakfast together. David isn't collecting the children until eleven. It'll give them plenty of time to pester you.'

She spent Friday in a whirlwind of effective, efficient preparation for the weekend and the coming week. Tackling routine tasks – shopping, cooking, washing, cleaning and tidying – at full tilt was satisfying and energising. When she got into bed on Friday evening, she felt the frisson that heralded Christmas and birthdays.

The alarm went off at seven which was as well because Bing was knocking the door at eight. Naomi and the children were still upstairs. Max was singing at the top of his voice, regular thuds on the ceiling suggesting he was jumping off the bed.

'Paul's here,' Miriam shouted and the children flew down the stairs, whooping and hurling themselves at him, bickering over who would sit next to him at breakfast. Naomi greeted him as though she'd known him forever.

Breakfast went on and on, the grown-ups trying to hold a coherent conversation whilst the children came and went, nibbling bits of toast, darting back regularly to make sure they weren't missing anything. They'd barely cleared the table when David was at the door, another excuse for Rosa and Max to explode with excitement. Naomi, usually keen to hand them over, invited David in, introducing him to Bing as if he were her long lost uncle.

'Coffee?' Naomi said.

As Miriam filled the filter machine, the two men chatted away and again she noted how well he fitted in. Rosa and Max. Naomi and David. She and Bing. They might be three generations of a happy family. At one point he caught her eye and winked, and she felt a lightness of spirit which had been absent for years.

After everyone had dispersed, they discussed how to spend their day.

'I want to do the prosaic things that old married couples do,' he said. 'Catch a bus. Change our library books. Always get our meat from the same butcher.'

'Quotidian, is that the word?'

'Far too fancy,' he said.

They took the bus into town and strolled through the mall, hand in hand, joining the army of Moat's invisible, middle-aged people, custodians of their own little histories. They ended up meandering around M&S, studying corduroy trousers and easy-grip socks. She persuaded him to buy a dark green crew-necked jumper and, for her, he chose an orange scarf.

'You're not looking sufficiently henpecked,' she said as they waited to pay. When the woman behind the desk trotted out the statutory 'Thank you for waiting,' he said there was nothing in the world more pleasurable than standing in an M&S queue with the woman of his dreams. And yes, he would like the hanger.

'Now can I take you to one of my favourite places?' she said. 'It doesn't quite fit in with your hankering for the banal but they do great coffee.'

'If you like it, I like it,' he said and kissed her on the lips, a noisy, passionate kiss, and she felt waves of envy and disapproval from the onlookers. Only when they reached the Arts Centre did it cross her mind that Callum or one of the students might be there. Whilst Bing went off to find the lavatory she ordered coffee and scones, scanning the crowded cafeteria, thankful not to see anyone she knew.

Fargo was showing at four o'clock.

'Shall we?' Bing said.

She'd seen it with Sam when it came out (he'd hated it) but pretended she hadn't and they sat in the dark holding hands. She was absurdly happy.

He offered to treat her to a meal in town but she had lashed out on a couple of steaks. 'My turn to cook,' she said. 'Naomi's out with her friends. She promised she won't be back 'til late.'

They made their way back to the house, Bing regretting not having the car and admitting that standing at a bus stop at six-thirty on a winter's evening was perhaps *too* 'prosaic'.

'I think we should live together,' he said when they were setting the table. 'Why don't you drive back with me tomorrow.'

'Be sensible,' she said, her breath sucked from her by his invitation.

'Don't you want to?'

'Of course I do.'

'So what's the problem?'

'There's no problem. But it's moving so quickly.'

'*Quickly?* I've dreamed of this for forty years.'

'I know. The thing is, we don't live in a vacuum. There are other issues to consider.'

'For example?'

'Well, have you spoken to your children yet?'

'I've told Leon and Camille, but not Pascale. Her blood pressure's sky high. They've taken her in for bed rest. It seems sensible to wait until after this baby arrives.'

'How did they react?'

'Leon didn't seem bothered. Camille? Well, she'll come round.'

'She wasn't happy about it?'

'She asked if we were seeing each other before Eloise and I split up. I told her that until two weeks ago we hadn't seen each other for forty years.'

'And?'

'She said if that were true, we were behaving like a couple of irresponsible teenagers.'

'So damned if we did and damned if we didn't?'

Back then it had been her parents, now it was his daughter. A fine irony.

'Pretty much,' he said. 'Naomi wouldn't object, would she?'

'She'd be thrilled. You're a superhero, come to rescue her mother from her dreary life. But I can't just up sticks. She relies on me to help with the children.'

'Naomi must know you aren't planning to live with them forever.'

True. In the turmoil of having to sell up, childcare had been a trade-off against a roof over her head. She'd never intended it to be a permanent arrangement, merely a breathing space whilst she sorted out somewhere of her own. There were options. Naomi could employ an *au pair*. Or let the granny flat and pay a childminder with the income. This wouldn't stop her helping should an emergency arise, and the children could come and stay in the school holidays.

'And there's my job,' she said. 'Can't we stay as we are until Easter? Three months would give Naomi time to sort something out. I can give notice at the college. And your children can get used to the idea of their father shacking up with his new woman.'

He made a sad face. 'If that's what you want.'

14

MOAT SEEMED NOT TO MIND her inspecting his work. During the course of her visits, she saw herself conjured into being by his wild, swirling brushstrokes. By contrast, he painted her shoes in painstaking detail, down to the nick in the reconstituted leather made by the zip on her backpack. This realism rendered them peculiarly lifeless. So much so that their only noteworthy feature was that she was wearing them. Moat had promised 'no gimmicks' but he knew the tricks of his trade and how to employ them, and by the end of the fourth week, she was pretty much there.

'Happy with it?' she said.

'I shan't know until it's finished,' he said, the softness in his eyes telling her he was.

Six months ago she hadn't known Callum or Moat existed or that, clothed or naked, it was flippin' hard to stand still for twenty minutes.

'How much longer will it take?' she said. 'I only ask because my life's got more complicated.'

Six weeks ago, she'd been unaware that Paul Crosby lived in the same city as her parents, and that he thought of her every single day.

'In a good way?' he said.

'I think so.'

Despite being asked not to, Camille made sure Pascale knew their father had a 'mistress'. Her irresponsibility angered Bing – 'She's always been the bolshie one.' They were obviously squaring up for a full-blown row, but before it had time to erupt, Pascale went into labour and the family's attention switched from the scarlet woman to the new arrival – Finbar Louis Paul Winter.

'You must be thrilled,' Miriam said when Bing phoned with the news.

'Yes. And relieved. Although the name's a bit of a mouthful.'

'When will you go to Edinburgh?'

'Friday. I've found someone to cover my surgeries.'

'Your going will mean a lot to Pascale,' she said.

'Maybe. It's complicated. Of course it means I shan't see you this weekend.'

'We'll survive,' she said.

'What will you do with yourself?'

'There's a film at the Arts Centre I'd quite like to see.'

'Will you go on your own?'

'Unless I can find a handsome young escort,' she said.

He said nothing yet she sensed her flip reply had rattled him.

When Miriam announced she would be moving in with Bing, Naomi opened a bottle of Prosecco. 'That's wonderful, Mum. I'm delighted for you. We'll miss you, that goes without saying. Like I said before, you deserve to be happy, and Granddad and Grandma will love having you on the doorstep.'

Miriam grimaced. 'Yes. Well. Of course I shan't leave until you've found someone to help with the children.'

'No worries. One of the mums is setting up as a childminder and she says she'll take them on. Her son's in Rosa's class so the kids know her already. She'll give them tea and I'll pick them up on my way home from work.'

It came as a shock to learn that her daughter had been making plans to replace her before she, herself, had known she was leaving. Naomi might have talked it over with her before making such a major decision. What sort of person was this 'mum' anyway? How would she deal with Rosa's tantrums and Max's need for cuddles? Would she be prepared to wipe his bottom? Would he let her? Did she understand that salt and corn syrup were lethal? It pained her to think of leaving the children – a physical hurt as real a jab to the heart. She would miss them terribly, and she hoped they would miss her, at the same time she couldn't bear them to be sad.

'I see.' She paused. 'What if they don't like her?'

Naomi patted her hand as if she were an old person who wasn't quite up to speed. 'David and I have talked it through. If there's a problem, we'll work something out.'

Picturing the fat manila envelope, tucked at the back of her underwear drawer, she said 'Childcare isn't cheap. I'd like to help out.'

'That's sweet of you, Mum. But let's see how things go.'

Her parents banked on her fortnightly visits. It gave them something to focus on and an excuse for her mother to cook too much food. When she informed them she wouldn't be coming at the weekend, her father said, 'That's a shame. We'll miss you. Both of you. We're getting to like this young man of yours. He's a nice boy.' He spoke of Bing as if he were a recent acquaintance and nothing to do with the teenager who had caused such consternation when he'd courted their daughter.

'Hardly a boy, Dad,' she said, 'but I'm glad you like him.'

Even though they thought him 'nice', she couldn't predict how they would take the news of her moving in with him. Although they'd surprised her by not kicking up a stink when she spent her weekends there. They'd planned to announce their intentions to cohabit this weekend – face-to-face – but made bold by her father's approving comments, she decided the moment was right.

'I've a bit of news. Paul's asked me to move in with him. We've talked it over. His job's there, and he owns the house, so it makes sense. And I'll be close to you, of course.'

She waited, ready for the explosion but all he said was 'I suppose you'll be telling me next that two can live a cheaply as one.' He gave a raspy little laugh, almost a cough. When he asked whether they'd be getting married, she said she wasn't sure, and again he seemed disarmingly sanguine. 'Well, you're old enough to decide these things for yourself.'

She hadn't realised how keyed up she was and his

acceptance – or, to be more precise, his lack of objection – came as a huge relief. Walking home from Moat's next day, the penny dropped. Better his daughter live in sin than she 'marry out'.

With the whole weekend to herself, she had chance to catch her breath. The matter of the storage locker had been preying on her mind. Her worldly goods, such as they were, couldn't remain where they were. They either had to go with her – or *go*. She'd made an inventory of what had been put into storage, but at the time she'd had other things on her mind. Everything needed to be evaluated. 'Keep' or 'dump' ought to be easy. Perhaps 'not sures' could have a temporary home in her parents' spare bedroom, where she could consider them at leisure.

The image of those lifeless rooms brought Danny sidling into her head. He wrote a few times a year. Never more than a page, and then without saying anything. After he left Fairfield, his addresses had always been post office boxes. She'd known he was somewhere in Denver, or Boston or Baltimore but there was never enough information for her to put a pin in a map. To say *this is where my brother lives*. Once in a while he'd phone, their conversation disjointed, sentences disrupted by long-distance time lag. In the beginning she got steamed up when she heard his voice. Before she knew it, she'd be ranting at him for abandoning them. Abandoning *her*. He'd slam the phone down and she'd end up sobbing and thinking of all the things she should have said. As time went by, she learned to remain calm. That way he stayed on the line longer. It was years since his last visit 'home' – a couple of days, and she'd never worked out why he'd come. She liked to think it was to make sure she was doing okay. He and Ava had parted company a long time ago – he'd revealed that much – but he'd been evasive when talking about his current circumstances. No matter how hard she listened, she picked up no clue as to whether she'd ever been replaced.

Her parents had concocted a fairy tale for the benefit of anyone who asked after Danny. Their go-ahead son had forged a wonderful life for himself in the land of opportunity – blah, blah, blah. And by the time they'd repeated it enough times, they'd brainwashed themselves into believing it. *Really?* A successful son who kept his location secret and never invited his parents to visit him in his life of plenty? *Please.* They're deluded, she'd said to Sam. He'd taken a softer line. Whatever gets them through, he'd said. Now Sam was gone, and the odds on her parents seeing their son again were plummeting. Danny had never asked but it must have been obvious she'd kept her word and Harold and Freda Edlin would die without knowing they had an olive-skinned granddaughter somewhere in the world. Last time she spoke to him she'd asked how he squared his conscience. He'd laughed – 'I don't have a conscience, Sis.' If that were true, she envied him.

Moat might not wish to know what made her tick but Callum was always ready to listen. She'd been glad to have someone – not a stranger but someone distanced from her family – in whom she could confide. She'd filled him in on the bones of her situation at their first encounter and more details leaked out over coffees and lunches on her days at the college. He'd heard about Bing's miraculous appearance and their more or less instant reconnection. He knew they were planning a life together and that she would be moving away.

'I feel rotten about letting you down,' she said.

'Don't be daft. I was in a pickle and you came to the rescue. I must admit I was flabbergasted when you offered to give the job a go.'

'That's why I did it. To shock myself, that is, not you. I wasn't in a good place when we met. I couldn't work out what I was *for*. I was afraid if I didn't do something drastic I'd fade away and no one would even notice I wasn't there.' She laughed. 'Sorry. I'm talking rot.'

'Well, whatever your reason, I never thought you'd stick it.'

'Didn't you?'

'Come on, Miriam. How many women of your age have the guts to take up life modelling?'

'Maybe you underestimate us,' she said.

'I think it's more the case that you underestimate yourself.'

'Really?'

'The students think you're the most interesting model they've had. And Moat says you're inspirational.'

She blushed at the unprompted compliments. 'I shall miss it.'

'You don't have to give it up because you're moving,'

he said. 'Evening classes are always short of life models. I could put out some feelers if you like.'

She smiled. 'Thanks, but I don't think so.'

He held her gaze. 'You get to choose what you do, Miriam. Promise me you won't forget that.'

'I promise,' she said.

Bing returned from Edinburgh with photographs of Finbar and a Celtic brooch for her. Apparently Pascale hadn't wanted to discuss her father's new relationship but it emerged that Eloise had intimated he and Miriam had been lovers for years.

'Why would she say that?' she said. 'She can't believe it's true.'

'Actually it was, in a way.'

'What d'you mean?'

'Every time we made love, I shut my eyes and pretended she was you.'

His revelation verged on the creepy – the sort of behaviour she associated with weirdos. Perhaps he intended it to be a compliment but if so it was wide of the mark.

'That's it,' Moat said halfway through their Wednesday session.

She was miles away, wondering what Naomi might like for her birthday. 'You've finished?'

'In as much as a painting is ever finished.'

She pulled on her robe and went to stand beside him. Light from the bright sky flooded across the canvas, emphasising the brush marks in the layers of paint. The improbable, subtle skin tones contrasted with the crude scarlet of the shoes. Her features were there but not there, as if blurred by her moving. It was in no way flattering but it was vital and dramatic. Moat's project had been about addressing the assertion that 'women become invisible with age'. Well no one could fail to notice this woman.

'Do I really look like that?' she said.

He sighed. 'Miriam, Miriam. You should be asking "is this what I *am*" not "is this what I *look like*".'

'Does it have a title?' she said.

'"Red Shoes".'

She'd expected something arty and obscure but if his aim was to explore the invisibility of older women, avoiding reference to the figure, without doubt, posed that question.

'Clever,' she said.

For an instant she glimpsed an ordinary man pleased to be congratulated on something he'd done, then the mask came down again and she realised she was no nearer understanding him than she'd been on that first day in the museum.

'I'll leave you to get changed,' he said. 'I'll go down and sort out the coffee.'

She dressed and packed the robe and the shoes into her rucksack. The sky had clouded over and raindrops stippled the roof lights. Off somewhere in the real world, a chainsaw whined. She would miss being up here, under the roof, in this hideaway that smelled of oil paint and coffee.

She took a last look at the woman staring out of the painting. Uncompromising. Purposeful. Vaguely feral. In fact everything she wished she could be. Although the quality, the intent, of the painting was entirely down to Moat, she felt a surge of pride. Perhaps she *had* been his muse. An area on the back of the hand glistened where the paint was wet. She touched it with the tip of her finger and, not knowing what to do with the resulting blob, smeared it across the skin on the back of her hand. A perfect match.

Moat was busy in the kitchen. 'Ahhh, there you are,' he said. 'We should celebrate.'

A plate stood on the table, piled high with cream cakes – éclairs, doughnuts, cream puffs – so many that she wondered if he were expecting guests.

'I wasn't sure what you like,' he said and she guessed he was unaccustomed to considering others.

'May I have an éclair?' she said.

They'd spent hours together in the most intimate circumstances but they'd both had a job to do. Here, in his kitchen, the dynamics were different. Now the painting was finished, she could tell him stuff about herself that he hadn't wanted to hear six weeks ago. But Moat was different from Callum. He wouldn't be interested and he certainly wasn't going to trade confidences. He watched her eat the éclair and, before she had chance to swallow the final mouthful, he pushed the plate towards her. To please him she took a doughnut, dumping the last bit in the bin when he excused himself and disappeared.

He returned with a parcel, clumsily wrapped in a Waterstones carrier bag. 'This is for you,' he said. 'A small memento.'

She took the package from him.

'Open it,' he said, nodding encouragement the way Max did when presenting her with one of his creations.

It was a framed pastel sketch of her head, in profile, the swirling lines making it distinctively Moat's work.

'What d'you think?' he said.

'It's beautiful. Thank you, thank you.'

He cleared his throat. 'If you're ever in a fix, it might be worth a few quid.'

'I'll never sell it,' she said. 'So what will you do with the painting now?'

'I'm not sure.'

'Wasn't it to be part of a project?' she said.

'It may be good enough to stand alone.'

She glanced at her watch. Time was slipping by. She needed to leave if she weren't to be late for the children. It wasn't as if she and Moat were friends. This had been a job and now it was finished, and they parted on Moat's doorstep with a self-conscious hug and no promise to keep in touch.

15

OVER THE RIVER. ON TOWARDS the dry ski slope. Up into fourth gear at the Royal Oak. Muscle memory kicked in. *Signal in plenty of time for the right turn. Easy round the blind corner.*

The house was on the far side of the town. She'd had neither cause nor desire to go back but rooting through the storage locker, binning the past, she'd decided it was time to lay this ghost. Eleven on a Wednesday morning. Not a soul to be seen. She parked the car a little way from the house and sauntered along, hoping to look like a stranger to any nosey parker peeping from behind a net curtain. Nothing to do with that poor woman whose husband had landed her in huge debt and then chickened out and killed himself.

But sauntering around, pretending to be someone else, wasn't going to lay any ghosts. In twenty years of living here, she had never *sauntered* along these tree-lined pavements. Hurrying to work or to collect Naomi from school, dashing to the supermarket or to pick up Sam from the office, every moment had been purposeful. Increasing her pace, she crossed to the opposite side of the road where her angle of vision was less acute and she could get a better view of the house.

The weeping willow had gone. And the honeysuckle she'd spent so long training along the fence. The windows, obscured by ruched blinds, looked like so many sightless eyes. 'Victorian' coach lamps – polished and perfect – guarded the front door. The lawn had been replaced by slabs – too pale and regular to be real stone. Two cars were parked on the slabs, a third on the drive, making the front garden look like a used car lot. Less than a year ago, she had been living happily here and now, through no fault of her own, her beautiful home was occupied by Philistines.

She hadn't married a gambler, she was sure of that. When it all came out, it was clear that Sam's gambling spree had been fast and furious – a matter of months from start to finish. He'd cancelled payments, withdrawn savings, forged her signature on documents and she'd suspected nothing. Covert, ruthless, unrelenting. (MI5 would have employed him in a flash.) Ten days after the truth had come out, he'd driven at full tilt into the stanchion of a bridge on the M1. If he'd intended her to get his life insurance money, he shouldn't have cancelled the payments. There had been no need for any of it – it wasn't as if they were short of money. No one – the medics, his employer, the bank – could offer an explanation. The best Doctor Tate could come up with was that some kind of chemical reaction had tripped a switch in his brain leaving her to agonise over it until it had drained her dry and left her incapable of functioning.

No one had ever asked what had happened to Sam's ashes and it wasn't something she was keen to reveal. It would have been judged the act of an unhinged woman but it had done her more good than a dozen sessions with a mealy mouthed counsellor. When Bing came along, her memories had started re-shaping themselves. Sam was becoming less of a villain, more of a victim. This had to be good for her and for Naomi who had loved her father so dearly. Poor Sam.

'Mrs Siskin?'

The voice came from behind her and she turned to see a postman loping towards her, his bulky satchel banging against his thigh.

'Phil?' she said.

Phil – if she'd ever known his surname, she'd forgotten it – had played a pivotal role in the Siskin tragedy. Bankruptcy coupled with death spawned a startling volume of mail and this outsider, barely recognisable but for his fluorescent vest and red bag, had delivered it to her door. She'd been too zonked out on pills to take account of the discomfort he must have felt, asking her to sign for those menacing envelopes. (They always required proof of receipt.) It can't have been pleasant, turning up, day after day, with the next instalment of bad news. When she finally surfaced, the poor man had behaved as though everything were normal, and for that she was grateful to him.

'How are you keeping?' he said.

'I'm well, thank you, Phil.'

'And your daughter? You've got two grandchildren if I remember rightly. One of each, isn't it?'

In his stint as their postman, they must have chatted. He must have mentioned his family or his football team or his dog. Yet she couldn't summon up one single fact and she felt a little ashamed.

'What a good memory you have. Yes, they're fine, thanks. In fact I'm living with them at the moment but I'm moving in a few weeks. To be near my parents.'

'Well, I hope everything works out well for you,' he said, his concerned tone suggesting he knew that what she'd told him was only part of the story.

She would have liked to know what he thought of the new people. Had they given him a Christmas box? (Sam used to give him ten pounds and bottle of whisky.) Ask and he would think her even more of a sad case than he already did. Instead she offered him her hand. 'Good to see you. Take care.'

His hand was warm, the skin on his palm dry and rough. *All those letters. All those frosty mornings.*

'You too, Mrs Siskin,' he said.

On her way home, she stopped at the coffee shop where she and her colleagues used to meet in the holidays. How or why the ritual had evolved, she couldn't remember. They saw enough of each other in term time. The café was outside the school's catchment area, but occasionally pupils would come in, take one look at their teachers and leave. They'd rung last summer to remind her of the standing arrangement, saying they'd love her to join them – if she felt up to it. And once, Naomi must have taken the children somewhere, she'd got as far as parking the car before realising she couldn't go through with it.

She stationed herself at a corner table where she could watch the comings and goings. The March sun filtering through the window. The fragrance of coffee. The clatter of cups and the hum of voices. Yes. She was glad she'd made this pilgrimage. Had she been facing a non-future, she wouldn't have summoned up the courage.

The coffee had always been excellent here and she ordered a flat white and an almond croissant. The waitress smiled. 'We haven't seen you for a while,' she said. 'Have you moved?'

This woman must have served hundreds – thousands – of customers since Miriam was last here but she was accustomed to being recognised, something she put down to her white hair and dark eyebrows.

'Yes,' she said (*almost* true). 'I happened to be nearby so I thought I'd call in for old times' sake.'

Bing established that AAA Storage had a depot not far from his house. He said he would gladly pay for her possessions to be relocated. It was a tempting offer but a fresh start called for a clean slate. She'd got rid of a lot of furniture, keeping only a selection of smaller pieces to furnish the modest flat she'd imagined buying. Now everything had changed. Bing's house had that student-cum-motel aesthetic. She had nothing against Ikea but shouldn't a man his age aspire to furniture with a pronounceable name? He took her gentle criticism in good part, agreeing that, where possible, they would replace his MDF with her solid wood. (Naomi had second dibs and the remainder went to the Salvation Army.) When she was nearly done, in the far corner of the locker she came across a sealed cardboard box. When she ripped off the tape and pulled back the flaps, she discovered a motley assortment of odds and ends which, in the nightmare of the move, she must have shoved into the box and proceeded to forget. Knitting patterns. A hot water bottle. A chipped bowl. A pack of pens. Half-burned tea lights. All went into a black bag. And at the very bottom was the folder containing the beginnings of the novel she'd always promised herself she would write.

She wondered whether Naomi's enthusiasm for her leaving was linked to David's more frequent visits. If they were seriously thinking of giving it another go, they would stand a better chance if mother/mother-in-law weren't hovering on the touchline.

'What will you do with yourself all day in your new home?' David said. He'd called to return the waterproof Max had left in his car. Naomi was at the dentist's, the children in the living room arguing and playing Scrabble. 'Will you go back to teaching?'

'Not sure they'd have me,' she said.

'Tutoring? It's a growth industry.'

'Perhaps.'

Callum had asked the same question and the matter had been much on her mind. She would need something to occupy herself and to generate an income. Fail to do so and she might find that she'd swapped child care for geriatric care – not a happy prospect.

Max rushed into the kitchen. 'What's ectoplasm, Dad?'

David screwed up his face, struggling to rustle up a plausible definition.

Max beat him to it. 'Rosa says it's like frogspawn but without the black dots, and it comes out of dead people's mouths. But that's not right is it?' He turned to Miriam. 'Can we have a something to eat?'

She took four Bourbon biscuits from the packet. 'Four divided by two is…?'

'Two,' he said, carefully placing two biscuits in each pocket of his hoodie. 'I love you, Gamma.' Grabbing her hand, he kissed it then flitted back to Rosa with his haul.

'The kids are going to miss you something rotten,' David said. 'We all are.'

Tears welled and she turned away. 'Come on. It's not as if I'm emigrating.'

'But you can't deny things will be very different for them.'

'For me too,' she said. She'd not always enjoyed playing the role of factotum but the strengthened bond with her grandchildren compensated for its drudgery. Being here, helping her daughter, had given her a purpose when there might easily (and dangerously) have been none. 'D'you think I'm crazy, David?'

'Heavens, no. You're not crazy, you're brave. Everyone deserves their chance of happiness but you need guts to grab it when it comes along. I've only met Paul a few times but it's obvious he worships you. He seems like a really nice guy.'

'Everyone thought Sam was *a really nice guy*,' she murmured, 'and look how that panned out.'

'Poor Sam. I know what he did was unforgiveable—'
'It was.'

'—but he was always warm towards me. Supportive, too. I don't know whether you were aware of this but after Naomi and I separated, he used to phone every few weeks to check how I was doing.'

Another secret Sam hadn't seen fit to share.

'He, *we* – were – *are* very fond of you,' she said. 'Sorry. The past year has played havoc with my tenses, and my pronouns.'

'We – *I* – have the same problem,' he said. 'So tell me, does Paul have a family?'

She gave him the run down on Bing's ex-wife, children and new grandson, sticking to facts, not mentioning their hostility towards her.

'Now I come to think of it,' he said, 'Naomi said something about organising a get together before you move. A chance for the families to get to know each other.'

Surprise must have shown on her face because he slapped a hand to his forehead. 'Bugger. It's meant to be a surprise, isn't it?'

Naomi's proficiency with social media would make tracking down Bing's children a piece of cake. A click here, a swipe there, and she'd know all about Leon and Camille and Pascale; a few more and she'd be jabbering away to them, assuming they couldn't wait to unite in one big happy family.

Miriam told Bing what was afoot. 'It's sweet of her to want to do this but I'll have to find a way of putting her off the idea. I can't tell her your children aren't as thrilled with the situation as she is. It might set her against them forever.'

The matter was taken out of her hands when David confessed to Naomi that he'd let the cat out of the bag.

'How could he be so dense, Mum?' Naomi said.

'Don't take it out on him. Besides, you know how I hate surprises.'

'That's as maybe but you can't carry on as if nothing is happening. What you two are about to do is a big deal.'

She groped for a plausible excuse to deflect Naomi from her ill-judged plan. 'The thing is… the thing *is*, Paul and I are going away.' She embroidered the fiction. 'A sort of non-honeymoon.'

Naomi took the bait. 'Where? Somewhere romantic?

'That would be telling.' Her daughter's expression softened and Miriam pushed home her advantage. 'We need time to ourselves. Without interruptions.' She flashed her eyes, hinting at bedroom romps. 'We'll have a party later, when things have settled down.'

She almost believed it.

She and Bing spoke twice a day, if not more. Her phone pinged constantly announcing yet another incoming text. It was fun. She loved the breathless, adolescent frivolity of reclaiming the years they'd spent apart. Back then, spontaneity hadn't been an option. A phone call – if it were to be private – meant walking to a public phone box with a handful of heavy pennies. Mail depended on stamps and collection times. Had tap-of-a-screen communications been around forty years ago, their story might have had a different outcome.

Next time they spoke, she told him how she'd wriggled out of the party.

'Actually I like the idea of a non-honeymoon,' he said. 'Let's do it. Where d'you fancy? Paris? Rome? We'll have to go *somewhere* or we'll be rumbled.'

She pictured him, sprawled on the sofa, shoes kicked off, tie askew, bushed after a day of demanding patients. 'Let's not tangle with airports,' she said. 'How about York? Or Chester? Somewhere half-timbered. With log fires and wonky glass in the windows.'

They ended up in a seventeenth-century inn in Ludlow. Besides wonky glass and pungent, snapping log fires, The Crown boasted a no-nonsense cook who served the best roast lamb Miriam had ever tasted. It rained and blew a gale but they had waterproofs and walking boots, and a selection of reading matter. They found a jigsaw in the bottom of the wardrobe (Holbein's Henry VIII, missing only two pieces). There was no Wi-Fi and only patchy mobile service, and they became happily and passionately detached from the world. Their room couldn't have been more different from Bing's teenage bedroom yet it held the same enchantment and, over a bottle of wine in front of the fire, they concluded that, by simply being together, they created magic.

Miriam felt her life was near perfect, and yet without intending to, she had become a keeper of secrets. Standing as they were on the threshold of a brave new life, this didn't seem quite right. Bing had never asked about the circumstances surrounding Sam's accident, or why she was living with Naomi, or what *precisely* she did at the college. She'd never quizzed him as to what had gone wrong between him and Eloise. Come to that, Naomi had never asked where her father's ashes had ended up.

And there was Danny. Two weeks ago, she'd written to fill him in on Bing and their plans for the future. She reminded him of that day he'd sat on her bed insisting she should always be true to herself and said he should be happy for her because she was doing exactly that. The scuffed envelope, flap now edged with particles of dust, was still in her handbag, another secret yet to be revealed. It wasn't that she feared his reaction to her news but what if he failed to reply? She would be worried sick that something awful had happened to him. There was a more selfish reason too. If he knew she was blissfully happy and living within a mile of their parents, he would be off the hook once and for all.

After dinner they ventured out for a walk. The rain had blown over and the air smelled of wood smoke. A near-full moon floated above the tree tops and they strolled, arm in arm, following the line of the town walls, dipping in and out of the moon shadows.

'Just think,' he said, 'we'll be able to do this every evening, for the rest of our lives.'

'But we won't, will we?'

He stopped in his tracks. 'You don't think we'll stay together?'

'No. Yes. Of course we will. But we mustn't ever allow ourselves to get in a rut. I don't want us to end up like Mum and Dad.'

'How d'you see us then?'

'Doing new things – going new places. Remember how we used to lie in your room, daydreaming about the future.' She paused. 'You've never asked about my years with Sam. Aren't you curious?'

'I don't care to think about it. In fact, as far as I'm concerned, it never happened.'

'I fear you're making a huge mistake. Secrets are dangerous.' She pictured the trite slogan painted on driftwood, dangling from a door handle. 'There's no escaping the fact that we have our own histories and we should have faced up to that months ago.'

'Other people might do that,' he said, 'but can't we make our own rules? Dwelling on the past is only going to—'

She kissed him into silence, nudging him towards a grassy area where the pavement widened. They sat on a bench, his arm around her shoulder, his warmth seeping through her coat. 'I've a suggestion to make,' she said. 'Why don't we both write everything down? Set out a timeline. A potted history.' His resistance was tangible yet she pushed on. 'Facts. No analysis. Just a page. I'll give you mine, you give me yours. We'll lock them away in a safe place, to be read if we feel the need.'

'You want us to write a PowerPoint presentation?'

She laughed. 'If you like. I don't want to make a big deal of this but I know the harm secrets can do. It'd be an insurance policy against…' Against what, she couldn't say but suddenly it seemed vital it be done.

'If you ask me it'd be more like boring holes in a

perfectly watertight boat,' he said, 'but if it's that important to you...'

They used stationery from the hotel folder, the embossed crown at the top of the sheet fixing forever where the enterprise had taken place. She left him in the room and headed off along the creaky landing to the alcove at the top of the stairs. An hour ago, the task had seemed straightforward but it took several attempts before she achieved the objectivity she was after. When she returned to the room, Bing was lying on the bed, a sealed envelope with her name on it propped against his reading lamp.

Moat sent her a few lines (soft pencil, on grainy watercolour paper) wishing her an 'interesting' future and thanking her for the part she'd played in what he was coming to think might be his 'most successful' painting. The students presented her with a book of Hockney portraits, its flyleaf animated by their signatures – orchestrated, she assumed by, Callum. A final lunch with him – not sandwiches in his room but moussaka at the Greek restaurant behind the college. They drank too much and became sentimental. She thanked him for the chance to reinvent herself. He said she was brave and beautiful. She told him how lucky his wife was. When she started wondering whether he was a good lover, she knew it was time to say goodbye.

Her last week at Naomi's was occupied with packing and making removal arrangements. Notifying banks and building societies and everyone else who needed to know her new address, took forever. Getting through – in every sense – to HMRC and the DWP was indescribably frustrating. No matter when she phoned, a smug voice announced they were 'experiencing a high volume of calls' and to call back later. Better still, do… whatever it was, online which naturally involved *yet another* password. (To hell with security, she listed passwords in an A6 notebook which she kept in her washbag.) Whilst she was on this secretarial jag, she rewrote *and posted* her letter to Danny, keeping it snappy and unapologetic, giving him the facts and (yet again) her email address, insisting he 'get in touch immediately'.

Rosa and Max quibbled and quarrelled non-stop. They refused to do their homework and, when she badgered them, they deliberately made a hash of it. They pestered for treats and sobbed for no reason. She knew why they were behaving this way. She felt cranky and weepy too, and did all she could to keep confrontations to a minimum.

Bing, on the other hand, was persistently upbeat, like a vicar at a funeral who insists the dear departed is 'moving on to a better place'. Her feelings on leaving Naomi's were never going to be clear-cut, couldn't he see that? This little family, this house, had provided sanctuary when she was at her most vulnerable. Without doubt, she was doing the right thing yet it didn't rule out the occasional jitters – even the temptation to bolt.

Saturday came. Bing had offered to drive down and give her a hand but she'd dissuaded him, saying he'd be more useful at his end, directing the removal men (which was true). She'd hoped this last breakfast with the children would be like any other morning but David turned up to say goodbye which further intensified emotions. Rosa – in tears – took herself off to her bedroom, and Max came near to hysterics when the removal men began loading her possessions into the high-sided van. The only thing to do was get in the car and drive.

Before she'd gone far, a headache settled at the base of her skull. She pulled in at a petrol station, and swallowed a couple of Paracetamol. Wandering over to the picnic area, she sat at one of the shabby tables, checking her phone. The log showed a couple of missed calls from Bing and a text saying he'd booked a table at a restaurant for this evening. When she rang, his line was busy and she left a message telling him not to worry, she'd stopped for a coffee and should be with him in a couple of hours.

Next she texted Naomi, apologising for leaving so abruptly and saying she hoped the children were okay. A text pinged straight back. They'd already perked up. She and David were taking them swimming then to Pizza Express for lunch. Clearly Naomi and David were making progress which had to be good news. And yet she couldn't help feeling a little miffed that the children had recovered so quickly.

There was a whiff of diesel fuel in the air but the sun was breaking through and the shrubs around the garage forecourt were budding up, hinting at spring. The van would be well ahead of her, hauling her bits and pieces towards her new life. It was time to be on her way.

16

BING'S HOUSE WAS THREE YEARS OLD, a modern, brick-built box – the sort of prosaic place Miriam had never imagined she would live in. According to the neighbours, the previous owner – a single man whom they thought had worked 'overseas' – had spent hardly any time there. He'd certainly done nothing to stamp his mark on the house, or the garden which consisted of lawn, decking, drive to the garage and panelled fencing – each component rectangular and unadorned. The estate agent had identified these failings as selling points. *A virtually new property, decorated throughout in stylish neutrals. Easy to maintain garden with great potential.* 'Stylish? It's like living in... a bowl of porridge,' Miriam said. 'Tell you what,' Bing said, 'you choose a colour scheme, I'll find a painter.'

She had fun doodling around with colour charts and trial paint pots. One of Bing's patients recommended a decorator who, thanks to a cancellation, was able to start immediately. The three-man team were in and out in ten days and by the time she'd trawled TK Maxx for throws, cushions, towels and curtains, the house had been transformed from porridge to fresh fruit salad.

So what next? At Naomi's, she'd been in perpetual motion – pairing socks, screwing tops on toothpaste tubes, searching for vital bits of Lego (*she missed the children*) and, more recently, there had been her session at the college and with Moat. Life here couldn't be more different. By mid-morning she'd done all that needed doing and with no one undoing her good work, once plumped, cushions stayed plumped; once tidied, drawers stayed tidy. Her greatest problem was finding excuses not to call in on her parents who would have liked her to visit every single day.

When she announced her intention of finding a job, Bing said there was no need but if she were bored, how about charity work? She wasn't yet ready to join that worthy band and she checked the local rag and the small ads pinned on the board in the supermarket. But nothing grabbed her. She was starting to lose heart and, yes, confidence. 'Sign on with an agency,' Naomi said. 'That's what people do.' All well and good but at sixty-one the prospect of selling herself to some agency woman with fake nails and a fake smile, who would ask all sorts of intrusive questions, gave her the heebie-jeebies. She was delighted, therefore, when, meandering down Angelgate one morning, she spotted a 'part-time help needed' sign in a bookshop window. Without hesitating she went in. The woman tidying the shelves was the owner, Hazel Nesbitt – a no-nonsense woman, ten years her junior, with a dry wit (and her own fingernails). The hourly rate was less than that for a life model, and a fraction of what she'd earned as a teacher, but she loved the idea of being amongst books again.

Angelgate Books, which specialised in books on ecclesiastical architecture, new and second-hand, did well for a small indie bookshop. Its bow-fronted window and brass door bell were charming, its location a cobbled passageway running off the cathedral green picturesque. When Hazel's husband had left her, her response had been to take voluntary redundancy and embark on a new project. Using her redundancy money and some of her divorce settlement, she'd opened the bookshop. The shop had a loyal clientele who valued her expertise and reasonable prices. Although she stocked contemporary and children's fiction too, she wasn't terribly up in it – one of the reasons she'd offered Miriam (who was) the job. The other reason was that her new venture – www.angelgatebooks.com – was proving more time consuming than she'd bargained for. The two women took to each other immediately and after only a few weeks, they'd laid the foundations of a firm friendship.

Bing glanced up from his newspaper. 'Off somewhere?'

'I'm taking Mum to the hairdresser's,' Miriam said. 'The parking's tricky and Dad's losing his nerve although he'd never admit it.'

Remarkably, her father still held a driving licence but they didn't venture far afield. On Thursday mornings, they drove the short distance to Waitrose to do the weekly shop but the rest of the time the car, polished and topped up with fuel, stood in the garage.

He folded his paper. 'How long will you be?'

'No idea. Why?'

'I was hoping we might take a stroll along the tow path. Maybe grab lunch at The Pheasant.'

She scooped her keys from the bowl on the dresser. 'But you're working today. I checked the rota.'

'I swapped with Kasha,' he said. 'She needs Friday off – something to do with her son's school. Damn. Any chance you could reschedule?'

'Not really. Mum's been stuck in the house for days. I don't want to disappoint her.'

He looked downcast and she bent to kiss his forehead. 'I'll tell them I have to be back for lunch.'

'We're in here,' her father called from the kitchen.

She found them standing shoulder to shoulder, for all the world as though they were propping each other up. 'What's the matter?' she said.

Her father pointed at an envelope sitting in the centre of the otherwise bare table. '*This* is the matter.'

She could tell from the banding on the blue envelope that it was from Danny. 'Is he okay?'

'Of course he's *okay*,' he said. 'We'd have heard soon enough if he weren't. I've been telling your mother that for months.'

'May I?' She reached for the envelope.

It contained a single sheet of paper covered with Danny's rangy scrawl. Considering the few words he'd written, he might have made an effort to make them legible. She put on an elaborate show of reading it, trying to give the impression there was more to it than a couple of sentences.

'That's nice,' she said.

Her father snorted. 'How can you say that? We write letter after letter – God knows how much we've spent on postage over the years – and he never replies. When he does, he avoids our questions. We don't know where he's living. We don't know if he has a job. We don't know whether—' He pressed his hand to his mouth as if holding back a flood of unspeakable misdemeanours whilst, inexplicably composed, her mother placed a hand on his forearm and tapped it absently with her fingertips.

What she didn't tell them was that Danny had emailed last week, the first communication from him since she'd sent that spiky note. What with the move, and the bookshop, and visits to Naomi's, she'd had enough to keep her busy. All the same, his extended silence had niggled and nagged, once in a while, erupting in a panic. She'd been on the point of writing again when an email from an 'unrecognised sender' (Danny, using a new address) landed in her inbox. Its tone was polite, not to say distant. He was glad to hear that she and Bing had reconnected although he didn't mention her moving in with him. He asked to be 'remembered' to Naomi and the children as if they were passing acquaintances. She was accustomed to his tirades against religion and capitalism and global warming. And, of course, his persistent sniping at their parents. At least those angry letters gave the impression he was connected to the family whilst this was as near as dammit a *pro forma*.

Secrets were empowering. In the early days, when the hurt had been at its most crippling, keeping news of Danny from them had been her way of punishing them for their part in her break up with Bing. By the time her anger had subsided to a chronic ache, secrecy had become a consoling habit, an invisible defence.

She made tea and dropped a handful of biscuits onto a plate, and they sat drinking tea whist the wall clock flicked away the seconds. Her mother looked paler than ever, the skin around her lips puckered in tiny wrinkles like the opening of a drawstring bag. *That will happen to me and there's nothing I can do to stop it.*

'Why don't I change Mum's appointment,' she said. 'We can go next week.'

'*No.*' Her father's hands were clenched, his fists a delta of purple veins. 'He's not going to spoil your mother's day with his… his piffle.' Her father slammed his fist on the table, rattling the cups. 'He'll get nothing when we go.'

Danny had always made it clear that he neither expected nor wanted anything from his parents. Despite this, they'd included him in successive wills and made sure he knew it, until their unwavering generosity had become a weapon. Exclude him now, and he'd probably consider it a victory.

This outburst brought her mother back from wherever she'd drifted. A smile settled around her mouth. 'Don't worry about me,' she said.

'How was it?' Bing said when she returned.

'Exhausting. Sad. Pathetic. It takes Mum forever to do the simplest things. She used to be so sprightly. Now she's not with it half the time.'

'She's pretty good for her age,' he said.

'You'll say that about me one day.'

'You'll never grow old,' he said. 'I won't allow it '

He set aside the sheaf of papers he was feeding into

the shredder. 'I love you, Miriam Edlin. If anything happened to you, I couldn't go on.'

'Of course you could,' she said, kissing his chin. 'And I haven't been Edlin for a long time.'

'Well, say the word and you can be Crosby.'

'I know,' she said.

'You're not having doubts?'

'No, no, *no.*' She slipped her hands up inside his sweater.

'What is it then? Is it the religious thing? D'you want me to convert?'

She'd never told him but, when she was at university, she'd spent an afternoon in the reference library reading up on the procedure for conversion. To an impatient nineteen-year-old it was a series of daunting hurdles which would take years to complete. Even then there was no guarantee it would win her parents over, and it would certainly alienate the Crosby family who were fervent agnostics.

'Of course not. It's perfect as it is, don't you think? Mum and Dad are very fond of you. They've no problem with our living together. It seems daft to rock the boat by getting married.'

He shook his head. 'Mim, my love, you're not making sense.'

'I know. But can't you humour me?'

How could they marry when she'd not met his children? And why didn't she come out and tell him how uneasy that made her? Naomi kept saying 'it's a bit rum' – and it was. They might disapprove of the liaison but weren't they just a teeny bit curious about her? Was it money? Did they fear their inheritance would be whipped from under their noses? It was up to him to let them know his estate would go to them.

Naomi's main concern was that she might be feeling isolated in her new home. 'Why don't I set you up on Facebook? I can't bear to think of you being lonely. There must be dozens of your old schoolfriends still in the area.'

The news of her moving in with Bing had filtered through to Angela Terry who was quick to phone, clearly delighted to have been instrumental in the reunion. Angela was easy to talk to, bright and funny, precisely the sort of friend Naomi wanted for her. Yet lurking in the back of Miriam's mind was Angela's confession that she'd once hated her and she decided to tread warily before getting too chummy.

Miriam put it to Naomi that she might not want to make contact with people she'd not given a thought to in years, a concept which seemed alien to her daughter.

'How about new friends?' Naomi said. 'What are Paul's workmates like?

'They seem a nice enough crowd,' she said.

And they did. Whenever she had occasion to call at the practice, everyone was welcoming. They seemed to be aware that she and Bing had been at school together although they didn't know the details of their reunion. They probably weren't terribly interested. Why should they be? He was a newcomer, and childhood-sweetheart stories weren't unusual these days.

As for *lonely*, Miriam had always been content with her own company and, when the weather was good and she had nothing pressing to do, she took herself off for a walk, meandering where the fancy took her. She and Bing used to cycle out this way before the rash of housing developments nibbled away at the farmland, rendering swathes of it unrecognisable. They'd bring an old army blanket and, if there was no one around, make love under cover of a hawthorn hedge. The risk of discovery. The fusty smell of old blanket. Summer breezes on damp skin. Even after all these years, the memory of it roused her and she could barely wait for him to get home from work.

'Now we've got the house straight, let's invite your children to visit,' she said. 'I wouldn't like them to think me stand-offish.'

'It'd mean a lot of extra work for you,' Bing said.

'Not necessarily. We could eat out. And they'd probably only stay a night or two.'

'Well, as long as you're sure.'

She removed the Sasco planner from the fridge door and spread it on the table and they identified a couple of possible dates. She was both excited and nervous at the prospect of meeting them.

Bing appeared unfazed by his children's negative response to their invitation.

'They must have given reasons,' she said.

He checked them off on his fingers. 'Pascale says the

trip's too much with the baby. Leon's going to be working away. Camille can't spare the time.'

'How can you be so sanguine?'

'What choice do I have? My children believe everything Eloise tells them. Always have. And, as I told you, she has it in for me. You've seen what happened with your brother. Families are a combat zone. You mustn't let it get to you. Onward and upward.'

Their rejection of the invitation was hurtful and, whatever he might say, threatened to cast a shadow over the future. 'Maybe I should talk to them,' she said. 'Convince them I'm not a threat. I couldn't bear to be the cause of a rift.'

'And I couldn't bear it if they were spiteful. Look. Let's give the dust time to settle then try again in a few months.'

When there were no customers in the shop, she and Hazel chatted. Sometimes they discussed strategies for boosting sales. Author talks. Competitions. Themed displays. As time went by, she grew to trust Hazel and felt comfortable discussing personal matters. Her parents. Danny. Sam's suicide, and the breakdown which had ended her teaching career. On the brighter side, how she and Bing had lost and found each other. 'You must think we're crazy.'

'You're certainly brave,' Hazel said. 'What seems extraordinary to me is that, in all those years, the two of you never tried to get in touch.'

When she'd accepted Sam's proposal, she'd vowed never to see, speak or write to Bing ever again. Sam hadn't demanded it, but if the marriage were to stand a chance, a clean break was the only hope.

'Were you never tempted?' Hazel said.

'Yes, of course. In the beginning it was unbearable. But then I found a solution. I killed him off. Not literally, but I pretended he was dead.'

'Good Lord. That's radical.'

'When I put my mind to something, I can be quite determined.'

'All the same…'

'Don't forget I was very young. Everything was black or white. Paul was out of my life forever and I had to find a way of living with that. I simply took that fact to its logical conclusion.'

Hazel wrinkled her nose. 'I still don't get why you had to give him up.'

'Three years of parental disapproval wore me down.'

'I don't have you down as a Miss Mouse. Quite the opposite.'

'It was different in those days. Parents called the shots. And you have to bear in mind there was other stuff going on. My brother had walked out and it was pretty clear he wasn't coming back. My mother was heading for a breakdown. My father was permanently angry, ready to lash out at anything. Their hopes were pinned on me and I did everything I could to please them apart from give up Paul. Their constant disapproval – the permanent look of disappointment – it was truly awful.

'I was barely coping then, in my second year, I went down with glandular fever. God, I felt lousy. Student

Health sent me home to convalesce. I was starting to pick up when my aunt turned up and proceeded to fill me in on missing bits of family history. Long story short, it explained why my parents were desperate I stay in the fold. I had no option but to give him up. We'd call it emotional blackmail now.'

'That's tantamount to abuse.'

'Maybe. But it wasn't as if Sam was an ogre. To be fair, he was kind, funny, patient. And my parents loved him. *Really* loved him.'

'He wasn't marrying your parents.'

'No. But he was replacing their son. They caught me when I was feeling low and it was a massive relief to be welcomed back into the family. I'll never know what they would have done had I married out.'

'You didn't have to marry anyone,' Hazel said.

'No, but they were never going to change their mind about Paul, and I'd been introduced to enough of what they considered "suitable" candidates to realise that Sam Siskin was as good as it was likely to get.'

'Well, whatever excuses you're generous enough to make for them, I say it was barbaric.'

The shop bell jangled and an elderly man came in with a list in his hand.

'Looks promising,' Hazel whispered and they set about selling books.

Whenever the children came, Miriam went flat out to ensure they had a good time. Bing was a natural, ready to down tools and play with them, interested in whatever they had to say. They adored him. When they stayed for a weekend, they went swimming or bowling or went to the cinema and, although it wasn't top of their list, they visited her parents – their great grandparents. A little wary of each other, they were all on their best behaviour. Her mother stoked them up with sugary snacks and her father told them meandering stories, irrelevant to their young lives. When the youngsters became fidgety, Bing was there ready to take the strain.

With the summer holidays looming, she asked Naomi how she would manage six weeks' childcare. She'd always been on the spot, able to lend a hand, but now she was a hundred miles away with a job and a partner. 'It's all under control, Mum,' Naomi said. 'They're booked in for a drama course. David's taking them camping. Then his parents are having them. I'll take a couple of weeks and we're almost there.' She hated the idea of her grandchildren waking up, confused as to where they were or who would be looking after them. Bing told her she was being silly. 'If Naomi says she can manage, you must assume she means it.'

17

ON WARM AFTERNOONS, HER PARENTS were content to sit on the patio making the most of any late summer sunshine, her father with his *Telegraph*, her mother with her library book. Miriam noticed how much time they spent dozing. How their appetite had faded. How they talked less and less, as if speaking demanded too much energy. She'd watched Mopsy, their old cat, go through a similar process until finally she'd curled up in the grass in a corner of the garden and quietly, without any fuss, died.

August rolled into September. Dewy cobwebs and chilly mornings. Schoolgirl, student, schoolteacher – Miriam's life had been measured in Septembers. Despite her disengagement from that world, the 'back-to-school' frisson – nervousness, anticipation, hope – was ingrained and she found herself wandering into WHSmith's, ogling notepads and pencil cases and bumper packs of felt tips, coveting leather briefcases in Debenhams.

Out of the blue, Callum rang, asking how she was, grumbling that his current model – a young man – was incapable of standing still for more than five minutes. It was good, if a little unsettling, to hear from him.

'Moat dropped in the other day,' he said. 'He was singing your praises. In fact he wanted me to ask if you'd consider modelling for him again.'

She laughed. 'You're joking. I live a hundred miles away. I have a job here. How's that going to work?'

'You could make it work if you had a mind to.' He paused. 'I've seen Moat's painting. It's – well – it's the best thing he's ever done. At least promise you'll give it some thought.'

Her parents took it into their heads to go on a coach holiday to the Cotswolds with their bridge-playing pals. Three nights. She was dubious but Bing said she should leave the decision to them. 'Sitting at home, monitoring every ache and pain – it's like being on a self-imposed life-support machine. The stimulation will do them good.'

When she asked her father whether he was sure they were up to it, he stuck out his chin and countered, 'Paul thinks it's a terrific idea. That's good enough for me.'

'Well, as long as you've thought it through.'

'Miriam. We're travelling for three hours in a luxury coach with on-board facilities. We'll be taking a comfort break at a service station. We're staying in a four-star hotel. Someone will carry our bags, cook our meals and make our beds. No one will force us to do anything we don't feel up to doing. If we die, we'll die in luxury and I'm sure they'll find someone to say Kaddish. Now let's talk about something else, shall we?'

A few days before they set off, she received a text from Frankie Slattery saying she would be 'passing through' and asking whether she could drop in. Miriam had kept her friend abreast of events with Bing and Frankie had responded with a sentence or two expressing surprise and delight, as vague as ever about her own situation, promising to 'tell all' next time they met.

'How long since you've seen her?' Bing said.

'A couple of years? She was supposed to come to Sam's funeral but she didn't show.'

'That's a bit off. I can't imagine why you've stuck with her.'

Sam hadn't been keen on Frankie either. On their first few encounters, she'd flung herself at him – but there had been no reason why she shouldn't. Sam Siskin was simply a bloke who turned up at the house occasionally. Frankie's blatant attempts to ensnare him were embarrassing but in no way a betrayal of the girls' friendship. By the time Miriam and Sam became a couple, Frankie was out of the picture but, once in a while, when she failed to follow through on a promise, Sam would remind Miriam to be wary.

'Correct me if I'm wrong,' she said, 'but you two were quite close at one time.'

'Briefly. And we weren't *that* close.'

She tangled her fingers through his. 'You will be nice to her won't you?'

He kissed the back of her hand. 'I'll do my best to be civil but please don't ask me to like the woman.'

Her father dug out his ancient AA maps of the Cotswolds as if he might be called on to take over navigation duties. They sought advice on what clothes, toiletries, medication, books to take and she had to stop herself pointing out they weren't going on a trek through the Himalayas. Their suitcases were collectors' items – built like tanks and without wheels. She was sure she'd taken one of them on her trip to America the year she left school. Once packed, they were impossibly heavy and she persuaded them to slim down their loads and lent them her lightweight wheel-along cases. 'I can't take you to the coach station but I'll organise a taxi if you like,' she said. Her father instructed her to get a quote from a couple of taxi companies but the coach station was less than three miles from the house and Miriam had drawn the line at that.

'I've barely seen you for days,' Bing said when she returned from another session with her mother who'd decided most of what she was taking needed dry-cleaning.

'They're off first thing tomorrow,' she said, 'so we'll have a few days' peace and quiet.'

'But you'll be at work and then Frankie's coming, and before we know it they'll be home again—'

'And we'll have to go for dental check-ups and to the supermarket and the tide will go out and come in.' She held out her arms. 'So let's make the most of our evening.'

Some time ago, her father had purchased a rudimentary mobile phone 'for emergencies'. He kept it on his desk, located in its holder-cum-charger and, when she checked, the five calls logged were those she'd made to demonstrate how to use it. As part of the pre-Cotswolds preparations, she'd gone over it all again and, in addition, shown him how to send and receive texts, writing step-by-step instructions on a piece of stout card. Throughout the morning, much to her dismay and Hazel's amusement, texts pinged into her inbox, the intimation of calamity never far away – 'Taxi £8', 'So far so good', 'Coach driver proficient', 'Arrived safely'.

At lunchtime, she spotted Bing peering through the shop window. She raised her hand but he pressed a finger to his lips and came in, joining the handful of customers.

'Maybe you can help me,' he said. 'I need a gift for someone special.'

She played along, wondering where this was leading. 'What sort of thing did you have in mind?'

'Something modern. Poetry maybe.' He lowered his voice a fraction but it was still loud enough for all to hear. 'It's for my mistress.'

Hazel was at the back of the shop, packing orders, and Miriam heard a barely-suppressed snort of laughter.

'This is very popular,' she said, selecting a slim volume with a blood-red cover.

'*Rapture*. Carol Ann Duffy.' He flicked through the index. 'Would *you* be pleased if your lover gave you this?'

She blushed, beginning to regret playing along with his nonsense. 'Yes. I would.'

He offered it back to her with a flourish and a dip of the head. 'In that case, it's yours. How much do I owe you?'

'What was that all about?' Hazel whispered when he'd gone and his attentive audience had returned to their browsing.

'You tell me.'

Hazel nodded towards a man who was clutching the remaining copy of Duffy's poems. 'Tell him he can repeat his performance any time he likes.'

18

THEY HUGGED, MURMURING NONSENSE AS they eased back into their friendship. Frankie had been a redhead when Miriam last saw her, now she was implausibly blonde. When she shrugged off her leather jacket, Miriam noted its torn lining. 'You look very… rock 'n roll,' she said.

Frankie tugged at a clump of hair. 'A DIY job. Big mistake.'

She found a vase for Frankie's offering of flowers. 'Tea? Coffee? Have you eaten? I could make you a sandwich.'

'Coffee sounds good.'

Frankie settled on a chair and glanced around the kitchen. 'This is nice. You always had a good eye.'

'It was wall-to-wall beige when I moved in,' Miriam said. 'It sucked the energy out of me although Bing didn't seem to mind it.'

'So he's still "Bing"?'

'Only to me.'

'You're kidding.'

Miriam shrugged. 'That's the way he wants it.'

'Surely your parents…?'

'When I told Mum we were back together she recalled "the boy with a funny nickname" but that's as far as it went. Dad treats him like a recent acquaintance. It suits them not to remember.'

'Well, I'll do my best but I can't guarantee anything.' Frankie flashed her eyes. 'Is *Paul* still devastatingly handsome?'

Miriam nodded towards the pin-up board and the recent photograph of the pair of them sitting together in Naomi's garden. Frankie took down the photo and studied it. 'Blimey. He's worn well. So have you. Look at your beautiful hair. You make a good-looking couple. Is he still sports mad? Oh, God, please tell me he doesn't play golf?'

'He swims a couple of times a week, and plays the odd game of badminton, but no golf.'

'Look,' Frankie said, 'about Sam's funeral. I still feel terrible. I should have been there but to put it bluntly, I was a bit of a mess. The last thing you needed was some screwed-up friend showing up.'

'I knew there must be a good reason for your no show,' Miriam said. 'To be honest, I was barely there myself.'

Puffing out her cheeks, Frankie exhaled noisily. 'Wow. That's a weight off. I wish everyone were as forgiving. I still find it hard to credit. Sam came across as Mister Sensible. Captain Cautious.'

'He did, didn't he? I've been over and over it and the conclusion I've reached is when you've been married as long as we were, you see what you expect to see. Or rather what it's convenient to see.'

'I wouldn't know about that. He certainly turned out to be a conniving, cowardly bastard, that's for sure. He lured you away from Bing and then he sold you down the river.'

'It wasn't quite like that.' Miriam stood up. 'Come on. Let me show you where everything is.'

After they'd finished the tour, she told Frankie about her job at the bookshop, and how Naomi and David were talking again, flicking through photos on her iPad to prove how Rosa and Max had grown. How beautiful they were.

'Your brother?' Frankie said.

'Nothing's changed. Your brothers?'

'Who knows?'

Miriam made a second pot of coffee. 'Last time we had a proper chat you were working for a letting agency.'

'I was. And I learned a lot. Mainly not to mix work and pleasure.' Frankie raised her cup. 'You wouldn't have something to pep this up?'

Before Bing returned it would be prudent to establish what had prompted Frankie's visit and digging out a bottle of cooking brandy, she added a splash to her friend's coffee. 'So what are you doing now?'

'Not a lot. I won't bore you, but it boils down to job, skills, savings, hope – none of which I have.' She gave a mirthless laugh. 'I swore I'd never get bogged down in that dreary stuff. So I guess you're right. We see what it suits us to see, and, ridiculous as it sounds, I never saw myself growing old.'

'Oh, come on. Sixty-one isn't old.'

'My mother only made it to fifty-one.'

Frankie poured another splash of brandy into her cup and downed its contents. 'What happens when I meet Mum in heaven and she's younger than me? How's that going to work?' She frowned. 'I've forgotten. Does your lot believe in heaven?'

'In principle. Do you?'

'Some days I do, and other days I... What was the name of our scripture teacher? Permed hair. Glasses on a chain.'

Miriam smiled. '*My lot* were excused scripture.'

'You were lucky. You *are* lucky. You *will be* lucky. See. I still remember my tenses.'

'You'll stay?' Miriam said, noting how the level of brandy had dropped, picturing a wrecked car and screaming sirens.

'Tempting but I'm not sure Bing – sorry, *Paul* – would be too thrilled.'

'Tosh. He'd love to see you. Let's get your things.'

The last time Frankie visited, she was driving a sporty, red number. Today it was a Jazz, bodywork scuffed, nearside mirror held in place with gaffer tape. The back seat had been levelled to accommodate a hodgepodge of holdalls, boxes and bin bags. A suitcase occupied the front seat, belted in like a dumpy passenger.

Frankie was right. Yesterday, when Miriam had mentioned inviting her to spend a night or two, Bing had been dead set against it. The more they discussed it, the more entrenched he became until finally he'd stomped out of the house. Miriam left it half-an-hour before ringing him only to discover his mobile was in the living room, on the arm of the chair. Time went on and she grew anxious. He'd gone out without a jacket and his keys were in the bowl on the hall table. She set about the ironing pile. When that was done, phone in hand, she watched the ten o'clock news followed by a documentary on... something or another. He'd returned after midnight, cold and contrite, bearing chocolates and a bunch of flowers from the all-night garage. They'd kissed and he'd apologised for behaving like a child, but it had shaken them both and done nothing to resolve the issue.

Frankie manhandled her suitcase onto the pavement. Miriam anticipated a joke or at very least a reference to the contents of the car, but nothing was said as if it were normal to travel with all one's possessions. Frankie insisted on hauling the cumbersome case upstairs unaided and, in the doing, took a chunk of paint off the newel post.

Miriam opened the door to the spare bedroom. 'You're in here.'

'Bliss,' Frankie flopped onto the bed. 'I didn't realise how knackered I was.'

'Where have you driven from? I forgot to ask.'

'Hastings.'

Miriam had assumed London or Bristol, or some other big city. 'Hastings? I don't think I've been there.'

'You've not missed much.'

Miriam left her to 'freshen up'. She'd bought fillet steaks for supper which she planned to serve with jacket potatoes and salad. Fruit and cheese to follow. She took everything out of the fridge and dug out a decent bottle of red wine from the stash under the stairs. Bing should be home around seven-thirty and they'd eat at eight. Checking her phone, she found a text from her father.

They'd been to visit a National Trust property close to where they were staying and were now putting their feet up before their evening meal. Good to think someone was having a stress-free time.

She waited ten minutes then went to the bottom of the stairs and called, 'Got everything you need?' There was no reply, no sound of activity. 'Frankie?'

The bedroom door was ajar and she tiptoed in. Frankie was lying on her back on the bed, out for the count. Her mouth was open and she was breathing noisily. She'd unbuttoned her jeans and her leopard-print top had ridden up revealing a yellowing bruise a few centimetres above her waistline. There was a similar mark on her forearm. A fall? A bump in the car? There were endless innocent explanations. Frankie mumbled and rolled onto her side. A shaft of evening sunlight hit the wall above the bed head. Miriam closed the curtains and draped a blanket over her sleeping friend.

She was rinsing salad leaves when she heard the *clunk* of a car door and, standing a little back from the window, she watched Bing take his bag off the back seat, lock the car and walk up the path. This reunion repeated itself most days but nevertheless her heart leapt as it had on that snowy day when he'd come to claim her.

He hung his head like a contrite schoolboy. 'I'm an idiot, aren't I?'

'You are,' she said offering her lips to be kissed.

He pointed to the jacket slung on the back of the chair. 'She turned up then?'

'Yes. She's upstairs. Asleep.'

He nodded. 'Same old Frankie?'

'Not really.' She described the bruises. 'She looks defeated. I've asked her to stay. That's okay, isn't it?'

'Of course,' he said, and she loved him for his acceptance.

While he changed, she cooked the steaks, setting Frankie's to one side. They ate in the kitchen, discussing whether to shop around for a better deal on house insurance and marvelling at her father's mastery of technology. Frankie might have been their delinquent daughter, banished to her room until she came to her senses.

She was stacking the dishwasher when Frankie came down wearing her dressing gown on top of her clothes. 'How long did I sleep?'

'Four hours.'

'Really?' She yawned and shivered. 'Sorry. I've buggered up your evening.'

'Don't be silly.' Miriam pointed to the remaining food. 'Help yourself.'

'Thanks. Maybe later. Where's Bing? *Paul.* I'm going to get this wrong.'

'I'm sure "Bing" will be fine. After all, you knew him before I did. He's watching the news. We'll be off to bed soon. Surgery starts at eight, and I need to leave before nine.'

Miriam had told Frankie about her job, yet the puzzled look on her face showed it had failed to register. 'The bookshop? I knock off at one. We could have lunch at The Angel. Unless you have other plans.'

'No. No plans.'

Miriam nodded towards the living room. 'Why don't you go and say hi? I'll finish up here.'

She pottered around, allowing her lover and her best friend ten minutes to negotiate their first encounter in over forty years.

The sun had come out and it was warm enough to take their lunch into the hotel garden. Frankie, wearing a long-sleeved T-shirt and black jeans, looked tired but less shambolic than she had yesterday. She'd toned down her make-up too.

'Any reservations about moving in together so soon?' Frankie said. 'I suppose you're used to the idea of marriage.'

'None at all. And we're not married.'

'But you will be.'

'Mmmm. Bing's keen but I sometimes think it'd be best to leave things as they are. His children wouldn't have to worry that some wicked stepmother was after their inheritance. And I know deep down my parents would prefer me not to marry "out", even if they haven't put it into words.'

'"My parents." "Bing's children."' Frankie rolled her eyes. 'Where are *you* in all this?'

'Precisely where I want to be.' She took a cocktail stick and stabbed an olive. 'Where are you heading next? You said you were "passing through".'

'Did I?'

'Look. It's obvious something's come unstuck. D'you want talk about it?'

'Not really. It's the usual pathetically predictable story. Bob owns the agency where I work. Correction – *worked*. We'd been having a "thing", pretty much since I started there. In fact he asked me to marry him. He's not the most exciting man in the world, but it might have worked. I was on the point of accepting when his son showed up. Dominic's a real charmer. Sex on legs, to be honest. So when he came on to me…' Frankie covered her face with her hands. 'Don't look at me like that. Mim.'

'Go on.'

'Naturally my job went down the pan. Everything was good for a few weeks then Dom started leaving his phone where he knew I'd see it. He was getting these suggestive messages from a girl called Chloe and—'

'You listened to his messages?'

'Oh, come *on*. Don't you check Bing's phone?'

'Absolutely not.'

'Well you should. Anyway, it was obvious he wanted me to find out. He never fancied me, I can see that now. He was using me to get at his dad. Some stupid feud. I confronted him and, well, it got out of hand.' She grimaced. 'I don't have much luck do I?'

When they were shunting their trays along the food counter, she'd hustled Frankie past the alcohol instead picking up a large bottle of Evian. Now Frankie's eyes wandered to the next table where four young women were sipping white wine and, without saying anything, Miriam went to the bar and returned with two glasses of Prosecco.

'Thanks,' Frankie said and they chinked glasses.

'Can I ask you something?'

220

'Oh, God.'

'You've had a lot of boyfriends – men – lovers – whatever you care to call them. Was there ever anyone you thought you might spend the rest of your life with? You don't have to answer.'

'You mean a *soul mate*?' Frankie hooked the air with her fingers.

'If you like.'

'As a matter of fact, there was.' She took a swig from her glass. 'His name was Andrew. Andrew Latham. He was a librarian, would you believe? We met on a bus, in Brighton. I seem to have spent half my life in Brighton. The bus broke down and it was raining, and we were heading in the same direction so we shared a taxi. He told me that getting in a taxi with a total stranger was reckless. That I shouldn't do things like that. But he never felt like a stranger.'

'What was different about Andrew Latham?'

'He wasn't sexy, for a start. Or even good-looking. He didn't care what he looked like – and neither did I. He had this wonderful calm about him, as though he'd found the answer.'

'Was he religious?'

'Well, he believed in me if that counts as religion.'

'Married?'

'No. And he never had been which was strange because he was lovely. Gentle. Kind. Funny. Considerate in bed. He taught me that simply lying still next to someone can be satisfying. I can't tell you how redemptive that was. I wish you could have met him. Sometimes I think I invented him.'

Frankie reached for Miriam's wine and drank it down. 'I expect you're waiting for me to tell you I ballsed it up. I didn't. Some cunt in a transit van ploughed into him when he was cycling to work. I heard the police sirens from the flat. You never imagine it's going to be your tragedy, do you?' She glanced around. 'D'you think they'd notice if I had a quick fag?'

'I'm sure they would. Let's find a bike shed for you to skulk behind.'

They wandered in the direction of the river. 'Aren't you going to give me a lecture?' Frankie said.

'On?'

'Pretty much everything.'

They found a low wall and perched on it and, while Frankie was fiddling with her lighter, a text came through on Miriam's phone.

'It's Dad. "Safe home. Early night. See you tomorrow around 3pm." Well that's tomorrow sorted for me.'

'I love your parents,' Frankie said. 'They were unbelievably kind to me when Mum was in hospital. Your mother used to feed me huge meals, as though nothing could go wrong if my belly was full.'

'She hasn't changed. Actually, that's not true. They've become inward-looking. They're not interested in anything that goes on beyond their road, or anyone outside the family.'

'Neither will I if I get to be their age.'

'I understand that, although it worries me that they're cutting themselves off. It's not good.'

'What about this trip they've just been on?'

'I haven't got to the bottom of that.'

'D'you think it'd be okay if I popped in tomorrow? I'd like to say hello before I leave town.'

'They'd love to see you.' They would and yet Miriam felt uneasy at the prospect of her parents and Frankie buddying up. 'What's the plan?'

'Find a job. A place to live.' She lit another cigarette. 'I know my way around an office, and I'm good with figures. I should be able to find something. That job you had at the college, how did you find that?'

'Word of mouth. It was only a few hours a week.'

'I need to work full-time. Or two part-time jobs would do. 'Specially if they were cash-in-hand.'

'No chance of making it up with Bob?'

Frankie wrinkled her nose. 'To be honest, he's a boring fart. And he makes this funny squeaking noise when he comes.'

They fell about giggling and they were eleven years old again.

Bing's tight smile revealed his displeasure at seeing Frankie's jacket on the peg.

'She's upstairs,' Miriam whispered. 'She'll be off first thing tomorrow. Honest. I thought we might eat out to make the evening a bit special.'

Il Barocco was one of their regular haunts. The food was authentic, the wine affordable, the atmosphere homely – perfect for an evening with her oldest and dearest friends. Yet she was on pins. Trapped in their seats, there was no alternative to conversation and whichever course that took

– reminiscence, catch-up or plans for the future – something problematic was sure to surface. Bing must have felt the same way and, like a couple of sheepdogs, whenever the conversation threatened to stray into hazardous territory, they herded it in another direction. But by the time coffee arrived, Frankie had drunk best part of a bottle of wine and refused to be distracted.

'So, Dr *Paul* Crosby. You were married to thingy.'

'Eloise,' he said.

'*Eloise*. That's the one. So what went wrong? Why did you divorce?'

Miriam folded her napkin – once, twice, three times.

'It worked for a bit and then it stopped working. I like to think fate was setting things straight. Clearing the way for Mim and me.'

'Well it took its bloody time.' Frankie held the upturned bottle over her glass, catching the last few drops. 'I gather Naomi thinks you're the dog's doodahs – but she would, wouldn't she? Her father turned out to be a shit and you're a knight in shining armour. She's had a tough time, poor kid. Not as tough as Mim, of course.' She swivelled the bottle so that it was a gun pointing at Bing. 'Don't you let them down or you'll have me to reckon with.'

Miriam loved her for making the childish threat.

Bing took Miriam's hand and squeezed it. 'I would never do that.'

'Good,' Frankie said. 'So what do your kids – you've got three, so I'm told – make of the situation? Do they see Mim as a wicked stepmother, or a fairy godmother?'

'Here.' Miriam pushed the tiny espresso cup towards Frankie. She could tell from Bing's expression he was wondering how much she'd confided in Frankie. 'We're taking it slowly,' she said.

Bing stood up. 'I'll get the bill.'

When they got back, she coaxed Frankie up the stairs, promising to wake her before she left for the bookshop.

'That wasn't too bad, was it?' she said when they were getting undressed.

'Beats me why you bother with her,' he said.

'Aren't the most enduring connections made through the gut not the brain?'

'But somewhere along the line, reason has to kick in.' He tossed his shirt towards the laundry basket. 'She's amoral and feckless. She drinks too much. She's... tacky.'

They got into bed and Bing lay on his side, facing away from her.

'Frankie's been my friend for fifty years,' she said. 'I knew her before I knew you existed. I'm well aware you don't like her. I'm simply asking you to accept that I *do*.'

19

THE CLOCKS WENT BACK AND by five o'clock it was dark. There were few days when it was worth pegging out washing. The garden chairs were stacked in the shed. Dahlia buds rotted on the stem, and the acer shed its fiery foliage, leaving the garden drab and inhospitable.

As a practice member, Bing was invited to all manner of 'dos' but he almost always wriggled out of them telling Miriam he spent enough time with work colleagues. When neighbours asked them in for coffee or drinks he concocted reasons not to go – 'start that and we'll have half the neighbourhood knocking the door for medical advice'. He was never happier than when they locked the door on the outside world. Miriam loved that too – the two of them, talking, reading, making love. She still couldn't believe how things had turned out and found herself touching his hand or the back of his neck, making sure he was there, that he was hers.

And yet.

Sam had been a gregarious man. Friends, neighbours, people from the office, were forever popping in. This wasn't always convenient but she'd enjoyed the unpredictability of it. Those difficult months when she was at Naomi's had been leavened by the household's chaotic schedule. And there had been the stimulation of working with Callum and Moat. Now she'd left that behind. From the moment Bing crossed the snowy road, before they'd exchanged more than a few words, their future had been inescapable. They belonged together, and that was that. But without realising it, she'd conflated belonging with Bing and belonging *here*, in this city when, in truth, she'd not belonged here for forty years. There were moments when she had the feeling she was drifting into a lazy backwater.

'You really should tell him how you're feeling.' Hazel said when she mentioned yet another declined invitation. 'How *are* you feeling?'

'Like a displaced person. And there's something wrong with that house. Something lacking.'

'You could always look for something with more character. Older perhaps. Nearer the centre of town.'

'I suppose so. I know I only have to ask. But what if it's me, not the house? When I was at Naomi's, I dreamed of reclaiming my life. Now I can't work out what that means. Or, to be honest, what I'm *for*. Don't get me wrong, I love working here, with you, but it's as if I'm marking time. Everything feels temporary. One thing I am sure of – Paul and I are permanent. We fit. Does that sound cheesy?'

'Horribly, although from what I've seen you do seem remarkably well-suited.' She paused. 'Aren't you being a tad optimistic in assuming you can pick up your relationship where you left off? It's been an awfully long time.' She raised her hands. 'Sorry. This is none of my business.'

'No. I asked for your opinion. I can see how it must

look to outsiders. A couple of sixty-year-olds who've messed up, snatching at a last chance. The thing is, we didn't mess up. Not in the conventional way. We would have stayed together – spent our lives together – were it not for my parents. I'm sure of that. Had I challenged them they might have relented. I'll never know.'

'Well, they've taken Paul to their bosoms now, from what you tell me.'

'Yes. I suspect it had a lot to do with their giving up on Danny. Heaven knows how they've squared it with their consciences. Frankly I'm amazed he's prepared to forgive them after the way they treated him.'

'He cares for you very much. He's doing it for you.'

'I know.'

'Harking back to your time apart. Doesn't the forty-year hiatus present difficulties? In effect, you're a couple of bookends but without the books. So much of a relationship depends on shared stories.'

'If I stop to think about it, it makes me sad. We've both seen the Taj Mahal but with somebody else. We've become parents but of different children. We have no friends in common – well, only Frankie and that's a mixed blessing.'

Hazel shrugged. 'Maybe I'm making this too complicated. Look at it another way. If you'd met Paul for the first time last January, would you two have got together?'

'Yes, I think we would.'

'So, regardless of how you reached this point, you're with the right person.'

Miriam smiled. 'Yes. I'm with the right person.'

'Just now, you mentioned feeling adrift. That's not surprising. You've been widowed in appalling circumstances. You've lost your home, your savings and the job you loved. You're missing your grandchildren. That's a lot to deal with even if you have rediscovered your soul mate.'

Miriam had not seen the children since term started, and when Bing went up to London for a few days (a symposium on sexually transmitted diseases), she rescheduled her sessions at the shop and headed off to visit them. The timing wasn't ideal – midweek, the children in school – but Naomi agreed that, whilst she was there, she'd do drop-offs and pick-ups as she used to do.

When Max spotted her across the playground, he launched himself at her, flinging his arms around her waist, not at all embarrassed to be kissed in front of his classmates. Rosa was torn. Walk home with her friends or her grandmother? (Friends.) She was going through a growth spurt, all knees and elbows, sallow-cheeked as if she hadn't slept. Miriam recognised her nine-year-old self in Rosa's gaucheness. Before too long, that wayward hair would be the bane of her life, those bold features defy make-up. She was obstinate, quick to fly off the handle. She'd make heavy weather of her teenage years. She'd fight with Naomi who'd never had much patience. In a couple of years she'd team up with her own Frankie – or, considering her insubordinate nature, become someone else's. That's why it was so important David be there, steadying the ship.

She slipped effortlessly back into the teatime routine. The remains of yesterday's casserole were in the fridge but the children weren't keen and, without putting up much resistance, she gave in to their request for fish fingers and baked beans. There weren't many advantages to being an absentee grandmother but one of them was that she could break the rules.

They were finishing their tea when Naomi came in from work. 'Could you bear to babysit? David's asked me to a private view. We won't be late back.'

'Where is it?'

'You know those gloomy old houses near the hospital? One's been converted into an art gallery. I'm surprised you didn't hear about it.'

Callum had mentioned a new gallery. Something to do with Lottery funding but she couldn't recall the details.

'It's work from the art students' degree show. You ought to pop over and take a look before you go home.' Naomi checked her watch. 'I should get changed.'

There had always been the possibility that Naomi would, through some casual encounter, establish the connection between her mother and the woman who'd been the college life model. But Miriam's time there had been brief and, as the months passed, her anxiety had faded. Tonight's private view, coming without warning as it did, rekindled her disquiet.

When David let himself in, she was clearing the table, struggling to persuade herself that, were Callum and Naomi to meet, he wouldn't blow the gaff. Rosa and Max, who were at the kitchen table playing *Hangman*, glanced up, said hi, and carried on with their game as though his turning up were a regular occurrence. He kissed her, told her she was looking as lovely as ever, asked after Paul, and put the kettle on. Everything pointed to the restoration of the family.

After their bath and two chapters of *The Witches*, the children went to bed without a fuss. Bing had phoned, but she'd been up to her elbows in soapy water and she didn't get round to returning his call until later. She apologised, explaining that she'd been getting the children to bed, exaggerating a little to account for her delay.

'I was beginning to worry,' he said. 'I pictured you skidding off the road and—'

'Have you been drinking?'

'What else is there to do?'

'You poor thing. London's such a dreary place.'

'Every where's dreary without you.'

She laughed. 'Now you're being pathetic.'

'What will you do tomorrow?' he said.

'Not sure. I might drop in at the college. See how they're coping without me.'

The idea had been gathering shape. It would be good to see Callum. He'd been a true friend when she needed one and she missed his wry take on life.

'Good idea,' he said. 'I know you enjoyed working there.'

She felt a pang of guilt. Callum had been right. She should have been straight with Bing. But now, ten months on, the moment had passed.

'What time will you be home on Friday?' he said.

They'd been through it several times and she tried to keep the irritation out of her voice. 'I'll set off as soon as I've dropped the children at school. So, all things being equal, I should be back by lunchtime.'

'Let's do something special on Saturday,' he said.

'I'm working, don't you remember? I have to make up my hours?'

'I'd forgotten. What a pain.'

'We'll do something on Sunday,' she said. 'The weather looks settled. Let's take a picnic and a Thermos and go for a walk.'

It was the kind of placatory tactic she employed with the children but it appeared to cheer him up.

Breakfast time was the inevitable scavenger hunt. Games kit. Reading records. Yoghurt pots and egg cartons. The permission slip for Max's class trip. And Rosa's elusive left trainer. They arrived at school with seconds to spare, the children darting into their classrooms with barely a backward glance. They loved her, of that she was sure, but she doubted they gave her a second thought when she wasn't standing in front of them. That was as it should be. Their young lives shouldn't be weighed down with missing and fretting.

She wandered back to the house, weighing up whether to visit the college or the new gallery. Naomi had said the refurbishment of the old house was stylish, the exhibition within it, uninspired. 'Many people there?' she'd asked. 'Quite a crowd,' Naomi said, 'the usual arty types. We spent the evening with the architects. David thinks they might offer him a job.' So she needn't have worried after all. Why would anyone remember her anyway? She'd worked at the college for two mornings a week over a period of less than six months. Outsiders might find it hard to credit but, within that environment, a life model was no more noteworthy than a bowl of fruit. But there was the possibility that a visit to the college might throw up an unforeseen problem and, with that in mind, she plumped for the gallery.

Naomi's assessment was spot on. The interior of the house had been transformed into something rather wonderful. Pale wooden floors. Off-white walls running up to midnight blue ceilings. Clever lighting that showed the exhibits off to advantage. One space flowing effortlessly into the next. (Scandi-meets-Quaker? She must ask David about it.) Everything came together in an arresting yet unobtrusive setting for what was, on the whole, mediocre work. She meandered around spending longer than she would had she not felt a certain allegiance to the work on show.

The young man on the desk was pretending to be busy, shuffling pieces of paper and peering at a screen. He even managed to look surprised when she approached the desk. 'Oh, hello.'

'It's a beautiful gallery,' she said.

'Isn't it just?' he said. 'We have a loyalty scheme, if you're interested. Do you live locally?'

'Until recently but I regularly come back to visit family.'

He gave her a leaflet. 'This gives all the details. Shows. Talks. Members are invited to private views.'

'Sounds good.' She dropped the leaflet into her bag. 'I'd best be off.'

'We've a visitor book if you'd care to leave a comment.'

He slid a hefty book towards her, flipping it open to a page headed with the day's date. The previous pages listed endorsements from last night's private view. Halfway down the first page she recognised David's architectural handwriting, a little further on Naomi's careless scrawl. No sign of Callum or Moat's signatures. It was amusing to note how visitors had avoided commenting on the art, praising instead the renovation and wishing the gallery success. She added her name and a woolly 'A great asset to the town.'

Not yet midday, she had several hours before she was due at the school. She could go back to Naomi's and do something useful but, while she'd been in the gallery, the wishy-washy clouds had given way to jewel-bright skies. The grand houses, high on this ridge, were surrounded by handsome trees planted, she guessed, when they were built. The trees had lost most of their leaves but the low sun enhanced the colours of those that remained. On the way here, she'd passed a modest shopping parade which included a deli-cum-coffee shop. It was too pleasant a day for housework and she pulled in to the parking space immediately outside. Having collected her flat white and lemon drizzle cake, she perched on a stool at the high counter near the window and folded her newspaper to the crossword.

She was doodling with an anagram when someone tapped her shoulder. 'Miriam?'

Turning, she came face to face with Moat, resplendent in duffle coat. 'Good gracious.'

She slid off her stool, unsure whether a handshake or a kiss was appropriate. He clearly felt equally bewildered and they ended up in a self-conscious hug.

'What are you doing here?' she said.

'If you recall, this is my home town. You?'

She explained that she was visiting her family and had been to inspect the new gallery. 'Have you been? It's very smart.'

'I'm on my way there now. I popped in here to stock up on olive oil. It's the best in town.' He pointed towards her cup. 'Another coffee?'

'Thanks.' She didn't need a second cup but she was overtaken by an unanticipated fondness for this tubby little man.

They ordered two coffees and relocated to a corner table, and she recalled their first meeting in the museum café when he'd demolished the Danish pastries.

'Can I treat you to a cake?' she said.

He grimaced. 'I'm on a diet. My sister—'

'You have a sister?'

'Is that so hard to believe? Barbara insists I lose two stone. Says she doesn't relish the prospect of nursing me when I'm struck down with something unspeakable.'

'I wouldn't have thought you'd take advice from anyone.'

'You don't know my sister.'

'Is she an artist too?'

He rolled his eyes. 'She's an aeronautical engineer. Psychopathically health-conscious. Terrifying woman.'

Moat lived in his late mother's house and she'd leapt

to the conclusion that he was an only child. Now he had a sister – a clever one at that – who bossed him about.

'Where does Barbara live?' she said.

'Hampshire, thank God. She lectures at Southampton University. I keep out of her way if I possibly can.' He turned to study the cakes on the counter. 'Oh, to hell with it. I'll have a slice of coffee and walnut.'

He squinted at her as if he were sizing her up before starting a drawing. 'You look well, Miriam. This liaison obviously suits you. Callum tells me you have a job in a bookshop.'

'It does. And I do.' It didn't take a mind reader to know where this was leading. 'Callum tells me you'd like to paint me again.'

'I would. And he told me you were making all sorts of excuses.'

'Oh come on. It's not practical, is it? I can't see how it could possibly work. There must be a host of models who'd love to do it.'

'Models are ten a penny. As I told you before, I'm looking for more than that. I found it in you.'

'I'm flattered.'

'Flattery is not my style, Miriam, as you well know. As far as practicalities go, where there's a will, and all that. Will you answer one question for me?'

Red shoes.

'If I can.'

'Did you get anything at all out of working with me? Honestly now.'

'You mean apart from fifteen pounds an hour?'

He rolled his eyes. 'Miriam, Miriam.'

'I was in a weird place when I met Callum.' She wrinkled her nose. 'I had no zest for anything. You know the apathy that follows a bout of 'flu? Even my grandchildren were too much at times. I was starting to think I'd never shake it off. To be honest I was on the verge of panic. Then I met Callum and – well, I don't know how or why but the job at the college set me back on an even keel.'

'You're avoiding my question.' He dropped two sugar lumps into his coffee. 'Did you get anything out of working with me?'

She imagined climbing the stairs to his studio, each tread, each riser, distancing her from the banality which had been bogging her down. The uncluttered studio. The smell of paint and coffee. Spring skies racing across the skylight. Peaceful, easy silence. Innocence.

'I did. I found it restorative,' she said. 'Interesting. Calming. I went to meditation classes after I was widowed. People said it would help. I didn't take to it, yet my sessions with you came as close to meditating as I'm likely to get.' Where was this coming from? Was she trying to please him? 'Paul reappeared around that time too, don't forget.'

They were interrupted by the waitress bringing Moat's cake and while they jiggled plates and cups, her thoughts flipped to Bing at his conference. She slipped her phone out of her pocket. One message. 'Love you. B xx'.

'Have you told *him* about our enterprise?' He nodded towards her phone and raised his eyebrows, and she felt she'd been caught doing something she shouldn't.

'I haven't,' she said, 'and I'm not going to. He cares so much – too much. *I* know modelling's a job but he might find that impossible to accept. Things are good with us. Life is good. I see no reason to rock the boat.'

'That's a real shame but I respect your decision. Should you change your mind, or if you'd like to call in and have a look at what I'm doing, you know where I live.'

She guessed he didn't invite many people to his house and she was touched by his offer of friendship.

They shook hands and went their separate ways, Moat and his can of olive oil to the gallery and she back to the house to make a cottage pie and pack her bag ready for an early getaway next morning.

20

LIVING WITH A DOCTOR ALERTED MIRIAM to the extent of winter's treachery. Vomiting, coughs and sore throats were rampaging. The red-tops threatened 'killer 'flu'. Most days Bing returned from work exhausted and crabby, exasperated at his patients' failure to understand that antibiotics did nothing to combat viruses. Whilst other doctors caved in to demands for them, Dr. Crosby's patients were treated to a lecture on global antibiotic resistance, and sent home to tough it out.

Her parents regarded winter as a personal affront. They dosed themselves with vitamins and cod liver oil. They broke out flannelette pyjamas and nighties washed so many times the pattern on them had faded to nothing. They draped heavy-duty curtains across front and back doors. They refused to venture out if it was 'too cold' or 'too wet' or 'too dark', then got in a right old state if, through these self-imposed curfews, they missed their weekly shopping trip. Miriam suggested setting them up with an Ocado account. They were dubious, fretting over delivery charges and the possibility of missing out on special offers. She won them over by explaining that there were even better online deals, and agreeing to add items from her own list if their total spend failed to meet the criteria for 'free delivery'.

Christmas had begun showing itself in October but

Hazel held out until the second week in December before decorating the shop – and then so minimally it was barely noticeable.

'Our regulars will shop here, regardless,' she said. 'They'll be relieved to get away from fake snow.'

'How are online sales doing?' Miriam said.

'Dismally. I can't compete with Amazon when it comes to those trashy celebrity books that appear at Christmas and get remaindered by February. Anyway, that's not what I'm about.'

'Can retailers afford to be judgemental?'

'I'm not a *retailer* – I'm a bookseller.'

As if to prove her right, a middle-aged woman came in and congratulated them on the shop's serenity. She browsed for twenty minutes and left with a second-hand copy of *The Work of Grinling Gibbons* and a poetry anthology.

'What are your Christmas plans?' Hazel said. She was closing the shop from Christmas Eve until after New Year. Her sister ran a B&B in Newlyn and her entire family convened there every Christmas.

'Doze off in front of the telly. Overindulge. Go for walks. All those ordinary things we've never had the chance to do together.'

'Do your parents celebrate Christmas?'

'Oh, yes. Crazy I know but they pretend Christmas has nothing to do with religion. They're experts in all kinds of self-deception.'

It was a tradition at Monkton Square to give staff members with young families first choice of leave. This meant Bing's days off were dotted here and there over the holiday period, giving them no time to venture far afield.

'I think you should ask your children to come here,' she said, 'I know they were stand-offish last time but they must be getting used to the idea of me by now and it really is time I met them.'

'No doubt they'll have made plans,' he said.

'We won't know unless you ask.' She handed him the phone and went upstairs to run a bath. He would find it easier were she not listening to their conversations, and she lay in the hot water, pretending to relax, waiting for him to report back.

Ten minutes. Fifteen minutes. Then a tap on the door and he came in and sat on the edge of the bath.

'Well?' she said.

'Pascale is tied up with her in-laws for the entire week. And Camille is off to France. But Leon has a couple of free days between Christmas and New Year, if that suits.'

Leon's acceptance felt like a major victory and Miriam clapped her hands. 'That's wonderful. What's his partner's name again?'

'Bente. She's Danish. You'll like her.'

He took a sponge, dipped it in the bath and trickled water across her breasts and down towards her navel. 'Look at you, lying there shimmering.' He dipped his head and she realised he was crying.

'What's the matter?' she said. 'Did Camille say something to upset you?'

'No. It has nothing to do with them.' He swiped his nose with the back of his hand.

'What is it then?'

'You. Us. For most of my life I lived with the agony of losing you. Now, by some miracle, we're together. I'm so happy it terrifies me.'

Their first Christmas together was to be a modest affair. Nevertheless, there were things to consider. Cards. Gifts. Catering. When would they see Naomi and the children? And there was Leon's visit to squeeze in – exciting and intimidating in equal measure.

Bing was all for not bothering to send cards. 'No one will notice. And as for presents, do we really need more "stuff"?'

'That's an appalling thing to say,' she said. 'The best part of Christmas is choosing gifts for people I love. What about Finbar? It's his first Christmas, poor little soul. You have to buy him something.'

'He's too young to know the difference between the gift and the wrapping paper.'

'Stop it. I shan't go on loving you if you're going to be such a killjoy.'

His frown dissolved into a grin. 'Of *course* we'll send cards. And I absolutely insist you buy gifts. Sack loads of the things.'

Christmas rituals evolve over many years until, after years of refinement, they jog along on autopilot. But they were starting from scratch. Ground rules needed laying down. Trivial yet fundamental decisions made. Angel or star on top of the tree? Presents opened in a pre-breakfast frenzy or eked out through the day? The meat – turkey?

Goose? Beef? And the schedule – eat at two or six or eight o'clock?

But before all that, there was the Monkton Square Christmas party. Last Christmas had been Bing's first at the practice. He was still very much the 'new boy' and he acknowledged it was the one social event they couldn't avoid. It was customary to hold the party at the surgery. When the old house had been converted, the top floor had been made into a self-contained flat for Doctor Leyshon, the practice founder. He'd retired years ago but the flat had been retained for employees or visitors needing temporary accommodation. (Bing had spent a few weeks there whilst he was looking for a place to buy.) A perfectly good flat lying empty for months on end was an extravagance but the consensus was that it added to the smooth running of the practice.

Miriam was looking forward to the party but when the invitation arrived – heavy cream card edged with gold, *Dr Paul Crosby and Mrs Miriam Siskin* handwritten in dark green ink – she was taken aback. She'd anticipated an informal do. Not exactly 'bring a plate' but certainly not 'black tie'. When she asked what sort of thing she should wear, he said 'You'll look stunning whatever you wear.'

'Sweet of you to say so but not helpful.'

'Okay. A dress. Something sparkly. Wafty. High heels. How's that?'

'Oh dear. When I cleared the house, I couldn't imagine ever going to another party. I ditched all but one of my party frocks. Stay where you are. I'll slip it on.'

Sam had adored parties – as host or guest. He loved

watching her get ready, suggesting what she might wear and how she should do her hair, whilst she, in turn, advised on his shirt and tie. She was quite able to make her own decisions but, gin-and-tonics to hand, the ritual had become an agreeable precursor to an evening out. The dress in question had been Sam's favourite – enough to earmark it for the charity bag – but she'd hung on to it because she couldn't bear anyone else to have it. She'd spotted it in a tiny shop in Chester when they were on holiday. (Naomi was thirteen or fourteen, hating every second she was forced to spend with them and they'd bought her a portable CD player to stop her whinging.) The dress was a simple shift. Velvet with silk trim at neck, sleeve and hem. Dusky pinkish-grey. When the fabric caught the light, it made her think of a pigeon's feathered breast. She tended to be drawn to bolder colours – dark red or purple – but from the moment she'd tried it on, it had belonged to her.

She twirled around. 'Will I do?'

From the front, the dress was demure, grazing her collar bone, sleeves reaching her elbows. But turn around and the neckline looped down below her shoulder blades in a soft fold.

'Mmmm,' he said. 'It's very… Actually I'm not sure I want everyone seeing so much of you.'

She was irritated by his put-down. 'They see a great deal more of me when I go to the swimming pool.'

By the time they arrived, the party was underway. Caterers hovered with champagne and canapés. A frillyshirted lutenist sat next to the Christmas tree playing something medieval. Open fire. Discreet decorations. Expensive perfumes. Animated conversation. It was a swish do.

'You look stunning,' Bing murmured, squeezing Miriam's arm. 'We can slip away when you've had enough. Just tip me the wink.'

She called in on Bing if she were anywhere near Monkton Square, and he'd introduced her to several of his colleagues. She recognised some of them this evening despite their unaccustomed finery. She had no idea whether they were aware of Dr Crosby's back story. He certainly wouldn't have told them himself but a version might have filtered back via the friend of Angela's friend.

The room spanned the front of the house and she estimated there were fifty or sixty guests. A group standing near the fireplace beckoned them and she was bombarded with a flurry of names she couldn't hope to remember. There was the usual party chit-chat – weather, school concerts, travel plans. From jokes and body language it was evident these people knew each other well. They were welcoming if slightly guarded as might be expected with a newcomer. Someone asked what she did, looking nonplussed when she told them she worked in a bookshop, as if Dr Crosby's partner should do something more worthwhile.

Groups dispersed and reformed and introductions were repeated. Bing was affable but contributed little to the conversation. She'd noted how rarely he passed on work gossip and, as far as she could make out, he wasn't pally with any of his colleagues. 'Wouldn't you like a "mate"? Someone to share a beer with?' she'd said. But, not for the first time, he insisted she was the only 'mate' he needed.

Around nine, when she was on the point of breaking out her emergency energy bar, waiters appeared with platters of snacks, delicious but barely bite-sized. In her teaching days, Christmas parties tended to get pretty 'lively'. On one occasion, following a few rounds of 'Truth, Dare or Promise', they'd been blacklisted and banned from ever returning to the restaurant. This party couldn't have been more different. Being on home turf seemed to ensure immaculate behaviour – the very opposite of what was generally expected from a house party.

She leaned close to Bing. 'I think they must all be on tranquilisers.'

'Perks of the job.' He ran a finger across the back of her neck. 'We can make our excuses if you've had enough.'

'What, and miss the karaoke?'

Bing went off to the bathroom. Almost immediately, a man to whom she'd been introduced earlier – Alan? Adam? Selway? Salter? – joined her. He was perhaps in his mid-fifties, handsome in an obvious way.

'First impressions?' he said.

'Of?'

'Monkton Square at play.'

'Honestly? You seem a very self-possessed crowd.'

He raised his eyebrows. 'What's that old adage? Don't foul your own patch. This is only the warm-up session. Some of us are going on to a club. Well actually it's a dive.

But the music's good – blues, mainly, and the drinks are cheap. Why don't you come along?'

'Thanks but my clubbing days are done,' she said, 'not that they ever began.'

'Nonsense. A gorgeous-looking woman like you.'

She felt her cheeks colour and she looked towards the door, relieved to see Bing coming to her rescue. He handed her a glass of champagne and nodded curtly to her companion. 'Your wife's not here, Stanway?'

'Clashing fixtures. You know how it is near Christmas. Look, we're going on to The Basement as soon as we can escape. Why don't you two come?'

Bing turned to her, his face impassive, yet there was no doubt what he wanted her to say. 'Miriam?'

'It's sweet of you to invite us,' she said, 'but I've an early start tomorrow.'

'Next time, maybe,' Stanway said. 'You're a lucky man, Crosby.' He gave an awkward bow and for one ghastly moment she thought he was going to kiss her hand.

Bing waited until he'd moved away. 'You look flustered.'

'It's hot in here.' She took a sip of champagne knowing it would make things worse. 'What does Stanway do? Surely he's not a medic.'

'Solicitor. We call him in when we need legal advice. I'm told he's good but I can't stand the man.'

'He is rather smarmy.'

'Was he bothering you? I'll break his bloody neck.'

She looped her arm through his. 'He's tipsy, that's all. And picking a fight with a lawyer wouldn't be a smart move.'

On the dot of eleven, the lutenist stowed his instrument in its case and the partygoers gathered up their possessions. Stanway and his clubbing pals already had their coats on and were edging towards the door. He turned and scanned the room and she tried not to catch his eye but he came over and made a big thing of saying how much he'd enjoyed meeting her and how he hoped to see her soon.

'The man's a creep,' Bing muttered at Stanway's retreating back and an echo of adolescent jealousy reverberated across four decades.

They shared a taxi home with Della, one of the receptionists, and her boyfriend. Miriam sat in the back, sandwiched between Bing and Della, Bing sitting bolt upright, staring out of the window. Conversation was perfunctory, Bing's input next to nothing. She guessed he was still miffed at seeing her with Stanway, unfair as she couldn't be blamed for the man's flirty behaviour.

The driver dropped them off first and, by the time they were getting ready for bed, a cold silence had settled between them.

'Would you unzip me, please?' she said.

'Turn around,' he said and yanked the zip so roughly she feared he'd tear the fabric.

'For goodness sake,' she said, 'what's eating you?'

'This dress,' he said. 'It's too revealing. I'll buy you something more suitable.'

'Suitable? Perhaps you'd prefer me to wear a burqa.'

'You're being melodramatic. I simply mean showing so much flesh is unbecoming.'

'My back is unlikely to drive men wild.'

'Well Stanway's tongue was hanging out.'

She picked up the dress, snatched her pyjamas off the bed and, not trusting herself to speak, went into the spare room, and lay in bed sobbing with anger and frustration.

Around four o'clock, she fell heavily asleep, only waking at eight when the front door banged. She hurried to the window in time to see Bing driving away. How absurd that a man like Stanway and an old dress had come between them. The dress was draped over the back of a chair, limp and inoffensive. Maybe she should chuck it out before it caused any more trouble. But why should she? No matter what Bing thought, it was a lovely thing. She threaded the dress onto its hanger and hung it at the back of her wardrobe behind her winter coat. One day Rosa might want to go 'retro' and she would be able to provide the perfect item.

She showered and went downstairs. Several sheets of paper were spread across the table, dense with Bing's handwriting.

Paul Crosby is an idiot.
Paul Crosby is an idiot.
Paul Crosby is an idiot.

Line after line – one hundred? two hundred? – the final line as painstakingly written as the first. He must have been at it for hours. She reached for her phone. She'd call him and they'd laugh and she'd forgive him.

And yet. This wasn't the first time he'd lost it then

come crawling back with an apology trying to gloss over the whole thing. To carry on as if nothing had happened. Their last bust-up had been when Frankie had visited.

Another thing. When she went out on her own, he'd started asking where she was going – with whom – what time she'd be back. When she got home he'd want to know who had been there. Sam had his faults but he'd always trusted her. She couldn't recall his ever cross-questioning her on her movements, or her friends. Perhaps he hadn't given a toss but she was more inclined to think he knew that in order to keep her she must have the freedom to be herself.

She placed her phone on the table. It would do him good to stew for a while.

21

THE PLAN HAD BEEN FOR MIRIAM's parents to come to them. She'd consulted as to what, and when, they would like to eat, done the 'big Christmas food shop' and sketched out a schedule. Bing was detailed to collect them at eleven o'clock, in time for coffee and mince pies. She was, to her surprise, looking forward to playing hostess and had taken great care with the decorations and the tree – a Norwegian spruce which scraped the ceiling.

Her father phoned on Christmas Eve as the street lights were coming on. As soon as she heard his voice, she knew what he was going to say.

'It's about tomorrow.'

'All set?' she said, determined not to make it easy for him.

'It's your mother. Her nerves are playing up. We think coming to you might be a bit much for her.'

'In what sense *too much*? It takes ten minutes, tops, to drive from there to here. And you don't even have to do the driving. All you have to do is sit by the fire and watch Paul and me rushing around.'

'You know how she is,' he said.

Miriam ploughed on. 'If you stay there, she'll end up having to cook.'

'Yes. Well. I've been thinking about that. Why don't you bring everything to us? It'll come to the same thing.

We can watch you rushing around here.' He laughed. He was enjoying this.

'What exactly is wrong with her?' she said. 'Does she need to see a doctor? Or a rabbi? D'you want me to take her to A&E?'

'Calm down, Miriam. All I'm saying is your mother's feeling out of sorts. She'll be more comfortable in her own surroundings.'

'You make her sound like an endangered species.'

'She is, in a way. We both are.'

Headlights shone through the kitchen window as Bing's car pulled up behind hers. She'd been looking forward to the moment when he came in from work and they could shut out the world and indulge in their own little Christmas celebration. And now this.

'I'll ring you back. Paul's just come home. I'll have to discuss it with him. It's his Christmas too you know.'

She thumbed *end call* and hurried to the front door. Before he had taken his coat off, she was telling him about her father's attempted blackmail, her words tumbling out in a torrent of frustration.

'Hey,' he said, 'it's no big deal. Your dad's right. It's not a nice thought but this may be their last ever Christmas. If you can cope in their kitchen, why don't we go along with their suggestion?'

'But I so wanted to spend our first Christmas together here, with our own tree and our own decorations. Besides the turkey will take at least four hours. I'd have to be at theirs by eight o'clock. I wanted to have Christmas breakfast here with you.'

'We'll cook it here. I'll set the alarm for five and it'll be cooked by ten. Think of the fun we can have when we come back to bed. We needn't stay late. They'll have had enough of us by seven. Eight hours isn't long in the scheme of things.'

'You're so much more patient with them than I am,' she said.

'I don't know about that. I simply don't think it's worth getting steamed up about.'

Theoretically, Christmas had nothing to do with them, nevertheless Harold and Freda Edlin embraced it with great gusto. Cards dangled from red ribbon looped along the picture rail and an array of candles, wicks still pristine after donkey's years, were dotted along the mantelpiece. The tree was 'first generation' artificial and the decorations had seen better days, but that was no different from half the households in the country. They drew the line at a crib – that simply wouldn't have done – but Miriam's mother had managed to sneak a string of glittery camels along the top shelf of the dresser.

All things considered, the turkey transfer went smoothly. They forgot the brandy butter and Christmas crackers, and the festive tablecloth which Miriam had bought when she last visited Naomi. But, having caused the disruption, her parents were in no position to criticise her failings. And they didn't. They seemed, if anything, invigorated by the modified arrangements, quipping about 'meals-on-wheels' and 'flying doctors'.

After lunch, they exchanged gifts – 'smellies', chocolates, diaries – making obligatory noises of surprise and delight. Miriam and Bing had left their gifts to each other under their tree to be opened when they got home.

Whilst the men were inspecting the slipped tiles on the garage roof, Miriam took the opportunity to ask her mother if she were feeling better. 'Better?' she said. 'That's a funny question.' And a funny answer – unless her father had been mischief-making again.

The phone rang and, in a flash, her mother was there, grasping the cumbersome old handset with both hands. 'Who's speaking, please?'

And seeing the frail figure, expectant, voice wavering, the penny dropped. They wanted to be at home in case Danny called.

Her mother's face slumped into a disappointed frown. 'Who is that?' Miriam held out a hand, offering to resolve the mystery, but her mother shook her head. 'Frankie? Sorry, dear. I didn't recognise your voice. It's very noisy at your end. Of course it would be…. Merry Christmas to you too…. Yes, we're having a lovely day.'

Miriam waited, expecting her mother to pass her the phone but instead she turned away. 'Thank you for your card, and the letter. We always enjoy your letters.'

Letters? Always?

The tête-à-tête continued. 'She's with us if you'd like a word…. Alright. I will. I'll let you go. You must be rushed off your feet. And don't forget. Anytime. Goodbye dear.'

'Frankie sends her love,' her mother said as if holding a long conversation with her best friend were the most natural thing in the world.

'She writes to you?' Miriam said.

'Now and again. She knows we like to hear what she's up to.'

Miriam had heard from Frankie only once since her visit. She was living in Birmingham where her ex-sister-in-law was managing a pub. It seemed she had a room and job there, doing a bit of 'this and that' which 'would do for the time being'. (She hadn't mentioned the two hundred pounds which Miriam had sneaked into her suitcase.)

Her parents' acceptance of Frankie Slattery had always baffled her. Initially, they'd discouraged the friendship. Frankie embodied everything that alarmed them. Smoker, truant, with self-inflicted tattoos and one outrageous hairstyle after another, she came from the kind of chaotic family they despised. But her humour...or candour...or sheer exuberance had eventually breached their defences. At the time, Danny had been occupying a great deal of their attention and perhaps they'd lacked the energy to police two wayward offspring. Later, when Danny was long gone and the thing with Bing came to a head, had they allowed her Frankie as a consolation prize?

The men came in from the garden, shucking off muddy shoes and asking whether it was time for a cup of tea. When she finally got a few moments alone with Bing, she hissed her exasperation at her father's determination to have things his way. 'There's nothing wrong with Mum. What the hell's the matter with him? Why does he always have to call the shots?'

'I understand why you're cross with him,' Bing said,

'but you have to remember he spent years and years running the show. Suddenly everyone's telling him what to do, how things should be. He feels emasculated. Mind games are all he has left.'

'I'm his daughter, not his chess opponent. And I don't know why you're so chipper. What if he starts playing his mind games on us? Don't laugh. It could happen.'

She glanced at her watch. Three more hours and they could go home.

Leon and Bente would be with them for barely twenty-four hours – and in bed for eight of those. A walk along the ridge overlooking the town would take care of a few more hours. It was the bits in between that bothered her. 'What if we have nothing to talk about?' she said. 'It doesn't matter,' Bing said, 'as long as we all rub along.'

They arrived on the dot of midday bearing potted hyacinths, wine and chocolates. Bing had shown her recent photographs of his children, but only when Leon was standing in front of her did she realise how like his father he was. Not only his face but his voice and the way he stood, head tilted to one side. It was as if she were looking at Bing when he was a boy – although Leon was thirty-two. They stood in the hall, muddling through introductions, covering their awkwardness with prattle about routes and road conditions. Eventually they managed to get themselves out of the hall and into the kitchen, where Bing poured glasses of sherry and everyone relaxed.

'Your kitchen, I like it. It's so homely.' Bente's perfect

English had just enough Scandi twang to make it appealing. Miriam had pictured her as a fresh-faced, big boned girl – patterned jumper and fur-lined boots – unshaven legs. She couldn't have been wider of the mark. Bente was petite and dark-haired with brown eyes behind round spectacles. She wore jeans, a black polo neck – cashmere by the looks of it – and elegant ankle boots, no bigger than size four. In fact not far off her mental picture of Eloise – a photograph of whom she had yet to see.

'I'll show you your room,' Bing said, ushering their visitors into the hall.

She put the pan of minestrone on the hob and counted out the cutlery. Overhead she could hear the rise and fall of voices. Footsteps moving from room to room. Easy laughter as if they were all more comfortable when she wasn't there.

Throughout lunch, Leon was civil enough, yet he didn't seem interested in her, directing most of his conversation to Bing. She'd worried that he might subject her to the third degree but, if anything, it was the opposite. Was he embarrassed? Whatever his reason, it cast her as the odd one out. As the meal progressed, she detected an underlying competitiveness between father and son. A dig here, a jibe there – sparring – testing each other. Maybe this behaviour was unavoidable as one generation gave way to another and the balance of power changed. Her father and Danny had been at each other all the time. But that was in an era when children were expected to defer to their 'elders and betters', something which Danny had refused to do.

After lunch, the breeze got up and the mist which had hung around all morning cleared. Bing suggested a walk along the towpath but Bente had forgotten her walking boots and, as Miriam's footwear was several sizes too large for her, it was decided 'the girls' would stay at home.

'It's a shame you had to miss the walk,' Miriam said as they settled in front of the fire with cups of coffee.

'Yes, but it's good that Leon spends time with his father,' Bente said. 'They don't talk enough. Men are bad talkers, don't you agree?'

She nodded, not entirely sure what she was agreeing with. Now she had Bente to herself, she had a chance to find out more about Bing's family but the young woman was canny and she must tread warily. 'Tell me about you. I know you're a surveyor but that's all.'

'Me? I was born and raised in Roskilde. You know it? We have a big music festival every year. My parents work in the biomedical research unit at the hospital. What else can I tell you? I'm thirty-seven. I have an older brother – Mads – he's a dentist.'

Bente didn't beat about the bush and this encouraged Miriam to continue. 'So how did you and Leon meet?'

'Friends of friends. They thought we would get along. Not so romantic, perhaps, but better than looking for a partner on the internet.'

'You have perceptive friends. How long have you been together?'

'Two years.' Bente pulled her knees up to her chin. 'Now it is my turn. I think you and Paul were childhood sweethearts?'

'Yes. Well. We weren't *children*. We were in the sixth form.'

'Ahhh. It was *puppy love*. And then you grew out of it. I understand.'

'I don't think you do. We didn't *grow out of it*. It was simply a matter of meeting the right person at the wrong time.'

'You believe there is a "right person"?' Bente hooked the air with her fingers.

'Don't you?'

Bente shrugged. 'It makes no sense. There are seven billion people on the planet. What are the chances?'

'Leon isn't the right man for you?'

'It's good with us now but when it stops being good we will shake hands and call it a day.'

'That sounds a little… clinical.'

'No. It is realistic. We're not robots. Time passes and, naturally, we will change. The important thing, is to identify what is right for us as we *are*, not as we once were.'

'That sounds, dare I say it, rather selfish.'

She shrugged. 'It is the truth.'

Bente's forthright words felt like a reproach and Miriam was compelled to defend herself. 'Paul and I were young but what we had was very special. But there was a lots of other stuff going on – particularly in my family. We were students, and living in different cities made things difficult. We'd go months without seeing each other and keeping in touch was much harder then. A few things went wrong. There were misunderstandings.

People interfered. I won't go into details but we allowed it to slip through our fingers.'

'That is sad,' Bente said, 'but maybe not unusual. Then what happened?'

'A man – a family friend – asked me to marry him. He was kind and funny. He cared more for me than I did for him but he didn't seem bothered by that. We had a reasonably happy marriage. I didn't forget Paul but I'd made choices, and promises and, after my daughter was born, life without him became easier.'

Miriam took the poker and jabbed at the fire, sending sparks spiralling up the chimney. 'My husband died a couple of years ago. It was a tough time. In fact I had a breakdown. I was quite ill. A year ago a friend told me Paul was divorced and living back here.'

'You must tell all this to Leon,' Bente said.

'I'm not after Paul's money if that's what he's afraid of. All I want is to spend the rest of my life with him. We messed up first time around. We deserve another try.'

To her dismay, she was crying.

Bente fished a pack of tissues from her bag. 'Here.'

She blew her nose and tossed the tissue on the fire, watching it blacken and burst into flame. 'I don't know what they've been told but we were out of contact for forty years. Not one single letter, or phone call, or message. *Nothing*. That sounds unbelievable but it's true.'

'All those years. Were you not interested to know what happened to your "right man"?' Bente raised her phone which had been on the arm of the sofa. 'It is very easy to find out.'

'Of course. But I had a husband and a daughter to consider. It wasn't their fault. I couldn't risk destroying their lives.'

Bente was silent for a while. 'I'm flattered that you tell me this but I do not wish to get involved. Leon is a grown man. Pascale and Camille are grown women. It's up to them to sort this out with their father.'

22

THE VISIT WAS BY NO means a roaring success but it was a start, and they left promising to 'do it again soon'. Bente was a self-possessed woman and Miriam had gleaned no real sense of her links with, and attitude to, Bing's family. (The only time they'd been mentioned – at least in her presence – was a passing reference to the baby.) She was crossing fingers that, despite her refusal to get involved, the essence of their fireside conversation would filter back to Pascale and Camille and, with luck, temper their mindset. She waited for Bing to reveal what he and Leon had talked about on their walk and, when nothing was forthcoming, she asked. 'Oh, the usual,' he said. 'I'm not sure what that means. Football? Holidays?' 'We didn't get into our situation.' 'I didn't realise we're a *situation*.' 'I mean it seemed wise to keep it light. Gain his confidence.'

Invitations to several New Year parties had arrived including one from her parents' 'over-the-road' neighbours but, having spent Christmas with her mother and father, they were off the hook and she was content to go along with Bing's plea that they batten down the hatches and have their own celebration. In the afternoon, she texted Hazel, Frankie and Callum with cheery greetings, and had a long chat with Naomi who was in nostalgic mood. 'Remember that brilliant New Year trip to Utrecht, Mum? I was thinking David and I ought to take the kids next year. They'd love it.'

When Naomi wasn't much older than Max, they'd driven to Holland for New Year. She couldn't recall why – something to do with Sam's cousin who lectured at Utrecht University. The city had been a picture. Trees festooned with lights. Musicians on every corner. The canal bustling with decorated boats. Exquisite window displays. A pervading smell of roasting chestnuts. As midnight approached, streets and squares had become thronged with families singing and celebrating into the early hours. It did no harm to be reminded of the good times.

Bing returned from afternoon surgery – the last of the old year – and they meandered into town to check all was in order at the shop. They spent half an hour browsing the shelves, buying each other a book and selling another to a passing regular, leaving an I.O.U. next to the empty till. On the way home, Bing bought her a bouquet of wintry flowers from the florist at the bottom of Angelgate and walking home, flowers cradled in the crook of her arm, she remembered that this time last year she was holed up in her parents' spare room, cooking up excuses to avoid going to the party.

As part of their stay-at-home pact, Bing was cooking dinner. Miriam offered to act as sous-chef but he would have none of it.

'In that case I'll have a bath,' she said. She turned on the tap and trickled bubble-bath into the flow, swishing it around with her new flannel – part of her Christmas gift from the children. She undressed, caught her hair up in a scrunchie and climbed into the fragrant water. She lay back and closed her eyes. It was raining, pattering on the windows, pinging off the porch roof. It was a relief not to be going out. Doubtless this was a symptom of ageing but, for as long as she could remember, the turn of the year had filled her with apprehension. Ramped up by the media, expectations were impossibly high, outcomes invariably disappointing. Yet there was no denying, for her this had been an *annus mirabilis*. Against all odds, she and Bing had found each other, something she'd long ago stopped dreaming could happen. As Bente had pointed out, these days, tracking people down was dead easy. The miracle of *their* reunion was that it had come about by chance, at a time when there was no obstacle, no reason why they couldn't be together. And now, if that weren't wonderful enough, Naomi and David appeared to have come to their senses. Yes, life was sweet.

Yet there were still matters to be resolved. This ongoing stand-off with Camille and Pascale for starters. It must be resolved, one way or another. And she needed to find something stimulating to do because, to be honest, there were times when she felt she was marking time. When she broached this with Bing, he'd told her that she mustn't be impatient, the right thing would turn up.

After Sam killed himself, when she'd been petrified that she would never get back on her feet, everyone – medics included – banged on about it being 'early days' and 'giving it time', like parrots, squawking the same vacuous phrases over and over, as if their repetition would eventually bring about an epiphany. *Good gracious. Why did I not think of that?* Their well-meaning attempts at encouragement belittled her plight. Only David – dear, insightful David – came close to understanding that time had the power to kill as well as cure.

Somewhere miles above, a plane murmured as it headed into or away from the coming year. It would be early afternoon on the East Coast – or breakfast time in California. Christmas had passed without word from Danny. It had been heartbreaking to watch her mother flinch each time the phone rang. The fact was, her brother was drifting further and further away. Soon he would be out of sight, and this made her feel both angry and sad. But she mustn't be greedy. She was happy and she was loved.

It was tempting to slip back into jeans and sweater but today was significant in the chronicle of their reunion. She chose a dress bought for an interview four or five years ago. She hadn't got the job but the dress was flattering and, Naomi assured her, made her look younger. She wore her hair down, the way Bing liked it, and dabbed his favourite perfume at the base of her neck. *There.*

'My God,' he said when she returned to the kitchen, 'I'd forgotten how beautiful you are.'

She laughed. 'I've been gone all of half an hour.'

'That's as maybe but each time I see you, you're even more beautiful. I love you so much it makes my heart ache. D'you know what? If the world were to stop this minute, that'd be fine with me.'

'Don't say things like that,' she said. 'You're scaring me.'

After they'd eaten, they took coffee and brandy into the living room. While he tended the fire, she studied him. How handsome – ageless – he looked in his white shirt and jeans. He was whistling. In the candlelight, his grey hair might be taken for blond, and he the twenty-year-old Bing she'd lost.

They flicked through the TV channels, pausing to watch snatches of things they'd seen before, eventually switching off and salvaging the half-finished crossword from yesterday's paper. The brandy had left them pleasantly slow-witted and they made no progress but it was enough to be together on the sofa watching the flickering coals, thoughts in free fall.

'I'll sort out a drink,' he said as midnight drew near. 'Don't go away.'

She plumped the cushions and snuggled down. Whatever Bente might think, there *was* a 'right person'. And if there *were* seven million people on the planet, she couldn't imagine Bente making a mistake, odds were that a handful would, at this very moment, be re-connecting with their soulmate.

Bing returned and set a bottle of champagne and two glasses on the coffee table. She patted the sofa but he remained standing, fiddling around with the fire irons.

'I've been mulling something over,' he said.

'Am I going to like it?'

'I'm not sure.'

He pulled an envelope from his back pocket and held it out for her to see. On the front was written 'A Brief History of Miriam'. She'd thought it rather witty but before she had time to comment, he turned it over. It was still sealed.

'You haven't read it?' she said.

'I get why you wanted us to do this,' he said, 'but I've decided I don't want to know about you and Siskin. I'm only interested in *us*.'

With that, he leaned forward and tossed the envelope onto the coals and they watched it scorch, curl and catch fire, burnt shards of paper rising and floating above the coals like black feathers.

Flopping down beside her, he spread his arms across the back of the sofa and let out a sigh. 'That's better.'

She waited, anticipating the question that would follow, knowing there was no ducking it.

'Have you read mine?' he said.

'No, I haven't.' She pictured his envelope, tucked at the back of a drawer in the spare room. 'I'm not even sure where it is. I have loads of stuff still waiting to be sorted.'

The fib – the *lie* – had popped out. So far, she'd felt no temptation to delve into details of his life with Eloise and whatever else he'd chosen to write. In all likelihood she never would. All the same, she wasn't going to be pressured into emulating his dramatic gesture. *His* history could stay where it was for the time being.

They toasted the coming year with champagne and kisses, intertwined on the sofa, listening to the whoosh and crackle of fireworks in neighbouring gardens. They lingered in the fire glow finally hauling themselves up the stairs when the embers had turned grey.

When she came out of the bathroom, he nodded

towards her phone which was lying on the chest of drawers. 'It was pinging. Anything important?'

A glance at the screen showed that Frankie and Moat had sent texts. 'The usual New Year stuff,' she said.

He was sitting on the edge of the bed with his back to her. 'So who's this *Moat*?' he said.

Her stomach flipped. He'd checked her phone. That wasn't on. In fact it was completely unacceptable. But making a big thing of his invading her privacy would invite too many questions. 'Moat? I'm sure I've told you about him. He's a painter. Pictures not walls.' *Stop there.* 'He used to come in to the college occasionally. To talk to the students.' *Leave it.* 'He's quite well-known.'

He nodded and she thought they were done with it. But she was mistaken. 'Why would he be texting you?'

She shrugged. 'Perhaps I'm included in one of those group message thingies.'

She scanned the text. *May the coming year exceed your expectations. Moat.* Her explanation might have been plausible were it not for his postscript. *Don't forget, if you should change your mind...*

'Tsk. He must have sent it to the wrong person,' she said. 'I imagine everyone's a bit tipsy tonight.'

Slipping off her nightdress, she kneeled on the bed and rested her chin on his shoulder. 'I do love you, Paul Crosby. You know that, don't you?'

Part IV

MIRIAM SAT ON THE STAIRS ready to greet any late arrivals, making the most of the barely perceptible updraft. The party was well underway and she was contemplating abandoning her post and escaping to her room when the doorbell rang.

A man – dark hair, mid-twenties – stood on the step. 'Edlin residence?'

'Yes,' she said.

'Taxi for Siskin.'

Crisp white shirt, silk tie. He looked nothing like the taxi drivers she was used to seeing and her misgiving must have been evident.

'Well, not exactly a taxi,' he said. 'I've come to pick up my parents.' He held out his hand. 'Sam.'

'Miriam,' she said. 'Have we met?'

'Afraid not.' He smiled, revealing white, regular teeth. *A man not a boy.* 'If we had, I'd surely have remembered.' He was looking at her with unmistakable admiration and she blushed, flummoxed by this stranger's openness.

Her father chose that moment to emerge from the living room. 'Sam, my boy. Come in and join the party. You'll have to excuse me for a moment.' He inclined his head towards the kitchen door. 'I'm on ice duty. Mim, why don't you find our guest something to drink?'

'I've a better idea, Dad,' she said, 'why don't *I* get the ice and *you* look after Mr Siskin?'

He laughed as if she'd suggested something preposterous. 'You'd rather talk to a pretty girl, wouldn't you, Sam?'

Without waiting for an answer, he pottered off, leaving her no option but to lead Sam Siskin through to the dining room and the remains of the buffet lunch.

'D'you know my father well?' she said.

'We've met a few times. He called at the house last week, actually. Some business he and my dad were doing.'

'Business?' She frowned. 'He's never mentioned you.'

It was Sam's turn to look uncomfortable. 'I've been working in Amsterdam.'

Now she was supposed to ask what he'd been doing in Amsterdam, and why he'd returned, but she was damned if she'd participate in what was her father's blatant attempt at matchmaking.

'Twenty-five years,' he said, pointing at the cake, pristine amongst plates of curling sandwiches and crumpled napkins. 'That's quite an achievement.'

'Not really. Once you've made your bed, you must lie in it. That's the Edlin motto.' This explanation of her parents' stoic and incomprehensible union hadn't crossed her mind until now but it made depressing sense.

'I'm not saying they *don't* love each other,' she said, relenting slightly. 'What I'm saying is, even if they *didn't*, they'd rather soldier on than admit it.'

He nodded, an indulgent smile playing across his face, and she wanted to throw the wretched cake at his head.

'Help yourself to a drink,' she said, 'unless you're in a rush to get away.'

Ignoring the dig, he poured a glass of lemonade. 'Aren't you having anything?'

'I've got things to do,' she said.

Every window in the house was open yet her bedroom, tucked beneath the eaves, was stifling. A mishmash of party food and the sweet sherry Aunt Bea had forced on her had coagulated in her stomach and she was feeling queasy. Taking a book from her pile of vacation reading, she flopped on the bed. But whichever way she turned, however many times she flipped the pillow, she couldn't get cool or comfortable. Even Gatsby was unable to take her mind off the heat, the twinges in her stomach and her quarrel with Bing.

It had started when he'd got hold of Terry Garner's picture postcard. 'Who's this from?' he'd said, waving it in front of her. 'Nobody. He's in my year,' she'd said. 'So why's he sending you "love and kisses"?' 'Don't be silly. It's a figure of speech. And who gave you permission to read my mail?' Like a snowball rolling down a mountain, their bickering had gathered momentum, until finally it careered out of control. That was three days ago and they hadn't spoken since. He'd better get his act together soon because next week he was off on some stupid family holiday.

The discomfort in her stomach intensified to a griping ache and, easing herself off the bed, she made for the bathroom. Perched on the edge of the bath, she rested her forehead on the cool porcelain of the hand basin. A shiver raised goosebumps on her arms and, dropping to her knees, she wrapped her arms around the lavatory bowl, bracing herself as she began to heave, each convulsion stronger than the last. She gagged a few times, sweat gathering at the nape of her neck. And then she was sick.

But it wasn't over yet and she stayed there until she'd gone through the loathsome business twice more. When there was nothing left to come, she got to her feet, sweat cold on her back.

'Miriam?' Her mother was at the door.

'I'm on the loo.'

'Well don't be too long. Your father wants to cut the cake.'

But what do you want, Mum?

She flushed the lavatory, rinsed her mouth and gargled. She cleaned her teeth and sluiced her face with cold water. When she checked the mirror, her face was pale, her eyes dark-ringed. Brushing back her hair, she caught it in a rubber band, giving an extra tug to ensure it was as straight as it could be. Back in her room, she shucked off her damp, rumpled dress and slipped into shorts and a cotton shirt. She felt lightheaded and her throat burned but she felt much, much better. Laughter filtered in through the open fanlight; someone was playing the piano. 'Some Enchanted Evening', her mother's favourite.

Poor Mum. Miriam had written to Danny begging him to come home for the party, saying how much it would mean to them – and her. He'd replied with a vague and selfish 'things are up in the air here'. At least he hadn't given a definite 'no'. But, as the days rolled by, she'd lost hope. Once again it fell to her to carry the weight of his absence.

The cake had been relocated to the coffee table in the living room and her parents were standing guard alongside it, looking proud yet self-conscious.

'Here she is,' her father said.

Heads turned towards her and she blushed as someone she didn't recognise took a photograph. She must have looked about twelve years old with her ponytail and shorts. Her father beckoned her to join them. From his off-centre smile she could tell that he was tipsy and when the three linked arms, they were almost a family again. Her parents joined hands and cut the cake, the knife blade fracturing the icing like the prow of an ice-breaker forging through the Arctic floe. A cheer went up and cries of 'speech, speech'. Her father had spent several evenings at his desk preparing a speech but when the moment came, overcome with the occasion, all that came out were sentimental remarks and incoherent jokes.

Uncle Michael – who had been their best man – took over, feigning reluctance whilst pulling his speech from his trouser pocket and she grabbed the chance to slip out of the limelight. Her uncle soon found his stride, listing the (unrecognisable) qualities of Harold and Freda Edlin's marriage, sidestepping the issue of Danny as if the happy couple had produced only one (perfect) child. He was exceedingly 'merry', as were the guests. Loosened ties, rolled shirtsleeves, smudged lipstick, loud laughter – against all odds, it was turning into a jolly affair. She was glad they were having a good time but she felt this celebration had nothing to do with her, and when no one was looking, she escaped into the garden. The shadows were lengthening but it was as hot as ever, the air still and heavy. She sat on a low wall, listening to distant church bells, watching a column of flying ants make its way in and out of a crack in the dusty brickwork.

Something made her look up. At the far end of the lawn, beyond the clump of red hot pokers, a dark-haired man was sitting on the grass, leaning against the trunk of the cherry tree. Raising her hand, she started towards him. 'Danny?'

But when he stood up she saw it was Sam Siskin.

August hurtled into September, the days clouded by her impending separation from Bing. Every hour became overly precious, burdened with expectation. A misjudged word or a tactless comment resulted in tears or sullen silence. As if that weren't enough, she had to endure the *drip, drip, drip* of parental disapproval until she could scarcely bear to be in the house with them.

She and Bing were coming out of the cinema when someone called her name. Sam Siskin was walking towards them, suited and carrying a briefcase. He stopped and she had no option but to introduce the two men. They shook hands and she thought that would be the end of it but Sam fell in with them, chatting as they walked. Had they'd enjoyed the film? When did term start? Would they like a lift? It was no trouble – his car was parked around the corner. Bing draped an arm around her shoulder and snapped a refusal, embarrassing her with his churlishness. But Sam smiled his good-natured smile and wished them good evening. As soon as he was out of sight, Bing gave her the third degree. Who exactly was this Sam? How many times had she met him? Why hadn't she mentioned him? Did she think him good looking? Worrying away at it until the evening was ruined.

Her parents were more demanding than ever, doing everything they could to ensure she had no time to spend with Bing. And Bing wasn't helping by going on and on about Sam Siskin. Hard though it was to admit, their attachment was becoming a source of pain as well as pleasure.

'Let's drop out,' Bing said.

'And do what?'

'*Be* together. You and me. Let's find a place where no one knows us. Where nothing can spoil it.'

She held him close. 'As soon as I've finished college, I'll find a job in London. We'll rent a flat.'

'But that's two whole years away.'

'It's not as if we won't see each other.'

'It's killing me,' he said. 'You're slipping away. I can feel it.'

A few days later, Sam brought some documents for her father. She kept out of the way, spying from the landing window, watching the two men laughing and chatting in the garden. If only her father could be like that with Bing, she could be rid of the permanent knot in her stomach.

No doubt about it, Frankie Slattery was a flaky friend – out of touch for months and when she did show up, making promises she wouldn't keep. But the thing about Frankie was that she never passed judgement or made assumptions. She had an offbeat take on things. For this reason, Miriam needed to talk to her. There were rumours she was living in Brighton with a man twice her age. Miriam called at the house, hoping one of the Slattery clan would know how to contact her, but the family had upped sticks without leaving a forwarding address.

Two days before Miriam was due back at college, Frankie showed up.

'God, I need to talk to you,' Miriam said when the screeching and hugging had subsided.

'Who is it?' her mother called from the kitchen.

'It's Frankie.'

Her mother had never known what to make of Frankie, clearly on pins whenever the girl was around in case she did something outrageous. (She wouldn't approve of her current look – improbably blond hair, heavy duty makeup, satin jumpsuit.) But, knowing how 'difficult' Frankie's home life was, she 'made allowances', treating her like an animal whose unpredictability was due to maltreatment.

'Hi, Mrs Edlin,' Frankie said. 'What's new?'

Her mother looked anxious as if she might give a wrong answer. 'Nothing that I can think of, dear. What are you doing these days?'

Frankie gave a bowdlerised version of her circumstances and as soon as they could, the girls escaped and headed for the park.

'What's the problem?' Frankie said. 'Tell me you're not still with Bing.' She rolled her eyes. 'God, you are, aren't you?'

'Please don't be mean. We love each other. We're soulmates.'

Frankie sighed. 'If it's all so perfect, why d'you need to talk to me?'

'It's really, really hard,' she said. And it came tumbling out. The pressure of separation. The misunderstandings. The opposition from her parents, and recently their unashamed attempt at matchmaking.

'Bing's a sweet guy,' Frankie said, 'but there are masses of lovely men out there. How can you be sure he's *the one* if he's the only one you've had?'

'You're suggesting I put myself about a bit?' Miriam said. 'That's worked for you, has it?'

'I'm not looking for a soulmate, Mim. I don't go in for that moon-and-June rubbish. It's bollocks.'

Miriam could see why someone whose father had walked out would take this line. 'Sorry,' she said, 'I didn't mean to snap. I'm feeling a bit raw, that's all.'

She treated them to choc ices from the kiosk near the park gates and they made their way to the bench where they'd shared so many secrets.

'Aren't you going to tell me about this new man of yours?' Miriam said.

'I thought you'd never ask. His name's Geoff Tarrant. He's forty-eight. Divorced. Two grown up children.'

'*Children*. Gosh. How did you meet him?'

'He advertised for a receptionist and I applied. He's an estate agent. You'd like him. He's kind and gentle and, before you start criticising, he's what I need right now.' Frankie cleared her throat. 'Mum's in hospital. Cancer. She's not going to make it.'

Miriam took her friend's hand, cold from gripping the ice cream. 'Oh, God. I'm so, so sorry. And here I am, wittering on.'

'You weren't to know. And life must go on, as they say.'

The park was hectic with children letting off steam on their way home from school. And there were mothers everywhere: mothers carrying things, mothers pushing prams, mothers waiting, mothers chivvying, mothers chatting. Mothers, alive and well.

After a while Frankie said, 'You know we've never hit it off – Mum and me. Apparently I'm too much like my dad, whatever that means. But she's still my mum. I kinda assumed we'd work things out one day, but she's out of it most of the time. Doesn't have a clue who I am. So we're not going to get the chance.'

Not knowing what to say, she put her arm around Frankie's shoulders. 'Your brothers? Are they doing their bit?'

'You're joking. Mick's in Borstal. Johnny's in denial.'

'Where are you staying? There's room at ours if you're stuck.'

'I'm in a B&B, near the hospital. It's fine. Honestly.' She jumped up. 'That's enough of that. What d'you reckon to my outfit?'

'It's very… shiny.'

Frankie set her face in a scowl and slunk along the tarmac path, hand on hip. 'It's Biba. Geoff chose it.' She grinned. 'Don't give me that po-faced look, Miriam Edlin.'

Frankie was perched on the bedroom window sill, whiling away the time until the start of hospital visiting. 'There's a man coming up your path.'

Miriam joined her and they peeped down into the front garden. 'I told you my parents are trying to set me up. Well, that's him. That's Sam.'

'You didn't mention the fact he's bloody gorgeous.'

'Is he? I hadn't noticed.'

There was a *rat-tat* on the knocker and before Miriam could stop her, Frankie was downstairs, introducing herself to Sam Siskin.

'Hello, Miriam,' he said when Frankie stopped flirting. 'Is your dad home?'

'Not yet. And it's Mum's whist afternoon.'

'No problem. I'll call back later.'

'Actually, we're about to have a coffee,' Frankie said, turning to Miriam and raising her eyebrows.

'I'd love a cup of tea, if that's possible,' Sam said and Miriam found herself making drinks while Frankie ramped up the charm, laughing too loudly, leaning too close to the 'bloody gorgeous' visitor.

When she could bear Frankie's flirting no longer, she tapped her watch. 'Isn't it time you were heading for the hospital?'

'Let me give you a lift,' Sam said, draining his cup. Miriam was amazed that he'd been so easily reeled in.

'That's very sweet of you,' Frankie said.

He turned to Miriam. 'Why don't you come? Your dad might be home by the time we get back.'

She couldn't help but smile. 'Okay.'

They'd dropped Frankie at the hospital and were making slow progress in the heavy traffic.

'Don't you drink coffee?' she said.

'I love coffee. But I've learned from experience that people are less likely to ruin tea. And d'you realise, that's the first time you've asked me a personal question?'

'Is that good or bad?' she said.

'It's an observation.'

When they got back, her parents were in the kitchen, visibly bewildered to see her walk in with Sam Siskin. She hastened to explain and they expressed regret that Frankie's mother was so ill. 'I never knew her, of course,' her mother said, the past tense laying Mrs Slattery firmly in the grave.

Sam appeared to be completely at ease in the kitchen – chatting, recounting anecdotes of his working day. When it was time for him to go, it seemed natural they all traipse out to see him off.

Later that evening, her father kissed her forehead. 'You're a good daughter.'

She couldn't recall when he'd last told her that.

The long vacation came to an end. Once again, Bing's term started before hers. This time their parting went to plan but their final evening together was fraught with tension. He kept on and on, making her promise she wouldn't so much as look at another man and neither of them could face the extravagant meal which had cost Bing a week's grant.

This year she was sharing a basement flat with two other girls. Trips to the launderette, meter money, scrappy meals, plumbing crises, tetchy neighbours – all conspired to gobble up time and money. Student life had lost its shine and 'second year blues' infected all three of them with chronic doubt. They questioned the competence of lecturers, the relevance of the course, the sanity of parents, the general world order.

Bing's timetable meant his free time came in useless chunks – a day here, half a day there – never long enough to allow him to visit her and, yet again, it fell to her to make trips to London. To be honest, life felt rather joyless.

Frankie travelled back to visit her mother every couple of weeks. When she did, she called in on the Edlins, something which Miriam's mother reported in her weekly letter. 'That girl's not as wild as she likes to make out,' she wrote. 'She's very loyal to her poor mother.' She wasn't sure she liked the idea of her mother and Frankie buddying up.

Mrs Slattery clung to life longer than seemed possible. Frankie was with her when she finally slipped away. 'As if she waited for her to get there,' her mother said. The funeral was scheduled for a Wednesday morning and Miriam's tutor gave her leave to miss lectures. Geoff, whom she'd assumed would come to support Frankie, was 'away on a business trip' and she ended up sitting next to Frankie, amidst the ragtag of Slatteries. The service was held in the bland crematorium chapel. Frankie was impassive throughout and Miriam wondered whether she was on medication. They were in and out in fifteen minutes. A woman had been in the world – and now she wasn't. Was this pathetic effort the best they could do to mark the shocking reality? Miriam decided she would rather be devoured by a lion, or fall into a volcano than disappear behind a beige curtain like poor Brenda Slattery.

Afterwards they stood outside in a shifty gaggle, smoking and looking wary as if they couldn't wait to be somewhere else. Miriam recognised Frankie's brother Mick. The expressionless man standing close to him was, she guessed, a Borstal employee. The mourners were heading for the pub but she managed to snatch a few minutes with Frankie before leaving to catch her train back to Manchester.

'Thanks for coming,' Frankie said. 'You didn't have to.'

'Don't be silly.'

'Your parents have been really kind.' She hesitated. 'Sam, too.'

'Sam?'

She shrugged. 'You did say you weren't interested.'

'I'm not.'

'A word of warning from Auntie Frankie. Your parents don't get to choose who you marry. Okay?'

They hugged, making the customary promises to keep in touch and as Frankie walked away she turned and shouted, 'In case you're interested, I don't stand a snowball's chance with Sam. It's you he wants.'

Freda Edlin wrote to her son on the first day of every month, marking the calendar with a tiny 'D', as if to prove she'd done it. Danny replied if and when he felt like it, but he also wrote to Miriam at her college address. It was plain from the references to Ava and Pearl that these letters were meant for her eyes only. Not even Bing knew about them. She kept the letters hidden in her ring binders, amongst essays on Chaucer and the Romantic Poets. The truth was, Danny was testing her, pushing her loyalty to its limit, but this wasn't a problem because secrecy had become a habit.

When she wrote to her brother she did her best to make her letters interesting. He didn't want to read about her rows with Bing or their parents' objections to their friendship. Instead she wrote about the 'stimulating' time she was having at college and the 'fascinating people' she encountered. She avoided mentioning her disappointment at his missing the party, or asking when he might next come home.

Sometimes it was hard to believe Daniel Edlin was a real person and not a version of the tooth fairy.

Partway through the spring term, Miriam was laid low with glandular fever which had gone undiagnosed for a few weeks, her exhaustion and sore throat attributed to overwork and late nights. In the end she went to Student Health where the doctor advised her to go home and take it easy for a few weeks. 'I'll pack tonight. Catch the first train tomorrow,' she told her mother when she rang to tell them.

She mustn't fall behind. She needed to pack her course notes. And books. But which ones? And where was that Keats essay? *Come on.* Washing her hair might perk her up. But someone had used all the hot water and, tearful, she crawled beneath the blankets.

She must have slept because she was aware of someone tapping her gently on the shoulder. 'Taxi for Edlin.'

'Mmmm? What?' Squinting against the daylight she saw Sam Siskin standing next to her bed. 'I don't understand. Why are you here?' She sat up. Her ears and her eyes ached and she was parched. 'What's the time?'

'Nine-thirty.' He pointed to the suitcase and rucksack near the door. 'You get dressed and I'll put your stuff in the car. Is this the lot?'

She didn't have the will to argue. She gulped down a tumbler of water and struggled into her clothes, explaining to her flatmate that she was going home and had no idea when she would be well enough to return. Louise's only concern was whether glandular fever was infectious.

A pillow and blanket lay on the back seat of Sam's car. 'Make yourself comfy. We'll soon have you home.'

There were questions to ask but she couldn't get the words together.

The family doctor reiterated what she'd been told – rest, fluids, time. He filled in a form confirming the diagnosis. 'Send this to your tutor. We don't want them thinking you're swinging the lead, do we?'

Bing weighed on her mind. He didn't know she was at home. She needed to speak to him in case he phoned the flat and got the wrong end of the stick. But she couldn't face the hoohah that would ensue if she asked to make a long distance call to *Paul Crosby* – not when her head was stuffed with cotton wool.

Time became variable – rushing then standing still. It took an effort to cross the landing to the bathroom. Her body smelled stagnant no matter how hard she scrubbed it. When she brushed her hair, her scalp felt tender. She was exhausted yet couldn't sleep. Her father solved this by buying her a snazzy little transistor radio – 'An early birthday present for my favourite daughter' – and she dozed through *Desert Island Discs* and *Woman's Hour*, rarely making it to the end of the afternoon play.

She'd been too woozy on the drive home to establish why Sam had come to collect her. It seemed he'd been at the house when she'd phoned. Her mother had gone into a flat spin and he'd offered to set off early next morning to bring her home. It had been extremely kind – or extremely calculated – on his part but, either way, she was grateful to him. She couldn't have coped with the train journey.

Whilst she was sleeping, one of her flatmates phoned to inquire how she was ('Louise? Or Lisa?' – her mother wasn't sure) and she seized her chance to make a long distance call. 'It's Louise. And would it be okay if I phone her back? I think I forgot to unplug my table lamp.' (Plugs left in sockets were on her parents' list of deadliest sins.)

After all that, Bing wasn't there and all she could do was leave a message with his housemate. 'Can you tell Paul I'm at home, ill? It's really, *really* important. You won't forget, will you?'

When her father came in from work, he perched on the end of her bed, telling her about the new secretary who'd managed to lock the filing cabinet and lose the key, doing his best to raise a smile. Her mother brought her a mug of Ovaltine. 'It'll build you up.' Miriam couldn't stand the sickly stuff but she drank a little and disposed of the rest when she cleaned her teeth.

All evening she was on pins, imaging the worst case scenario – *Bing comes back late, gets her message, panics and phones in the middle of the night* – and she lay in bed, door ajar, pretending to read, all set to rush down if the phone should ring.

Not long after ten, she heard the plugs being pulled out and bolts being drawn on the front door. The stairs creaked as her parents came up to bed, whispering in case she was asleep. She imagined them a few feet away, undressing and climbing into bed, lying side by side in the darkness, fretting about her. They loved her, and she loved them, which made everything so much more complicated.

Her mother was at the hairdresser's when Bing's letter plopped on the mat. She tore it open, expecting words of comfort, instead finding a few terse sentences.

Miriam. I don't understand. Why are you refusing to speak to me? If you are going to dump me I'd rather you come straight out and do it. I have important exams coming up and I can't concentrate. Paul

It was as if she'd come in halfway through a conversation and she had to read it a few times before the penny dropped. Bing must have phoned and her father or mother – father most likely – had blocked him. Whatever they said had clearly wounded him. ('Miriam'. 'Paul'. So cold.) This misunderstanding needed to be resolved before it wreaked more damage. She tried ringing Bing again, her anxiety increasing with each unanswered jangle. How were they ever to sort this out? When she was able to get to the phone, he was at lectures. By the time he came home, her parents were guarding the telephone, watching her. Her mouth tasted foul and everything ached. All she wanted was to creep back into bed.

Aunt Bea arrived with a bar of Dairy Milk and a clutch of glossy magazines. Freda Edlin's older sister was endowed with a double helping of the wit and confidence she lacked. The moment she walked through the door, the house came alive.

'How's my lovely niece?' she said.

'Cheesed off.'

'What does the doctor advise?'

'Bed rest. Peace and quiet. Blah, blah, blah.'

Aunt Bea grimaced. 'Sounds deadly.' She lifted Miriam's chin with her finger and squinted at her face. 'Mmmm. You could do with a pick-me-up.'

Raising her voice she called, 'Freda? I'm taking this young woman out for a spin.'

'Where are we going?' Miriam said.

'I thought we'd take afternoon tea somewhere smart. See how the other half lives.'

The Angel Hotel was in the centre of the city, near the cathedral. She'd passed by dozens of times but never dared set foot inside.

'We'll have our tea in the lounge,' Aunt Bea said. 'It's cosier.'

She surveyed the scene. A log fire. Waitresses in brown dresses and cream pinafores. The aroma of coffee and cigarette smoke. The hum of conversation punctuated with fluting laughter. They drank black tea with slices of lemon from glasses in filigree holders. They chose cakes from a tiered stand – Miriam, a strawberry tartlet, Aunt Bea, a meringue. A man wearing a bow tie sat down at the piano and began playing something vaguely classical. It was worlds away from the Kardomah where she and her mother used to go after buying her school shoes or visiting the dentist.

'This is heaven,' she said, 'but it must cost a fortune.'

Her aunt squeezed her arm. 'A little tip. No matter how fancy the place, you can always afford afternoon tea.'

Miriam settled back in her chair and closed her eyes, swaddled in the murmur of conversation. 'I'd like to stay here forever. Away from the hassle. Not having to think of the future.'

Her aunt patted her hand. 'Poor Miriam. It's been hard for you since Danny left. I still don't understand what happened. He was the sweetest little boy. Loving. Polite. Biddable. Then he went off to university and he changed beyond all recognition. Your Uncle Michael and I wondered whether he'd been brainwashed. The Moonies, or whatever they call themselves.'

'I do miss him terribly. Mum and Dad seem to forget his absence affects me too. I've suddenly become an only child. It wouldn't be so bad if I had another brother or sister.'

Her aunt's eyebrows dipped. 'It's not my place to tell you this…'

Miriam raised herself up in the chair. 'Tell me what?'

'Oh, dear. I'm really not sure…'

'*Aunt Bea.*'

'Well, I suppose you're old enough. And it might help you understand why your mother's… the way she is.' Aunt Bea leaned closer. 'Did you never wonder why there was five years between Danny and you?'

'Not really. I assumed it panned out that way.'

Her aunt shook her head. 'Your mother lost two babies before you.' She paused. 'She was quite far into both those pregnancies. It was harrowing.'

Her mother, lying amongst bloodied sheets.

'The doctors advised them against trying again, but your mother took it into her head that one child didn't make for a proper family. And you're the proof of her determination.'

Her mother? Determined?

'Dad didn't bully her into it?'

'Absolutely not. As a matter of fact, he did his level best to dissuade her. You might find this hard to believe but your mother can – or could – be very stubborn. She fell pregnant again first time of trying and she sailed through the pregnancy despite having Danny to look after. Then, by all accounts, an easy delivery. And you were such a beautiful baby. It was a miracle. "Everything's too perfect, Bea," she used to say. "Something's bound to go wrong." And it did. Danny left.'

'But they knew he'd go sooner or later. That's how it works. I'll be off before long.'

Her aunt nodded. 'Of course. But there are right ways and wrong ways of leaving, and anything that causes that much pain can't be right.'

Aunt Bea edged still closer until Miriam felt her warm breath on her cheek. 'When Danny changed from that sweet boy to a cruel, selfish stranger, your mother was distraught. And then when he upped and went to America, it drove her right to the edge. If she didn't have you…'

And there, in the lounge of the Angel Hotel, Miriam Edlin let Paul Crosby slip away.

Part V

23

MAX WAS OFF SCHOOL WITH a summer cold. Naomi took a couple of days leave but then something came up at work and she needed to go in.

'Can't David help out?' Miriam said.

'He's in Sheffield, giving a big presentation. He'll rack up masses of brownie points if he can swing the contract for his firm. Sod's law, his parents are in Italy.' She paused. 'I don't suppose there's any chance…? I wouldn't ask but there's no one else.'

Hazel, bless her, said she could manage on her own for the rest of the week but Bing wasn't keen on her going. They'd booked tickets for a concert in the cathedral and it meant her missing it. 'It needn't stop you going,' she said. 'You could take Hazel as a thank you for giving me the time off.'

He looked unimpressed. 'No thanks. If you ask me, dropping everything and driving half across the country to look after a child with a bit of a sniffle is ridiculous. Can't Naomi find someone local?'

'Obviously not. And if Max is feeling ropey, I'd like to look after him. It's what grandparents do.'

'You more than do your bit. Besides, the kids will soon be old enough to look after themselves. There'll be no need for you to go dashing back and forth. You've done enough of that.'

It was becoming apparent that she and Bing had conflicting attitudes to grandparenting. Finbar was well into his second year and Bing had been to see him only three times. He and Pascale Skyped once in a while (on the last occasion Miriam had managed to exchange a few polite, if strained, sentences with her) but a face on a screen was no substitute for the real thing. If Bing didn't shape up, the poor mite would grow up thinking his grandfather was a TV presenter.

She set off before six and arrived at Naomi's in time for breakfast. Max was feverish, his damp curls flattened against his head, eyes looking darker than ever against his wan cheeks. When he saw her, he raised a smile, reaching out his hand before falling back on the pillow in a fit of coughing. Rosa played up, saying she didn't want to go to school, obviously reluctant to leave her and Max together. It took several promises from Miriam – 'We'll have pancakes for tea. And we'll play that board game you like' – and threats from Naomi – 'No school today, no sleepover on Friday' – to get her out of the door.

Max's cough had kept him awake most of the night but, as so often happens, daylight and familiar sounds – passing cars, a lawn mower, the radio in the kitchen – proved soothing and before long he was asleep, his breathing slow and steady. Later, when she laid the back of her hand against his forehead, he felt cooler, and she remembered how a sick child had the power to twist the heart. How the slightest improvement lifted the spirits.

This house had been her home for a year. She'd grown accustomed to its smell and the noises it made. She knew where things were, and what needed doing, and as Max slept she busied herself, putting on a wash and tidying the kitchen. She pictured Bing, halfway through morning surgery, and sent him a text letting him know she'd arrived safely and that she loved him. She made a coffee and flipped through the local newspaper. There was a new show on at the gallery but she doubted she'd have time to fit in a visit. When she popped upstairs, Max was asleep, snuggled right down in his bed, his snot-encrusted nose pressed against his beloved teddy.

The room she'd occupied (and still thought of as hers) had, before that, been David's office. When he moved out, he'd taken everything with him but she'd noticed his bits and pieces were creeping back. The bed had been pushed tight against the wall, and a desk and bookshelves had appeared. Today, there were more of his clothes in the wardrobe and his precious guitar was propped in the corner.

Max woke and announced he wanted to come downstairs. She made him comfortable on the sofa with his pillows and duvet, and persuaded him to drink a glass of water and eat a few mouthfuls of bread and honey. They watched a television programme about polar bears, Max holding her hand, occasionally touching it to his cheek. Remembering how difficult it was to concentrate on anything when your child is ill, she took a photograph of a smiling Max and sent it to Naomi as reassurance. She'd made the right decision in coming, whatever Bing thought.

Terry, who picked up the children from school and

gave them tea at her house, brought Rosa straight home. She'd thought better of her morning strop and was making an effort to be nice to her brother, keeping him company and offering to fetch whatever he needed, even lending him her new felt tips. It heartened Miriam to see that, when it came to it, her wilful granddaughter could be so considerate.

Rosa was in her final term at primary school. After the holiday, she would be off to Richmond Grove. Unsurprisingly, the school, rated 'outstanding' after a recent Ofsted inspection, had been oversubscribed and hearing she'd been allocated a place there had been a relief. Not only was it a good school, it was within walking distance of the house, a huge plus in Miriam's opinion. Not having to face a daily bus journey would make adjusting to her new environment that bit easier. Miriam was – *used* to be – acquainted with the members of the English department at Richmond Grove and, from what she'd heard, it was a happy school. Most importantly to Rosa, she would be going with her two best friends. She was impatient to begin her new adventure but everything about adolescence was touch-and-go and Miriam was already holding her breath for her granddaughter who, in Frankie's opinion, had 'a touch of the Scarlett O'Hara's' about her.

'You look shattered,' Miriam said when the children were settled and she and Naomi finally sat down together.

'Max landed up in with me last night,' Naomi said. 'I didn't get a wink of sleep what with the coughing and fidgeting. He seems a lot brighter today. I don't know what you two have been up to but he tells me you have *magic hands.*'

Miriam smiled. 'I said if stroked his back, I could make him better.'

'Well, it's working. He loves having you around, Mum. We all do. Thanks for coming. Traipsing over here must be a real chore.'

There had been times when she'd resented her role as child-carer. Now she could imagine nothing more rewarding than looking after these delightful children. She was no longer in a position to spend any length of time with them. This pained her more than she dared acknowledge. She wished she could find something to fill the hollow left by their absence. She despised ambition, yet she envied those who were driven. Nothing had ever *possessed* her and now she regretted that. She needed something to grab her. Stretch her. Was she being fanciful? Maybe all that stuff about self-fulfilment and 'be whatever you want to be' was piffle. Perhaps life was simply a matter of getting on with it.

'It's been a while since we've seen Paul,' Naomi said. 'I hope I've not offended him. He was rather offhand last time we came to see you.'

'In what way offhand?'

'I asked after his family. I said we should all meet in the school holiday. Get to know each other. He was – well – dismissive like he was the last time I suggested a get-together. Frankly, I find it weird.' Naomi held her gaze. 'You'd tell me if anything were wrong, wouldn't you?'

There was *something* wrong but Miriam wasn't sure

what, or how serious, it was. It was hard to put into words, and she feared that were she to tug at the threads of her unease, everything would unravel.

'He gets stressed,' she said. 'I don't think people realise how relentless a GP's job is. Every person who comes through the surgery door is ill – or imagines they are. He says he spends more time convincing *well* people that there's nothing wrong with them than finding out what's wrong with genuinely *ill* people. Doctors are supposed to be objective about life and death but that's not easy, especially where children are involved. Some of his cases really get to him.'

'I understand all that,' Naomi said. 'but wouldn't his life be a bit less stressful if his family gets to know you? The kids and I met Paul on day one. We were involved from the word go and it's been brilliant. You've met Leon once, and his daughters never.' She sighed. 'Let's not beat about the bush, for some reason they're cold-shouldering you and I can't bear that. He must realise how hurtful that is.'

'Our getting back together was bound to throw up a few issues,' Miriam said.

'So you keep telling me. He loves you to pieces, anyone can see that. Why is he letting them get away with it? It doesn't stack up.'

'I'm not sure what went on when he and Eloise separated. Perhaps they think being friendly with me would show disloyalty to their mother.'

'*Perhaps?* God, Mum, after everything with Dad, you must know how important it is to share things with your partner.'

Naomi's allegiance was gratifying but having her fall out with Bing was unthinkable. Risky too. Should the two of them get into a slanging match, he could easily let slip the circumstances of their split. Should Naomi discover that her beloved grandparents had blackmailed her into marrying a man of their choosing, the fallout didn't bear thinking about.

By Thursday evening, Max was almost back to his old self but Naomi agreed that he would benefit more from spending the day in the fresh air than in a stuffy classroom. Miriam expected an 'it's not fair' tantrum from Rosa but after school she was off to her friend's for the long-awaited sleepover and she raised no objection. 'We're going to camp in the garden,' she said, making sure her brother knew she was getting the better deal.

Miriam and Max spent an hour in the park, 'collecting'. She'd devised this game when the children were younger, often reluctant to drag themselves away from whatever they were doing when it was time to go home. The quest for a leaf or a discarded bus ticket had been enough to lure them away from the sandpit or the swings. As they grew older, the rules were rewritten. 'Finds' had to be out-of-the-ordinary, or display a noteworthy characteristic. A bus ticket passed the test if the integers in its serial number added up to twenty-one. A leaf had to be an extraordinary colour – and then it must be pressed and mounted on card to prevent it curling. She'd rescued a small display cabinet from a skip, cleaned it up and repainted it, and the children had adopted it as their 'museum of odds and ends'. A stag beetle (dead) was currently the star of the show.

Today Max was hunting for the perfect feather, combing every inch of grass around the pond. She'd never been keen on the geese which were waddling around looking particularly angry and she placed herself between him and the aggressive mob until he found a tiny iridescent feather which he judged worthy. They wandered on to the café where she made him scrub his hands – twice – before letting him choose an ice cream. A young woman appeared from the kitchen with a tray of glasses and Miriam sensed her watching them. Eventually she came over to their table. 'It's Miriam, isn't it?' she said.

'That's right.' She looked at the girl. Ex-pupil? No. They called her 'Miss'.

'Caz,' the girl said. 'From the college. You sat for us.'

Miriam had a first-rate memory for pupils, especially the troublesome ones, but her relationship with the art students – well – she'd *had* no relationship with them. She'd been sitting, standing, lying on a dais, and they'd been a sea of faces. They'd exchanged the odd word but there had been no need to learn their names.

'Caz. Of course. Gosh, that seems a long time ago. How are you?'

'I'm good, thanks.'

'What are you doing here?'

'Reducing my overdraft. I fit this,' she raised her tray, 'around my college work.'

Max was folding a paper napkin in half, then in half again. He spent hours doing this, determined to prove that it *was* possible to fold a piece of paper more than seven times.

'You moved away, didn't you?' Caz said.

'That's right. I'm back for a few of days to look after my grandson. He's off school with a cold.'

Max, still intent on his napkin, gave a gluey sniff.

'Still modelling?' Caz said.

She shook her head. 'I was only helping Callum out until he could find someone permanent.'

'You did a great job. Everyone thought so.'

Max looked up from his mangled napkin, his eyebrows drawn down in a slight frown. 'Were you making models, Gamma?'

She improvised. 'Everyone was drawing and making things.'

'Did you make a coil pot?'

'I didn't but I wish I had.'

'Did you like it better than working in the bookshop?' His trusting gaze held hers.

'I think I did,' she said.

Max tried to persuade her to stay an extra night, employing all his wheedling charms.

'I have to go home, sweetheart,' she said. 'I promised Paul. He gets lonely when I'm not there.'

Max wasn't ready to give up. 'But *we* get lonely when you're not *here*, don't we, Mum? And there's three of us so that adds up to more loneliness.'

Naomi settled it by saying that *of course* they missed Gamma, but a promise was a promise and Gamma always kept her word.

'Thanks again, Mum,' Naomi said as she was putting

her bag in the car. 'Sorry we didn't have time for a decent chat. I've been thinking. Why don't you and I have a night away? A spa break. Or just a break. Away from snotty kids and needy men.'

'That sounds wonderful.'

'Good. Let's do it.'

The traffic was light for a Friday evening and she allowed her thoughts to wander. A night in a swish hotel with Naomi might be fun. They'd not done anything like that in years. What did she say? 'A decent chat.' The reference to 'needy men' was obviously a dig at Bing (David was the least needy man Miriam had come across) and she guessed her daughter's unqualified enthusiasm for him had taken a knock. She felt a hint of unease. A *froideur* between Bing and Naomi would spoil things.

He greeted her with roses and a box of her favourite marzipan chocolates. He'd re-stocked the fridge and the laundry basket was empty.

'I'm impressed,' she said. 'Maybe I should go away more often,

He wrapped her in his arms. 'Don't say that. Not even in jest.'

24

HAROLD EDLIN WAS OBLIGED TO renew his driving licence every three years. This involved his answering questions on his health and the state of his eyesight. The decision as to whether his application was successful rested solely on his responses and, to Miriam's surprise, required no input from his doctor. Although her father was deemed capable, she sensed that retaining his licence was more a point of honour than a desire to get behind the wheel.

These days her parents used their car infrequently and, when they did, they travelled short distances and chose familiar routes. This was reassuring in one respect, yet troubling in another. Their world was shrinking, their perspective on it skewed by media scare stories. Once in a while, she and Bing took them out for a 'spin'. A glimpse of life beyond their self-imposed boundaries bucked them up and freed them, if briefly, from the drip, drip, drip of doom and gloom. They didn't venture too far afield, limiting travel time to an hour at most, choosing a National Trust property or beauty spot with benches and a view. There were plenty of places nearby that fitted the bill. Bing was so good, so patient with them, turning a deaf ear to her father's incendiary opinions, winking at her when her mother got the wrong end of the stick. He pretended he enjoyed these jaunts but she knew he was doing it for her.

'That was lovely,' her mother said, when they returned from visiting a Georgian house, noted for its formal gardens. 'I didn't think we'd ever go there again, did you Harry?' She gave a trill laugh. 'Life's still full of surprises, isn't it?'

Miriam went to organise a cup of tea and by the time she got back her mother had fallen asleep in her armchair. Her father was in the garden, talking to Bing about his plan to grass over two flower beds. Her mother had given in some time ago and allowed her to organise a cleaner to come in for a few hours a week. Persuading her father to hire a gardener, proved more of a sticking point. She knew the problem wasn't cost, rather the implication that he was no longer up to the task. Bing pointed out to him that the critical ingredient when creating a successful garden was the vision behind it. 'Any fool can push a mower,' he said. Her father had raised his eyebrows. 'I may be old, young man, but I'm not gullible.' But then, because he was ready to take advice from Bing where he refused it from anyone else, he added, 'Perhaps I will if we can find the right man for the job.'

She took the tea tray outside and the three of them sat on the patio in the shade of the sun umbrella, nattering about this and that. Richie, the next door neighbour, appeared on the far side of the hedge separating the two gardens. 'Got a moment, Paul?'

Her parents didn't have a great deal to do with Richie and Valerie but they were friendly enough and knowing they were on the spot in case of an emergency was reassuring. The men talked for a while, their conversation involving much nodding and pointing. Finally Bing went next door to help manhandle fencing panels which needed stacking behind Richie's garden shed.

Her father seemed unusually relaxed as if, in that moment, everything was how he wanted it to be.

'Should I check Mum's okay?' Miriam said.

'Let's leave her. A snooze would do her good. She doesn't have the stamina she used to have.'

What must it be like, Miriam thought, to reach an age when each day lived was a bonus yet there was little you could do with it apart from see it through? It took a kind of courage to get up every morning and face the increasing probability that *this* day would be your last. Longevity – blessing or a curse? Live long enough and she'd find out.

'We never get a chance to talk,' he said.

'That's not true, Dad. You see a lot more of me these days.'

'I do. But you and I never get to *talk*. There's always someone around – Paul or your mother. Or you're dashing off somewhere.'

She reached for his hand. 'Well I'm here now.'

After a few moments he said 'Are you happy, Miriam? You seem to be, but I need to know for sure.' His question was disconcerting. As a rule, he steered clear of what he'd probably label 'airy-fairy topics'. 'Well, *are* you? And don't give me all that "it depends what you mean by happy" nonsense. A simple yes or no will do.'

'In that case, yes, I am happy.'

'I'm glad. You deserve to be.'

His eyes were fixed on the end of the garden as if he

were searching for the rest of what he wanted to say. 'I've been thinking.' He gave an odd little laugh. 'That's about all I'm good for now. There were things we did – they seemed right, at the time but,' he shook his head, 'I'm not so sure.'

'Everything's fine, Dad. There's no need to say anything. It was a long time ago.'

'It was. And you were so young. Nineteen?'

'Mum was nineteen when you were married.' She spoke quietly, more to remind herself than to challenge him.

'Your mother left school when she was fifteen. You had to grow up fast in those days. Take on responsibilities. The family counted on your money. Back then, teenagers hadn't been invented. You were either a child or an adult. There was nothing in between. Your mother'd held down a job for two years when we started courting. Then we had the war. When you were nineteen, you were still a child. It wasn't your fault. That's how it was.'

'You never talk about the war,' she said.

'Some things are too terrible to speak about. The only way to cope is to lock 'em away. It's not foolproof. When you least expect it, someone shows you an old snap or you read an article in the paper and it all comes flooding back.'

'That's what I'm saying, Dad. There's no point in raking over things that happened decades ago. The important thing is to make the most of the here and now.'

'That's as maybe. But it doesn't stop me wanting to set things straight between us.'

Bing and Richie were laughing on the other side of the

hedge, wrestling with fence panels, firmly planted in the present.

'It wasn't only my age that bothered you, was it?' she said.

'No it wasn't. I won't pretend we were happy at the prospect of your breaking with tradition.'

'You mean marrying out?'

'I've never liked that phrase. It gives the wrong impression. Times have changed. Religion or *culture* as we're supposed to call it, doesn't mean what it did back then. It used to be about respect for your forebears and the sacrifices they made.'

'Doesn't faith come into it at all?'

'That's a tricky one.'

She laughed. 'Now there's a conversation we must have some time.'

It was pleasantly warm sitting there, watching the shadows lengthen. Her father's eyelids drooped occasionally and his head nodded forward but, stubborn man that he was, he refused to surrender to sleep.

'If you thought me so immature, why did you push Sam at me?'

'Sam Siskin was a man, not a boy. He was steady. We trusted him to take care of you.'

'You thought I needed taking care of?'

'Didn't you feel that way about Naomi?'

'Of course, but we accepted she had to work things out for herself. We didn't agree with everything she did but our job was to offer advice when she asked for it and support when she made a mess of things. I wish you'd talked to me, Dad, instead of going all tight-lipped. It felt as if you were punishing me without giving me a chance to explain my side of the story.'

'You never said anything.'

'I should have done. And I might if Aunt Bea hadn't told me about Mum. The miscarriages. The depression. How badly Danny had treated you. She made me realise how close Mum was to the edge. I dared not pile hurt on hurt.'

'Bea told you?'

'Yes. When I was home that time, with glandular fever. I assumed you'd put her up to it.'

He shook his head. 'Bea, may she rest in peace, always was a meddler.'

'I'm sure she thought it for the best. We all do the wrong things for the right reasons at times.'

He lifted her hand and kissed it. 'You're quite something, d'you know that? We'd never have welcomed Sam into our family if we'd known what he was like.'

'There was nothing to know back then. And he *did* take care of me until that disgusting addiction took hold.'

Her father took a deep breath. 'I'd like to know your mother will be well looked after if I go first. But you mustn't – *must not* – take that on. There are plenty of nice places for old folk in these parts. In fact we've been to look at a few. We've put money away against that eventuality. When that's all gone, you'll have to sell this house.'

'Dad—'

'Shhh. Let me finish. If your mother goes first, I intend staying here. I can have meals-on-wheels or whatever they call it now and you can show me how to work the microwave. If I can't manage the stairs, the dining room would make a nice little bedroom. There's no need to harp on about this but I wanted to tell you while we had a bit of time to ourselves.

'We've made our wills. Whatever's left after we've gone, will come to you. You'll find copies, along with details of everything I just told you, in the black document box in the bottom of our wardrobe.'

She could only assume that they had, as they'd sworn they would, left Danny out of their wills. They must have agonised over it. He was less often in her thoughts these days but he was their son and they must think about him every day. Looking across the table at the frail, proud old man who had reached some kind of acceptance of his situation, she wished they could always have been this honest with each other. But after all this time it would be too cruel to tell him that, somewhere in the world, he had a second granddaughter called Pearl.

He turned to her, the ghost of a smile on his lips. 'You're a good daughter. And Paul's a good man. You deserve to be happy. I hope you can forgive us.'

Miriam pulled her chair close to her father's and twined her arm through his and they stayed like that, without saying any more, until Bing returned.

25

BING HAD SHOWN UP AND everything had made sense. Seeing him, hearing his voice, smelling his skin, had revived feelings she hadn't experienced since she was twenty. It was heady stuff – febrile, delicious, curative. Yet occasionally disappointment settled on her like a layer of dust, taking the shine off things.

'You seem preoccupied,' Hazel said.

The observation caught Miriam off guard. 'Do I?'

'We could knock off early and go for a coffee if a chat would help.'

In most friendships, there are talkers and there are listeners. It was in Miriam's nature to listen. Admitting to someone that things weren't quite right, didn't come easily to her. But unlike Naomi or Frankie, Hazel could be relied on to be objective, non-partisan. Although she was on nodding terms with Bing, she hadn't met Miriam's family. If she intended sharing her very personal anxiety with anyone, Hazel would be the one. They ended up in the bar of the Angel Hotel. It was that between-time – too late for afternoon tea and too early for drinks – but they decided a bottle of white wine might ease conversation.

Hazel settled back in her chair, and raised her glass signalling she was ready to listen.

'When I married Sam,' Miriam said, 'I found myself

living in a nice enough house with a nice enough husband. I had a nice enough job. But when you're twenty-two, "nice enough" is – well, it *isn't* enough. I had nothing to complain about yet I couldn't help thinking *is this it*? Is this how it's going to be forever? Compared with the future Paul and I had dreamed of, it fell pathetically short.'

'You must have had an inkling what being Mrs Siskin would entail.'

'That's the thing. I knew exactly how it would be and I accepted it. God only knows what was going on in my head. Was I punishing myself for betraying Paul? Or trying to make my parents love me more? Perhaps I wanted to make them feel guilty. There was definitely an element of self-flagellation involved.'

'You never considered leaving Sam and going back to Paul?'

'How could I? He'd never have trusted me after what I'd done. Besides, I fell pregnant almost immediately. Carrying another man's child was not the ideal way to prove my undying love. Naomi was born and suddenly the stakes were higher. This innocent little soul who was only in the world because of me, deserved to grow up in a stable environment. I had no alternative but to knuckle down. It wasn't so hard. Naomi was an easy, delightful baby and Sam was besotted with her. He was cut out to be a father. Patient. Gentle. He would have loved half a dozen. We tried but it didn't happen. We were sad and disappointed but we'd become a solid family unit. Things toddled along. We had our ups and downs – which family doesn't? – but nothing major. Naomi grew up and married David.

Rosa and Max came along and Sam doted on them. Silly old me assumed it would go on that way forever.'

The bar was beginning to liven up. Miriam glanced at her watch. Bing wouldn't be home for a while.

'When Sam bankrupted us, I wanted to kill him. Unfortunately he got there first.' Her voice caught. 'Is that a terrible thing to say? Put yourself in my shoes. I'd done everything expected of me for *forty years* and he hadn't the balls to face up to what he'd done.

'I lost the plot. It all seemed futile. Too much of an effort. But then Max would give me a cuddle, or Rosa would giggle at something I said, and I knew I had to hang in there. Their father had left them. Their grandfather had left them. I couldn't go too.

'I muddled on, helping Naomi with the kids and the house. To my great relief I started to heal, to dare to look at the future, and I realised that being an adjunct to other people's lives wasn't going to be enough. That's when the job at the art college came up – just a couple of mornings, but it made a huge difference. I began believing in myself. Regaining my confidence, I suppose. Not long after that after, I found out Paul was divorced. You know the rest.'

Hazel re-filled their glasses. 'So what's happened?'

'Nothing. That's the problem. We've lost momentum. We've stalled. It's as if finding each other was the end of the process as far as Paul's concerned. He's happy with things as they are, but I signed up for more than a part-time job, redecorating the kitchen and pottering in the garden. If Romeo and Juliet had made it to sixty, I can't think they'd be satisfied with a trip to the garden centre.

on Sunday afternoon. After waiting for each other for forty years, there's got to be more to our story than that.

'No doubt you'll say I must have it out with him. Explain how I'm feeling. But what would I say? I need more from life than you're giving me? What's that going to do to him?'

'Sorry to be so predictable,' Hazel said, 'but look at it another way. You're doing him a disservice in allowing him to go on thinking everything's fine. The longer you leave your discontentment festering away, the more poisonous it'll become. Surely he'd rather hear a few home truths now than end up making you miserable.'

The wine was making talking – *telling* – too easy. 'There's something else,' Miriam said. 'When I go out on my own, he wants to know where I'm going, who I'm seeing. He gets in a state if I'm ten minutes late home. Sam was a hopeless timekeeper. If he bumped into a friend, he'd stop to chat. Or he'd go for a drink. It was bloody irritating at times but the upside was he was happy for me to do the same. I didn't realise what a gift that was. How liberating. Paul pretty much has a post-mortem on my every move. Or that's how it's starting to feel. It's like being under curfew.'

She held out her phone. 'Look. He's called three times in the past twenty minutes.' She took a gulp of wine. 'When we go anywhere, he won't leave my side. He doesn't like my talking to other men. And he can't bear those dinner parties where they split couples up. He seems to think every chap I come across is hell-bent on seducing me. For God's sake, I've got a bus pass.'

She sighed. 'I might as well get the whole lot off my chest while I'm at it . Naomi's been pushing for a get-together – Paul's family and ours – but whenever the subject's raised he comes up with some random excuse why it can't happen. It's eighteen months now and I still haven't met Camille. You must admit that's bizarre.'

'He's happy to spend time with your family, though?'

'Happier than I am. He can't do enough for my parents. The kids adore him. We *all* adore him.' She puffed out her cheeks and exhaled noisily. 'I hate having these negative thoughts.'

Hazel lifted the bottle of wine but Miriam rested her hand on the top of her glass. 'Your getting back together – it all happened very quickly,' Hazel said.

'It must seem like that to outsiders, but as soon as we saw each other we knew. It was preordained. What was the point of waiting? We were both free. We weren't hurting anyone. And we weren't getting any younger.'

'Maybe you were a tad—'

'Ingenuous?'

'*Optimistic.* You aren't those two starry-eyed youngsters who parted when the Beatles were in the charts.'

'Maybe not. But we're fundamentally the same. Our *natures* haven't changed.'

Hazel looked sceptical. 'Your *context* has. You must have heard that old saying about not being able to step twice into the same river. You've advanced a couple of generations for one thing. Your priorities are bound to be different. You have to honest with yourself. How do you want things to be? What needs to change to bring that about? When you've fathomed that out, you have to sit Paul down and talk it through. This is a two-way thing, don't forget. He may come back with a list of things that aren't working for him. You'll have to negotiate.'

'You make it sound so easy.'

'Other people's problems generally are.'

Miriam glanced at her phone and grimaced. 'Come in Miriam, your time is up.'

'Shall I write you a late note?'

'Don't. That's a bit too close to the mark.' She dropped her phone into her bag. 'Sorry to be such a wuss. Next time, it's your turn on the couch.'

As her bus crawled through the traffic, she re-played their conversation. She hadn't intended pouring it all out. That bottle of wine – bad idea. She'd made Bing out to be a control freak which was unpardonable and disloyal. Hazel had offered no silver bullet but her advice was rock solid. *Talk to him.* Why was that so difficult? Was she frightened to admit there were flaws in their flawless partnership? What was the worst that could happen?

She'd never dodged a row with Sam. When a niggle escalated into an out-and-out quarrel, they'd each given as good as they got. To all intents and purposes, theirs was an arranged marriage. Knowing she'd rather have been with another man, Sam might have been tempted to pander to her in order to win her affections. He'd never done that, which, on reflection, might have gone a long way to account for the quiet success of their marriage.

Bing was in the kitchen, whistling and chopping vegetables.

'Sorry I'm late,' she said, 'Hazel and I went for a drink. We were chatting away and I lost track of time. It was noisy and I missed your calls. Sorry.'

Excuses. Apologies.

'No big deal. I only wanted to know if we had any ginger.' He raised the knobbly root. 'Found it in the fridge, behind the cottage cheese. Stir-fry okay?'

He'd changed into khaki shorts and T-shirt. His hair was sticking up at the back. He looked like a schoolboy. Running her hand up beneath his T-shirt, she grinned. 'Wonderful.'

26

EVEN AFTER NAOMI HAD LEFT school, they'd had no option but to take their holiday in August. Year on year, they'd paid over the odds to sit on teeming beaches and queue for museums and restaurants. Miriam had dreamed of the day when she could potter around the Algarve in May or rent a villa in Tuscany during the grape harvest. Holidaying in term-time was no longer a problem and they booked a week's leave for September. Bing fancied heading off the beaten track. Iceland or the Shetland Isles. Naomi recommended Budapest. Hazel suggested a long weekend in New York. Miriam didn't mind where she went – although she had a hankering to swim in the sea.

Two days before term ended, the weather broke. Wind played fast and loose with garden furniture. A ferry was forced to anchor off Holyhead for hours, waiting until the storm abated. Rain battered her petunias, and cohorts of slugs appeared from nowhere to feast on lupins and pansies. After weeks of hot days and balmy nights, the drop in temperature came as a shock to everyone. Miriam, who had been living in sleeveless dresses, dug out her jeans and sweatshirts, feeling sorry for families who had splashed out a small fortune on what they'd hoped would be a fortnight in the sun.

The turn in the weather brought more customers into the shop. They made space for additional children's books and introduced morning story sessions. Once in a while, Hazel asked, 'Okay?' and Miriam would nod. 'Fine thanks.' They didn't revisit their conversation but she was surprised how much better she felt as a result of it. Perhaps she'd simply needed to let off steam. *Of course* Bing wanted to spend time alone with her. *Naturally* he worried for her safety when she was out alone. He would be a strange lover if he didn't. And the business with his children? She'd met Pascale a couple of weeks ago when she'd flown down from Edinburgh to attend a friend's wedding. First uncomfortable moments negotiated, Miriam expected Bing and Pascale to relax into family gossip, questions, laughter or even a row. But they appeared to be keeping each other at a distance, steering clear of personal matters, their conversation focused on travel arrangements and the quality of coffee at various coffee shops. As Miriam watched father and daughter, she was struck by their lack of physical contact. The 'sorry' when they inadvertently touched. It was unnaturally civilised. Pascale had barely acknowledged Miriam. She'd not enquired about her family, or how she and Bing knew each other – details which had intrigued Naomi. Perhaps she was trying to hurt her father by snubbing his new partner. From the way she kept checking her phone it was clear she couldn't wait to be on her way and when they parted there was no mention of another get together. 'There. I told you it would be fine didn't I?' Bing had said as they drove home. If 'fine' amounted to negotiating a scant hour without confrontation, yes, it had been 'fine'. But Miriam was no further forward in understanding how

Bing's family worked or what was causing their standoffishness. She was left feeling the episode had been a box-ticking exercise on Bing's part. Leon. *Tick*. Pascale. *Tick*. Only Camille still to go, and as she'd started a new job in Toulouse there was little chance of their meeting in the near future.

On her way home from work, she called at Boots. Naomi's birthday was only a week away and she'd asked for a specific face cream. Miriam could have ordered it online, saved herself the trouble of wrapping and posting it, but it was important to put in a bit of effort when buying a gift for someone you loved. When she let herself in, the house felt chilled after a morning's rain and while the kettle boiled she went upstairs to find a sweater. Hearing a car door slam, she glanced out of the window. Two female police officers were getting out of a car. Plonking their hats on their heads. They looked comical in their bulging fluorescent jackets. Out of place in this quiet cul-de-sac. One was holding a notebook, glancing between the page and the front door, obviously checking the house number.

Her stomach lurched. Bing? Or the children?

She ushered them in and they sat in the kitchen, their hats side-by-side on the table like two pudding basins. They were solemn and inscrutable and, as they went through the rigmarole, introducing themselves and checking she was, indeed, Miriam Siskin née Edlin, daughter of Harold and Freda Edlin, she realised, with a sense of relief, that it was her parents. And, after asking if there was anyone she would like them to contact – 'No. I'm okay but please tell me quickly,' – they told her.

It was a car accident. They were coming out of a side road, turning right across the traffic flow. Her father had missed seeing the oncoming car which had ploughed into the driver's side, killing him outright. Her mother had been injured and was at the hospital undergoing assessment.

'Will she be okay?' Miriam said.

The women looked uncomfortable. 'I'm afraid we don't have any more information at the moment.' 'I'm sure they're doing everything they can.'

'Where did it happen?' she said.

They showed her a map, one of the policewomen pointing to the spot with a nicotine-stained finger.

'They must have been coming back from Waitrose,' she said. 'The other driver?'

'Minor injuries. We'll be taking witness statements, of course, but from what we understand, he did everything he could to avoid hitting them.'

'My husband died in a car crash,' she murmured as though it might count against her if she didn't tell them.

One of them made her a mug of tea, ladling in sugar until it was undrinkable. They kept calling her Miriam, as if they'd know her for years, asking if there was anything she needed. They used language Max would have understood when he was three, repeating everything slowly and clearly as if she were deaf. They were doing their job but they were bloody irritating.

'I need to see my mother,' she said.

'It might be as well to phone someone?'

Now that maddening 'upspeak'.

'My partner's a doctor,' she said. 'He'll be in the middle of surgery. I don't like to disturb him.'

'I'm sure he'd want to be with you?'

She took her phone through to the living room. Bing was between patients and when she told him he said he would come right away. He was calm. Businesslike. He would know what to do. She told Tweedledum and Tweedledee that he was on his way, that she would be fine, that they really didn't have to stay, but they insisted. 'Procedure' no doubt. They sat in the kitchen, trussed up in their roly-poly jackets, talking about shifts and meetings. All the while radios clipped to their collars garbled curt messages which they ignored. Other tragedies, other lives about to change forever. All in a day's work. It wasn't their fault but they were sullying her home and she wanted them gone.

When Bing turned up, he took over, noting down telephone numbers and instructions. Every now and again, he looked at her, raising his eyebrows, silently asking how she was coping. When there was no more to be done, he ushered the police women out of the door.

'Poor love,' he said, pulling her close.

'All I could think was thank God it wasn't you, or Naomi, or the children. Isn't that terrible?' She puffed out her cheeks. 'Poor Mum. Has anyone told her?'

'I rang the hospital. She's sleeping.'

'You mean unconscious?'

'Yes. And that's a good thing. It'll make it easier for them to assess what's going on.'

323

She pictured Sam after the accident, broken and bloody, unrecognisable but for his clothes. But her mother was alive. She couldn't possibly look as bad as he had.

'D'you think they'll let me see her? Just for five minutes? Will you come with me?'

'Slow down, Mim. We'll go soon. But first I'll make some toast and—'

'Please, no more tea.' She pressed her palms to her face. 'What's the matter with me? I try focusing on Dad, and my mind shoots off in another direction.'

'You heard this news – what? – an hour ago? Of course you can't deal with it.'

'I'll have to identify him, won't I?'

'I can do that.'

'No. I want to.' She buried her head in her hands. 'What is it with this family and cars?'

He went upstairs to change and, unable to keep still, she followed him.

'This can't be happening,' she said.

'A feeling of detachment is normal. It's a—'

'I *know* all that. I'm fed up with being told everything I feel is *normal*. My father dying isn't *normal*. My mother lying in a coma isn't *normal*.' Her word came out in gulping sobs. 'And don't say a good cry will do me good or I'll scream.'

Naomi took the news better than Miriam had feared. She must have known the call would come before too long – her grandfather was, after all, a very old man. And the circumstances, although shocking, didn't alter the fact he was dead. When all was said and done, he hadn't suffered. She was more distressed about her grandmother, wanting to come right away, but Miriam dissuaded her, advising her to wait until the situation became clearer.

When she got around to 'phoning Danny, she got a chirpy *this number is no longer available* and her emails bounced back from every address he'd ever given her.

Her mother lay on her back, enveloped in the sombreness of the ICU. Apart from a few tubes and the bouncing traces on the screen, all to indicate anything was wrong were the bruises on her cheek and arm. Seemingly the collision had been not much more than a bump. But when you're old and frail, it didn't take much. She stayed with her mother, holding her hand, talking, singing to her, only leaving to sleep and to set in motion the formalities associated with her father's death. Naomi came as soon as she could organise childcare, going to pieces when she saw her grandmother. Miriam spent all her time consoling her, but having a diversion – something practical to do – was better than sitting there, waiting.

On her way home to shower and change, she called at the house, bracing herself against the sight of crockery stacked next to the sink, waiting to be washed up when they returned from their shopping trip. A skim of Oxtail soup – their last meal together – had congealed in the white china bowls but she couldn't bring herself to wash them.

She dug out the document box her father had mentioned. Screeds of instructions, set out in his looping script, raised a smile. Good old Dad. Micro-managing from beyond the grave. But 'the grave' was a problem. He'd requested a traditional funeral which stipulated burial should take place within twenty-four hours of death – impossible as there had to be an inquest. 'He'd understand,' Bing said.

Her parents' solicitor and her fellow executor was a family friend. She'd known Simon Newman for years and it was a comfort having him there, reducing what seemed insurmountable problems to minor glitches. There were things needing immediate action and, as surviving spouse, the responsibility for these would normally have fallen to her mother, but he assured her there were ways of working around the difficulties which her condition presented.

Bing was a star. He checked her parents' house, saw to their mail, fended off enquiries, kept up with the washing and made sure she ate regularly. More importantly, he used his influence to find out whatever medical details were to be known.

Her mother clung to life for five days, finally slipping away painlessly (Bing assured her), quietly following her beloved husband wherever he had gone. The redeeming feature of the tragedy was that Harold and Freda Edlin were laid to rest on the same day, in the same place. Miriam was astonished and moved by the turnout. Most of their contemporaries were dead and she'd expected the mourners would be limited to close family and a few neighbours, but Bing had done sterling work getting the word out. Frankie was there, and Hazel, and several of her father's surviving work colleagues. Even a second cousin she'd not seen since her parents' silver wedding (the day Sam appeared on the doorstep). The double funeral of the old couple captured the public imagination and the story made the front page of the local paper.

'It's as if they planned it,' Naomi said when everyone had gone.

This possibility had crossed Miriam's mind. But no, they wouldn't do that to her, not after Sam, and certainly not with thirty-six pounds-worth of groceries in the back of the car.

27

THERE WAS MUCH TO SORT out. Banks, pensions, tax, insurance, utilities – the list went on and on, every step of the process made more complex by the five days Freda Edlin had survived her husband. Simon steered her through the maze of paperwork and, on the whole, everyone she dealt with was patient and helpful. Her greatest cause for anguish was her continuing failure to make contact with Danny. Simon told her there were firms who specialised in tracking missing people. At her request, he contacted Denton and Ryde who had a good reputation in that field and they set a search in motion.

Bing pressed her to abandon her job to allow herself 'time' – whatever that meant. She refused. 'I'll need something to do after this is finished.' Hazel solved it by finding a student who was looking for summer work and was delighted to step in until autumn term started.

Every couple of days, Miriam drove to the house, surprised to see how well it was surviving without them. Usually it was a flying visit to pick up mail and check nothing was amiss. Occasionally she stayed longer, sipping a coffee and allowing herself to remember. Standing in the kitchen she felt them close by, heard them chatting upstairs, smelled her mother's Kugelhopf – hot and fragrant. Glance out of the window and she and her father were sitting in the garden, forgiving each other.

Within the space of one week, she'd been orphaned. No warning, no time to prepare – although their age should have prepared her. As memories surfaced, she processed them like Kodak film, adjusting focus and brightness, fixing each one to prevent its fading. Her parents had vanished so quickly and she couldn't risk losing the fine detail of their lives. She took to cutting flowers from the garden and putting them in vases in the living room and on the kitchen windowsill. Flowers in this house – their home – made more sense than those she left at the cemetery.

Four weeks after the accident, she went to look after the children, grateful for five days' respite from the sea of papers that littered the dining table. Naomi said if it proved too much, David's parents would take over, but being with the youngsters, a hundred miles away from the memories and dreary legalities, was the best antidote to the melancholy which was suffocating her. Naomi had talked to Rosa and Max, explaining what had happened and why Gamma might be 'a bit sad'. But their great-grandparents had lived far away. They'd seen them infrequently and, when they did, they'd been forced to be on their best behaviour. The two wrinkly old people had been less interesting than the exhibits in the 'museum of odds and ends'. If they felt any sorrow at all it was for her – Gamma – and that was soon forgotten.

Their September break amounted to a week in the Lake District. The sun shone. Their room looked out across

Windermere. They ate good food, went on walks, took boat trips and made love. Bing told her she was looking better. 'Fresh air. Peace and quiet. Just the ticket.' But she found it difficult to engage with any of it, unable to shrug off the feeling that she was treading water.

Despite supplying them with a list of Danny's various addresses and phone numbers, Denton and Ryde had so far drawn a blank. 'D'you think he's dead?' she asked. They said if he were, they should find records. That it was almost as if he were doing everything he could to cover his tracks.

'If he doesn't want to be found, isn't it time to let go?' Bing said.

'Maybe he's ill. Or in trouble. What if he's destitute? I'm going to have more money than I need.'

'Your parents made their wishes clear enough. You don't intend overriding them?'

'*Dad* made his wishes clear but I'm not sure it's what Mum wanted. She never went against him. If she'd recovered, she might have changed her mind. Danny's not knowing they're dead – that's what's getting to me.'

'He never considered you, or your feelings. Not once.'

'I'm not pretending this is rational. I'm simply telling you how I *feel*. I realise it's costing a lot but I'm not ready to give up.'

He assured her money had nothing to do with it. He said that instead of frantically searching for her brother, she should be grieving for her parents. 'The two things aren't mutually exclusive,' she said.

330

Although she was loath to admit it to Bing, she knew that sooner or later she would have to give up. But it was a well-known fact that spells, wishes, quests took a-year-and-a-day to reach fruition. And that's how long she would give Denton and Ryde to find Danny.

Probate came through. Papers were sorted and filed away and the dining table reclaimed. After three months spent tying up the loose ends of her parents' lives, Miriam decided it was time to address her own. The main issue was the house. She'd received enquiries from several neighbours 'asking for a friend' if she was planning on putting it on the market, and more than a few notes had been pushed through the letter box, registering an interest in the property. It was reassuring to know the house would sell quickly but the very fact that so many strangers were aware that it was unoccupied, made it vulnerable. She'd removed anything of value and also the things most valued by her (not the same). Nevertheless knowing how easy it would be for someone to break in and trash the place made her anxious. To give the impression of occupation, she set lamps to come on when darkness fell. She moved the curtains, sometimes leaving them open, other times shut. It wouldn't deter a determined mischief-maker but it was the best she could do.

'I know how much you love the house,' Bing said one evening when they were getting ready for bed, 'but I can see it's preying on your mind.'

'You're saying I should sell?' she said.

'If you think that's best.' He shucked off his socks. 'Or we could sell *this* house and move in there. Just a thought.'

His suggestion brought her up with a start. It was the first time he'd mentioned moving but to come up with this plan… he must have been considering it for some time.

'I don't know,' she said. 'It's a possibility, I suppose. I'd have to think about it.'

'Of course. I was thinking that, with winter coming on and all that… Anyway, it's up to you.'

'It is,' she said, perhaps a little too sharply.

She did love the place. Its dipping roof, elegant chimneys, bay windows. Its burnt-red bricks and crisp pointing. It looked solid, as if it would endure. But it would always be *their* house. If she and Bing took it on, it would be like slipping into their shoes. When Sam's creditors came knocking, she'd had no option but to sell. This time she was beneficiary not victim. This time she had a choice.

Their clothes hung in wardrobes and filled drawers. She made a couple of attempts to sift through them but each shirt, each 'cardi', each pair of shoes – particularly slippers – brought her to a tearful halt. Perhaps she'd gone at it too soon. Bing offered to bag the lot and take it to Tenovus. Sensible, maybe, yet disrespectful. Cowardly. She considered asking Hazel to give her a hand but decided it might not be a good idea for two of her worlds to collide, especially in such highly-charged circumstances.

'I'd come and help,' Naomi said, 'but I'd be useless. I only have to think about them and I'm in shreds. Have you thought of asking Frankie?'

They'd exchanged a few words after the funeral. Frankie had been rushing off to meet someone – or so she said. Miriam guessed she was in one of her pickles but it hadn't been the time or place to talk and since then she'd had other things on her mind.

Bing was dubious. 'You know how needy the woman is. How she likes holding centre stage. You'll end up listening to her problems.'

'That mightn't be so bad. It would be a distraction. And there's another reason to ask her. She spent a lot of time with them over the years. I don't like the idea of a stranger going through their things.'

This time Frankie came by bus explaining that she was 'between cars'. She was more subdued than usual but Miriam put this down to her making an effort not to rub Bing up the wrong way. First thing next morning, equipped with a packed lunch and a supply of large carrier bags, they headed over to the house.

Standing in the hall, sniffing the air, Frankie said 'If I were blindfolded, I'd know exactly where I was. It's always smelled comfortable here.'

'Is *comfortable* a smell?'

'Don't be picky. Every house has its own a smell.'

'Does ours? Bing's?'

Frankie frowned. 'Mmmm. Can't say it does. Maybe it hasn't absorbed enough history.'

They made a start with things that held the least emotional charge – towels, bedding, table linen – keeping the best, assigning anything grotty to a black bin bag. As they went through the cupboard, she noted with sadness that many of the items were brand new, still in their wrappers. Packs of pillow cases. A mattress cover. A set of Christy towels – peach-coloured to match the bathroom – given them by Naomi a couple of Christmases ago.

She held up another new towel. 'It makes me mad. What were they thinking?'

'They were proud,' Frankie said. 'They were keeping them in case they ended up in hospital or bed-bound. They'd have hated strangers seeing them with manky towels and tatty sheets.'

When they'd finished sorting the linen, they turned their attention to the spare room and the clothes her parents kept for 'best'.

'I can't stop seeing their clothes as second skins,' Miriam said. 'Those coats in the hall, those dressing gowns on the back of the bedroom door… hanging there, waiting for them to come back and slip into them.' She buried her face in her mother's camel coat, the brooch on its lapel scratching her cheek. 'This still smells of that awful scent she loved.'

They worked their way through the wardrobe and moved on to the tallboy. The clothes were dated – wide lapels, unnecessary buttons and belts – but top quality and made to last. Someone might find a use for them and they folded them into carrier bags. Shoes were a different matter. They were intimate. Slip a hand inside, and she could feel the indentations made by their toes. Her father had had a thing about his feet. The only time they appeared naked was on a beach and, even then, he squirmed them down into the sand away from public gaze. Their shoes – every last one – would go to landfill where they could slowly and privately rot away.

It was a one of those twinkly October days, the low sun accentuating the yellows and ochres of the foliage. The lawn was flecked with fallen leaves and the chrysanthemums were hanging on, bold and scruffy. Really it was too chilly for a picnic but, needing to escape briefly from their melancholy task, they found a sheltered corner of the garden and took out their sandwiches.

'We haven't talked about you,' Miriam said. 'You're still at the pub with your sister-in-law?'

Frankie shook her head. 'It's been taken over by Wetherspoon's. Cath's moving to Spain with her boyfriend.' She laughed. '*Boyfriend*. He's getting on for seventy.'

'So…?'

'Something will turn up. It always does.' She delved into her bag and produced a half-bottle of brandy, adding a dash to their mugs of coffee. 'We should drink to your parents.'

They chinked mugs – 'Mum and Dad', 'Harold and Freda' – and Frankie lit a cigarette.

Miriam pulled her collar up around her ears. 'Remember skiving off behind the bike shed for a fag?'

'What are you on about, Miss Goody Two Shoes? You didn't smoke.'

'No, but hanging out with the infamous Frankie Slattery, gave me street cred – or whatever we called it back then.'

Frankie tilted her head back and exhaled, a plume of cigarette smoke curling in the breeze. 'How did they manage to make school so deadly dull? I reckon they were trying to bore us into submission, don't you?' She took another pull on her cigarette. 'I had this friend who let me copy her homework. Full marks every time. The suckers must have thought me a genius. Of course it all went tits up when exams came around.' She brushed ash off her sleeve. 'I'd enjoy school now. I'd see the point of it. Maths. History. Maybe not Scripture. But that's the trouble, isn't it? Everything comes at the wrong time.'

A stiff breeze was getting up, whipping the pampas grass and driving them, shivering, inside. Frankie found a radio channel playing sixties pop and singing along to the vacuous, unforgettable tracks, Miriam almost forgot that the cardigans and skirts and jackets she was shoving into bags were her parents' second skins.

They worked steadily and, by mid-afternoon, they were done. 'That's it,' Miriam said, tying the top of the umpteenth bin bag. 'The rest can stay for now. Thanks for helping, Frankie. Not exactly a fun visit for you but I couldn't have tackled it on my own.'

'Don't be daft. So what next for you? There's nothing to keep you here.'

'There's Bing's job.'

'He could work anywhere in the world.'

'I suppose he could, but he's happy at Monkton Square.'

'I expect he is, especially now he has you all to himself.' She hesitated. 'Is this how you imagined it would turn out?'

'This?'

'You know what I mean. When you told me you were back with Bing, the first thing that came into my head was at least *someone* gets their happy ending.'

'I *am* happy.'

Frankie raised her eyebrows. 'Or are you just *happier*? Not that difficult when you consider the crap you've had dumped on you.'

'It's not that simple.'

'Isn't it?'

'I love being with Bing. It's as if I've found the missing bit of me.'

'And when you're not with him? Let me guess. You don't know what the hell you're doing here.'

'I'll soon find something interesting to do.'

'Interesting? Here? Come on, Mim. The world's your oyster.'

She laughed. 'I'm sixty-three.'

'So? You're clever. Gorgeous-looking. Fit and healthy. Think big. You could go travelling. Or start a business. You could write a bestseller. Or learn Chinese. You could...' Frankie waved her arms around as if the very air were filled with possibilities waiting to be grabbed.

'Funny you should mention writing. I was sorting through the stuff I'd put in storage and I did unearth the first few chapters of a novel I started years ago. I'd forgotten all about it. It's probably rubbish but—'

'There you go. And it won't be rubbish. You were brilliant at English. Get stuck in. It'll probably win the Booker. But getting back to you and Bing. At school, you were *the golden couple*. Scarlett and Rhett. Posh and Becks. What's gone wrong? Where's the thrill? It's all so bloody safe. It's like he's got you back and he's determined to clip your wings.'

'You're being melodramatic.'

'No, I'm deadly serious.' She took Miriam's hand. 'You've been at everyone's beck and call for as long as I've known you. Your parents. Sam. Naomi. Not to mention me. This is *your* time. Use it wisely. With your genes you could live another twenty-five years.'

'Bing and I love each other and always will so it's not my time but *our* time.'

'Okay. Message received if not entirely understood. I've said my piece.'

Miriam wasn't relishing what could easily be a challenging evening but Bing was on his best behaviour and Frankie at her least confrontational. As dinner progressed, she found herself relaxing. Thinking how pleasant it was to be with her oldest and best friends. Mellowed by food and wine, they fell to talking about their school days, and she dug out the photograph of all of them outside the coffee bar. She passed it to Frankie. 'I meant to show you this last time you were here.'

'Oh. My. God.' Frankie ran her finger along the row, calling the register. 'Colin. Judith and Lisa. I don't think I ever saw them apart. D'you think they were gay or just wet? There's Little Pete. And us. Wow.' She angled the frame towards the light. 'If we'd known then what we know now, we wouldn't be looking so pleased with ourselves.'

338

'Would you like to know what lies ahead?' Miriam said.

'God, no. Who in their right mind would?'

'Shall Bing get a copy done for you?'

Frankie handed the photograph back to Miriam. 'Thanks, but I'll pass. It's too sad.'

Next morning they returned to the house and loaded the bags into the car – some to go to the charity shop the rest for the tip.

'Okay if I have a little wander before you lock up?' Frankie said.

Miriam went into the garden to pick the last few chrysanthemums. The tattered blooms bore no resemblance to the perfect specimens found in M&S but her mother had been very proud of them. Seeing them in her precious cut-glass vases, would make her happy.

'Would you like to choose a keepsake?' Miriam said when they were back in the kitchen. 'Sooner or later everything will have to go. There are some bits of costume jewellery in the dressing-table drawer. Or maybe a photo?'

'I would like a memento if you don't mind,' Frankie said. 'I loved coming here. It was a real oasis. They were so kind to me even though I wasn't their cup of tea. Maybe it's easier to tolerate flaws in the people you don't have a stake in. Your mum was a sweetie. My idea of what a mother should be. She used to feed me up and send me off with a bag of leftovers. Kept me going for days. And your father. He was a force to be reckoned with. Dogmatic. Bombastic. *Extremely* clever. I can see where you got your brains from. He could be very funny – very

339

caustic – but he had a real soft centre where you were concerned.'

'If he did, he managed to hide it most of the time. We had our moments, he and I. Poor Dad. The Sam business knocked the stuffing out of him. He blamed himself for bringing him into our family. I'm sure he saw Bing's reappearance as a chance to salve his conscience. Only a few months ago, he and I reached a kind of resolution. I'm so glad we did.'

Frankie chose the marcasite brooch which had been pinned to the lapel of Freda Edlin's coat. It depicted a swallow in flight. Miriam couldn't be sure but she thought it had been a present from Aunt Bea.

28

HER PARENTS WERE CONSTANTLY IN her thoughts but the trauma of their loss was fading, leaving her feeling as if she were recuperating from a prolonged bout of 'flu. But she was unquestionably on the mend. Her appetite improved. She suffered fewer violent dreams. She was able to concentrate long enough to read a novel – something she'd failed to do since their death. And – a real indication of improvement – she felt well enough to return to the shop.

Her rehabilitation was, however, tainted by the old whisper. *Is that all there is?* Determined to tackle this, she scoured the internet, looking for jobs or courses or *anything* that fired her imagination and fitted her capabilities. She forked out twenty pounds on *How To Write An Impressive CV* (complete with DVD and templates) but no matter how she tarted it up, her employment history boiled down to teaching English at a couple of run-of-the-mill comprehensive schools. It didn't help that most job specifications were pumped full of jargon and even after several readings, she had little idea what the wretched job entailed. She made the mistake of mentioning to Naomi that she was looking for something which would stretch her and her daughter deluged her with details of outlandish posts in exotic places, obviously reflecting her own fantasies.

Naomi brought the children for a weekend. Rosa, full of her new school, insisted on showing them every one of her textbooks. Max seemed delighted by his sister's elevation to 'big school' which Miriam guessed had a lot to do with his no longer being labelled 'Rosa Garrett's kid brother'. When asked if there was anything in particular they wanted to do whilst they were there, they reeled off a list. Swimming (with Bing). Football in the park (with Bing). A takeaway Chinese (in a box shaped like a house). It was their first visit since the funeral and Miriam thought Naomi might want to visit the house or the cemetery, but she mentioned neither.

As they sat around the kitchen table, juggling foil containers and struggling with chopsticks, Miriam recalled Hazel's question. *What's most important to you?* It was a no brainer. She wanted – needed – to be embedded in her family's daily lives, not parked on the periphery, morphing into an ageing relative to be dutifully visited a couple of times a year. As Frankie had insisted, doctors could work anywhere. People relocated all the time. So what was the problem? If Bing's goal was to keep her to himself, *he* was the problem. His track record with his family wasn't encouraging. Why would he want to integrate with hers? Besides, if she were to talk him into moving, she would be duty bound to be deliriously happy every minute of every day – a ghastly and unrealistic prospect.

Torrential rain and ferocious gales swept the country taking out bridges and railway tracks and bringing floods to Cumbria, Scotland and Wales. The city escaped the worst of it but it was bad enough. Water surged up through storm drains. Traffic had to be re-routed to avoid low-spots where surface water collected in menacing pools. The river burst its banks in several places, creating lakes complete with bobbing gulls. When she checked the empty house, leaves had blocked the drains and the patio was under a couple of inches of water. There were puddles on the sills in the living room and a wet patch on the bathroom ceiling. The bedding felt damp.

'I've been thinking,' she said to Bing, 'whatever we finally decide to do, it would be better if the house were occupied through the winter months.'

'You want to let it? Mmmm. That might work.'

She wrinkled her nose. 'Wouldn't that involve safety certificates and contracts and heaven knows what else? No. I was thinking more of an informal arrangement. Offering it to someone for a few months. They could keep an eye. Be a sort of caretaker.'

He raised his eyebrows. 'I take it you mean Frankie.'

'Well, yes. She knows the house inside out. She'd be my first choice.'

'And your second choice would be...?'

'Don't be so grumpy. It's just a thought. It'd mean we needn't fret about damp and frozen pipes and intruders.' She paused. 'I wouldn't have to spend so much time there.'

'Have you thought this through?' he said.

'Not in fine detail. I wanted to discuss it with you. It feels wrong that a house belonging to me is standing empty whilst my best friend has nowhere decent to live. Mum and Dad liked Frankie. They'd think it was a good thing to do.'

'Wouldn't it be simpler to sell and have done with it?'

'Simple doesn't necessarily mean right,' she said. 'And what if Danny comes back? He's going to need somewhere—'

'Mim, my love, Danny isn't coming back. This has been going on long enough. It's time to let him go.'

'No. You can't say that. You aren't allowed to decide whether he's alive or dead.'

He held his hands up in submission. 'All I'm trying to say is that your brother's absence is blighting your life.'

'D'you think I don't know that? I'm worn out with it.' She began to cry. 'What's the matter with my family? They're incapable of dying normal deaths.'

She felt Bing's arms around her. 'Shhhh. Don't upset yourself. Look. If Frankie moving in for a while eliminates one of your worries, why don't you ring her now? See how she's fixed.'

She left several messages before Frankie got back to her. She was in Gloucester, working in a hotel and renting a room in a 'friend of a friend's' flat. Details were sketchy but judging by what *wasn't* said, the set-up was grim. Miriam had been pondering the best way to put her proposal. 'We were wondering if you could do us a favour.' She explained that the house needed looking after through the winter and that Frankie would be doing them a great service by moving in. Acting as a sort of concierge. Of course, if she were happy where she was… Frankie wasn't daft. She knew what was going on but she played along with it. She'd think about it. Were she to say yes, she'd have to find work of course – but she should be able to pick something up, especially with Christmas on the horizon. Could she have a couple of days to weigh it up? She phoned back next evening accepting the offer and they agreed she would move in as soon as she could get herself organised.

When Miriam told Naomi of the arrangement, she detected a note of reticence in her daughter's 'what a great idea, Mum'. And she began having a few doubts of her own. If Frankie failed to find a job, she'd be at a loose end, without money or friends, or anything to keep her busy. More troubling still, what if she acquired a band of hangers-on – lame ducks needing a roof over their heads? 'Am I doing the right thing?' she asked Hazel.

'It's your house. It's up to you what you do with it.' Hazel paused. 'It might be wise to lay down a few ground rules.'

'I'm not sure how I would do that, or what those rules would be. Frankie's not a teenager who can be told.'

'Fair enough.' Another pause. 'Didn't you tell me that she and Paul were once an item?'

'For a few months. When we were at school. Then she got bored and passed him on to me. Why d'you ask?'

'Is that likely to cause a problem? Old girlfriend back on the scene. That sort of thing.'

'Absolutely not. For one thing, they don't get on.'

'So will *that* cause a problem?'

Miriam had a set of keys cut and stocked the fridge with essentials. She aired the beds, washed the towels and bumped up the central heating, occasionally stopping to remind herself that she was landlady not hostess. Frankie arrived with two suitcases and a backpack. (How could a woman of her age have so few worldly goods?) Noting how defeated she looked, Miriam knew she'd been right in offering her friend respite. Frankie must have been mulling over the implications of the set-up and they were hardly through the door before she was reassuring Miriam that should she decide to sell the house, or want to live there herself, or should she change her mind about *anything*, she had only to say the word.

'I won't smoke in the house. Or pester you and Bing. And you must make a list of jobs. I want to be useful. You'll tell me if I'm doing anything wrong, won't you? To be honest, things haven't been brilliant recently. I've done more than my fair share of stupid things but I'm not going to fuck this up.'

Driving off, leaving her friend on her own, Miriam was a whisker away from inviting her back for dinner. But for this arrangement to succeed, Frankie must stand on her own two feet.

'Did you discuss household bills?' Bing said.

'What?'

'You can't be thinking of paying the woman's running costs.'

'Of course not. She can be irresponsible but she's not stupid. She knows she's getting a good deal.'

'I should bloody well hope she does.'

'We'll sort out the bills in the next day or two but I can't start straight in asking for money before she's even unpacked.'

'It's the perfect time if you ask me.' He shook his head and shrugged.

'She's changed, Bing. She's determined not to screw this up.'

'This *is* Frankie Slattery we're talking about?'

'Please don't be snarky. We're not going to fall out over this are we?'

'Of course not.' He sighed. 'Sorry if I seem negative but I worry she'll let you down.'

'I'm sure it's the right thing to do. She says she'll start looking for a job tomorrow.'

'I may be able to help there. The dentists on the other side of the square are looking for a receptionist. Their new girl's walked out on them and they're desperate.'

'Really? She's done loads of admin work. And she's terrific with people. It sounds ideal.'

Frankie went for an interview and started immediately. Within a few weeks, by all accounts she was running the place. The dentists sent over a bottle of whisky for Bing as a thank you for finding them such a 'treasure'.

The issue of household bills was soon sorted out. They would cover standing charges – Frankie would cover the balance. When Miriam put this to her, Frankie confessed to having no money at all. This came as no great surprise to Miriam who insisted on lending her four hundred pounds to tide her over. 'Best we keep this between us,' she said. 'Pay me back as and when.'

'I don't know how to thank you, Mim.' Frankie dipped her head. 'I haven't forgotten the two hundred you hid in my suitcase that time. It may take a while but I'm going to pay back every penny. For once in my life I'd like to do things properly.'

'Is Paul happy with her being there?' Hazel said.

'He's getting used to it. To be honest, it's not made much difference. We don't see a lot of her. I pop in for an occasional chat and to pick up bits of mail. She's had dinner with us once. She's doing her best not to intrude.'

'Doesn't she have any family?'

'A couple of brothers but they've always been useless. She never mentions them. She puts on a brave face but it's obvious she was at rock bottom. As far as I can make out, she's had no support from anyone in a long while.'

'Except you, that is. Not many people would do what you're doing.'

'It's no big deal. We're not desperate for the money and in fact hanging on to the place is probably the smart thing to do with house prices on the rise.'

'There's more to it than that though, isn't there?' Hazel said.

'I suppose so. My parents liked her. They didn't have a clue what she was about but I think she brought a breath of fresh air into their conventional lives. If they'd known she was struggling, they'd have offered her a home, I'm sure of that.' She paused. 'Having someone they were fond of living there, makes their absence easier to cope with. Does that make any sort of sense?'

Hazel nodded. 'Absolutely. My parents bought their house when they were newlyweds. They lived in it all their married life. Every square inch of it was steeped in them. When Dad died there was no question of Mum moving. All her memories were there. When she died, I had no choice but to sell. Having strangers move in whilst they – or their *essence* – was still tangible, was an affront to their memory. It pained me to walk past the place. Real physical pain. Your parents will be comfortable sharing their home with your friend until they're ready to leave.'

Miriam shivered. 'That's it exactly. The essence of them *is* still there and I suppose it will be until I can bring myself to accept they really have gone.' She held out her bare arm. 'Look, I'm all goosebumps.'

Christmas had been a mirage, off in the distance, blurry and illusory, but when the calendar flipped to December, Miriam was forced to acknowledge its reality.

Naomi invited them to go there, peppering her offer with 'no pressure' and 'don't feel you have to'. Bing's children, it seemed, all had 'longstanding commitments' which ruled them out, and made things easier. She had no idea what Frankie was planning to do. She'd made a crowd of friends at work and was going to a Christmas 'do' at the golf club. But Christmas Day itself was sure to be tough. The thought of her eating her solitary Christmas meal and, more than likely, drinking herself into oblivion was distressing.

As The Day drew nearer, Bing said he would be happy to go along with whatever she wanted. She'd love to be with the children on Christmas Day but she knew he'd prefer to stay at home. And then there was Frankie. She dithered for a few days until Max clinched it by emailing imploring them to come, saying Christmas wouldn't be any fun without them. And should he *happen* to get the Lego set he 'needed', Bing would be welcome to help build it.

'Why don't we drive to them on Christmas morning?' she said. 'We can have a Christmas Eve celebration here. Just we two.'

'I'm always banging on about myself,' Frankie said when Miriam called with a Christmas card. 'How are *you*?'

'I miss them, of course I do, but sometimes I feel sad that I don't feel *sadder,* if you know what I mean. I've been trying to remember my last conversation with them. I have a feeling it had to do with tinned tomatoes. They got it into their heads that processed tomatoes are the elixir of life. They'd stockpiled dozens of tins of the wretched things.'

'Better tinned tomatoes than incontinence pads,' Frankie said.

'You're right. They were old but in remarkably good health. They went together. They didn't suffer. That's probably as good as it ever gets. All the same, it doesn't stop my wishing I'd been able to say a proper goodbye.'

'Poor Mim. We rely on you, don't we? Bing. Naomi. Me. Perhaps, once in a while, you ought to let us down. Make us realise how much you do for us.' She clapped her hands. 'I nearly forgot.'

She took a notebook from her handbag, 'I.O. Mim' written on the cover. Inside were two crisp notes. 'Here's another twenty. That brings it down to four hundred and ninety.'

'Are you sure?' Miriam said. 'Don't leave yourself short over the break. Look, will you be okay?'

'Didn't I tell you? One of our dental nurses – Jen – works with the homeless. She asked me to lend a hand over the holiday. Quite a turn-up, don't you think? I'm usually the charity case but, thanks to you, I'm in a position to help someone else. It feels really good.'

29

WHILST MIRIAM WASN'T PAYING ATTENTION, Hazel had acquired an admirer, a lanky Scot called Gavin who taught music and was excruciatingly shy. Judging by her new hairstyle and the perfume she'd taken to wearing, it seemed she was quite keen. This year, instead of going to Devon, she was spending Christmas at home with Gavin. Miriam was delighted that she'd found someone to appreciate her honesty, humour and wisdom. Other good things were happening too. David was officially back with Naomi and, fingers crossed, Frankie was making a go of her job. After months of sorrow and uncertainty, the year was ending well for those whom she most loved.

Angelgate, with its bow-fronted shops and soft street lights, was made for Christmas. The Salvation Army playing on the cathedral green and the scent of roasting chestnuts, enhanced the ambience. Last-minute shoppers wandering down the cobbled lane, were lured into the bookshop with the offer of free gift-wrapping and a tot of mulled wine. They'd sold out of Moleskine notebooks earlier in the week, and the big hit of the season was a pricey book on gargoyles, a tie-in with a popular television series. 'Thank God for sexy TV presenters,' Hazel said.

As the light faded, customers evaporated. 'Have fun,' Hazel said as they set the shop straight and collected their bits and pieces. 'I hope everything goes to plan.'

'This will be my third Christmas as a widow, my first as an orphan,' Miriam said. 'Generally people do it the other way. I'm glad we're going to Naomi's. I won't have a chance to be gloomy. You have a lovely time with your Gavin. He's a sweet chap.'

'He is,' Hazel said, 'but I'm not sure he's *my* Gavin. We get on fine but I'm growing selfish in my old age. And lazy. I love my life the way it is. I'm not looking too far ahead. Having a nice man to spend weekends and holidays with, and, yes, have sex with, that may be enough. I hope Gavin's content to go along with that. If not, I won't stop him moving on.'

They went their separate ways and, as Miriam stood at the bus stop, she recalled her conversation with Bente – 'when it stops being good we will shake hands and call it a day' – and she felt a surge of respect for both women's resolve not to settle for second best.

Bing was already home and the house smelled of freshly-brewed coffee.

'What's all this?' she said pointing to half a dozen packages piled on the kitchen table.

'They're from patients. Bribes to keep them alive.' Bing lifted up what could only be a bottle. 'I spend hours telling them to cut back on sugar and alcohol. Come Christmas, they give me booze and chocolates.'

Whilst they pottered in the kitchen, she told him how Frankie was spending the next few days. He seemed less than impressed. If she – Frankie – wanted to gain his approval, she needed to do more than dole out hot meals and blankets once in a blue moon. Miriam wished they would set aside their differences. Their mutual mistrust impacted on her. They should recognise that and at least pretend to get along.

She'd bought turbot from the fishmonger in the market and, to follow, a selection of cheeses from the deli opposite the shop. Bing unwrapped his bottle-shaped gift, on the off-chance that Mr Jenkins had defied expectations and given him something white, dry and delicious, but it was supermarket rosé and they broke out the Pouilly-Fumé, bought when it was on offer at Waitrose.

After they'd cleared away, they sat by the fire listening to Britten's 'Ceremony of Carols'. 'I remember singing this with the school choir.' she said. 'My parents would have had forty fits if they'd known, but I honestly didn't think of it as having anything to do with religion.'

'Do you believe there's a god?' Bing said. 'I don't think I've ever asked.'

'I try not to but, once in a while, my defences drop. You?'

'No I don't. But seventy-five percent of doctors do.'

'That's astonishing,' she said.

'Isn't it. I've got this theory. If things go pear-shaped, they can square it with themselves.'

'How?'

'They pass the buck. It's God's will, and all that.'

'But you told me you believe in destiny. Isn't that the same thing?'

'Not at all. Destiny isn't wilful or whimsical like God—'

'Who doesn't exist.'

'Exist or not, he's caused you and me enough grief in the past,' he said. 'Let's not let him spoil our second Christmas together.'

The sky was streaked with slivers of luminous yellow and a skim of frost decorated the fields. The boot was stashed with gifts and goodies, and a carrier bag containing flask and mince pies was sitting on the back seat. They pootled along, marvelling at the lack of traffic. There was something subversive about taking to the open road on this, the most prescribed day of the year. They could be jailbirds out on a spree, making the most of their freedom before recapture and incarceration. They drank their coffee in a layby, exchanging Christmas greetings with another couple who were also *en route* to a family gathering. On any other day but this, chatting to strangers, offering them mince pies, would be unthinkable. But today regular rules didn't apply.

When they reached their destination, they sat in the car, enjoying a final few moments to themselves. 'Thanks for coming,' she said. 'If I were at home it would be all too easy to wallow in Christmases past. We shan't have a chance to do that. Children don't go in for self-pity. And if they do reminisce, it's about something funny or scary. I'm sure they'll tell you about the time the smoke alarm went off and we couldn't stop it. The noise was intolerable. I could feel it damaging my ear drums. David ended up ripping it off the ceiling and dumping it in a bucket of water. I do love David. I'd given up hope of their getting back together but he hung in there. I'm not sure I would have put up with

Naomi's nonsense. She got to be very prickly. Mind you, my living there probably didn't help.'

'Come on, Mim. You were twenty-four-seven childcare.'

'*And* a twenty-four-seven reminder that her father was dead,' Miriam said. 'I sometimes forget that. Anyway, thanks. I know you'd rather be at home. Next year you get to choose how we spend Christmas.'

'I can tell you that now,' he said. 'I shall whisk you off to a desert island.'

She laughed. 'Sounds wonderful. Can I bring my eight discs?'

'Seriously, Mim, much as I love being with your family, I must admit I prefer having you all to myself.'

As if to drive home his point, the front door opened and Rosa and Max, flushed and boisterous, charged out – 'I've got *Star Wars* Lego, Gamma.' 'Dad dropped the eggs.' 'How many nights are you staying?'

David, wearing a butcher's apron, was close behind. 'Welcome to the house of fun. We're in desperate need of a bread sauce expert.'

The kitchen was in chaos, ever surface piled high with the makings of the Christmas meal. Naomi was juggling pans, bemoaning the size of the oven. 'Merry Christmas, you two. Help yourselves to whatever you fancy. I recommend a large glass of something.'

After a brief discussion they concluded that bread sauce was overrated and it was struck off the 'to do' list, and while Bing disappeared to set up Rosa's new digital radio, Miriam cleared debris and set the table.

After lunch, the children's five o'clock start caught up with them and they fell to bickering. David suggested he and Bing take them out to blow away the cobwebs. Max was up for it but Rosa refused point blank, asserting that everyone should be allowed to spend Christmas Day as they pleased. After 'the men' had gone, she tied herself in knots, unable to make up her mind what to do, finally flouncing upstairs to her room and slamming the door.

'Hormones and Christmas,' Naomi said, 'a deadly combination. She's at that tricky age. Although I can't say she's ever been easy. Was I like that?'

'Not as far as I remember. You didn't get difficult until you were in your thirties and then you were David's problem.' Miriam took a fresh tea towel from the drawer. 'It's wonderful seeing you together again. It can't have been easy but I'm sure you've made the right decision.'

'It was touch and go for a while but we came to our senses and realised what was important. Now it's better than ever.' She grinned and hugged herself. 'Did you and Dad ever wobble? Apart from at the very end.'

'I can't say we did. If anything, we went through our bad patch before we got married.'

'Anything to do with Paul? I know you were teenage sweethearts.'

'In a way, but it resolved itself.'

'You've never told me the whole story.'

'Water under the bridge. If I'd not married your father, you and my precious grandchildren wouldn't exist. That's good enough for me.'

Naomi wrinkled her nose. 'We never did get our

357

weekend, did we? Shall I see if I can find something before Easter?'

'I'd like that.'

Rosa was stamping around overhead, making sure they could hear her. 'I bet she's dying to come down,' Miriam said. 'She's afraid of losing face. I'll pop up and see what I can do.'

'You're so patient with her, Mum. Sometimes I feel like giving her a slap. Don't look so shocked. I would never do it.'

Rosa had fixed a sign to her door. *PRIVATE. Knock before entering.* Miriam tapped the door and waited to be summoned. Rosa's face was pink and puffy and, for some reason, she'd pulled all her clothes out of her chest of drawers and heaped them in the middle of the floor. 'Are they back yet? What are they *doing?*' she said, her face contorted with anguish.

'There's nothing open today. They'll have gone to the park.'

'I expect they're having fun without me.'

'Come here.' She held out her arms, and Rosa burrowed against her and, after a few moments, the child's body relaxed.

'Do you still feel sad, Gamma?' she said. 'About… you know.'

'Now and again. And when I do, I think of you and Max and it cheers me up.'

'I hate Max.'

'And why's that?'

'He's a pain. He comes in my room, looking at my

things. He follows me around. He talks to my friends. He copies my drawings.'

'Well, you're his big sister. He thinks you're the bee's knees.'

'The bee's knees?'

'Yes. The cat's pyjamas.'

Rosa giggled, drunk with tiredness and spent emotion. She ran her fingertips beneath Miriam's jaw line. 'Your skin's so soft.'

Miriam stroked the pale skin on the inside of her granddaughter's slender arm. 'Yours is too. Especially here.'

Rosa gently pinched the flesh on Miriam's neck and smiled affectionately. 'But I'm not squidgy.'

'That's true. Come on. Let's go down. I haven't seen all your presents.'

By agreement, the television remained unplugged and the evening drifted pleasantly away. David's family had infected the children with a love of party games and they'd prepared a list of the ones they wanted to play. They began with 'Chinese Whispers', the adults deliberately mishearing to ensure a hilarious outcome. 'Name-in-the-hat', 'Charades' and 'Up Jenkins' (involving a coin, the kitchen table and sleight of hand) followed until, to the adults' relief, Naomi called a halt. The children, wilting and wan-faced, knew that their staying up depended on immaculate behaviour and they sat quietly, reviewing their stash of gifts. The day had panned out as Miriam hoped. Bing had thrown himself into it – helped with the catering, stacked and emptied the dishwasher (twice), bagged acres of wrapping paper, and dropped whatever he was doing when the children demanded his attention. She'd had barely a moment to think about her parents, or Frankie ministering to the homeless (or hosting an epic knees-up). Or even Danny.

She and Bing had exchanged gifts before setting out – a silk negligée and a book of poetry; the leather wallet he'd coveted – so when he appeared with a plate of mince pies, she was surprised to see a small package – no bigger than a matchbox – nestling amongst them, her name on its gift tag.

'What's this?' she said.

'It's for you,' Bing said.

'But I've had all my presents.'

'It's a little extra one. I hope you'll like it.'

Sensing something interesting afoot, the children, looked up. 'Open it, Gamma,' Max said.

'*I* think it's a ring,' Rosa said, as if this were another party game.

Conscious that all eyes were on her, Miriam untied the ribbon and folded back the wrapping paper. Inside was a leather-covered box, its hinged lid secured with a miniature hook-and-eye. Inside the box, held by folds of satin, sat a gold ring with a greenish-blue stone.

Rosa, squealing, jumped up and down. 'Told you, didn't I?'

'What are you on about?' Max said.

'It's an engagement ring, stupid,' Rosa said. 'Paul's going to marry Gamma. Can I be bridesmaid? *Please*.'

Max frowned. 'Has he even asked you, Gamma?'

Before Miriam could think of a thing to say, Bing dropped onto one knee. 'Let's ask her now, shall we? Miriam, my dearest love, will you do me the honour of becoming my wife?'

She was dumbstruck by his proposal. Horrified by the manner of its delivery. How could he be so crass? Did he not appreciate the pressure this put on her? He was still kneeling, smiling up at her, awaiting her response.

'What d'you say, Miriam? Will you make me the happiest man in the world?'

David was the first to break the silence. 'Come on you two. Let's get you up to bed. Say goodnight to Gamma and Paul.'

'But Dad—'

'No "buts". Chop, chop.'

Placing a hand on the their shoulders, he manoeuvred the children towards the door, Naomi following close behind.

'Please get up,' she said.

He moved towards her, arms outstretched, but she took a step backwards. 'What were you thinking? You can't spring this on me. And in front of everyone, too.'

'*Spring* it on you? You know how I feel – and always have.'

'That's not the point. Did it not cross your mind that I might not *want* to marry you?'

'What are you saying? Don't you love me? Don't you want us to be together forever?'

'You know I do. But it doesn't follow that we have to get married.'

He looked wounded. 'Why are you being so hostile?'

'I'm not. I simply object to being bullied. Because that's what it feels like.' As their voices rose, she remembered that Max's bedroom was directly above. 'If we're going to shout at each other, can we at least do *that* in private?'

He followed her out to the car, and they sat in the back, a cushion wedged between them. 'You're forever telling me how important your family is to you,' he said. 'I thought you'd like them to be involved.'

'Involved? You're suggesting we get them to vote on it?'

'That's ridiculous.'

'Is it? You actually said, "let's ask her now, shall we?".'

'Who cares what I said? It's what I meant that matters.'

Christmas night. Ten o'clock. It was freezing cold and here they were, huddled in the back of the car, arguing semantics. Suddenly she was laughing.

'What in Christ's name is funny?' he said.

'Everything. Max, hell-bent on following protocol. Rosa, desperate to be a bridesmaid.'

'I'm desperate to be a husband but that doesn't even raise a smile.'

'Poor Bing,' she said. 'I've never been good at surprises. I'm sorry I reacted the way I did. And yes, of course I'll marry you.'

They stayed in the car for a long time, misting up the windows, stopping short of making love as they agreed it would be foolish to risk injury when a comfortable bed awaited them.

'Where's the ring?' he said when they were back in the house. She pulled the box from her pocket. 'Here,' he said, 'give me your hand. Let's do this properly.' He slipped the ring on her finger. 'I was thinking April. How does that sound?'

The house was silent. Naomi and David were either asleep or afraid to return to the war zone. Bing had sneaked a bottle of pukka champagne into the fridge but they decided it should wait until tomorrow when they could all share it. Instead, they made inroads into David's single malt. By the time they were getting into bed, it was Boxing Day and they were too squiffy for anything more than a cuddle.

Naomi was emptying the dishwasher when Miriam came down. 'Sorry about the drama,' she said. 'The whole thing caught me on the hop.'

'It was a somewhat unusual proposal. When we heard the front door go, we thought you'd thrown him out.'

'Not quite. We sat in the car and had a blazing row.'

'And?'

'And then I accepted.'

'Congratulations. That's wonderful – and something of a relief. I was afraid we were in for a miserable Boxing Day.'

Rosa appeared, carrying her sketchbook. 'Did you say yes, Gamma?'

'I did.'

'Good, because I've been working on my outfit.' She flipped open her notebook and pointed to a drawing of a girl in orange dungarees and a floppy-brimmed hat. 'I can do yours if you want me to. Purple's your favourite colour, isn't it? D'you like feathers? I do.'

Max and David turned up and the kitchen was soon bustling. 'What's the plan for today?' David said through a mouthful of cereal.

'Lego,' Max said. 'Paul promised he'd help me.'

'Maybe Paul and Gamma would like some time to themselves,' Naomi said.

'I don't think so,' Max said. 'They're always together. Where *is* he anyway?'

'He'll be down soon,' Miriam said. 'He has a few phone calls to make.'

She sat between the children, helping Max fold paper aeroplanes, admiring Rosa's growing portfolio of wedding garments, watching the minutes tick away.

Max had all but abandoned hope by the time Bing appeared. When Miriam raised her eyebrows, he shrugged and shook his head. Rubbing his hands together he said, 'Max and I have work to do.'

Boxing Day floated lazily by. They worked their way around the edges of a jigsaw puzzle, watched *Toy Story* for the umpteenth time, ate too much and laughed at limp cracker jokes. Rosa designed several wedding dresses for Miriam, more appropriate for a pop star than a bride in her sixties.

She'd got out of the habit of wearing a ring – her wedding ring was stashed away awaiting the appropriate time when she would pass it on to Naomi – and Bing's aquamarine looked out of place on her hand. It clunked against her cup and snagged her sweater and she was conscious of its rigidity between the adjacent fingers. Aquamarine wasn't what she would have chosen – too big and sparkly – but it was unquestionably arresting and, every now and then, she caught Rosa eyeing it.

'Would you like to try it on?' she said.

Rosa's eyes widened. 'Am I allowed?'

The ring was too large even for the child's thumb. Naomi solved the problem by digging out a pair of satin gloves, left over from a fancy dress party. Rosa slid it over her gloved finger, dancing around the room, entranced by the ring, in awe of what it symbolised. Miriam recalled Max once asking if she were granted a super-power, what would it be. Watching her granddaughter hovering on the brink of adolescence, she would without question choose the power to make time stand still.

Miriam would have liked to stay another day or two but Bing had to get back. 'Why don't *you* stay, Mum?' Naomi said. 'I'm sure Paul can manage.' But packing Bing off alone didn't seem the right way to begin their formal engagement.

Three days of incarceration with 'nearest and dearest' was evidently as much as anyone could handle and it seemed the entire populace had chosen today to make their escape. Their road home took them within a block of Moat's house and, as they waited at the traffic lights, her thoughts returned to the hours she'd spent there. Her involvement had been brief but exhilarating. She might almost have dreamed the whole thing. The pastel portrait, hidden under the stairs in her old suitcase, was the only thing to prove it had happened.

30

LIKE ROSA, FRANKIE COULDN'T WAIT to slip the ring on her finger. 'What does Naomi think?'

'She's thrilled. They all are.'

'And Bing's family? Or shouldn't I ask?'

Miriam grimaced. 'Camille's refusing to speak to him. Pascale and Leon are in denial.'

'I don't get it. You'd think they'd be grateful their father will have someone to take care of him in his dotage.' She passed the ring back to Miriam. 'He must have blotted his copybook, big time. Something to do with his divorce, perhaps? Why *did* they split?'

Miriam shrugged. 'I suppose the marriage ran out of steam.'

'You *suppose*?'

'We agreed raking over the past would achieve nothing.'

'But he knows about Sam?'

'Vaguely.'

'What does that mean?'

'He knows he died in a car crash. I did offer to tell him the whole story, but he didn't want to know.' She pictured the envelope, curling and burning. 'He says he can't bear to think I had a life with another man.'

'For goodness sake. How old is he? Five?'

Miriam clapped her hands. 'Let's talk about something else. Tell me, how was your Christmas?'

'Depressing. Stinky. Knackering. And there was a great long list of rules.' She marked them off on her fingers. 'Volunteers weren't allowed to be alone with "clients". We weren't allowed to ask personal questions. Or tell them anything about ourselves. I understand why but it's flippin' hard. You don't realise how you depend on that sort of stuff when you meet someone for the first time. Obviously you can't sit there in silence. You have to natter about something. It's very different from speed dating.'

'You've *speed dated*?'

Frankie grinned. 'Who hasn't?'

'So what did you talk about?'

'Weather. Music. Food. Don't laugh, at one point I was discussing football.'

'Would you do it again?'

'Who knows where I'll be in twelve months. But I'm definitely going to help Jen with the soup run.'

'Good for you.'

Miriam's approbation was tempered with unease. It wasn't in Frankie's nature to keep her distance. Neither was she the best judge of character as her history of calamitous liaisons proved. Warm, empty house. Soft heart. Frankie's new-found altruism could, all too easily, go awry.

Bing remained intransigent on the issue of Danny and Miriam had resorted to shoving Denton and Ryde's invoices into her bag before he had chance to spot them. This month's arrived early. It felt different – bulkier – and she could barely wait for Bing to leave for work before opening it.

Along with the regular invoice, the envelope contained a letter from James Denton.

Dear Mrs Siskin,

Regarding the work we are carrying out in respect to your brother, Daniel Edlin and his wife and daughter, Ava and Pearl Edlin. Our operative in the United States has reported a lead in the case. I must stress that this might prove to be inaccurate or indeed, a dead end. Whilst this is encouraging, I advise caution.

I would be grateful if you could phone me at your earliest convenience.

Yours sincerely
James Denton

Although it was late, Denton was still at his desk.

'Tell me quickly,' she said. 'What's this "lead"? Is Danny alive?'

'I'm afraid I can't answer that, Mrs Siskin. The lead I spoke of refers to a Pearl Edlin who taught at a school in Prescott, Arizona, in the early nineties. Her date of birth ties in with the information you provided. She worked there for three years. We're trying to discover where she went after that.'

'So nothing on my brother?'

'Nothing so far I'm afraid.'

'Would more money help? Or could you—'

'These things take time, Mrs Siskin. The man we have

368

engaged is expert in this field. If there's anything to be found, I assure you he'll find it.'

Miriam felt sick with disappointment. She wanted to scream at the pompous fool who failed to understand that not only had she inherited her parents' worldly goods but also their torment over Danny's disappearance. She was longing for her brother not some girl she'd never met. *Arizona?* He'd never given her an address in Arizona. The nineties were a long time ago. Her niece – if it were her niece – could be anywhere. If they were to track her down there was no reason to think she and Danny had stayed in contact, especially if his split with Ava had been acrimonious.

Bing was tetchy when he returned from the surgery. She'd made up her mind to tell him about Denton's news as soon as he came in but it would be a mistake to raise the issue whilst he was in this foul mood.

'Anything wrong?' she said.

'If you must know I bumped into that creep Stanway.' He paused, his eyes fixed on hers. 'Why didn't you tell me you'd seen him?'

She hadn't recognised the man when he came into the shop. 'Alan Stanway,' he'd said. 'The party at Monkton Square.' 'Of course.' 'I heard you worked here so I thought I'd drop in and say hello.' 'You might consider buying a book whilst you're here,' she'd said. 'Sure. Half a dozen if you'll let me buy you a drink.' She'd been stunned at the man's gall. 'I don't think Paul would be too happy,' she'd said. He'd winked. 'I won't tell him if you won't.' And she hadn't told Bing because – well, because of the state he'd got himself when Stanway had cornered her at that Christmas party.

'I didn't mention it because it wasn't worth mentioning,' she said.

'Really?' Bing said. 'He was smirking all over his fat face as usual. He couldn't wait to tell me you agreed to go for a drink with him. Did you?'

'What do you think?'

'I don't know. No. *No*.'

'So why even ask me? It's degrading having you interrogate me like this.'

Miriam favoured holding the reception at home. 'We'll get caterers in. It'll be nice.'

Bing dug his heels in saying the occasion warranted more than a few sausage rolls in the living room. The Angel Hotel already had one wedding booked for that day but the manager – a close friend of Hazel's – offered them the small dining room which accommodated a couple of dozen guests. Short of roping in Bing's work colleagues, she couldn't see how they could rustle up anywhere near that number and they accepted. She stuck to her guns on everything else. No designer dresses, apart from Rosa's, no extravagant flower arrangements, no flashy cars. They'd ask David to take photographs. The local bakery could supply the cake and she would enjoy making the invitations.

Bing failed to conceal his frustration. 'We've waited forty-odd years, don't you think we deserve a bit more razzamatazz?'

Her father had gone overboard when she married Sam, but having capitulated on her choice of husband, what had been the point in her objecting to the rest of the circus? So. Vintage cars; two hundred guests (few of whom she'd met); a klezmer band, for crying out loud. And that ghastly lace dress – rigid and bright white. Having formulated the masterplan, her father had left her mother to sort out the details. Miriam hadn't hindered preparations but neither had she helped which, looking back, had been horribly unkind.

Naomi, too, was disappointed at her mother's modest plans. 'It's your wedding, Mum. Isn't that important?'

'Of course but there are other things to consider.'

'Such as?'

'Paul's children. They haven't said whether they'll come or not. It's bad enough as it is but if we opt for an elaborate "do" and they don't show, it'll be doubly mortifying.'

After months of Miriam's stonewalling, Naomi had abandoned her ambition to meld the families and, shrugging, she let it rest there.

Ceremony and reception booked, Miriam put preparations on hold until after Easter. That would give her more than enough time to organise what amounted to a delicious lunch with people whom she loved.

31

THE CLOCKS HAD GONE FORWARD and the world was greening into life. Miriam was in the garden, raking up the remains of winter debris and enjoying the warmth of the spring sunshine. The front door banged signalling Bing's return with the newspaper and, she hoped, something delicious to accompany their morning coffee. Shucking off her wellington boots, she went inside to track him down.

He was in the kitchen, *The Sunday Times* spread out on the table.

'There you are,' she said. 'Have you put the kettle on?'

He shoved the paper towards her. 'Did you know about this?'

She glanced down, anticipating a headline about NHS cuts or the closure of a local factory. Instead she saw Moat. Moat in his duffel coat and silly hat. Moat. And alongside him his painting of her.

'Christ, Miriam,' Bing said. 'What were you thinking?'

'I can—'

'No. Don't say anything.'

'Please. Let me explain.'

'What's to explain?' He jabbed at the photograph. 'You're here for all to see – every naked inch of you.'

'Bing—'

'I don't want to hear it.'

He grabbed his car keys and by the time she got to the window he was reversing his car out of the drive. She beat on the glass but he chose not to see her, and she stayed there, staring at the space where his car had been. When it was obvious he wasn't coming back she returned to the newspaper, scanning the article, catching a phrase here, a sentence there, struggling to make sense of it. The upshot was that 'Red Shoes' had been awarded some major new prize. Tens of thousands of pounds.

She forced herself to read it from beginning to end, not easy when her thoughts were skittering. The judges hailed Moat as 'a natural successor to Lucien Freud'. There was stuff about his background, his training, his previous successes. His thoughts on the Turner Prize and contemporary art in general. Now this big breakthrough. And he spoke of his 'inspirational model'. No name but the hair, the eyes, the posture – she'd forgotten how perfectly he'd captured her.

Across the country, people would be flicking though the paper. When they reached this page, what did they see? A naked woman, or a work of art? What did they think? Were they appalled that a woman *her age* had the audacity to expose her flesh to public scrutiny? Did they assume she was Moat's mistress? Did they see a pair of cheap red pumps or Moat's 'invisible woman'? Perhaps they glanced at it and turned over to – she flipped the page – the interview with Jarvis Cocker.

Bing had been gone for forty minutes. Long enough to regret his overreaction – although she held out little hope of that. He'd never been rational when it came to her. She laid her head on her folded arms. When they first got together, the prospect of his finding out about her modelling had preyed on her mind. Time had gone by and they had moved on, and her unease had faded. When, on the odd occasion, she spoke to Callum, the last time had been before Christmas, they chatted about everyday things – family, books, films – never her work at the college. And Moat? She'd last seen Moat in that café when he was buying his olive oil. All she could recall was eating cake and telling him there was no possibility of her working with him again.

Her phone roused her and she snatched it up. It was Callum. 'D'you happen to take *The Sunday Times*?' He sounded apprehensive.

'Why didn't you warn me? Paul's gone into meltdown.'

'I only found out yesterday. Moat knew a few days ago but the story was embargoed until last night's award dinner.'

'So why didn't *he* warn me? He must have known that the interview – the picture – would be in today's paper.'

'To be honest, I doubt it crossed his mind. You know what he's like.' Callum paused. 'You must have realised that, sooner or later, the painting would go on public display. Moat doesn't paint for fun, Miriam. It's his job. It's the way he earns his living.'

'I didn't give it much thought.' (Not true. In her mind's eye, it had remained in Moat's house, taking pride of place at the top of the stair on the first-floor landing.) Besides, a painting on some rich connoisseur's wall, or in a gallery in… in Aberdeen, is entirely different from a full-page spread in a national Sunday. Another thing. He finished it two years ago. Where's it been all this time?'

'He told me he was keeping it in his locker, waiting for the right occasion.'

'Right for him maybe but it couldn't have come at a worse time for me.' She folded the newspaper so she couldn't see herself. 'Sorry. I should be yelling at Moat not you.'

'You've no reason to yell at anyone, Miriam. And your bloke has no reason to throw a wobbly. Sorry but he's a twat if he doesn't know a masterpiece when he sees one.'

She gave a mirthless laugh. 'He didn't stick around long enough to study the brushwork. Whatever's going on in his head has nothing to do with its artistic merits.'

'Poor Miriam. You've nothing to feel bad about. Modelling's a perfectly respectable occupation. It's not as if you were a stripper.'

She imagined David's parents, her ex-colleagues, Alan Stanway, sitting down with their Sunday papers and their small-minded attitudes. 'Respectable in your world, perhaps.'

'I'm truly sorry this is causing you grief. I feel responsible for getting you involved.'

'You mustn't. I volunteered.'

'But I introduced you to Moat.'

'And I could have turned him down.' Her phone buzzed indicating a caller was waiting. 'Look, I'd best go.'

'Keep in touch,' he said.

This time it was Hazel. 'I'm in awe. And don't pretend you don't know what I'm talking about.'

'Am I that recognisable?'

'Unmistakable. Unless you have an identical twin. Why didn't you let on?'

'I'd forgotten about it.'

'Come off it. You'd have to be an amnesiac to forget something like that.'

'You're right. But it was in another life and I was another person. Tell me truthfully. Are you shocked?'

'Impressed more than shocked. It's a wonderful painting. I can quite see why it won.' Hazel paused. 'Knowing how… protective Paul is, I wouldn't have thought he'd be altogether thrilled.'

'He's not. In fact he stormed out and I have no idea where he is.'

She explained how the whole thing had come about. Callum and the art college. How Bing's reappearance had coincided with her agreeing to pose for Moat. How she'd decided not to jeopardise their second chance of happiness by telling Paul something he need never know. 'I can see now what a terrible mistake that was,' she said.

'Is he angry with you for doing it, or angry with you for not telling him you did it? They're very different things.'

'I might find out if he ever comes back.'

Lunchtime came. She made a cheese sandwich but after a couple of bites it went in the bin. The sort of prize money Moat had won would attract attention way beyond the rarefied world of fine art. She would be fooling herself if she pretended the story would appear in only one paper. It was unlikely that the identity of his model would escape investigation. That Miriam Siskin might slip under the radar.

Needing to occupy herself, she tidied the dresser drawers. As she untangled string and hunted for missing pen tops, remorse gave way to anger. The past presented a hazard to any happy future, but whenever she'd pointed that out to Bing – suggested they get theirs out in the open – he had resisted. He maintained their relationship was built on trust, yet the first time his was put to the test, he'd bolted. Callum was right. She'd done nothing wrong. Had nothing to be ashamed of. Bing was behaving like a petulant adolescent. She should leave him to stew. And yet. What hope was there for them if they failed to confront this now? She texted *Please come home so we can talk.*

She'd stopped listening for his car when it finally pulled up. He'd forgotten his house keys and had no option but to ring the doorbell. For a dizzying second, she thought he was going to take her in his arms but instead he pushed past her and ran upstairs, and she heard him crashing about, opening and closing drawers.

She followed him up to their room. 'What are you doing?'

He pointed to the holdall on the bed. 'What does it look like?'

'Don't be absurd. This is me, remember?'

He grabbed a handful of socks and shoved them in the bag. 'That's just it. Who the hell are you?'

'For goodness sake, stop being so melodramatic.'

'You have some nerve criticising my behaviour. Who flaunted herself in front of some... weirdo? And what about the one you're always texting? Did he come along and watch?'

'Stop it,' she shouted. 'Okay. I should have told you. But I saw you and I loved you and I couldn't bear to risk losing you. I was afraid you wouldn't understand.'

'You're damn right there.' He scooped a handful of underwear from the drawer. 'So after you *saw me* and you *loved me*, did you continue stripping off for this… this pervert?' A vein bulged on his temple. 'You did, didn't you? Are there any more pictures like this likely to appear in the press?'

'What if there are?' she said. 'Read the article and you'll find out how well-respected Moat is.'

'I don't care if the little turd's Leonardo da-fucking Vinci. You've allowed your body to become public property.'

'Instead of *your* property, is that what you mean?'

'Why did you do it? Were you trying to prove something?'

'If you must know, yes, that's precisely what I was doing. If you'll just stop packing, I'll explain everything.'

'I don't want to know, Miriam. I don't want to talk about it, or think about it.'

'If that's the case, we have a real problem.'

Before he could respond, her phone rang.

'If that's him…' he said.

She turned the phone towards him so he could see the caller's name. 'It's Naomi if you must know.'

Not knowing what Naomi was going to say and fearing that Bing might get involved, she went into the spare room. As her daughter prattled on – a recipe, a haircut, Max's school trip to London – it was clear she knew nothing about the painting. Finally she ground to a halt. 'Are you okay, Mum? You seem distracted.'

'Sorry. I'm in the middle of something. Can I call you back?'

She waited, giving Bing the opportunity to come and find her. When it became obvious this wasn't going to happen, she ran downstairs and got in her car. For a while she drove around aimlessly eventually, like a homing pigeon, ending up at her parents' house.

'My God,' Frankie said, 'you look terrible. What's wrong?'

'Everything. Bing and I've had a massive row.'

Frankie shrugged. 'Brides get jittery before the wedding.'

'No. This is serious. *Really* serious.'

Having extracted Frankie's promise not to interrupt, she told her everything. When she'd finished, Frankie clapped her hands. 'An artist's muse, eh? Atta girl. Like I said, the world's your oyster.'

Miriam's tears welled. 'Thanks.'

'For what?'

'Not making this about Bing.'

'Why would I do that? It's your body. You can do what you like with it. I've yet to see this painting, but I doubt it's one of those soft-porn-masquerading-as-art jobs. For starters, you're too scrawny for that sort of thing.'

'Should I take that as a compliment?'

'More a vote of confidence. Look. You just told me how close you were to falling apart. If this modelling job helped you get yourself together again, Bing ought to get down on his knees and thank God you met this Moat.'

'He refuses to listen to me.'

'Well he's a prick. I warned you months back, he wants to keep you for himself.'

Miriam flexed her neck. 'I feel as if I've been hit by a truck. I don't know what to think. Or what to do. Should I go back? Have another shot at talking to him? That's if he's still there.'

'Only you can decide that one. Watch out though, he's looking for any excuse to clip your wings. He'll do everything he can to turn this to his advantage. Whatever you do, don't lose your nerve.'

32

HE WAS IN THE LIVING ROOM, sprawled face-down on the sofa. A whisky bottle and empty glass stood on the carpet within arm's reach. She'd pictured several scenarios but not this one. He was angry, hurt, confused – she understood that – but resorting to alcohol? She expected better of him.

The kitchen was as she'd left it and she guessed he'd not eaten since breakfast. This gave her an idea. She wouldn't prod him into consciousness and demand they thrash this out. That was too crude a tactic, guaranteed to worsen the already grim situation. No. She would leave him to sleep on for a while then wake him gently and offer him something to eat. Sitting down to a meal might present them with a way back.

She was filling the kettle when she noticed that the newspaper was no longer on the table. She checked the pedal bin and the recycling box, finally tracking it down to Bing's office where it lay in the waste paper basket next to the shredder. She shivered. She hadn't expected him to pin the picture on the cork board but reducing her to slivers of paper felt like a brutal assault.

Fishing her mobile from her pocket, she thumbed her daughter's number. Naomi would be clearing away supper and piling things – gym kit, reading books, tuck money – in the hall ready for the morning scramble. It wasn't the ideal time to call but she needed to talk to her. To tell her everything. To establish her daughter's position.

'I'm sure you're up to your eyes,' she said, 'but can you spare a moment?'

Naomi picked up on the earnestness in her mother's voice. 'Hang on a sec. David? Can you sort your children out? They need baths. And Max's nails could do with trimming.'

She heard the children complaining and David laughing, their voices fading as Naomi put some distance between them. What followed was a difficult, one-sided conversation. Her daughter said barely a word and several times Miriam paused her story to ask, 'Are you still there?' She'd been through it with with Frankie but this mother-to-daughter disclosure called for great delicacy. It was imperative she strike the right note – neither defiant or defensive – so much easier were she sitting opposite Naomi, able to read her expression, her body language.

'Naomi?' she said when she'd finished.

'You'll have to give me a minute, Mum. It's a lot to digest.'

She sat on the top stair watching the curtains on the landing window as they caught the evening breeze. After what seemed an eternity, Naomi said, 'What d'you want me to say? That what you did was amazing? Wonderful? The best thing ever?'

'No. But I hoped you'd understand it was a job and it helped me get through a really difficult patch.'

'I probably could if you were someone else's mother.

But you're not and I have to say the whole thing's freaking me out. How old is this Mount, anyway?'

'*Moat*. Mid-fifties? Why d'you ask?'

'When you said he was "up-and-coming", I imagined him to be much younger. Is he married? Or gay?'

'Neither of those. Does that make a difference?'

'Yes. Alone, naked, with an unmarried straight man who's not much younger than you... I dunno. The art school gig seems harmless in comparison.'

'How d'you reach that conclusion?'

'Safety in numbers. The lecturer guy was there to chaperone. Besides, eighteen-year-olds were hardly likely to fancy you, were they?'

'So nakedness, *per se*, doesn't bother you?' she said, smarting a little at Naomi's ageist pronouncement.

'It's not something I've ever considered.'

'Not true. Think about it. Every time you look at a nude painting you consider it.'

'That's entirely different. I don't suppose anyone can be objective when it comes to a looking at a naked parent.' She hesitated. 'Did this have anything to do with Dad?'

'Of course it did. Your father stole my future. Because of him, I lost my job, my home and, for a while, my sanity. In fact everything I thought I could count on. Don't misunderstand me, I loved living with you – spending time with the children – being useful – but I was starting to fade into the background. Turning into wallpaper. To put it bluntly, the future held nothing for me.'

'Let me get this straight,' Naomi said. 'You encounter

a stranger who offers you a job as a life model and, hey presto, you turn your life around. You must admit that's a bizarre solution to any sort of problem.'

'It wasn't quite—'

'What's more, you lied to me. You told me you worked in the college office.' *Not true.* 'And if getting paid to take your clothes off was so acceptable, why did you keep it secret?'

'Because I knew it would cause a rumpus. I don't know if you're interested, but the pay was insignificant. And I was never late collecting the children.'

'Knowing you went straight from stripping to the school gate isn't all that comforting, Mum.'

'You mean I should have gone through some sort of decontamination process? Ritual cleansing, perhaps. And I wasn't stripping.' She sighed. 'Can we stop sniping?'

'I assume Paul has no problem with it. Naked bodies are his bread and butter, as it were.'

Rosa chose that moment to come looking for her mother, moaning that Max had hidden her watch and saving Miriam from having to fudge a reply. Naomi shooed her out, promising she'd be there in a few seconds.

'You'd like the painting,' Miriam said.

'I'm not sure I want to see the thing. I've got to go, Mum. Rosa's having a meltdown.'

Miriam felt better now she'd spoken to those who mattered – Naomi, Frankie, Hazel. It hadn't been easy but it was done. In a few days, this would be old news. Before long Moat's prizewinning painting would find its way into some private collection, to be seen only by a handful of rich people.

Bing had turned onto his back and was snoring. When she ran a hand down his arm, he murmured, lifting his head, raising a hand to shield his eyes from the glare of the low sun. He smiled then his smile faded and he turned away, burying his face in the cushion.

'We should eat something,' she said. Without waiting for his reply, she returned to the kitchen. A few minutes later, she heard footsteps on the stair and, not long afterwards, the thrum of water in the pipes. A lover's tiff could be patched up in bed, where bodies could be trusted to say what needed to be said. This falling-out was in a different league and she resisted the impulse to go to him.

When he came down, he'd shaved and was wearing a clean shirt and chinos. He said nothing and his expression gave little away.

'Cheese on toast?' she said. 'One round or two?'

'One, please,' he said, as if self-denial were virtuous.

They moved around the kitchen, setting the table, performing intricate choreography in order to avoid brushing against each other. As he passed, she caught a whiff of whisky beneath minty mouthwash. When the food was ready, they sat at opposite sides of the table, paying the toast and the cheese the attention afforded to a rare delicacy. Any second now, he would look up and smile and apologise for being an arse and tell her if she wanted to cavort naked on the cathedral green, it was fine by him because he loved her and he trusted her and he was proud that she'd been so courageous.

'Where did you go?' he said.

'To see Frankie.'

He snorted. 'I bet she she's loving every minute of this. I wouldn't be surprised if she put you up to it.'

She laid down her knife and fork. 'Don't you think it's time we had a grown-up conversation?'

'Don't be so bloody condescending. I'm still trying to get my head round it.'

'How can you if you won't let me explain?'

'I know everything I need to know.'

'You mean all you *want* to know.'

For the first time since coming back with the newspaper, he looked her full in the face. 'Why is this happening to us?'

'Because you're letting it,' she said. 'You've dreamed up some crazy story and convinced yourself it's true.' She softened her voice. 'Can I ask you something? When you look at a painting of a nude woman, do you think *what a slut*? No. You decide whether it's a good painting or not. At least that's what civilised people do.'

His face was impassive. 'So when we wrote down our potted histories, did you include your modelling career?'

'Yes, as you'd know if you hadn't chucked it on the fire.' *One little lie.* 'I'm not asking forgiveness, Bing. Why would I? I've done nothing wrong. I'm asking for acceptance.' She paused. 'I have to accept your seeing *and touching* naked women every day.'

'A-ha. I was waiting for you to bring that up.'

She slapped the table, setting the cutlery rattling. 'You need to cut out this self-pitying nonsense right now.'

He gave a stifled cry and, without hesitating, she went to him, cradling his head to her breast, stroking his hair, offering him the chance to gather her in his arms and put an end to this. But he remained unresponsive.

'Maybe it's best I spend tonight at Hazel's,' she said. 'We'll talk tomorrow when we're both thinking straight.' How reasonable and improbable this sounded.

She shoved a few things in an overnight bag. When she went to call Hazel, she had second thoughts. If Gavin were there, staying in her small flat would prove awkward. She'd ring Frankie instead. Bing wouldn't like it but it was none of his business. Her call went straight to voicemail and she remembered Frankie mentioning she was going to the cinema with a friend. She left a message, telling her she was coming but not to rush back, she would let herself in.

The house had, as Frankie said, its own smell – an amalgam of furniture polish and something dog-like (although her parents had never owned a dog). It was still there but much fainter than it had been. The place was remarkably spick-and-span – not a used coffee mug or discarded magazine to be seen. She peeped in to Frankie's room – *her* room. No rumpled duvet. No tangle of clothes on the bed. No jumble of make-up on the dressing table. No wastepaper basket brimming with soiled tissues. Her mother would have approved of the new tenant.

As dusk turned to darkness, she meandered from room to room, casting around for something to do, flicking through the TV channels but nothing grabbed her. Without anything to take her mind off the horrid day, it became impossible to rein in her anxiety and she set off for a walk, wending her way along streets she'd known since childhood. Eventually, her meandering led her to the old Crosby house. It lay off the beaten track and she'd no had reason to come this way for years. Judging by the row of doorbells and array of wheelie bins alongside the garage, the gracious old house had been converted into flats. What a shame. It had once been a happy, shambolic, family home, with Bing's liberal-minded parents and his clever, carefree sisters at its warm heart.

She stood beneath the street light, gazing up at the room under the eaves where she and Bing had lain together, spending heady, breathless hours pledging their love and planning a life together. And suddenly she understood. In the euphoria of their reunion, Love had beguiled and bamboozled them into believing the future had been on hold, marking time for forty years, waiting for them to return and repossess it.

The tring of her phone brought her back to the present. 'Where are you?' Frankie said.

'Walking. Remembering. Regretting.'

'Oh, God. I don't like the sound of that.'

'I'm not going to jump in the river if that's what's worrying you. Put the kettle on. I'll be there in ten minutes.'

She picked up the pace and before long she was dunking chocolate biscuits with Frankie, bringing her up-to-date.

'I've left him to get a grip and reflect.' She sounded more confident than she felt. 'Can I stay here tonight?'

'Of course. But he won't like it. He's already accused me of luring you away from him.'

'When was that?'

'A couple of weeks ago. I popped over to the surgery with some mail for your dad. He more or less told me to stop pestering you.'

'Why didn't you say anything?'

'I knew it would upset you and seeing as how I'll be going soon, it didn't seem worth it.'

'Going?'

'As in moving on. Much as I love living here, this place,' Frankie extended her arms as if trying to encompass the whole house, 'was only ever going to be a safe haven whilst I got my act together.'

'And you're doing that, aren't you?'

'Yes. I think I am.'

Only then did Miriam register the fact that her friend was wearing a little black dress and pearl earrings. 'You look very chic. I thought you were going to the cinema.'

'We changed our minds. We went for a meal in that new Thai place.' To Miriam's amazement Frankie was blushing. 'He's a dentist. A widower. I don't want to say too much. It's early days.'

'A-ha. And does your dentist have a name?'

'Francis. Frank. Don't laugh.'

'Frankie and Frank. It has a certain…'

'Monotony?'

'I didn't say that.'

'It's okay. A dose of tedium might be what I need.'

Frankie grinned and tapped her front teeth. 'And I could certainly do with a new bridge.'

'Well, if Frank makes you happy, I like him already.' Miriam yawned. 'I think I'll have a quick bath before I go to bed.'

'Why don't you sleep in your old room?' Frankie said.

'I'll be fine in Danny's...' she grimaced, 'I mean the *spare* room.'

'No news from the States?' Frankie said.

'Nothing... concrete. I'll give it another six months.'

She undressed and lowered herself into the water. Her parents had been so proud of this bathroom, spanking new in the eighties, now dated and shabby. They'd lain in this bath, naked and vulnerable, frightened of so many things. Had they ever talked – *really* talked? Laid their souls bare so that there was nothing more to know? It hadn't appeared that way – but how much could an outsider know about the workings of a marriage? Raising her knees, she lay back, head half-submerged, hair swirling like seaweed around her shoulders. Max used to love doing this, giggling as she talked to him, her voice distorting through ears filled with bathwater. Nothing stayed the same forever. These days he made sure the door was shut when he was in the bathroom.

She been trying not to dwell on her horrid day. She'd left promising they'd talk tomorrow. All the same, she'd expected Bing to text if only to check she was safely with Frankie. His failure to do so didn't bode well. What was he doing now? Sleeping? Drinking? He'd got himself into a dreadful state and another night of self-torment could push him to do something stupid. What if he got in the car?

There was no chance of her sleeping and, dressing quickly, she went to find Frankie. 'I need to go home,' she said. 'Never go to bed on a quarrel, isn't that the perceived wisdom?'

A shadow crossed Frankie's face. 'Sure you'll be okay?'

'He's furious with me but he'd never hurt me.'

Frankie pushed back her fringe, revealing a scar which started on her forehead and disappeared into her hair. 'The guy who did this was a pussycat until the time he lost it.'

Reaching out, Miriam traced the scar with the tip of her finger. 'Poor Frankie.'

33

THE HOUSE WAS IN DARKNESS. Bing's keys were on the hall table. No sign of a note – but there wouldn't be. He wasn't expecting her back until the morning. He must be in bed. She was debating what to do when a text came through. *We LOVE the painting. D says he's lucky to have such a gutsy, gorgeous m-in-l. N xx.* She guessed that David – dear David – had been instrumental in Naomi's conversion but, however it had come about, having the pair onside was a huge relief and boosted by this small victory, she made her way upstairs. The bedroom door was closed. Locked.

She rapped on the door. 'Bing? Can we talk?'

'Go away.'

She slapped the door with the flat of her hand. 'Why won't you open this door?'

'Why won't you fuck off?'

'Be careful what you wish for,' she shouted.

Hand shaking, she cleaned her teeth, scrubbing violently until her frothy spit was speckled with blood. Then she took herself off to the spare room, slamming the door, making sure to shake the whole house. She got into bed and lay there, conscious of the rapid *thud, thud, thud* of her heart, feeling the tightness in her throat.

She and Sam had regularly fallen out but they'd always been good at talking and listening. Unravelling their differences. Bearing no grudges. There had been none of that today. The man who claimed to be her soulmate had shunned her, drunk himself senseless then shunned her for a second time. She wiped her tears on the corner of the pillowcase. The first time she came to this house, they'd made love in this bed. Afterwards she'd lain awake, fretting that her parents would, once more, make her choose between them. But they'd confounded her by welcoming him, pretending they'd played no part in what had taken place forty-odd years ago. *Poor Mum. Poor Dad.* At least they were beyond being hurt.

Callum had urged her to tell Bing. But no, she'd known better. Now her cowardice – that's what it was – had caught up with her. Could she have played it differently this morning? How? He hadn't given her a chance. Dashing off to Frankie's had been a mistake, too. She should have stuck it out. Held her ground. Made him listen. Now he was camped on the moral high ground, waiting for her to get it wrong again. He was punishing her for having done something *he* didn't like. Something that didn't chime with *his* vision of her.

The envelope was in the tallboy, tucked beneath papers relating to her parents' estate. She slid it out, running her finger across the embossed logo. What secrets did Paul Crosby's past hold? Ammunition for a counter-attack? She hesitated. This mustn't escalate into a tit-for-tat battle. On the other hand, she couldn't simply stand here, taking whatever he cared to chuck at her. Sliding her finger under the flap, she opened the envelope and removed the sheet of notepaper, the crease in it as sharp as the day it was folded.

What…? It was blank on both sides. Not a single word. Not even a declaration of love. Without stopping to think, she was across the landing, pounding and kicking the door, screaming his name.

He opened the door. 'What the hell's got into you?'

'This has got into me. *This.*' She flung the sheet of paper in his face. '*You* have the nerve to accuse *me* of being secretive.'

He squinted into the light. 'You told me you'd lost it.'

'Well hard luck because I've found it again. What were you playing at?'

'If you really want to know I thought your "let's confess what we did in the past" was a duff idea but you were dead set on it. If I'd refused it would have spoiled our weekend.'

'It had nothing to do with *confessing*. It was about honesty. Openness. When you agree to something, you don't get to pick and choose whether you'll do it or not. You don't get to call the shots. Do we have a future, you and I? From where I'm standing, it's not looking good.'

'Don't say that.'

'Why shouldn't I? It's the truth. I have no idea what's going on in your head. Unless you tell me, we don't stand a chance.'

'Okay. Okay.' He dragged his palms across his face. 'Siskin was bad enough but at least he's dead. I know that's a rotten thing to say but you asked for the truth. Now there's this Moat. I can't stop thinking of him. Ogling you. Touching your breasts—'

'Bing. You're going to drive yourself mad.' She laid her

hand on his chest. 'We've got ourselves in a terrible mess but there's no point in trying to unravel it now. We're both shattered. Overwrought.'

She led him towards the bed. They were good at love-making. From that first time in the Crosby's garden, they had been able to satisfy each other. But sex now would offer no more than a quick and temporary fix. He seemed to understand that and they lay, hand in hand, her head on his shoulder. Before long he was asleep, his breathing slow and regular, his hand heavy in hers, but each time she drifted towards nothingness, events of the day dragged her back. Two days ago they were planning a wedding. Tonight it was touch and go. Today's revelation had come as shock. All the same Bing's conduct had been intolerable. His accusations – his outbursts – unwarranted. She doubted he'd ever approve of what she'd done but no one had *died*. No one had *disappeared*.

At breakfast time, they were excessively polite to each other, treading warily, assessing the damage. 'We need to start talking,' she said, 'and listening too.'

'Message received,' he said.

'You look under-slept,' Hazel said as they were sipping their first coffee of the morning.

Miriam yawned. 'The dawn chorus woke me at some ungodly hour.'

'Bastard birds.'

To Miriam's relief, Hazel made no reference to the painting or Bing's reaction to it. None of her acquaintances or ex-colleagues contacted her. If she and Bing could resolve things, perhaps it was a matter of sitting tight and letting the whole thing blow over.

With stock to unpack, orders to dispatch and a steady flow of customers, the day raced away. She barely had time to think about their quarrel and when she did, it had miraculously shrunk to no more than a spat. But it was clearly a case of distance lending enchantment and, by the time she was unlocking the front door, her stomach was roiling. She took a pack of mince from the fridge. Bolognese or chilli? Hard to enthuse about either.

'Sorry I'm late,' Bing said when he got in. 'All these sick people kept turning up, demanding attention.' He leaned over and took an olive from the dish. 'Mmmm. Something smells good.'

'It's only bolognese.'

'Perfect. I'll dig out a bottle of red.'

She was tempted to remind him where yesterday's drinking had led. To suggest they keep clear heads. 'I'll stick to water,' she said, hoping he would take the hint.

Humming to himself, he took a bottle from the wine rack, pulled the cork and poured himself a generous glass. 'Cheers. How was your day?'

'Busy,' she said. 'We had a big delivery to sort and… Look, we agreed to talk.'

'We will. I promise. But can we eat first? I'm ravenous.'

She faltered before she was halfway through her plate of food, her appetite doused by what lay head. He seemed not to notice and downed a second helping and two more glasses of wine. When they'd finished, he began clearing the table. 'Can you leave that for a minute?' she said.

He followed her into the living room and she sat in the armchair, indicating he take the one opposite.

'I feel like a naughty schoolboy,' he said, holding out his hand. 'Six of the best please, Miss.'

'Don't make a joke out of this. It's too important.'

'Sorry. You're right.' He cleared his throat. 'About yesterday. I was out of order. I should have listened to what you had to say.' He pushed himself forward in the chair. 'But you have to look at this from my point of view, Mim.'

'Do I? Why?'

'*Come on.* What if my private parts had been splashed all over the newspaper? How would you feel?'

'What-ifs aren't terribly helpful,' she said.

'So what *would* be helpful?'

'Your keeping calm. Allowing me to explain.'

She was as objective as she could be whilst doing her best to convey her emotional state, her dread of the future, when she'd met Callum Robertson. Once or twice Bing went to interrupt but she silenced him with a raised hand. Throughout, she tried to maintain eye contact, but he kept glancing away, looking out of the window or at the blank TV screen, as if what she was saying had nothing to do with him.

When she'd finished, he said, 'So basically you did this… this *thing* because you enjoyed doing it?'

'For God's sake, you're making it sound like some repulsive self-indulgence. Were you not listening? For six months I worked as a life model. I met interesting people. I learned a lot about myself and a bit about art. I felt alive

397

for the first time since my husband died. I'm glad that I did it. Proud that I did it. My only regret is that it's causing you such unhappiness.'

'Then why keep it to yourself if it was so… so fucking life-affirming?'

'Why? I was scared to tell you in case you rejected me. And please don't shout at me.'

'Why go on doing it if you were so sure I'd disapprove?'

Disapprove?

'Because I'd said I would.' She paused. 'And, to be honest, I liked knowing I was needed – not for my childcare or cleaning skills, but for being myself.

'Good God, Mim, *I* need you. Isn't that enough?'

'But what d'you need me *for*? To keep in a cabinet like some kind of trophy? And that envelope-burning stunt – what was that all about? At the time I persuaded myself you wanted to prove you loved me, *no matter what*. The truth is, you couldn't stomach the fact I'd had a life without you. You won't want to hear this but it was a nice life too. I lost sight of that for a while.' She tugged at a tail of cotton dangling from the cushion cover. 'As for your blank sheet of paper – what am I to make of that? Are you saying I shouldn't give a hoot what you've been up to for the past forty years? Surely that's for me to decide. Believe it or not, you don't have the monopoly on approval.'

'So this is my fault?' he said.

'*No*. We're supposed to be fixing things, not apportioning blame. I don't know what more to say. How to convince you I've done nothing wrong. Or why I should *have* to convince you – although it's vital you believe it. Would it help if you talked to Moat?'

'I'd kill him.' He looked up, his face flushed. 'And you're right. The thought of your *nice life* with anyone else is intolerable.'

'You'd prefer I'd been unhappy all those years?'

'Of course I would. *I* was.'

His admission astounded her. 'But Eloise? And your children? Everything you shared. Does that count for nothing?'

'I never shared much with them. No point. I was marking time.'

She shivered. 'That's a shocking thing to say. And it's so sad for your children.'

'They'll survive,' he said and held out his arms. 'Come here. We're going to get through this, you and I.'

His change of mood caught her off guard and, out of habit, she went to him. He rocked her gently from side to side, as if she were a child seeking consolation. 'Promise you'll never contact that Moat person again. Or any of his arty friends.' He stroked her hair. 'It wasn't your fault, Mim. I see that now. You were ill. You weren't thinking straight. Those men took advantage of you. I'll tell you what. Let's pretend none of it happened. In a couple of months, we'll be married. From then on, it'll be just us. You and me. That's what we want, isn't it?'

'WHAT'S THE TIME?'

'Getting on for twelve-thirty.' Moat peers at her over his canvas. 'Why? Am I boring you?'

She smiles. 'Never.'

Flexing her neck, she settles back in the chair. It is warm up here, the sky – the little she can see of it – marbled with fair-weather cloud.

Today would have been Sam's seventy-second birthday. *Sam.* She likes to think he'd forgive her for what she did. He'd probably laugh and say he'd always wanted his ashes to be scattered on water. And the rest of it? Would he applaud her willpower? Her determination to stay true to herself, no matter how painful that proved to be? He'd certainly be proud of his grandchildren. Rosa, channelling her stroppiness into campaigning for green energy, and showing a real aptitude for maths. Max, growing up too quickly for her liking, a sweet boy with more than a touch of his – Sam's – patience and good humour.

Moat sets down his brushes. 'That'll do for today.'

She takes off the elbow-length gloves, slips on her robe and goes to check progress. This painting – the fourth in his 'Invisible Woman' sequence – is in its early stages, yet already she can see how it will complement the others.

'Remind me,' he says, 'when's our next session?'

'Thursday. And may I ask a favour? Can I bring someone with me?'

'Are you out of your mind, woman? I'm not some… some street artist.'

She tells him who it is, pressing him gently – 'I'll bring chocolate éclairs' – until he surrenders with a gruff, 'If you must'.

She plants a kiss on his cheek. 'Cut that out,' he says, failing to conceal his pleasure. 'Has Callum been in touch about this party of his?'

'Yes. Are you going?'

'Good God, no.' He shudders theatrically. 'All those arty types talking bollocks.'

'Well, if you change your mind, I'll give you a lift.'

The fresh-paint-and-new-carpet smell which lingered for months, has surrendered to the smell of home. Her home. When she was searching for a place to buy, several properties fitted the bill. The wisteria festooning the wall at the end of the garden clinched it. The house isn't dissimilar to Moat's – three-storeyed, terraced, late Victorian. A little smaller perhaps but with the same shabby homeliness. ('It's "tired",' the surveyor said, 'but it'll see us all out.') She has commandeered the box room as a writing room but there's still plenty of space for her grandchildren when they need to escape from their parents. And for Pearl whenever she feels like making the trek from San Diego.

She straightens the bedspread and takes a final look around. Towels. Tissues. A bowl of fruit. And, on the table next to the bed, half-a-dozen black-and-white snaps. She came across them the other day, sandwiched between her father's old ledgers. She riffles through them. They are on a beach. Danny must be around Max's age, his crinkle-edged teeth too big for his face. She is a gawky little thing in a shapeless bathing costume. Aunt Bea is there too, cigarette in hand, and her parents are laughing and waving at the camera. She returns to the photograph of Danny. Wherever he is, he must be happy that she and his daughter are becoming close friends.

A cup of tea and then off to the station. If last time is anything to go by, Pearl will be shattered after her flight. It wouldn't do to keep her waiting.

No man steps twice into the same river,
for it is not the same river and he is not the same man.

Heraclitus : 535 – 475 BCE

ABOUT HONNO

Honno Welsh Women's Press was set up in 1986 by a group of women who felt strongly that women in Wales needed wider opportunities to see their writing in print and to become involved in the publishing process. Our aim is to develop the writing talents of women in Wales, give them new and exciting opportunities to see their work published and often to give them their first 'break' as a writer. Honno is registered as a community co-operative. Any profit that Honno makes is invested in the publishing programme. Women from Wales and around the world have expressed their support for Honno. Each supporter has a vote at the Annual General Meeting. For more information and to buy our publications, please write to Honno at the address below, or visit our website: www.honno.co.uk

Honno, 14 Creative Units, Aberystwyth Arts Centre
Aberystwyth, Ceredigion SY23 3GL

Honno Friends
We are very grateful for the support of the Honno Friends: Jane Aaron, Annette Ecuyere, Audrey Jones, Gwyneth Tyson Roberts, Beryl Roberts, Jenny Sabine.

For more information on how you can become a Honno Friend, see: http://www.honno.co.uk/friends.php